TEMPT ME TWICE
SELECTION OF THE
DOUBLEDAY BOOK CLUB

ROMANCING THE ROGUE

"The charming characters make it a more-than-satisfying read . . . Smith has the ability to take a usual storyline (long-lost relative) and spiral it just enough to make her tale unique. A delight to read and a pleasure to savor."
—*Romantic Times*

"Smith offers colorful characters that sweep into your heart as their story unfolds before your eyes."
—*Romance Reviews Today*

"Once again, phenomenal storyteller Barbara Dawson Smith has crafted a dramatic tale that puts tears in your eyes one moment, then has you chuckling the next. *Romancing the Rogue* is a fast-moving tale with plenty of wit and intrigue that'll keep you guessing until the end."
—*Old Book Barn Gazette*

"Smith's writing is smooth, and her characters lusty and likeable."   —*Publishers Weekly*

MORE . . .

* RomEx Reviews

TEMPT ME TWICE

BARBARA DAWSON SMITH

St. Martin's Paperbacks

TEMPT ME TWICE

Copyright © 2001 by Barbara Dawson Smith.

ISBN: 0-312-99891-0

Printed in the United States of America

St. Martin's Paperbacks edition / September 2001

St. Martin's Paperbacks are published by St. Martin's Press, 175 Fifth Avenue, New York, NY 10010.

10 9 8 7 6 5 4 3 2

ACKNOWLEDGMENTS

THANKS to Joyce Bell, Christina Dodd, Betty Gyenes, and Susan Wiggs—fellow writers and dear friends. Thanks also to Marilyn Clay and Margaret Evans Porter for their timely research help, and to Connie Brockway for adding the right twist at the right time. Jennifer Enderlin, Matthew Shear, and the fine folks at St. Martin's Press have my continued appreciation. Lastly, my heartfelt gratitude goes to all the booksellers, librarians, and readers who have read and recommended my books. Bless you, everyone!

CONTENTS

PROLOGUE

NOT for the first time in his life, Lord Gabriel Kenyon discovered a lovely girl waiting in his bed. But for once he was too stunned to relish the sight.

Kate Talisford sat huddled against the pillows, the white counterpane drawn up to her chin. The light from the candle on the bedside table glowed on her pert nose and high cheekbones, the curly red-gold hair that spilled over her shoulders. Her wide green eyes revealed a blend of wariness and bravado.

She looked like a virgin sacrifice.

Aware that her parents and sister occupied rooms nearby, Gabe eased the door shut. In a stern whisper, he said, "What the deuce are you doing here?"

"I'm waiting for you, m'lord."

Her honeyed voice and alluring smile startled him anew. He shouldn't be lusting after Professor Henry Talisford's adolescent daughter. "It's past midnight," Gabe snapped. "Get back to your own chamber this instant."

"No. I've something to tell you." Watching him with a fervid, almost fearful intensity, she sat up straighter, the coverlet clutched to her throat. "Something important."

"We can talk in the morning."

"But you're leaving in the morning. You and Papa."

Of course, she only wished to quarrel again. While he'd

been downstairs in the study, poring over the map of Africa with Professor Talisford, Kate had been plotting this last-ditch battle to stop him. She must have slipped beneath his bedcovers to stay warm in the chilly night air.

He was perverted to think she'd come to make him a lewd offer.

Stepping around the open trunk in the middle of the small chamber, Gabe approached the bed, which was nestled beneath the sloping eaves. "I'm sorry you're distraught. But you can't stop us from departing."

"Oh?" she said in the sugary, un-Kate-like voice that played havoc with his imagination. "If you'd listen to what I have to say—"

"There's no point in wasting your breath." In a firm, big-brother tone, Gabe went on. "You're of an age to know better than to visit a man in his bedchamber. If anyone finds you here, your reputation will suffer."

She scooted backward against the pillows. "Don't treat me like a child. I'm a woman now."

So he could see. All the more reason for him to depart on the morrow. "You're sixteen and still in the schoolroom."

"I'm nearly seventeen . . . and I happen to be in your bed."

"Exactly where you shouldn't be," he said, reaching across the coverlet for her hand. "Now run along. It's too late to bicker."

"I'm not here to bicker." Her white teeth chafing her lower lip, Kate regarded him with that curious aura of seductress and schoolgirl. Then she drew a deep breath and, with a dramatic sweep of her arm, flung back the coverlet. "My darling Gabriel, don't leave me. I love you too much. I vow I'll die without you!"

A modest white nightgown cloaked her from throat to toes, though Gabe could see the hint of feminine curves.

He stood, paralyzed, his hand outstretched and his mind in the gutter.

Forcing a laugh, he lowered his arm. "Only yesterday you put salt in my tea and water in my inkwell. What was that colorful description you used? Ah, yes, you said I was a louse who deserved to be squashed."

"I was hiding my real feelings," Kate said with theatrical passion. She slid out of bed to stand before him, her hands clasped so tightly the knuckles showed white. "But this is my last chance to confess the truth," she recited in a rush. "I've loved you from the moment you came to draw sketches for Papa's book. You're the handsomest, most wonderful man I've ever met."

"Balderdash," he said. Her confession had a rehearsed quality that nonetheless stirred him. "You can't know more than a dozen men—and that includes the baker, the green-grocer, and the vicar."

"I know my own heart," she said, her voice quavering a little. "Please, let me show you how much I love you. Make me yours, darling."

She threw herself at him so unexpectedly, he almost fell over the trunk with its load of clothing and paints and sketchpads. By instinct, he caught her in his arms. Her soft breasts made a cushion against his chest, imprinting him with the forbidden warmth of nubile youth.

Just as swiftly, he thrust her away. "Don't be absurd. I'm ten years your elder and not in the habit of seducing naïve girls."

"I'm not naïve," she insisted. "I know all about what men do with women."

"I rather doubt that."

A charming blush tinted her fair skin. "I *do*. They . . . kiss. On the lips."

"Far more than that."

"They lie together, too. In bed."

Her clear-eyed expression proved that she didn't understand the particulars. Despite the serious circumstances, he
fought back a grin. "The woman also must remove every
stitch of her clothing. She must permit the man to touch
her as he wills, no matter how embarrassing the act might
be."

Kate blinked rapidly. The blush on her cheeks deepened
to a rosy hue. "Fanny says it's the greatest pleasure in all
the world."

"Fanny," he scoffed, picturing the bold maidservant with
her horse teeth and frizzy hair. "So that's who taught you
your shameless behavior. I'll speak to your mother about
having her replaced."

"All Mama thinks about is her gardening . . . and all *I*
think about is *you*, m'lord."

Kate kept her determined gaze trained on him as her slim
fingers plucked at the fastening of her bodice. A button
went flying, landing on the planked floor with a tiny *ping*,
but she paid no heed. Sweat broke out on his brow. He
could see the taut peaks of her breasts. Her ripe, womanly
breasts.

With an age-old charm, she murmured, "Please, Gabriel,
don't go to Africa. Don't take my father away. If you with-
draw your funding, he won't be able to afford the trip. He'll
stay home, where he belongs. And in return, I'll be . . . your
mistress."

For one mad moment, his loins controlled his logic. He
wanted to see her naked, to kiss her senseless, to tumble
her down onto the linens . . .

Snatching a shirt from the trunk, he hurled it at her.
"Cover yourself."

Kate clutched the garment to her bosom. "But . . . you
said the woman must remove her clothing."

"I didn't mean *you*," he said through gritted teeth. "I
was trying to make you see your own error."

"It's no error," she declared, her chin held at a defiant tilt. "I'll do anything to keep my family together."

"It would shatter your family if they found out you'd sold yourself to a man."

Her gaze wavered. "Papa needn't know. He's too wrapped up in his books."

That much was true. Surrounded by the ancient tomes and artifacts in his study, Henry Talisford could go all day without remembering to eat, let alone paying heed to a household of females. Cordelia Talisford, too, pottered in her flower garden with only a distracted regard for her two daughters. Kate and twelve-year-old Meg were left to run wild under the dubious supervision of a few servants.

Striving for paternal firmness, Gabe grasped Kate's arm and propelled her toward the door. "I decline your proposal. And don't you ever again show such idiocy as to offer yourself to any man other than your future husband."

Kate dug in her bare heels. With a stubborn fierceness, she turned on him. "This expedition is idiocy, that's what. Papa is a scholar, not an adventurer. He's far too old to survive a trek through the jungle and desert."

"He's forty, and in the prime of his life. Like me, he's been longing to explore Africa since he was a boy."

"No he *hasn't*! I would have known. He would have told *me*."

The glimpse of pain in her struck Gabe with guilt, a guilt he steeled himself to ignore. "You should be proud of him—he wants to give you and your sister a legacy. When we find that ruined city, we'll bring back enough gold and ivory to make you and your family very rich, indeed."

Kate crossed her arms. "I don't need wealth. I'm not a noble wastrel like you, squandering money on a foolish expedition."

"There's nothing foolish about it. The professor found a reference to the ancient city in a stack of dusty old manuscripts. I know the treasure is there, just waiting to be discovered."

Even as he spoke, Gabe knew that no woman could understand his burning purpose. He and Henry Talisford would be searching for a fabled lost civilization buried deep in the wilds of Abyssinia, beyond the uncharted source of the Nile. His fingers itched to draw all the strange new sights that no other explorer had seen before. At last he would step out of the shadow of his older brothers and achieve a renown of his own.

Michael and Joshua had disliked the notion of him setting off into dangerous, unknown territory, but at least they'd sent him on his way with a slap on the back and an admonition to take care. As for Grandmama, well, no female could fathom a man's thirst for adventure.

"Professor Talisford and I shall depart for the coast at first light," Gabe stated. "Nothing you say or do can change that."

"No!" Kate said wildly. "I'll follow you, then. I'll go with you and Papa. You can't stop me!"

With the mane of unruly red-gold hair rippling around her shoulders, she looked as fierce as a Celtic princess. He had to put an end to her folly, once and for all. "We'll send you straight back, then," he said harshly. "Neither your father nor I have any use for an irksome little girl."

She flinched, her lower lip quivering. The wounded look in her eyes was almost more than he could bear. On a choked sob, she hurled the shirt back at him. "I loathe you, Gabriel Kenyon. I'll loathe you forever. I hope you die in that jungle!" Then she darted out of the chamber, and her pattering footsteps vanished down the corridor.

Gabe crouched down to pick up the small white button that had lately graced her bosom. He despised hurting Kate, but even more, he despised himself for desiring her. Why the hell should he feel so remorseful, anyway? Someday, she'd thank him for saving her from her own foolishness.

Muttering a curse, he flung the button onto the empty bed.

CHAPTER I

A BEASTLY VISITOR

NEAR OXFORD, ENGLAND
1812

"I have the best news," Meg cried out, dancing into the parlor of Larkspur Cottage, her pelisse swirling around her black mourning gown. "Actually, two bits of wonderful news."

Straightening her aching back, Kate Talisford looked up from her packing and smiled as her younger sister plopped the market basket onto a cane-bottomed chair. Meg brought a ray of sunshine into the gloomy, partially stripped parlor. Their late mother's collection of floral paintings had been sold, leaving lighter squares against the age-dulled paneling. The oak bookshelves stood bare and forlorn with only a few wisps of dust scattered here and there. A daily maid helped out with the heavier tasks like the scrubbing and the laundry, but lately Kate had been too busy to do any other cleaning. To see their childhood home reduced to such a state left her feeling as hollow as the half-empty rooms, and she welcomed Meg's return.

"What news, dearest?" Kate asked, wrapping a silver candlestick in a length of old flannel. "Has Mrs. Wooster had her baby?"

"Gracious, no. She was waddling around the market like a fat Christmas goose. But here's what I wanted to show you." Rummaging in her basket, Meg pulled forth a bedraggled bit of paper. Her shoes made a light scuffing sound on the shabby rug as she hastened forward to thrust a handbill at Kate. "Look, the traveling players are in town! I just now saw them setting up their tent at the edge of Christchurch meadow. There'll be games and a puppet show and booths selling sweets. Oh, may we go to the fair this evening?"

Setting down the candlestick, Kate glanced over the advertisement, and for a moment, she caught her sister's excitement. How she wanted to watch the juggler and the magician, to laugh at the antics of the jesters and to savor hot meat pasties and sugary comfits. A few hours of escape tempted her. But practicality squashed her longing. "We mustn't squander our savings," she said regretfully, handing back the paper. "And don't forget, we've quite a lot of packing yet to do."

"We could stroll around without purchasing anything." Meg clasped her hands to her bosom. "*Do* say yes. I believe I shall die if I don't go."

Kate couldn't help smiling. Meg reminded her of herself at the tender age of sixteen, when she too had viewed the world as an unfinished canvas, full of rich color and exciting possibilities, her soul brimming over with fervent yearnings. And the zenith of her youthful madness had taken place in an upstairs bedchamber, when she'd thrown herself at an unsavory adventurer.

She shut the door on that wretched memory, unwilling to probe the ashes of anger. Dwelling on past mistakes accomplished nothing. Rather, she was grateful for the humiliating experience, for it had taught her the value of caution and sober sensibility. It had been a first, painful step toward maturity.

"We'll see about the fair," she said noncommittally. "It depends on how much work we can accomplish in the meantime." When Meg opened her mouth to plead again,

Kate held up her hand. "Now, what is your second bit of news?"

Slipping out of her pelisse, Meg hung the garment on a wall hook. "I saw John Thurgood strolling on the High Street today," she said, her blue eyes sparkling. "Oh, my heart, he's grown another inch over the Easter holidays. His chest is so broad and manly. And that dark gaze quite makes me shiver." Feigning a dramatic shudder, she twirled a path around the old green chairs and the threadbare brown chaise.

Kate wasn't overly concerned to hear of Meg's latest infatuation; her sister fell in and out of love daily. No doubt by tomorrow, Meg would have set her cap for another prospect. "John Thurgood is a graduate scholar and too old for a girl of six and ten. And where are your gloves, pray tell?"

Her sister stopped dancing and glanced abashedly at her bare fingers. "Oh . . . drat. I must have left them by the bridge."

"Folly Bridge, perchance?"

"Why, yes." Removing her plain black bonnet, Meg dropped it on a table. "Walking made me warm, and I stopped for a drink of water," she said over her shoulder. "I couldn't very well get my only pair of gloves wet, could I?"

Kate gave her sister a stern, knowing stare. "I wonder if you may have been distracted. Perhaps balancing on the rail of the bridge? In full view of the townsfolk?"

Meg had the good grace to blush. "So, Weasly Beasley has already come to call. I daresay that old tattletale is determined to discredit me."

Their busybody next-door neighbor had indeed interrupted Kate's packing to pass along the tidbit. "Mrs. Beasley couldn't discredit you, dear, if you didn't give her cause. That bridge is ancient and unsafe. You shouldn't go near it."

"Tra-la, tra-la." Meg waltzed to the mirror and tidied her silky black hair, the perfectly smooth, always obedient hair that Kate sorely envied. "The traveling players walk the high wire. Why should I be denied such fun?"

"Because you're a young lady, and you must behave yourself." Kate stepped around the crate and touched her sister's sleeve. "Oh, Meg. Surely you can see that."

Meg snorted. "Fie on propriety, I say. We're leaving here anyway, so what matter is it?"

"We're moving into town," Kate corrected. "And it matters because if ever I can complete Papa's book and earn some money, you'll have a season in London. In the meantime, you mustn't acquire a reputation for silly behavior."

Meg pursed her mouth in a pout. "There'll never be enough money for London, and you know it. There's never enough money for anything. We can't afford one new gown between the two of us. Even our mourning dresses are left over from when Mama . . ." She plucked at her drab black skirt, and tears glinted in her eyes so that she looked like a desolate little girl.

Kate blinked hard to stave off her own tears. Not long after their father had departed on his ill-fated trek through Africa, Mama had succumbed to a lung ailment after being caught out in a cold downpour while tending her beloved garden. By necessity, Kate had become both mother and father to Meg. To make matters worse, they had lost their comfortable savings when the bank manager had embezzled the funds of the investors. She and Meg had managed to recoup only a small nest egg, barely enough on which to subsist.

Of course, Meg didn't know about the opportunity to acquire five hundred gold guineas that Kate had declined recently. At times, particularly when she lay alone in her bed, pondering in the darkness, she wondered if she'd made the right decision.

Embracing her sister, Kate pressed a lace handkerchief into her fingers. "Don't weep, dearest," she murmured. "We must look forward, not back to things we cannot change."

Meg dabbed at her eyes. "If only Papa and Lord Gabriel had brought home a shipload of treasures. Gold and diamonds, ivory and emeralds. Imagine, we could have set those snobby Londoners on their ears."

Kate stiffened, remembering Lord Gabriel's grandiose promises. How carelessly he'd breezed into their lives, offering to fund her father's dreams, then whisking Papa away on a grand adventure. From time to time, Papa had sent them a jotted note along with an artifact like the ivory tusk of an elephant or a primitive jar. In turn, they had written to him, leaving letters at mail drops in remote outposts, never knowing if he'd received their missives or whether he'd ever even learned of his wife's death.

Only a fortnight ago, their hopes for his safe return had been dashed forever when a family friend had brought back news of Papa's death in Egypt at the hands of thieves.

Kate drew a long, steadying breath. "I would as soon have Papa back empty-handed. So long as he was alive."

"I, too," Meg said hastily. "Oh, Katie, I didn't mean to sound so greedy. It's just that . . . life is so much more bearable when one has money."

Kate couldn't quarrel with that, so she drew her sister to the shelves by the hearth. "Come, help me pack these dishes."

Obedient for once, Meg took down a blue china plate and tucked it in the straw inside the crate. "I do wish we weren't moving away from here. And to such dreary little rooms above that noisy, smelly marketplace."

"We must economize. The rent is a fraction of what we pay here." Kate wrapped a teapot in a sheet of old newspaper, trying not to remember her mother pouring tea, laughing gaily and chattering about her beloved flowers.

"With only the two of us now, we don't need so much space, anyway. We have to be practical."

"I hate economizing, and even more, I hate being practical." Meg gazed longingly at the open window, where the fresh scents of April drifted on the cool breeze. "If only we could go to the fair later . . ."

Kate nested the teapot in the crate. "May I remind you, the cart will be here in three days' time to take away our things. The new tenants will move in on Saturday. And we haven't even begun with Papa's study."

"Let's work faster, then," Meg said, opening a drawer at random and dumping the contents into a nearby wooden crate. She replaced the drawer, brushed off her hands, and said, "See? There's nothing to it."

Kate eyed the jumble of old quills, pruning shears, and balls of string. "I wanted to sort through all that. We can't fit everything into our new home."

"Then you would have more space if I were to join the traveling players," Meg grumbled. "At least *they* lead a life of freedom and leisure."

Did she mean it? Would she truly run away from home? "This is nothing to jest about," Kate said sharply. "Promise me you shan't go off on a lark with that troupe of ne'er-do-wells."

Meg cast her a defiant glance. "I could enjoy being acclaimed as a famous actress. Don't forget, I played Juliet at Miss Minchen's Academy last year." Clasping her hands, she intoned, " 'Come, nurse; I'll to my wedding bed. And death, not Romeo, take my maidenhead!' "

"It's a far cry to go from a school stage to a real one. You'd spend long, tiresome hours memorizing your lines. On rainy nights, you'd shiver in a tent or a wagon without even a fire to keep you warm. You'd trudge through mud and snow to the next town, and all for a few pence tossed into a hat—"

Meg let out a screech.

Kate wondered that her diatribe could have sparked so profound a reaction from her sister. But Meg wasn't looking at her. She stared goggle-eyed at the open window.

Kate followed her gaze and choked back a gasp. On the sill perched a dark furry beast with humanlike features and long hairy limbs protruding from a boy's breeches and shirt. That black, inquisitive gaze surveyed the interior of the cottage.

"Merciful heavens," she said breathlessly. "A monkey? A chimpanzee, if I'm not mistaken."

"Yes," Meg said in wonderment. "He looks just like the one in the drawing done by Lord Gabriel Kenyon—the one Papa sent to us."

Kate felt the little clench that Lord Gabriel's name always elicited in her, even as her mind whirled with confusion. "But . . . where did the beast come from?"

"The fair, of course! He must have escaped from the traveling actors." Her alarm vanishing with mercurial swiftness, Meg walked toward the chimpanzee. "What a darling creature! Are you lost? Can't you find your way back home?"

Babbling a string of gibberish, the chimpanzee stretched out to his pint-sized, bow-legged height.

"Do be careful," Kate said, hastening after her sister. "He's a wild animal and might bite."

"Nonsense, he looks quite tame. And I do believe he's just a baby. Doesn't he have a dear, sweet face?"

There *was* a certain charm to those simian features, Kate allowed. His dark eyes shone like those of a mischievous child. Succumbing to curiosity, she ventured closer and stopped beside Meg, who stood within arm's reach of the chimp.

"What do you suppose we should do with him?" Meg whispered as if he might understand her and take offense.

"Return him to the fair, of course. But how?"

"I'll take him." Eagerly, Meg reached out for the beast.

Kate stepped swiftly forward. "Wait! He's better off handled by his trainer. Why don't you run along and alert the players—"

In a lightning-quick movement, the chimpanzee thrust out a gangly arm and snatched the ivory comb that secured her tight bun. Kate clapped her hands to her hair—too late. A cloudburst of smaller pins popped out and rained onto the carpet. The too-thick, curling red-gold hair that was her bane tumbled down to her waist.

"You little thief!" Kate sputtered. "Give that back!"

She made a grab for him, but the chimpanzee bounded to the top of an empty bookshelf. There, he waved the comb in his leathery fingers, rolled back his lips, and loosed a series of high-pitched squawks.

Meg's eyes danced with laughter. "What a rum cove! I do believe he's funning you, dear sister."

A bubble of hysterical mirth escaped Kate. Marching to the bookcase, she tilted her head up and held out her hand. "Naughty boy," she scolded. "I'll take that comb back now."

Hooting, the chimp walked back and forth atop the oak bookshelf, sending little showers of dust downward to tickle Kate's nose. When he balanced the comb atop his head, he bore an uncanny resemblance to an ugly matron.

"Weasly Beasley," Kate couldn't help observing. "That's who he looks like."

Giggling, Meg clapped her hands to her cheeks. "Gad-a-mercy, you're right! He's the spitting image of that hag."

"But not for long. I won't let him steal Mama's favorite comb." Kate carried over a stool, lifted her skirts to step onto it, and reached for the chimpanzee. Even as her fingertips brushed one shaggy, crooked leg, he scampered down to the other end of the shelves. She moved the stool, but again he loped out of her reach.

Clearly enjoying the game, the primate chortled, displaying a set of broad teeth.

Meg dragged over a chair to the opposite side of the bookcase. "You stay down there," she told Kate. "Between the two of us, he can't get away."

But the chimp outsmarted them. He took a flying leap at the window and clambered up the faded gold draperies. Balancing on the wooden rod, he looked down on them and screeched in triumph, holding up the comb like a prize of war.

The sisters exchanged an exasperated glance. "You'd better run for help," Kate said. "I'll stay here and watch that he doesn't get into more trouble."

Nodding, Meg dashed into the small foyer of the cottage. Kate heard the squeak of the door opening, then her sister's startled exclamation. "Oh, my heart and soul!"

"What's wrong?" Kate called.

Meg didn't answer, and Kate could hear her speaking to someone in the low, trilling, breathless tone she used with men. Blast Meg! She mustn't dally with one of her suitors at such a moment.

Keeping an eye on the chimpanzee, Kate sidled toward the archway that led to the foyer. She pasted on a polite smile and glanced out, intending to hurry her sister on her way.

Instead, she witnessed her second shock of the day.

The tall figure of a man blocked the doorway. His face was cast into shadow by the backdrop of brilliant morning sunshine, and Kate had to squint to discern his features: high cheekbones, jutting jaw, ocean-blue eyes. Like a pirate aboard his ship, he stood with his booted feet planted apart in a bold stance. The breeze ruffled his dark hair into an attractive disarray. His attention on Meg, he grinned at something she'd said and his white teeth shone against skin burnished by the sun to a rich teak hue.

He looked up, straight at Kate. His smile died.

So did hers.

CHAPTER 2

THE GUARDIAN

KATE held herself rigidly upright lest she swoon for the first time in her life. Her palms felt damp and cold. Her mind reeled, resisting the identity of the man standing before her. Lord Gabriel Kenyon.

In a sickening flash, she recalled their last meeting four years earlier, when she'd thrown herself at him like a lovestruck ninny. Not only had his rejection lacerated her tender heart, it had left her with a lingering scar of humiliation, torment, and anger.

Because of this man, her father was dead.

"Don't you remember Lord Gabriel?" Meg said, a coquettish note in her voice. "I vow, I didn't recognize him either until he introduced himself. After all, I was only a girl of twelve when he left—"

"Meg," Kate interrupted. "Go on to the fair. Find out who owns that monkey."

Scowling, Meg opened her mouth to protest, but Lord Gabriel cut her off with a wave of his hand. "I do."

His deep voice raised the hairs at the nape of Kate's neck. Feeling slow and stupid, she struggled for icy manners. "I beg your pardon?"

"Jabbar belongs to me."

"Jabbar?"

"The chimpanzee. The rascal ran away from me." With the confidence of a man strolling into his own home, Lord Gabriel strode past her and entered the parlor.

Trailed by an eager Meg, Kate marched in his wake.

She caught his male scent, spicy and exotic. He had left England a brash young man soft from his rich, pampered life. Now, to her critical eyes, he projected the aura of a menacing stranger. He had grown more muscular, his face hewn from the hard angles of experience. His years in the wilds of Africa had affected his sense of propriety, too. With his unbuttoned blue coat, no cravat, and shaggy hair, he looked in need of a decent valet. The shocking display of his bare throat and the form-fitting doeskin breeches only enhanced his half-savage appearance.

Beside him, Kate felt like a drab little mouse in her old black dress, the one with the torn lace on the sleeve that she hadn't found the time to mend. A mouse with a tangle of curly, unbound hair that streamed down to her waist in rumpled disorder.

Because *his* chimpanzee had stolen *her* comb.

Pursing her lips, she said, "I'll thank you to remove your wild animal from the premises at once."

Her prim manner only seemed to amuse him. "Jabbar is domesticated, house-trained in fact. He's just a youngster." Going to the window, Lord Gabriel tilted back his head and regarded the chimp, who was balanced on the drapery rod. "Think you're king of the castle, do you? Come down now. Make your apologies to the ladies."

Jabbar looked as sheepish as a boy caught with his hand in a jar of sweets. He hunched his furry shoulders and peered at his master. Then slowly he clambered down the gold chintz curtain as if it were a jungle vine. Hanging his head, he approached Lord Gabriel.

"I won't bail you out of this one," Lord Gabriel said in a stern voice. "You'll give it back to her yourself."

Jabbar looked from him to Kate and back again.

"Go on," Lord Gabriel prodded.

Knuckles balanced on the threadbare carpet, the monkey loped toward Kate. He fingered the ivory comb with uncannily human regret, and then handed it to her. Amazed in spite of herself, she watched as the chimp turned and leapt into Lord Gabriel's arms.

Meg clapped her hands. "What a pretty trick! However did you train him so well, my lord?"

His smile charming, Lord Gabriel held the chimp as casually as he might hold a human child. "Training is wasted on him—the scamp is too inquisitive for his own good. And too fond of mischief. On the voyage to England, he even crept into the wheelhouse and steered us off course."

Jabbar snaked a leathery hand into Lord Gabriel's pocket and pulled out an orange. Chortling, he drew back his lips in a grin.

"He *is* a darling," Meg crooned, though her limpid eyes lingered on Lord Gabriel. "Where did you get him?"

"I liberated him from a trader outside Khartoum. His mother had been killed by poachers."

"How dreadful! May I hold him?"

"He's heavier than he looks."

"Fiddle-faddle. I can manage."

With a slight smile, he handed the chimpanzee to her. "You do seem a girl who can manage whatever you set your mind to doing."

Their flirtatious exchange sparked a fiery resentment in Kate. Blast Lord Gabriel for charming her naïve sister. He should realize that Meg had practiced her wiles only on the callow boys of the university town. A sixteen-year-old knew nothing of handling ne'er-do-well rogues.

Nor had Kate at one time. Her heart ached for the foolish girl she'd been, believing she could change him. Ever since then, a shrewd, no-nonsense manner had enabled her to parry their creditors, to take charge of the household after Mama's death, and to provide sensible guidance for Meg.

So why, Kate wondered, did a breathlessness catch at her lungs? She was no silly, romantic girl anymore.

Surreptitiously, she twisted her hair into a topknot and jammed in the comb so firmly that her scalp hurt. Retrieving the smaller pins from the floor, she ruthlessly fastened every stray strand in place. She wanted to step out to the foyer and check her appearance in the mirror, but subdued that feminine vanity.

When she turned, she saw Lord Gabriel watching her with a fixed concentration. A tremor flashed through her, shaking her hard-won confidence. Just as quickly, she denied the sensation. Lord Gabriel Kenyon was a callous barbarian. She felt only a hard knot of fury that he had dared to come back here to Larkspur Cottage after funding the expedition that had claimed Papa's life.

Gripping her hands at her sides, she said, "This has been most entertaining, my lord. However, you've caught us at a rather hectic time."

His intense gaze shifted to the wooden crates, some empty and some filled with books and bric-a-brac. "You're moving," he stated with some surprise.

"On Friday."

"Where?"

"Into town. This cottage doesn't suit us anymore."

"Why not?"

"Why must you ask?" she countered. "Oxford is a beautiful place. We'll be nearer to the market and the church." It was indeed a lovely town, she told herself firmly. She liked the broad, cobbled streets, the ancient medieval buildings, the colleges bustling with young scholars and old professors in academic gowns. She and Meg were certain to be happy there. Perhaps they could even find friends in the literate society that Papa had once frequented as a professor of ancient cultures.

"We'll be living in tiny rooms right over the market," Meg blurted out, holding the chimp. "You see, we haven't any money. The bank lost it all, right after Mama died."

Again, his gaze sharpened on Kate, and he inspected her from the top of her severe hairstyle down to the frayed hem of her gown. "Tell me what happened."

"It's over with and done, and we have enough to manage," Kate said, directing a quelling glance at her sister.

"Why hasn't your great-uncle provided for you?"

Because Nathaniel Babcock is as irresponsible as most men, Kate wanted to say. "The last we heard, he was touring Italy with his latest paramour. Now, I presume you're here to offer your belated condolences in regard to my father."

"Yes," Lord Gabriel said, his voice deepening to a gravelly pitch. His piercing gaze flitted over their mourning garb. "Who gave you the news?"

"We were informed weeks ago by a family acquaintance. He was visiting Cairo . . . when it happened." Kate swallowed against the thickness in her throat. The notion of weeping in front of this heartless man horrified her. Tears were useless, anyway; her father had been gone for four years already. She had learned to manage quite well without him.

Yet it was painful to accept that Papa wasn't ever coming home. That she could never again embrace him, never again see his blue eyes magnified by his spectacles or smell his comfortable aroma of pipe smoke.

"Who told you?" Lord Gabriel repeated.

Before Kate could recover herself, Meg said dejectedly, "Papa's friend, Sir Charles Damson."

Lord Gabriel's face hardened to a cold mask. "Damson? He came *here*?"

Meg stroked Jabbar's furry arm. "Yes, he was ever so kind. He even lent me his handkerchief to dry my tears."

Kate wondered at the tension that resonated through the small parlor. Why did Lord Gabriel's eyes hint at a violent rage? "Do you know him, too?"

"He's a collector of antiquities," he said tersely as if that explained everything.

Perhaps it did. Perhaps he resented Sir Charles's camaraderie with Papa. Certainly, Sir Charles Damson had been the more considerate friend. Informing her and Meg of Papa's passing clearly had ranked low on Lord Gabriel's list of important tasks.

"We'll be forever grateful to Sir Charles," she said. "*He* cut short his Egyptian holiday on our behalf."

"Is he still in Oxford?" Lord Gabriel fired back.

"No, he returned to London." To needle him, Kate added, "Though I do wish he'd stayed longer. He's a pleasant, polite gentleman."

"Yet not so fine as you, m'lord," Meg piped up, giving Lord Gabriel another adoring smirk.

He turned his watchful gaze on her. "How long was he here?"

"He took tea with us, of course." Sniffling, Meg clutched the chimanzee tighter against her. "Luckily, Kate had baked a cake that morning, but we didn't have enough in the larder to invite him to stay for supper."

"Then he left straightaway?"

"Why, yes—"

"And he hasn't returned since?"

Kate had had enough of his arrogance. Stepping forward, she said firmly, "No, Sir Charles hasn't come back. Though I do wish he would. At least *he* doesn't badger us with impertinent questions."

The harshness smoothed from Lord Gabriel's tanned features, and he aimed a beguiling look at Meg. "Do me a favor and take Jabbar out into the garden. As you can see, his manners leave much to be desired."

The pungent aroma of fruit spiced the air as the chimp busily peeled the orange and dropped the skin to the carpet.

Meg fixed her worshipful eyes on Lord Gabriel. "But I

was hoping to hear all about your marvelous adventures in Africa—"

He steered her to the foyer. "You shall. Later."

"I don't know how to care for a monkey. What if Jabbar escapes?"

"He won't. He's in need of a mother. He likes you already."

Meg made one last futile attempt to stay with the adults. "It isn't proper for a gentleman to be left alone with a lady."

"You'll be right outside." Opening the door, he gave Meg a little push.

In another moment, Kate spied her sister through the window, walking with the chimpanzee down the flagstone path to a stone bench in the overgrown rose arbor. As Jabbar ate the orange sections, Meg glanced back at the cottage with an all-too-familiar impatience.

Lord Gabriel scooped up the peelings and dropped them out the window. Tall and muscled, he dominated the parlor, making the very air seem thicker, charged with the force of his presence. Uneasy, Kate again remembered the last time they had been alone, when she had behaved like a besotted ninny. Did he ever recall that mortifying episode? Did he think back on her declaration of undying love and laugh at her naïveté?

It didn't matter; his opinion meant less than nothing to her. A typical man, he'd gone off on his grand adventure with nary a thought for those left behind. Now, thanks to him, Papa lay buried in a foreign land.

Lord Gabriel picked up a cowrie shell and examined it, idly stroking a long brown finger over the pale, fist-shaped surface. "In the Sudan, the tribal people use these shells as currency to purchase a bride."

"In England, it's a paperweight." Kate crushed her curiosity about all the fascinating sights he had seen over the past four years. "I'm sure you haven't come here to discuss obscure native customs."

He set down the shell and regarded her. A faint devil-try—and something else she couldn't identify—deepened the creases at the corners of his eyes. "Prickly Kate. Won't you at least invite me to sit down?"

"Pray have a seat, my lord," she said with polite for-bearance.

He waved his hand. "Ladies first."

She perched on the chaise, automatically taking the threadbare spot, and folded her hands in her lap. Too late, she realized her mistake. Lord Gabriel had the audacity to settle down right beside her. As if to embrace her, he stretched out his arm across the back of the chaise.

Instantly wary, she inched nearer to the upholstered arm. But he still sat so close she could see each individual black lash shading his keen blue eyes. He looked weathered, rug-ged, steeped in experiences she could only imagine. Things she didn't *want* to imagine.

"What did you wish to discuss with me?" she prompted.

"Tell me why Damson came here."

"I told you why—to inform us of Papa's death. He didn't want us to hear the news by gossip or letter. I ap-preciate his thoughtfulness."

Lord Gabriel's jaw tightened, as did his voice. "What exactly did he say to you?"

"He told us what had happened, of course. And he of-fered his condolences."

"Did he say how he'd learned the news?"

Wondering at his pointed questions, she gave a curt nod. "An Egyptian official told him . . . Papa was attacked by thieves on the night before he planned to set sail for En-gland. They broke into his room at the inn, looking for valuables. When Papa tried to stop them, they struck out at him . . ."

Kate bit her lip to stop its quivering. Papa had been intending to return home to her and Meg. They would have been a family again. And this time, she'd have been a good, helpful, loving daughter. She would have organized his notes, edited his writings, and aided him in publishing a book about his study of ancient cultures . . . perhaps a whole series of books.

Now, to honor his memory, she must do it alone.

Lord Gabriel's large hand came down over hers in her lap. "I'm sorry, Kate. You can't imagine how much."

His shockingly masculine touch threatened to spark the powder keg of emotions in her. Half of her was tempted to throw herself into his arms. The other half wanted to slap the sympathy off that sun-browned face.

She pushed his hand away. "Why didn't *you* save Papa? Where were you when my father was fighting for his life?"

An unfathomable blankness hid his thoughts. "I was out."

"Where?"

"It isn't important. And you're right. I should have been there. If I'd arrived only a few minutes earlier . . ."

"What?" she demanded. "Tell me everything."

"Suffice it to say, Henry lay stricken by a fatal blow. The brigands overpowered me." He paused, his expression grim. "I don't remember anything else until I awakened in a hospital three days later."

"Three *days*?" she said, doubting him. Sir Charles hadn't mentioned any injury. "Surely you weren't insensible that entire time."

"I'd lost a lot of blood. I had a raging fever. It took me a month to recuperate."

Kate could see no visible scars. He appeared hale and healthy, untouched and invincible. "How were you wounded?" she asked without a care for propriety.

"Stabbed," he said. "In the back."

She winced involuntarily, her spine stiffening. Swallowing queasiness, she asked, "Did you see the men? Could you identify them?"

"No." His reply was quick, terse, angry.

"Do you know if they've been caught and punished for their crime?"

He narrowed his eyes, staring at some distant point beyond her. "They haven't. By the time I was able to search for them, the trail was cold. They'd vanished into the vastness of the desert."

Savagery brooded on his dark features, but Kate didn't entirely trust him to stalk the murderers. He was the sort of man who looked out for his own interests. Had he really bothered to conduct a thorough search? "I wish I'd been there," she said, barely able to leash her own ferocity. "I'd have gone after them myself."

His gaze snapped back to hers. "Don't be ridiculous. Henry wouldn't have wanted you there. Africa is no place for a lady."

Neither your father nor I have any use for an irksome little girl. The cruel words he'd flung at her so long ago returned with a bitter vengeance. "And England is no place for an ill-mannered brute like you."

His mouth quirked in a way that was half grimace, half smile. "You're right, of course. Though I didn't come here to quarrel with you. I wanted to give you this." Reaching into an inner pocket of his coat, he withdrew a folded paper and pushed it into her tense fingers.

Kate slowly opened it, the parchment rustling. She stared down at a drawing, exquisitely rendered in pen and ink, of a modest stone cross on a hill shaded by several exotic palms.

"It's your father's grave," he said quietly.

Her chest tightened and her eyes blurred. With supreme effort, she restrained the hurt and loss that threatened to overwhelm her. She hadn't expected kindness, not from this man.

Hardly trusting herself to speak, she took a deep breath. "I don't know what to say," she whispered, her voice raw.

Lord Gabriel took hold of her shoulders, his fingers firm and his face taut. "Kate, I would gladly have traded my life for your father's. If you believe nothing else, believe that."

Kate believed nothing of the sort. His regrets came too late. Four years too late. Rising to her feet, the sketch gripped in her hand, she said coolly, "I accept your condolences, my lord. If that's all you've come here to say . . ."

As handsome as sin, he stood up to loom over her. "As a matter of fact, it isn't. I wanted to know if the professor's belongings arrived safely."

"Yes, a few weeks ago."

"Then you've examined the contents of the crate."

"No." She swallowed hard. "I've been busy. I haven't had the time." *Or the fortitude.*

"I see." His mouth eased into the semblance of charm. "If you wouldn't mind, I'd like to take a look."

"Look for what?" she scoffed. "The treasures you promised to bring back?"

Darkness flickered in his eyes, then vanished behind his amiable mask. "My sketchbooks are packed in there. I want them back."

So much for compassion. Lord Gabriel wished only the return of his property. Pivoting away, she tucked the precious drawing in the old, leather-bound Bible. "Leave me your address," she said politely. "I'll send them on to you."

"Don't trouble yourself. It'll only take a few moments to retrieve the books. I presume the box is in the study?"

Lord Gabriel stepped past her, heading for the corridor. His boldness enraged Kate. Picking up her skirts, she surged forward at an unladylike speed and planted herself directly in his path. "I beg your pardon!" she said in her iciest voice. "I haven't given you leave to wander about my home at will."

"Forgive me," he said with a smile that surely had the power to melt maidens from London to Zanzibar—though it caused only a clench of distaste inside Kate. "I forgot myself," he went on. "I did live at Larkspur Cottage once, if you'll recall."

How could she ever forget? Lord Gabriel had been her father's favored colleague. The man who had financed Papa's dreams. Not caring if she was rude, she said, "Until I have the opportunity to sort through Papa's effects, they shall remain undisturbed. By you or anyone else."

His gaze sharpened, his smile fading. "Has somebody asked to see that box?"

Shaken by his astuteness, she compressed her lips.

"Was it Damson?" he prodded, taking a menacing step toward her.

"As a matter of fact, Sir Charles offered to purchase the entire contents of Papa's study. For five hundred guineas." Kate instantly regretted letting herself be goaded by him. Not even Meg knew about that offer. As desperately as they needed the funds, Kate couldn't bear to sell so much as a scrap of paper with Papa's scribbling upon it.

Lord Gabriel scowled. "Damson must not touch any artifact that Henry sent back from Africa."

"Nor will *you* since they are in *my* possession."

He glowered another moment, and she feared he would thrust her aside and take whatever he wanted by brute strength. Instead, he plunged his fingers through his hair, further mussing the sun-streaked brown strands. "Be reasonable, Kate. As your father's partner, I have a stake in the curios we collected."

"No."

"Then I'll double Damson's offer. A thousand guineas."

"You can't be serious."

"I assure you, I am."

Kate braced her shoulder against the timbered wall. A thousand gold guineas? Meg could have a London season, entertain suitors, and marry respectably. Then Kate could live modestly off the remainder while she completed her book.

But there would be no book if she sold the fruits of Papa's research. No legacy to memorialize him. No way to absolve herself of a lingering guilt over never saying goodbye to him four years ago.

"You believe money can buy you anything," she said. "But it can't buy what belongs to me."

Watching her intently, Lord Gabriel took a step closer, crowding her with his too large, too masculine presence. "There's no need to answer now. Take some time to think about it."

"I've given the matter enough thought. The answer is no. Your wealth has brought this family enough trouble."

"Then consider Meg. It's clear that you both need the funds."

She stiffened. "What we need or don't need is no concern of yours."

"Oh, but there you're wrong. Your welfare is very much my concern." A grim smile graced his hard mouth. "You see, Kate, in the event of his death, your father appointed me your guardian."

CHAPTER 3

THE LUCIFER LEAGUE

"My dear Miss Talisford, there is something vital you should know," Sir Charles Damson said later that afternoon. "Shortly before his demise, your father asked me to act as protector toward you and your sister."

Kate's mouth dropped open as she stared at the baron's fine, pale features. Sir Charles looked like the paragon of elegance with his styled, flaxen curls, the apple-green coat with its gleaming gold buttons, the perfectly tied cravat. When he had appeared unexpectedly on their doorstep, just hours after the unsettling encounter with Lord Gabriel, she had welcomed him warmly, inviting him into the parlor while Meg went to fetch their tea. His flattering attention had soothed her injured sensibilities; he had even brought the bouquet of pink tulips that decorated the mantelpiece. Sir Charles was witty and respectful and pleasantly predictable.

At least he had been so until this moment. It couldn't be merely a bizarre coincidence that two men on the very same day would claim guardianship of her and Meg. One of them had to be lying.

Lord Gabriel, she decided instantly.

Yet suspicion wormed its way into her confidence. "Why would Papa make such a request of you?" she asked. "He couldn't have known what would happen to him."

Sir Charles shook his head sadly. "I found it rather odd myself. When we met in Cairo, he seemed rather ill at ease.

Later, I could only conclude that he'd known he was being stalked by thieves."

Cold prickles crawled over Kate's skin. The explanation made horrid sense. So why hadn't Lord Gabriel mentioned it? Even worse, if he'd been aware of the danger, why had he done nothing to protect her father?

"I can see this is all quite shocking to you," Sir Charles went on, looking apologetic. "That is why I hesitated to broach the topic when last we met. May I say, Miss Talisford, I greatly respect and admire your independent nature."

His concern was so genuine, Kate felt disloyal for her doubts. Yet she felt compelled to ask him the same question she'd asked Lord Gabriel. "Have you a document proving your guardianship?"

For a full three seconds, Sir Charles stared at her. Then he inclined his head in a nod. "Not with me, alas. My solicitor in London holds all my important papers."

Reeling at the news, Kate stared at the baron. "The agreement is signed by my father?"

"Of course. If you like, I can make arrangements for my man to deliver the document, though it might take a few days."

Putting a hand to her brow, she didn't know what to say. Unlike Lord Gabriel, who claimed only a verbal understanding with her father, Sir Charles actually possessed a legal paper with Papa's signature. As highly as she regarded Sir Charles, she felt uneasy being dependent on any man, let alone one who was merely an acquaintance to her.

"This is all so sudden," Kate murmured. Then something occurred to her. "I've a great-uncle who will provide for us, I'm sure."

Sir Charles narrowed his eyes. "I thought you had no family left."

"There's Great-uncle Nathaniel. So you see, we needn't depend on the charity of others."

"I wouldn't dream of offering charity," the baron said quickly. "That's why I thought to purchase the contents of your father's study, as a fair exchange for both of us. Have you reconsidered my proposal?"

"My answer remains the same. I shan't sell anything yet."

"Are you quite certain? Pardon me for saying so, but the proceeds would prove a great help to you and your sister."

Kate compressed her lips. That fact had been pointed out to her more than once today. And she found it strikingly odd that both her visitors wanted Papa's effects.

"I'll let you know if ever I change my mind," Kate said to placate him. Hearing the rattle of the tea cart in the corridor, she lowered her voice to a whisper. "I must ask that you mention nothing of money matters to Meg. It would only distress her."

"Of course, but . . . ye gods!" Abandoning dignity, Sir Charles shot out of his chair as Meg pushed the cart into the parlor, followed by a knuckle-walking Jabbar. "Where did that beast come from?"

Before Kate could think of a logical reason for an illogical situation, the chimpanzee spied their visitor and let loose an ear-splitting screech.

"Quiet now!" Meg scolded in a schoolmarm voice. "This is our guest and dear friend, Sir Charles Damson. Sir Charles, this is Jabbar."

Kate refrained from mentioning the foolishness of introducing a monkey to a lord of the realm. She hastened forward to help Meg with the tea cart. "Forgive me, Sir Charles. I should have warned you about the chimpanzee."

The look of stark horror melted from the baron's refined features, and with a tolerant smile, he strolled toward the chimp. "By Jupiter, he gave me a start. Not at all what one would expect to encounter in the home of two such pretty ladies."

Jabbar bared his teeth and growled, puffing out his hairy chest.

Sir Charles stopped and chuckled. "Why, if it weren't absurd, I'd say the little fellow's jealous. One can't blame him for wanting to keep the two of you all to himself."

Meg preened. "How kind of you, sir. I can assure you, Jabbar wouldn't harm a flea."

The chimp chose that moment to leap up and down, beating his fists on his chest in a distinctly simian challenge. His angry hooting echoed through the small parlor.

"Or so we hope," Kate muttered under her breath. Not for the first time, she regretted the weak moment when she had succumbed to Meg's pleading to keep the animal. Her only excuse was that she'd been utterly flummoxed by Lord Gabriel's claim to guardianship.

A claim she'd rejected as ridiculous. A claim he'd sworn to honor.

"I'll inspect these rooms you're renting in town," he'd said. *"To see if they meet with my approval. If not, I'll arrange for a more suitable place for you and your sister to live."*

"You'll do nothing of the sort," Kate retorted. *"I don't need your approval."*

"Yes, you do." His face was firm, unyielding, ominous. *"You and Meg are my responsibility now. That means you're both subject to my decisions."*

"Then I'll meet you in a court of law," she'd flung back. *"You'll have to prove your claim."*

Thinking back on his arrogance made Kate burn. Lord Gabriel had had the audacity to laugh at her threat. He knew as well as she that a judge would rule in favor of a rich man, brother to the Marquess of Stokeford and a member of one of the most powerful families in England. Especially if Great-uncle Nathaniel spurned his duty toward her and Meg.

But now, circumstances had taken a new twist. If Sir Charles truly did possess a document signed by her father, she would be forced by law to accept his guardianship.

Frustrated by the tangled situation, Kate snatched up a scone from the tray and gave it to the chimp. "Take him to his cage in the kitchen," she told Meg.

"But—"

"Do it, please."

Meg marched off with a screeching Jabbar in tow. Gathering the shreds of her composure, Kate made a show of pouring three cups of tea from the pot she'd hastily unpacked not half an hour ago.

"You must tell me where you obtained that wild creature," Sir Charles said, resuming his seat on a gold-striped chair, its shabbiness accentuated by his refinement. "Surely your father didn't send it all the way from Africa."

"No. Jabbar doesn't really belong to us," Kate said, stirring a lump of brown sugar into Sir Charles's teacup. She clenched her teeth at the memory of how Lord Gabriel had overridden her objections and indulged Meg's plea to keep Jabbar. It was the last time, Kate vowed, that she would let him dictate to her. "Jabbar is staying here only temporarily. His owner couldn't keep him at the inn for fear of alarming the other guests."

"His owner?"

"Lord Gabriel Kenyon." The name tasted bitter on her tongue. With effort, she maintained a pleasant expression, hoping Sir Charles hadn't detected the malice in her tone.

A strange alertness darkened his pale gray eyes. "What's that?" he said. "Kenyon was here?"

Meg stepped back into the parlor alone. "Yes, and he saved Jabbar from some evil traders. He said we could adopt him if we wished." She giggled. "Adopt Jabbar, that is."

Kate cast her a warning glance. Meg obstinately lifted her chin.

With his gloved fingers, Sir Charles stroked the diamond stickpin that anchored his immaculate cravat. "Well, well. Kenyon certainly took his time returning from Cairo. More than two months have passed since the attack. Did the rascal mention what kept him away for so long?"

"He was recovering from his wounds."

"Those robbers stabbed him," Meg said, wilting dramatically onto the chaise. "Why didn't you tell us he'd almost died?"

"Poppycock. I was told his wounds were minor." Taking a drink from the dainty cup, the baron lifted an eyebrow as if to cast doubt on Lord Gabriel's tale. "Your father hinted . . . perhaps I shouldn't say."

Kate leaned forward. "Hinted what?"

"That he didn't entirely trust Kenyon." Sir Charles held up a hand. "But it was only an impression I had. There's probably nothing to it."

Or was there? Kate wondered. "If only Papa were here to ask."

The baron's face softened. "I didn't mean to distress you. Remember that your father adored you . . . both of you. On the day before he died, Henry told me how very much he looked forward to seeing his dear, sweet daughters again."

A lump formed in Kate's throat. "Did he say . . . anything else?"

"Only that he regretted staying away from England for so long." Sir Charles smiled, encompassing Meg in his kindly perusal. "He was a man of few words, as you know, and for him to voice such sentiments, even to a friend, can only underscore the depth of his feelings for you two."

Kate swallowed hard. Strange that Papa had so seldom mentioned Sir Charles to her. But the baron was right; Papa had been a reticent man, especially with his family. And she hadn't been a biddable young lady who had invited his confidences. It was a fact she would always bitterly regret.

No longer able to speak of her father without weeping, she changed the subject. "Will you stay long in Oxford this time, Sir Charles?"

"Only tonight, I fear. Then I must travel to my estate on the Cornish coast. I'll be hosting a large house party at the end of the month." He wrinkled his nose in a wry expression. "Alas, one can never quite trust the servants to arrange things properly."

"A party?" Meg said, fairly bouncing on the chaise. "Will all the *ton* be there?"

"Only those who matter," he said with a smile. "One must be particular about one's friends, of course."

"Tell me, are you inviting"—she lowered her voice to a loud whisper—"the Lucifer League?"

Sir Charles froze, his teacup suspended midway to his mouth. "Where have you heard of *them*?"

Kate set down her cup with a clatter. "Meg? What on earth are you talking about?"

"A group of noble pagans who worship the ancient gods," Meg said in shivery delight. "They have lewd ceremonies and call upon the devil himself. At chapel, I overheard the boys whispering about it."

"You shouldn't listen to tales told by prankish boys who ought to be listening to the sermon," Kate chided.

"It isn't a tale, it's the truth!"

"Only partly so," Sir Charles said, brushing at his yellow nankeen pantaloons. "The Lucifer League is a harmless club of aristocrats who are bored with society."

All wide-eyed curiosity, Meg leaned toward him. "Do you know any of them?"

"In my elite circle, one can't help being acquainted with these gentlemen," the baron said, shrugging. "As to their sins, I suppose they practice the same vices as other coves. I daren't say more in the presence of innocent young ladies."

"But can't you at least tell us—"

"Meg," Kate said sharply. "That's enough."

Meg closed her mouth, though her slippered foot tapped out a rebellious message on the rug.

Sir Charles sipped his tea. "For myself, I prefer more genteel company. May I say, two such lovely flowers of English womanhood would enhance my little gathering. I'd be honored if the two of you would attend."

Meg stopped tapping and perked up.

"That's very kind of you, but my sister is not yet out," Kate said, swallowing her own secret yearning to attend a society party. "It wouldn't be appropriate."

"I'll be seventeen on the thirtieth of April," Meg declared. "Jane Fairfax attended her first ball on her seventeenth birthday."

"You are not Jane Fairfax."

Pouting, Meg crossed her arms. "You never let me do *anything*. I'll probably be twenty-five before you even let a man pay court to me."

Mortified by her sister's rudeness, Kate frowned a warning at her. "We're in mourning, pray remember. Out of respect for Papa, you shall wait another year."

"A pity," Sir Charles said with obvious disappointment. "But as your guardian, I extend an open invitation to the two of you to visit Damson Castle in Cornwall."

Meg's eyes grew large. "*You're* our guardian?" She cast an accusing glance at Kate. "You never told me that."

Kate tensed. As pleasant as the baron was, she felt a natural aversion to trusting him or any other man. "I knew nothing of the arrangement until today. I shall have to consult Great-uncle Nathaniel on the matter."

"But he's away in Italy," Meg said, turning adoring eyes on the baron. "While Sir Charles is right here in England. Dear Sir Charles, it's so admirable and gallant of you to take us under your wing."

Reaching out, he fervently clasped her hand. "Thank you, my dear. Indeed, I would be happy to fulfill your every wish."

"Nothing is settled," Kate said firmly. "It will be weeks before I hear from our uncle."

But Meg and Sir Charles had eyes only for each other. "Now that you mention it, sir," Meg said, "there *is* a favor you might do for us."

He pressed his palm to his neatly buttoned coat. "Ask and it's yours."

Sliding a defiant look at Kate, Meg said, "There's a fair in town. Perhaps you'd be good enough to escort us to it this evening."

CHAPTER 4

HIDDEN TREASURE

"WALK over! Walk in! Witness the dangers of tightrope dancing. Only one penny admission."

Kate fished in her reticule and drew out two coppers. Before she could hand them to the bewhiskered hawker, Sir Charles tossed him a few coins, which the stout man deftly caught in his hairy fist.

As they walked into the torch-lit tent, she tried to give her pennies to Sir Charles. "Please, I won't have you paying for us. It isn't proper."

He smiled benevolently. "Nonsense, my dear. I'd be insulted if you didn't allow me the pleasure of acting as your guardian in this at least."

For all his gracious manner, she felt uneasy accepting his largess, for it struck at both her pride and her prudence. Accordingly, she had posted a letter to her great-uncle, asking him to assume the role of their protector—on paper at least. It didn't matter that Great-uncle Nathaniel was a roué who would balk at accepting responsibility for his two grandnieces. So long as he signed the consent, their blood relationship would prevail over any other claim in a court of law. Then, while he stayed in Italy, she could live her life without interference from any man.

In the meantime, there could be no wrong in letting Sir Charles escort them to the fair. It did her heart good to see her sister enjoying herself.

Blue eyes sparkling, Meg motioned them to the front of the throng, where she'd found a place on the crowded bench. "Hurry, the show's about to begin! We can squeeze in right here."

She linked arms with Sir Charles and drew him down beside her as the spectators shuffled position to make room. Unfortunately, Kate came up short of space, and she only just managed to find a seat a few rows behind them, squashed in between a group of rowdy university students and Mrs. Islington, a bovinelike matron who greeted her with a nod, then resumed chattering with her husband, the butcher, who sat at her other side.

To make matters worse, the people behind Kate kept moving around, and someone's knees poked into her spine. She sat erect and rigid, uncomfortable in such close quarters with strangers. It was worse than being late for chapel and having to squeeze into the packed gallery. But at least she could be thankful she hadn't seen the gossipy Mrs. Beasley, who had gone off that day to visit one of her married daughters.

Lifting her gaze to the tightrope, Kate experienced a tingling rush of anticipation. A woody scent drifted from the layer of sawdust in the center of the tent, where a high rope stretched between two tall poles. Strutting back and forth before the benches, the grizzled hawkster called everyone's attention to a small, wiry man dressed in black breeches and a yellow shirt.

The barefoot man climbed a ladder to the top of the wooden pole. As he stepped out onto the rope, Kate gripped her fingers in her lap. Arms outstretched, the man took a few cautious steps on the swaying rope and then executed a wobbly somersault to the wild clapping of the crowd.

"Jabbar could do much better," said a husky voice in her ear.

Kate jumped, glancing first at the students, then back over her shoulder, where a familiar pair of ocean-blue eyes glinted at her. A jolt struck the breath from her lungs. Lord

Gabriel, the cur. It was *his* knees that prodded her lower back.

As before, he was dressed casually without gloves or hat, his shirt open to reveal his strong brown throat. He looked big and masculine, more like a common laborer than an aristocrat, and to her shame, she felt a thrill all the way down to her toes.

Instantly hostile, she whispered, "What are you doing here?"

"Same as you. Enjoying myself." In the torchlight, his gaze held a certain naughtiness. "Or perhaps as a spinster on the shelf, you're only here to chaperone your sister."

"I'm not—" She broke off a terse retort that she was twenty years of age and far from an old maid. "I'm not here merely to chaperone my sister, and well you know it."

"Then you should pay closer attention to her, for she's sitting with"—glancing past her, he narrowed his suddenly stony eyes—"Sir Charles Damson."

"There weren't enough seats for all of us in the front row."

"A gentleman would have let the ladies sit together."

Kate had wondered at that very thing. But what harm was there in letting her sister benefit from the attentions of a well-mannered aristocrat? Especially one who was kinder and more generous than the blunt, overbearing Gabriel Kenyon.

"Sir Charles *is* a gentleman. Now, if you'll excuse me, I'd like to watch the show."

Pointedly, she returned her attention to the tightrope dancer, who had tied on a blindfold and walked backward across the swaying rope. As the crowd oohed and aahed, Meg clung to Sir Charles's arm in exaggerated fright. Perhaps her sister *was* being overly familiar, Kate thought with chagrin. She resolved to have another talk with Meg about appropriate conduct.

Lord Gabriel's warm breath tickled Kate's ear again. "You told me Damson was in London."

She bristled at his accusatory tone. "He was kind enough to stop for a visit on his way to his estate."

"So he's going on to Cornwall. When?"

"Tomorrow." She twisted around in her seat, ignoring the *harrump* from the plump woman beside her. "How do you know where he lives, anyway?" she asked in a brusque whisper. "I thought you scarcely knew Sir Charles."

His gaze bored into her. "I own an estate some ten miles from his. And I forbid you and your sister to associate with him."

"Forbid?" she cried out. When several curious spectators turned to stare at them, she lowered her voice so the cheers of the crowd muted her words. "I'll befriend whomever I please."

"You'll do as I say."

She only just stopped herself from slapping his face. He would *not* make her behave like a hoyden. "As to that," she said coolly, "Sir Charles would disagree with you. He says that Papa appointed *him* my protector. His solicitor even has a document with Papa's signature."

Something fierce and wild entered Lord Gabriel's eyes. "It's a forgery. Don't believe him, Kate. He's a liar."

"And who are you? The Archangel Gabriel?"

"I've never lied to you."

"You promised to bring back untold treasures from Africa."

He didn't bother to deny it. Instead, he put his face close to hers, so close she could detect the faint spiciness of his skin. "Listen to me, and listen well. Damson has the morals of a sewer rat. He owns a vast collection of ancient artifacts . . . unsavory artifacts."

"Unsavory?" she scoffed. "What do you mean?"

"Vulgar. Indecent." His gaze flitted to her bosom, awakening a strange tension there. His voice was a mere breath of sound. "Erotic."

Her mind leapt with curiosity and struck the blank wall of disbelief. Did such artifacts exist? And if he spoke the truth, why would Sir Charles want Papa's curios? "Don't be absurd. My father didn't own anything like that. Anyway, it's no crime for a man to spend his money as he chooses."

"Damson doesn't always spend money to get what he wants."

It took a moment to catch his meaning. Aghast, she whispered, "Dare you call him a thief?"

"Yes."

"On what grounds, pray tell?"

His eyes held hers with piercing directness. "Suffice it to say, I have my reasons."

His unwavering tone reawakened her uneasiness about Sir Charles. Was she wrong to trust him? Or was Lord Gabriel simply a troublemaker? Erotic artifacts, indeed. "Reasons," she hissed. "More likely, the hot African sun has broiled your brain."

"This is no jest, Kate," he said, his fingers gripping her shoulder. "Henceforth, you and your sister will stay away from Damson. I require your obedience in this."

The pressure of his hand spread warmth through the depths of her body. A warmth that appalled her. She shrugged off his offending hand. "I'll follow my own counsel," she said with icy politeness. "You've taught me well to trust no man. Least of all *you*."

BY the flickering light of the oil lamp in her hand, Kate walked through the darkened cottage. Silent for once, Jabbar loped beside her. As they stopped in front of a door, she steeled herself for the task ahead.

Upstairs, Meg slept the sound sleep of carefree youth.

Kate hadn't been so fortunate. She had tossed and turned, plagued by thoughts of Gabriel Kenyon and his outrageous accusations. After the tightrope event, the knave had had the effrontery to follow them around the fair, staying out of sight of Meg and Sir Charles. More than once, Kate had spied that boldly masculine figure standing in the shadows of an oak tree while she and Meg sampled sugary comfits at a booth, laughed at the puppet show, and tossed leather balls at a target in hope of winning a prize. Kate had been tempted to spin around and hurl the missile straight at that smirking face.

If he were so disapproving of Sir Charles, why had he not come forward to challenge the man? It only proved Lord Gabriel knew he wasn't her guardian. He hadn't wanted to risk a confrontation.

Now, she looked down at Jabbar's gleaming black eyes and murmured, "I hope you realize you're the only trustworthy male I know."

The chimp rolled back his lips in a toothy grin, making her glad she'd liberated him from his cage. His mournful chattering in the kitchen had attracted her attention when she'd wandered restlessly downstairs. She didn't feel so alone now.

Turning the handle, she opened the door and stepped into her father's study. The air smelled musty, unused. A haunting whiff of Papa's pipe tobacco started a deluge of memories. During her childhood, he'd been gone more often than not, excavating Celtic or Roman or Viking ruins at far-flung sites in Britain. The scent of his pipe smoke was the first sign that he'd returned, and she would dash downstairs to embrace him and then all would be right with the world.

Aware of a raw pain inside her, Kate walked forward and set down the lamp on the old, scarred desk. Papers and discarded quill pens littered the surface. Jabbar bounded onto a sagging chair by the fireplace, seemingly content to observe her actions.

The cluttered room looked exactly as Papa had left it. The shelves were crammed with textbooks, shards of pottery, and primitive stone tools. The windowsill held a collection of ancient runic carvings. A Roman helmet hung from the fireplace andiron. On the mantelpiece stood a small terra-cotta horse, its ear chipped from the time she had sneaked in here as a child and borrowed it for her doll's riding lesson. Papa had scolded her soundly, lecturing her on the need to safeguard the relics of the past. His obvious disappointment in her had been worse than any whipping. He had exiled her from this sanctum, and she still felt a lingering shame over the incident, as if she didn't quite belong here.

How odd to think it was all hers now. Hers and Meg's, though her sister had no interest in these old curios.

Running her fingers over the dusty books on a shelf, Kate longed to understand her father's fascination for ancient artifacts—as she'd once longed to earn his full attention. He had just started accepting her help in his study, recopying notes for him, when Lord Gabriel Kenyon had entered their lives.

From the start, she'd fallen madly in love with the dashing aristocrat, even as she resented him for his friendship with her father. She couldn't compete with his amazing ability to sketch a scene with a few deft strokes of a brush or pen. Nor could she stay angry with him, for his devilish smile had melted her naïve heart. His restless enthusiasm for adventure had infected her father, and shortly thereafter, Lord Gabriel had funded the expedition to Africa against Kate's protests. Kate had known then that he wielded far more influence over Henry Talisford than did his own daughter.

She could still remember the searing pain of that reali-

zation, and her wild determination to do something—anything—to keep Papa home. If not for Lord Gabriel
providing the means, Papa would never have abandoned
his family.

*I loathe you, Gabriel Kenyon. I'll loathe you forever. I
hope you die in that jungle!*

After running out of his bedchamber, she'd returned to
her own room and locked the door. She'd stayed up half
the night, distraught and furious, alternately cursing Lord
Gabriel and resenting her father for being fooled by him.
When Papa had knocked on her door the next morning,
she'd refused to come out of her bedchamber.

After pleading with her, he went away at last, and she
would always remember rushing to the dormer window,
tears streaming down her cheeks, as he and Lord Gabriel
had ridden off on horseback. Meg and Mama had stood in
the cottage garden, waving until the men disappeared from
sight.

But Kate had been too choked by pride and pain to join
them.

Ever since, she'd bitterly regretted not saying good-bye
to Papa. She'd sent him off without a kiss or even a kind
word. How could she have been so childish, so cruel?

She took a deep breath to ease the constriction in her
throat. Wallowing in remorse accomplished nothing. Better
she should focus her mind on the burning desire to preserve
her father's legacy. As soon as she and Meg were settled
in their new quarters, she would organize the mounds of
papers and sort through years of research notes. She would
compose that book Papa had always talked about publishing, yet had never taken the time to write. She would make
up for her selfishness.

But tonight she had a more troubling purpose. She intended to find out why both Sir Charles and Lord Gabriel
showed such a keen interest in Papa's effects.

Resolutely, Kate turned her attention to the crate that had been delivered at an outrageous fee by a freight company from the London docks. Fumbling in her pocket, she brought out the small pry bar she'd found in the garden shed and pushed the blunt edge under the wooden lid.

"Here we go," she said to Jabbar, who cocked his head and watched from the nearby chair.

With a screeching of nails, the lid popped up and she lowered it to the floor. A musty, exotic scent wafted from the box. Crumpled news sheets cushioned the contents. She removed the papers, which were printed with squiggly Arabic writing. Inside the crate lay an assortment of objects swathed in lengths of unbleached linen. Picking up the largest one, she unwrapped the cloth. It was a mask, carved from a single piece of wood, with gruesome teeth, flaring nostrils, and slitted eyes.

When she showed it to Jabbar, the chimp squawked and leapt up onto the back of the chair. "It *is* rather frightening," Kate said. "Let's see what else we can find."

One by one, she uncovered a drum made from a dried gourd, primitive wooden carvings of animals, and a variety of powdered herbs wrapped in small pouches. There were no precious stones, no ivory, no gold. Yet Papa must have considered all these things to be treasures. He had taken the trouble to transport them through jungles and across deserts. She imagined him lovingly wrapping each item for the voyage to England . . .

Or had Lord Gabriel prepared the crate for shipment? Was she growing maudlin over a task that that rogue had performed?

Blinking hard, she glanced at Jabbar. "Your master won't lay claim to any of this. He can go to the devil for all I care."

Hooting, the chimp slapped his hairy legs.

"You think I'm jesting, do you? Just wait and see, then.

He can have his sketchbooks, but I shan't give him anything else, not so much as a string of clay beads."

Kate continued to unpack, but found nothing she would consider worth five hundred gold guineas—or a thousand, for that matter. Several large, leather-bound books rested at the bottom of the crate, along with a few smaller ones. She lifted them out, hefting the volumes in her arms, and settled down on the floor in front of the chair. Jabbar perched on the arm and peered over her shoulder.

The spicy scent of leather emanated from the books. It made her think of bazaars and minarets and other foreign scenes. With a quiver of anticipation, she wondered what strange sights Lord Gabriel had captured on paper. Slowly she opened one of the smaller, thicker books, and her heart tripped over a beat. She looked not at drawings, but at her father's precise penmanship.

Of course. She'd been so intent on Lord Gabriel that she had almost forgotten to consider the notes Papa would have accumulated on the long journey. Misty-eyed, she smoothed her fingertip over the inked words, imagining him bent over the notebook with quill in hand and inkpot nearby, the firelight glinting off his round spectacles and serious expression, a lock of brown hair falling onto his high brow.

The pages crackled as Kate slowly turned them. She skimmed over tales of encounters with tribesmen and treks through vast jungles and unending deserts. As she riffled the pages toward the end, a paper fluttered out, landing on the threadbare rug in front of the hearth.

She picked it up and found herself staring at a scandalous picture. An inbred prudishness made her avert her eyes. Just as swiftly, morbid curiosity lured her gaze back to the display of lush eroticism.

Rendered in lifelike watercolors was the statue of a naked, golden-skinned woman with an elongated neck, jew-

eled earrings, and an enormous, pendulous bosom. Her
hands were pressed to her lower belly, and her fingertips
brushed a huge diamond that nestled at the apex of her
thighs.

The statue must be worth a fortune, Kate realized in
mingled shock and interest. Had Papa really found such a
valuable object?

Hastily she paged through the notebook, seeking a reference to the treasure. At last, her gaze fell upon a description of his discovery of an ancient temple in the mountains
southeast of Khartoum. In cramped script, he filled page
after page with details about the crumbling columns and
stone altars and fading inscriptions on the walls. There had
been a cubbyhole that had been overlooked by robbers,
where the statue had rested undisturbed for untold hundreds—perhaps thousands—of years.

Stricken by excitement, Kate clutched the drawing in her
trembling fingers. This statue was surely worth a thousand
guineas—or more. It must be what both Lord Gabriel and
Sir Charles were seeking.

But wouldn't Lord Gabriel already know its
whereabouts?

A righteous anger scorched her. And by heaven and hell,
why hadn't he told her about the statue?

CHAPTER 5

AN UNWELCOME OFFER

GABE was stepping out of the copper bathtub, buck naked and dripping wet, when someone knocked on the door.

The persistent sound aggravated the pounding in his skull. "Damned innkeeper," he muttered to his valet. "Fetch the breakfast tray so he'll cease that infernal racket."

His dusky face impassive, Ashraf held out the towel. "If you have a sore head, master, it is Allah's punishment for drinking spirits."

"I'll keep that in mind."

Grimacing, Gabe took the length of linen and vigorously rubbed himself dry. The early morning light hurt his eyes. Ashraf glided toward the door, his white robes swishing, but Gabe wasn't fooled by that bland expression. His valet had taken a keen delight in throwing open the shutters of their dingy room here at the Rabbit's Hole Inn. For all his subservient manner, Ashraf took every opportunity to show his disapproval of Gabe's many vices.

The previous evening had been the least of them. After watching Damson bid farewell to Kate and Meg Talisford after the fair—and restraining the need to throttle the villain—Gabe had procured a bottle of Scotch whisky and settled down in the cold gloom of a hedgerow to watch Larkspur Cottage, for he felt uneasy knowing that Damson was in Oxford.

His brooding thoughts had centered on his plan to trap the baron, his own guilt and fury over Henry's death . . . and Kate Talisford, whose hatred he richly deserved. There was a maturity to her now that fascinated him, and a thorny restraint that made him relish his role as her guardian.

He couldn't forget how ravishing she'd looked in the entryway of Larkspur Cottage, her green eyes wide and vulnerable, her thick red-gold curls tumbling to her waist. Although his conscience told him she was forbidden, he'd wanted to haul her close, to bury his hands in all that lush hair, to kiss her senseless.

Of course, that was before he'd found out what a shrew she'd become.

Tossing down the towel, he stalked to the four-poster bed to find his clothes laid out in perfect order. He stood there a moment, rubbing his bristly jaw. He shouldn't be thinking about seducing Kate, but safeguarding her from Damson. His instincts urged Gabe to kill the blackguard, while his intellect warned him to bide his time, for his plan of revenge hinged upon Damson believing that Gabe didn't realize the identity of his attackers.

The trouble was, Kate trusted Damson. How in holy hell was Gabe to protect her without giving away his secret plan?

"Master."

Irritated, he turned to see Ashraf standing before him, palms pressed together. Gabe glanced around. "Where are my bacon and eggs?"

"It is not the innkeeper."

"Who is it, then?"

Ashraf stared at him suspiciously. "A female."

"The maid? Send her away."

"Nay, m'lord. I fear your visitor is a lady."

"The devil you say—" Gabe bit off the curse and shot a glance at the partially open door.

True to form, Ashraf bristled with indignation. "Master, it is my duty to point out the sin of indulging a weakness of the flesh before you have even said your daily prayers."

"It's you who pray five times a day. Now tell me her name."

"Miss Talisford."

"Bloody hell." Although he'd suspected as much, Gabe scowled. Here he stood, naked, unshaven, and surly. Seizing his breeches, he stepped into the garment and fumbled with the buttons. "Don't just stand there, man. Send her downstairs to wait in the common room. I'll meet her there in a few minutes."

The door flew open, banging against the wall. Kate Talisford's clear voice rang out. "You'll see me now, Gabriel Kenyon. I will not be put off."

Prim and proper in a black gown and unadorned bonnet, she glowered at him from the doorway. Her gaze fell to his bare chest, and she blinked rapidly, her lips parting. Then she sucked in a breath and met his eyes straight on. "I must speak with you. Immediately."

"Leave us," he told Ashraf.

"If you insist, master." Radiating censure, the valet bowed and walked to the door.

Gabe half expected her to rebuke his order and ask the servant to stay as chaperone. This new, straitlaced Kate surely wouldn't want to be left alone with a half-clothed rogue in his bedchamber. But after a moment's hesitation, she stepped to the side, and Ashraf pulled the door shut with a reproachful click.

Very intriguing.

Conscious of the newly healed scars on his back, Gabe didn't turn as he reached down to pick up his shirt. Just to annoy her, he took his time donning it. Now that he'd weathered the initial shock, he could ignore the hellish throbbing in his skull and enjoy the situation. "Good morning, Kate. May I say, you seem to have a habit of invading my bedchamber."

Her cheeks flushed a charming pink at odds with her

severe mien. She'd thrown herself at him four years ago, begging him to ravish her. He wondered if that impetuous girl still lurked inside her, and what she'd do if he pressed her down on the bed right now.

She'd probably bite off his tongue.

Kate remained standing by the door, a black crow with the face and figure of a temptress. "I know about the statue," she stated.

His blood ran cold. He scrutinized her stern expression, trying to gauge the extent of her knowledge. "Statue?"

"Don't pretend ignorance, my lord. You may be a filthy, deceitful, unscrupulous thief, but you are not a half-wit."

"I'm not filthy, either—I just stepped out of my bath." To fluster her, he made a show of tucking his shirt into his breeches. Her gaze wavered slightly, but she kept her eyes glued to his face, never once glancing below his neck. "Come and sit down," he coaxed, gesturing at the single chair by the fire. "You look as if you're ready to bolt."

She remained by the door, her gloved fingers clasped together at her waist. "I'm ready to hear some explanations from you. First and foremost, why you never thought to tell me that my father had found the fabled lost city. That he'd made the greatest discovery of his life."

Bloody hell. "I did think about it," he said, flashing her his most charming smile.

"I haven't come here to trade witticisms," she snapped. "I read my father's journal, and I want to know all about this statue."

She was like a dog gnawing a bone. Restraining his annoyance, Gabe said, "The statue came from a ruined temple. Henry believed it to be an ancient fertility goddess, predating the time of the Egyptian pharaohs."

"Where is it now?"

"I wish I knew."

She gave him a withering look. "You were willing to

pay one thousand guineas for the contents of that crate. You must have believed the statue was hidden inside it."

"You're wrong, Kate. I knew the goddess had been stolen."

"Oh? Then you did the deed."

"No." Keeping a tight lid on his temper, he leaned his shoulder against the bedpost and crossed his arms with deliberate relaxation. "The statue was never in the crate. We couldn't leave it unguarded on the dhow in the harbor. We kept it with us at the inn."

He watched the rounding of her eyes, the little tremor that shook her. "Are you saying . . . whoever killed my father . . . also stole the statue?"

"Yes."

She closed her eyes a moment, and he shifted his bare feet uneasily, fearing she might lapse into weeping. This was exactly the pain he'd hoped to spare Kate. He hadn't wanted to involve her in such an ugly, dangerous affair. His plan had worked—until Damson had come sniffing around her and Meg.

When she looked at him again, her eyes shone clear and cold. "Sir Charles said thieves were following Papa, and Papa feared for his life. That's why he asked Sir Charles to act as my guardian."

Gabe snapped out an oath. "He isn't your guardian. Henry would never have signed such a paper without telling me."

Planting her hands on her slim hips, Kate took a step toward him. "You must have known Papa was being stalked. So why did you go out that night? Where exactly were you while my father was fighting for his life?"

She'd struck a nerve on that one, but Gabe wouldn't tell her why. "Henry wasn't being stalked. Else he would have told me so immediately."

"So who am I to believe? Sir Charles, who came straight

back to England to offer me his condolences? Or you, who hid the true circumstances behind Papa's death?"

He'd hidden more than that. For her own protection, he didn't want to tell Kate any more than necessary. But now he wondered if his silence might well prove the greater danger to her. "Damson is a liar and a thief—"

"Not that again." Marching forward, she braced her gloved hands on the copper rim of the tub and glared across it. "Why are you so determined to discredit him?"

"Because," he said tightly, "Damson stole the statue."

In the early morning light, her face went as pale as milk, her eyes huge and impossibly green. A few wisps of red-gold hair had escaped the confines of her bonnet to curl like corkscrews on her brow. For a long moment, she stared at him until a little sound of disbelief huffed out of her. "Then you're saying . . . he also killed my father."

Gabe nodded curtly.

"No . . . it can't be true," she whispered, shaking her head. "That's a wicked lie."

He crossed the bedchamber and took hold of her elbow. "Sit down before you swoon."

She let him lead her halfway across the broad-planked floor. Then she wrenched away and pivoted to face him. "Don't coddle me. Have you any proof to support your accusations?"

Gabe's mind went back to that darkened chamber in Cairo . . . to the robed figure standing in the shadows, a short distance from Henry Talisford's crumpled form. Swallowing a glut of rage, he said, "I saw Damson holding the statue. One of his minions attacked me from behind. A weasel named Figgins."

"It was nighttime. How can you be so sure?"

"Any artist remembers faces. Figgins has distinctive features—deep-set eyes, squashed nose, bony angles like skin stretched over a skull."

Kate stood very still, and he wished to hell he could read her mind. But she was no longer the openly expressive girl who wore her heart on her sleeve. Turning away, she walked to the window and looked down at the quiet back street. "Dear God," she murmured, her voice thin. "This is impossible. Yet . . . if what you say is true, then I've welcomed my father's murderer into my home, drunk tea with him, enjoyed his company."

Gabe stepped to her side and touched her shoulder. "Damson has fooled a lot of people. I warned you to stay away from him."

Her chin shot up, her gaze snaring his. "And you refused to tell me why. Was I to take *your* word for it?"

"Better mine than his."

She gave an unladylike snort. "You told me yesterday that you didn't recognize those men. If you lied to me once, you could be lying to me now."

Gabe hissed out a breath through his teeth. "It's the truth, I swear it. I never expected him to visit you. Or to offer you money for your father's possessions."

"You said Sir Charles collects . . . unusual artifacts. So why would he pay so much for beads and spears and drums?"

Gabe shrugged. "Maybe he's looking for directions to the temple, to see if we missed anything of value. We'd barely begun to excavate the site."

"Then why were *you* so anxious to pay me a thousand guineas? And don't say you merely wished to thwart Sir Charles."

He gazed down at her angry, accusing face and cursed his idiot chivalry. "You and Meg need the funds."

"I won't accept a penny from you."

Gabe swore under his breath. "Kate, I don't like this predicament, either. But I made a vow to your father, and I intend to honor it."

How keenly he recalled that night in the desert, when Henry had reread a much-folded letter from Kate, informing him of his wife's death. Though a reticent man, Henry had had tears in his eyes when he'd spoken of his daughters, left to fend for themselves. As a precaution, he'd asked Gabe to watch over them, and Gabe had agreed reluctantly. The last thing he needed was to be responsible for two young women—one of whom despised him.

"My great-uncle will see to our care," Kate said, her tone dismissing his claim. "There's no need for you to trouble yourself."

"Henry thought otherwise. He considered Nathaniel Babcock a corrupting influence on you and your sister."

Kate gave a disbelieving laugh. "And you're not?"

A cord of tension constricted Gabe's chest. If only she knew, renouncing his duty would be a relief. "You ought to be grateful to me. I could have walked away."

"I wish you had." Kate cast him a scathing glance up and down. "Understand this: you will not dictate my life."

Frustrated by her stubbornness, he took a step forward, crowding her against the roughly paneled wall. "Understand *this*: I'm in charge of you now. You and Meg. Henceforth, I intend to provide for both of you."

For the barest instant, her pupils dilated slightly, betraying a physical awareness of him. He felt it, too, in the hot rushing of his blood. Whether she wanted to admit so or not, he did have power over her. The power of his charm. He could use that charm to his advantage.

"At least accept the money in exchange for your father's writings," he said, softening his voice to a persuasive pitch. He thought of his long-burning desire to make a name for himself, to achieve a fame outside the shadows of his two older brothers. "I need Henry's journals. I want to publish a book about our travels together."

Her mouth dropped open. "You? *I'm* writing a book."

"We'll collaborate, then," Gabe said on inspiration. The notion of spending long hours with Kate Talisford appealed to him. Perhaps once he'd dealt with Damson, he could enjoy her company, banter with her, find out all her secrets.

Her lips curled in sour distaste. "I'd sooner collaborate with Jabbar. He's far better company than you are."

He chuckled. This was the Kate he remembered. The fiery, clever Kate. "Jabbar can't draw as well as I can. You need me, Kate. Remember *your* attempts at drawing?" With her pad and pencil, she'd observed him at work in her father's study. Gamely she'd attempted to sketch, too, but her awkward stick figures had testified to an appalling lack of talent.

Pinkness swept her clear skin. "I'm quite capable of managing without your help, my lord."

Without touching her, he braced his hands on the wall on either side of her. "Call me Gabe," he murmured. "There's no need to practice formalities between friends."

"We aren't friends. Not anymore."

Yet her lashes lowered slightly, betraying the fact that she too felt the spark between them. The spark that had been there since she'd been a saucy sixteen-year-old. "We were friends once," he said. "Remember when I went to sketch Folly Bridge? You were so intent on spying on me that you fell into the river."

"That isn't true! You *pushed* me."

He chuckled. "I bumped into you, I'll admit. But how was I to know you were standing right behind me, peering over my shoulder?"

"You knew. You had that look in your eyes."

"What look?"

"That wicked look. It's there right now." Pressing her back against the wall, she regarded him primly. Although she could have ducked under his arms easily enough, she made no attempt to escape him.

Perhaps he hadn't destroyed her girlish ardor, after all. Certainly *he* had never forgotten the feel of her lithe body in his arms or the softness of her breasts. Now that she was a woman, he was free to court her.

The thought came out of nowhere, and he summarily rejected it. He had no right to touch her. Kate Talisford was a lady, not a courtesan he could dally with and then toss aside. He was duty-bound to let no man sully her innocence.

Least of all himself.

But the temptation was there, so strong he could almost taste it. He wanted to reawaken the passionate girl inside the prudish woman. The dingy brown draperies protected them from view of the street below. He could kiss those full, inviting lips, and no one would be the wiser . . .

By degrees, he lowered his head until he could almost feel the warmth of her breath. The faint flowery scent of her soap wafted to him. It made him want to bury his face in the tender hollow of her throat. "Say my name," he commanded again. "I want to hear you say it."

"Lord Gabriel."

The breathy catch to her voice encouraged him. "Coward," he said on a low chuckle. "I believe you're afraid of me. Or perhaps . . . intimidated."

"Gabriel," she spat out. "There, are you satisfied?"

Her hands flashed out to shove him away. Caught off guard, he stepped backward and bumped into the bedpost, which only served to magnify the throbbing in his skull.

Kate walked to the chair and took up a dignified stance behind it, her gloved fingers resting on the rounded back. "I'll thank you to keep your distance, *Gabriel*. We've strayed from the topic of the goddess."

Perversely gratified by her show of fire, he let his eyes roam up and down her slim figure. "Have we?" he drawled.

Her telltale blush deepened. Her voice tight and controlled, she said, "*If,* as you *claim,* Sir Charles did steal the statue and smuggled it into England, then where has he hidden it? At his estate?"

He grimaced. "Possibly. That's why I stayed out of sight last evening. The less he sees of me, the better."

"Why do you say that?"

"I intend to break into his house. To retrieve the goddess." The cold, angry need for retribution invaded him. He didn't tell her the rest, that once he had the proof in his hands, he'd see Damson pay for murdering Henry Talisford.

"I have a better idea," she said. "Sir Charles has invited me for a visit. So I can simply walk in the front door."

"The devil you say!" Struck by icy fear, Gabe aimed his finger at her. "You won't go near his house. I forbid it."

"And let you abscond with a valuable statue? I think not." She regarded him with steely resolve. "My father paid for that artifact with his life. As his heir, I'm claiming it."

"*I* found the statue. While Henry was digging up shards of pottery, I noticed a gap in the stones behind the altar."

One delicate eyebrow arched, Kate regarded him as she might a tiresome menial. "Then I'll grant you twenty-five percent of the sale price."

"Twenty-five—" he sputtered. "The goddess isn't for sale. She belongs in a museum."

"If the directors want the statue badly enough, then they'll pay the price. That one diamond alone must be worth a fortune."

She wore a look of headstrong determination. He didn't need for her to capsize his plans and endanger herself in the process. "The statue is priceless," he said. "Nevertheless, I'll give you a thousand guineas for your share. That's more than generous."

She shook her head, the black ribbons on her bonnet swaying. "I want no more or less than my due. We'll find the statue together, have it appraised, and then split the proceeds."

A cynical laugh broke from him. "Give up, Kate. You aren't going with me."

"We'll see about that." Her lips pinched, she marched toward the door. "Good day, Gabriel."

His bare feet slapping the floor, he strode forward and caught her by the wrist. For all her steely strength of will, she felt soft and fragile to the touch. He fought the urge to put his arms around her, to hold her close and protect her from harm. To have what could never be his.

Gruffly, he said, "I'll be watching you, Kate. And take care. When Damson wants something, he'll stop at nothing to get it."

CHAPTER 6

THE BLACK SHEEP

A raucous noise yanked Kate from the oblivion of sleep.

Her heart racing, she sat up straight in bed and blinked into the darkness. The black lumps of furniture dotted the dense gloom. The only sound was the faint ticking of the clock on her bedside table. Straining her eyes, she could barely make out the time—three o'clock in the morning. Had she been dreaming? She felt sluggish and disoriented, vaguely aware of having been lost in a strange, unsettling fantasy about half-naked savages who looked rather like Gabriel Kenyon . . .

The screech pierced the air again, a ghostly howling from the bowels of the cottage. The cacophony raised a flurry of goose bumps over her skin. Then she realized the source of the wild cries.

Kate bounded from the bed, her toes curling against the cold, bare floorboards. She seized her dressing gown from a chair, threw it on, and ran for the door.

In the narrow passageway, she nearly collided with Meg. Her hair tied up in little rag curlers, Meg had lit a candle, and her panicky eyes glimmered in the pale glow. "It's Jabbar," she whispered. "Gad-a-mercy, there must be a burglar! He'll murder us!"

Kate forced herself to speak calmly. "Hush. You're being dramatic. It's probably nothing."

"Nothing! What else could frighten him so?"

"The scrape of a tree branch on the window. Or the barking of Mrs. Beasley's dog." As they spoke, they made

their way to the top of the stairs. Kate thrust out her arm
to stop Meg from descending. "I'll go first."

For once, her sister didn't argue. Gripping the rail, Kate
felt her way down the steep wooden risers and wished desperately that they weren't two women alone. *Coward*, Gabriel had called her. It galled her to admit he was right. If
only she possessed real courage instead of this false bravado. Her palms felt cold and damp, and she kept a close
watch on the murky depths of the entryway. If someone
really had broken into the cottage . . .

The chimpanzee's long, drawn-out wailing grew louder
as they reached the ground floor. If it weren't for Jabbar,
she'd haul her sister out the front door and flee to a neighbor's cottage. But they couldn't abandon the poor creature.

At the base of the stairs, she grabbed a folded umbrella
from the stand by the door and brandished it like a weapon.
Meg hung back, though clinging to Kate's sleeve. Together,
they navigated down the corridor, past the piles of packing
boxes, and into the shadowy kitchen.

Jabbar jumped up and down in his large bamboo cage
in the corner. His lips were peeled back in a ferocious
scowl, his hair bristling. When he saw them, his fearful cry
diminished to an anxious chattering.

Thrusting the candle at Kate, Meg hastened to the cage
and unlocked it. The chimp leapt into her arms, nearly
knocking her over, clutching at her like a frightened child.
"You're safe now, darling," she crooned, petting him.
"Silly boy, there's nothing wrong."

Kate checked the back door, relieved to find it securely
latched. Yet she couldn't shake a shivery sense that something *was* wrong. Returning to her sister, she said, "I'll have
a look around just to be certain."

When she started toward the front of the cottage, Jabbar
increased his babbling again.

"Perhaps he wants to show us something," Kate said dubiously.

"There's only one way to find out."

Meg let him down and he loped out of the small kitchen, pausing only to look back and see if they were following him. Kate cautiously trailed the monkey down the corridor to her father's study, where he slapped his palms against the closed door and screeched again.

Meg grabbed Kate's arm. "There must be someone in there," she hissed. "Let's send to Lord Gabriel for help. Or Sir Charles—oh, but he's gone to Cornwall."

Meg didn't yet know about Sir Charles's crime, Kate thought with a twinge of guilty unease. Until she found the proof of his culpability, she hadn't wanted to unduly alarm her sister. The less Meg knew about the baron's possible role in their father's death, the better.

With a confidence she didn't really feel, Kate handed the candle back to Meg. "We've naught to fear. After all that racket, any intruder will be long gone."

Hefting the rolled umbrella in one hand, she slowly turned the handle and gave the door a push.

A gust of chilly night air nearly doused the candle. Meg cupped her hand around the flame as they walked just inside the doorway. Kate's gaze veered to the window, where the draperies flapped in the night breeze. A smashed pane showed where someone had reached inside and opened the casement.

Swallowing a gasp, she glanced around the small study. Everything else looked exactly as she'd left it. The tribal mask leaned against the crate, the beads and other mementos were scattered on the desk. Though shadows lurked in the corners, she could see by the feeble light of the candle that no one hid there, waiting to spring out at them.

Meg surveyed the window in horror. "Katie, we've been robbed!"

Cautiously, Kate lowered the umbrella and glanced around. She thanked heaven for the prudence that had induced her to hide Papa's diaries and Gabriel's sketchbooks in her bedchamber. "I don't believe he took anything of value. Jabbar must have frightened him away."

Meg knelt down to give the chimpanzee a hug. "What a clever beast you are—far better than a watchdog." She glanced up at Kate. "Isn't it lucky that Lord Gabriel gave him to us?"

Lucky. Kate suddenly wondered if Gabriel had left the chimpanzee there on purpose. To sound a warning in the event of an intruder.

Unwilling to voice the thought to her sister, Kate hid her jittery suspicions. A part of her still resisted believing the horrid story that Gabriel had told her. How could she be sure he wasn't lying to hide his own guilt? Yet now she couldn't forget the last thing he'd said.

When Damson wants something, he'll stop at nothing to get it.

KATE was in the study later that morning, stowing books in a wooden box, when she heard the rumble of male voices interspersed with Meg's excited tone. A huge history of Roman England fell from Kate's nerveless fingers and thumped onto the desk.

Gabriel was here.

She took a deep breath to steady the wild surge of her heartbeat. Smoothing back her tightly pinned hair, she tucked in a few stray corkscrews that always seemed to escape despite her best efforts. Just as quickly, she scorned her vanity. She didn't care what Gabriel thought of her. At the inn, she had seen him at his worst, an unshaven, half-naked scoundrel who looked capable of any dark deed.

That image bedeviled her. Who had tried to break in here, Sir Charles Damson? Or Gabriel himself?

After the foiled robbery, she'd returned to bed, but fear of the intruder's return had kept her wide awake. So she had lit an extravagance of candles and busied herself with household tasks. Not only had she finished a considerable amount of packing, she had spent hours in the kitchen, and the fragrance of her baking permeated the cottage.

Upon reaching the doorway, she stopped short. Two men strolled toward the study. Lord Gabriel looked far too rakish in a charcoal-gray coat, opened collar, and black breeches. Beside him, a dapper, white-haired gentleman in a finely tailored blue suit escorted a smiling Meg on his arm.

Happy surprise leapt in Kate. Abandoning dignity, she dashed forward and threw her arms around his tall, lanky form. "Great-uncle Nathaniel!"

He hugged her, too, spinning her around as if she were a child of five. "Call me plain Uncle Nathaniel, else you'll make me feel like a doddering old pensioner."

"But . . . how did you get here so quickly?" she asked in confusion. "I only just wrote to you yesterday."

He raised his white eyebrows. "Wrote to me?"

"Yes, I had news to tell you—"

"We'll have time enough for that in a moment. First, let me have a look at you." Clasping her by the shoulders, Nathaniel Babcock held Kate at arm's length. As always, he had a devilish smile and the jaunty air of a man who enjoys life. "Why, Katherine Talisford, you're all grown-up and pretty as a princess. Both you and Margaret."

"How kind of you," Kate said wryly as she glanced down at her old black dress. "I fear we weren't expecting visitors."

"You're ravishing, and well you know it," Gabriel said. He gave her his hallmark smile, the smoldering smirk that caused an instantaneous tightening deep inside her. "I met up with your uncle at the garden gate," he went on. "Recognized him at once. I vow, he hasn't changed a bit."

Uncle Nathaniel elbowed him in the ribs. "I'm no longer as wild as you young bucks. But don't tell your grand-mother that."

"You know his grandmother?" Meg asked with interest.

"Aye," Uncle Nathaniel said. "Lucy, one of the famous Rosebuds. By jings, those three were beauties in their day."

Kate glanced quizzically at Gabriel. "The Rosebuds?"

"Grandmama and her two childhood friends—" Gabriel stopped, frowning over Kate's head and staring into the study. "What the deuce—? Your window is broken."

Kate followed his gaze to the window. "We had a little . . . incident last night. It was nothing, really."

"I'll be the judge of that." He strode past the boxes and examined the shattered pane that Kate had patched with a sheet of oilpaper. "Who did this?"

"A thief," Meg said in a dramatic rush. "He came to rob us, but Jabbar screeched terribly loud and frightened him away before that awful man could steal anything."

Gabriel spun around, his face harsh. "You saw him?"

"Well, no, but it had to be a man. It was horrid! Kate was very brave, much braver than I. She marched around, holding an umbrella like a cudgel—"

"Whoa, slow down!" Uncle Nathaniel said. Worry intensified the lines of age on his face. "Are you saying a ruffian tried to ransack the place? And who the devil is Jabbar?"

"My chimpanzee." Biting her lip, Meg slid a glance at Kate. "Or rather, Lord Gabriel's chimpanzee. He's in the kitchen if you'd care to meet him."

"Later," Lord Gabriel said tersely, his gaze snaring Kate's. "Have you summoned the magistrate?"

She shook her head. "There was no point. The man was long gone by then."

"You're sure nothing was stolen?"

His sharp blue eyes pierced her, and she knew he was asking about her father's journals. Trying to gauge his possible guilt, Kate looked him up and down. "Not so much as a petrified bone," she stated. "I'm quite certain of that."

"Nothing in here but a pile of old rubbish, anyhow," Uncle Nathaniel commented, picking up a bronze coin of Celtic origin and rolling it between his fingers. "Never did understand why Henry collected this clutter. Where did all these boxes come from?"

"We're moving," Meg said, thrusting out her lower lip in a pout. "Into teeny-tiny rooms in town."

"Leaving Larkspur Cottage?" Uncle Nathaniel asked in astonishment. Tossing down the coin, he wagged a gnarled finger at them. "Why, I'll wager you gels want to be closer to all those fine lads at the university. Mind you, don't trust any of those young rogues, d'you hear? Else I'll have to tell your papa."

A brief, painful silence descended on the study. Meg sniffled. Gabriel opened his mouth as if to speak, but Kate flashed him a quelling look.

"Papa isn't coming home," she said quietly, taking her great-uncle's arm. "That's why I wrote to you. Come into the parlor, and I'll tell you everything."

In short order, they were seated around the hearth with cups of hot tea. The last time they'd seen their maternal great-uncle was at their mother's funeral, so Kate gave him a brief summary of their situation, beginning with the embezzled funds and ending with Henry Talisford's death. Out of a desire to protect Meg, she said nothing of murder and the missing statue. Gabriel stood at the window, staring out at the garden, an unreadable expression on his face.

Uncle Nathaniel sorrowfully shook his head. "All the years I was in Italy, I had no notion of the hardships you gels were suffering."

"Didn't you receive our letters?" Meg asked.

He aimed a guilty, sidelong glance at her and Kate. " 'Fraid I don't bother with the mail these days. Too many dun notices."

Kate hid her disappointment. Much as she loved him, Uncle Nathaniel was another undependable male, a gambler and a black sheep. It was a scandalous family secret that he lived off the largess of his mistresses.

"I'll gladly give you all I have to my name." Uncle Nathaniel rummaged in an inside pocket and withdrew a handful of coins. "Alas, 'tis only six pounds and a few shillings. 'Pon my word, I've had a run of bad luck at the tables. First night back in merry old England and I near lost the shirt off my back."

Kate waved away the money. "We have enough to live on."

"But I must take care of you now." Uncle Nathaniel snapped his fingers. "I've a capital notion! You two shall return to Italy with me. Ah, the wine, the cuisine, the love in the air. 'Tis a paradise, indeed."

"Do let's go," Meg said, clapping her hands. "Please, Kate. Italy would be a bigger adventure than going off with the traveling players."

The prospect of seeing new sights and exploring ancient Roman ruins tempted Kate. How lovely to think of escaping their money woes, to travel the world . . . The trouble was, she couldn't count on Uncle Nathaniel to provide for them. The last thing they needed was to be stranded in a foreign country without tuppence to rub between their fingers. "I'm afraid it's impossible, dear," she said gently. "Our home is here. There's the book I intend to write, don't forget."

There was the statue to find, too. And in the process, she would bring her father's murderer to justice. She glanced at Gabriel, but he was gazing out the window and her fierce look was wasted.

"You're too young to tie yourself down," Uncle Nathaniel said, helping himself to another slice of ginger cake. "A dear friend of mine, the Contessa di Sarona, would be delighted to have you as her houseguests."

"An Italian contessa?" Meg breathed, her face alight with interest. "Do tell us more. Is she fabulously rich?"

"Meg!" Kate chided. "Don't be impertinent." She knew about her great-uncle's *friends*. Clearly, the contessa was one of his paramours.

Uncle Nathaniel grinned. "Rich? Why, Elena wears enough diamonds to dazzle your eyes at midnight. She rides in a golden coach pulled by six white horses and lives in a villa on the shores of Lake Como. She always entertains dozens of visitors and surely wouldn't mind two more—"

"I'm sure it's all very pleasant," Kate broke in, "but we shan't invite ourselves to a stranger's house. I was hoping you'd agree to stay here with us, Uncle. Only for a few years, until Meg reaches her majority."

Nathaniel Babcock shifted uneasily in his seat. "But I was planning to go back to Italy. Soon as I can round up the funds."

As soon as he could coax a rich widow into lending him money. But if Kate had her way, he would be changing his plans. "You're our guardian now," she said firmly. "You must do what is best for us. And that means staying here in Oxford."

"I'm leaving, but you can't remain in England alone," Uncle Nathaniel averred. "Not with a ruffian on the loose. It wouldn't be right."

"They won't be alone," Gabriel said suddenly. Turning from the window, he flashed Kate a hard, calculating look. "They'll go to a place where they'll be safe. To my grandmother at Stokeford Abbey."

His words hit Kate like a slap. She sat up straight, her

fingers gripping her skirt. "We most certainly will not. Tell him, Uncle."

A considering look on his face, Nathaniel Babcock rubbed his jaw. "Stokeford Abbey, eh? Fine estate, noble company, why 'tis the very place for two orphaned girls."

"*I* think it's wonderful," Meg said, stars shining in her eyes. "May I bring Jabbar?"

"Of course," Gabriel said with a charming bow. "You're all invited for an extended stay."

Kate leapt to her feet. "No," she said fiercely. "We've no connection to your family. Uncle Nathaniel is our guardian, not you."

Smooth as a serpent, Gabriel turned to her great-uncle. "Henry asked me to provide for Kate and Meg. If it's agreeable to you, of course."

" 'Pon my word, it's more than agreeable," Uncle Nathaniel said with alacrity. "I'll be pleased to see Lucy again, too."

Then, as Kate watched in horror, the two men shook hands to conclude their transfer of guardianship.

CHAPTER 7

THE ROSEBUDS

No wonder Gabriel was so autocratic, Kate thought disparagingly as she stepped out of the traveling coach two days later, a battered leather valise weighing on her arm. Any man who had grown up in such grandeur would think himself superior to ordinary folk.

Awed in spite of herself, she lifted her eyes to the massive, pillared front of Stokeford Abbey. Somehow, she had been expecting a simple country manor, not . . . *this*. Painted by the setting sun, the ivy-covered stone and medieval archways bespoke an ancient, noble heritage. According to Gabriel, the house had been built around the ruins of an old monastery, a fact illustrated by the scores of vaulted windows that marched along the enormous façade. His childhood home was now the residence of his elder brother, Michael, the Marquess of Stokeford. The mansion reeked of wealth and privilege and breeding, a life utterly foreign to her humble upbringing.

Kate's stomach curled. She and Meg didn't belong among the aristocracy. She wanted to climb back into the coach and head straight for the familiar trappings of home.

But it was too late. They no longer had a home. The new occupants of Larkspur Cottage, an elderly couple who were fond of gardening, would have moved in today. And as loathsome as it was to let Gabriel dictate her life, she couldn't risk another encounter with thieves. For her sister's safety, Kate had relinquished their small, rented rooms

in Oxford and boxed their belongings for storage here at
the Abbey.

A white-wigged footman reached for the leather case.
"May I, miss?"

She gripped the handle. "Thank you, but I prefer to carry
it myself."

Looking somewhat startled, the servant turned to help
her sister down from the coach. At a loud hoot from Jabbar,
the footman leapt back in alarm, the freckles standing out
on his pale face.

Meg picked up the chimpanzee, gave the disconcerted
young man a sunny smile, and then bounded toward Kate
with unladylike haste. "Can you believe the magnificence
of this place?" she whispered, her eyes shining. "It isn't a
house. It's a palace! To think we're going to live here."

Before Kate could speak past the lump in her throat,
Uncle Nathaniel ambled over to join them. "Yes, I do believe we'll all be quite comfortable," he said with a jaunty
grin. " 'Tis my duty to see my dear nieces properly settled."

"May I remind you both, this move is only temporary,"
Kate said in a low tone. "We're a family, and we mustn't
be dependent on anyone else." She looked pointedly at her
great-uncle, but he didn't look abashed in the least.

"Wait until you have a taste of luxury," he said with a
broad wink. "Then you'll count yourself fortunate to have
a wealthy benefactor."

Kate pinched her lips together. It served no purpose to
debate principles with her great-uncle. For the time being,
she needed to reside here at the Abbey so that she could
keep a watch on Gabriel.

Little did Meg and Uncle Nathaniel realize, the goddess
had been another determining factor in her decision. Gabriel meant to leave her and Meg with his grandmother
while he went off to reclaim the valuable artifact. But Kate
had no intention of meekly submitting to such a plan.

To put it simply, she didn't trust the man. He might hide the statue, declare he hadn't found it, and she'd be powerless to prove otherwise.

Her gaze veered across the courtyard to Gabriel's tall form. He stood by the baggage cart, giving orders to several footmen, who sprang to unload the luggage. A groom was leading away his mount. Gabriel had ridden alongside their coach, which meant that every time she'd glanced out the window she'd been confronted by the sight of him. But at least she'd been spared his disturbing company.

He tossed his leather gloves to Ashraf. There was something vaguely sinister about the dour, dark-skinned valet in his long white robes. Kate wondered how much Ashraf knew about the statue. Where had he been on the night it was stolen? That was a question she intended to have answered.

Not for the first time, she was glad she'd taken the precaution of secreting her father's journals in the heavy case she carried. She wouldn't entrust them to Ashraf or Gabriel—or anyone else for that matter.

Then Gabriel pivoted, and his deep blue eyes met hers. A gust of wind ruffled his burnished, dark hair. His mouth curled into a half-smile as he caught her in the act of staring. Without breaking their eye contact, he strode straight toward her.

Warmth poured through her in a limb-weakening rush, a warmth she disdained. He looked exceptionally rakish today in a hunter-green coat, buckskin breeches, and black knee-high boots. If his bold manner weren't enough, his scorn for cravats gave proof that a less-than-civilized man lurked behind those sun-bronzed features. She could imagine Gabriel tramping through mountains and deserts, living off the land and befriending primitive tribes, as her father had alluded to in his notebooks.

On the journey here to Devon, she'd had plenty of time

to read Papa's cramped penmanship. She had hoped to determine why her father had trusted Gabriel so implicitly. But Papa had mentioned his traveling companion only briefly. He had devoted the pages to scholarly accounts of native toolmaking and detailed descriptions of poking through ancient rubble. The text had been rather dry and scientific—until that final, chilling entry, made on the day before he'd died.

Did Gabriel know of Papa's meeting with Sir Charles Damson? He must.

Reaching her side, he flashed a smile at her and her companions. "Welcome to Stokeford Abbey," he said. "What do you think of the old pile?"

" 'Tis so ancient it makes me feel young and spry," Uncle Nathaniel said.

"Are there ghosts?" Meg asked, her eyes as wide as saucers.

Gabriel chuckled. "Only in the attics. Or so Grandmama used to tell her grandsons to keep us out of there."

"Lucy always did know how to manage the boys." Uncle Nathaniel rubbed his palms together. "I hope she's at home today."

"She lives at the Dower House," Gabriel said. "It's across the river, not half a mile distant. I'll send word to her of our arrival."

Just then, a footman opened the immense front doors, and a trio of elderly women hastened out onto the covered porch. The first one was a dainty lady with a halo of white hair and a gown of angelic blue. Right behind her scurried a matron with a plump, merry face, a gown of green silk decorated with a profusion of lace, and a matching turban on her head. Bringing up the rear was a tall, dignified woman, garbed in sober gray, who walked with the aid of an ivory-topped cane.

The white-haired leader paused at the edge of the porch,

lifted a frail hand to her mouth, and stared down in obvious shock at Gabriel.

His smile deepened, and the warmth in his expression startled Kate. Bounding up the wide marble steps, he caught the old lady in his arms. He swung her around so that her blue skirt whirled, and she clutched at his broad shoulders.

"Gabriel Kenyon!" The firmness of her tone belied her fragile appearance. "Set me down this instant!"

He lowered her to the porch. "Is that all you can do, Grandmama? Scold? You should welcome your prodigal grandson home."

"After staying away for four years, you deserve a stern reprimand. But I'll demand a proper kiss instead."

He landed a loud smack on her wrinkled cheek, and she returned his embrace. Kate watched them with guarded interest. She must be mistaken to see an affectionate side in Gabriel Kenyon. He was a charmer, that was all, a charismatic man who knew how to beguile people. She would remain cool and aloof to his allure, never forgetting that she had one purpose and one purpose alone: to retrieve the statue.

The other two old ladies gathered around, smiling fondly and murmuring to each other. Then the regal one lifted her cane and made a beckoning motion to Kate's party. Clutching the valise, Kate accompanied her sister and great-uncle up the broad steps to the porch.

With a lace handkerchief, the dowager Lady Stokeford dabbed at the happy tears that shimmered in her blue eyes. "Heavens, you'll think me a watering pot. Who are you two lovely girls? And . . ." She blinked at the chimpanzee in Meg's arms. "My gracious! Who is that beast?"

Stepping out from behind Meg, Uncle Nathaniel kissed Lady Stokeford's hand. " 'Tis I, dearest Lucy, and may I say, you're even more ravishingly beautiful than ever."

The dowager extracted her hand from his. "I meant *that*

creature," she said dryly, pointing at Jabbar. Then she tilted her head to the side and looked more keenly at Uncle Nathaniel. "Are we acquainted, sir?"

"My stars, 'tis Nathaniel Babcock," the plump lady blurted out. Giggling like a girl, she clasped her hands to her rosy cheeks. "Why, I'd recognize that naughty grin anywhere."

"Indeed," the lofty, dignified woman pronounced in a scathing tone as she looked him up and down. "I thought we'd seen the last of you fifty years ago."

"I decided to let bygones be bygones," Uncle Nathaniel said mysteriously. He stepped between Meg and Kate, sliding his arms around their waists. "As you can see, I'm chaperoning my two pretty nieces."

Lady Stokeford arched a slender eyebrow. "I would suspect they are your *grand*nieces."

"A mere technicality," Uncle Nathaniel declared. "Be that as it may, I'm their only living relation."

"And he's given his consent for me to act as their guardian," Gabriel said, taking Kate's arm as if he owned her. "Grandmama, may I present the daughters of Professor Henry Talisford, Katherine and Margaret, lately of Oxford."

Despite the ferment of angry frustration inside herself, Kate set down the valise, stepped away from Gabriel, and curtsied. "We're pleased to meet you, my lady."

"Everyone calls her Kate," said her sister. "I'm Meg." She smiled proudly at the chimpanzee in her arms. "And this is Jabbar, my—or rather, his lordship's pet monkey."

For once, Jabbar behaved with impeccable manners. His black eyes bright and inquisitive, he clung to Meg and observed the strangers.

The dowager gazed askance from the chimpanzee to her grandson. Then she introduced her companions. The round, cheerful woman was Lady Enid Quinton, who apparently had a nose for gossip. "We shall have a grand time," she said, her brown eyes dancing. "The arrival of two such pretty houseguests will cause quite a stir in the neighborhood."

"Hush, Enid," said Olivia, Countess of Faversham. "The girls are clearly in mourning. We must respect that."

Lady Stokeford looped a comforting arm through Kate's. "My dear, I hope we haven't overwhelmed you. We're delighted to have you and your sister here. Young people always liven up the place."

"We appreciate your hospitality." Kate spoke the polite cliché with sincerity. In spite of the quandary of guardianship, she liked Gabriel's grandmother.

As Kate reached down for her valise, Lady Stokeford made an imperious motion to her grandson. "Have you left your manners in the wilds of Africa? For shame, letting a lady carry her own baggage."

"Miss Talisford likes her independence," Gabriel said, sweeping away the valise and handing it to a footman before Kate could protest. Looking annoyingly pleased with himself, he took her other arm, trapping her in between himself and his grandmother.

His closeness unsettled Kate, his firm touch and his male scent, redolent with leather and spice. But she couldn't object to his highhandedness without causing a scene. By the devilish twinkle in his eyes, he knew so, too.

If his grandmother noticed his possessiveness, she made no reference to it. A smile softened her mature features as Lady Stokeford gazed fondly up at her tall grandson. Clearly, she saw only the best in him. "I could scarcely believe it when Rumbold told me there was a procession of vehicles coming up the drive. It's been so long since you deigned to visit me. Shame on you for not sending ahead a note."

"There wasn't time," Gabriel said. "I decided only two days ago to bring Kate and Meg here for a visit."

The dowager raised her eyebrows, but she didn't inquire further. "Ah, well, no matter, the Abbey is always ready these days. I'll settle Kate and Meg in the west wing in the two bedchambers directly across from mine."

"Aren't you living at the Dower House?" Gabriel asked.

"Goodness, no! Not since Michael's marriage. It was far too lonely there all by myself."

Gabriel stopped, bringing all three of them to a halt in the doorway. "The devil you say. Michael has remarried?"

"Of course. I told you so in my letter."

"Which must have gone astray," he said with a wry quirk of his mouth. "So tell me, who is the lucky woman?"

The Rosebuds shared a covert smile. "Her name is Vivien, and she's a most delightful young woman," Lady Stokeford said. "I must add, at least one of my grandsons has done his duty in presenting me with great-grandchildren. I think it high time you settled down and made your contribution, as well. Don't you agree, Miss Talisford?"

Feeling awkward, Kate scrambled for a response. There was steel behind that guileless smile, a steel she couldn't help but admire. "I believe the family is the bedrock of civilization," she said with as much tact as she could muster. "Unfortunately, some men take longer to realize its value."

"Brava! You're very wise for one so young." Lady Stokeford gave her an approving nod. A certain calculation on her face, she glanced from Kate to Gabriel. "Perhaps you could teach my grandson a thing or two."

Gabriel winced. "Two against one makes unfair odds. Now, you mentioned great-grandchildren. Has Michael sired more than Amy?"

Nothing could have been designed better to distract his grandmother. "Oh, yes," she said, her face lighting up with beatific joy. "There's baby William now, too. If you'd come home more often, you wouldn't miss so many important events." Head held high, she led the way into a foyer the size of Larkspur Cottage.

Kate looked for the footman who had taken her valise, but he had vanished, presumably to deliver it to a guest chamber. Another footman accepted her cloak and bonnet. Discreetly she smoothed her hair, tucking in the springy strands that had inevitably escaped their mooring. Once again, she was hard-pressed not to gawk like a bumpkin at her surroundings. She had known Gabriel belonged to a wealthy, aristocratic family, but seeing the proof of it shook her anew.

A broad, curving staircase soared upward, flanked by tall columns and archways. The sand-colored marble floor had been polished to a high sheen. Costly statues filled niches in the walls, and a crystal chandelier sparkled in the late sunlight that streamed through the high windows. The place reminded Kate of a great cathedral. She might have tiptoed reverently, but was forced to keep up with Lady Stokeford and Gabriel, who walked through the foyer without even glancing at its grandeur.

What could have induced him to forsake his exalted heritage for the wilds of Africa? she wondered. How could he have left his grandmother, who clearly loved him in spite of his faults? He must have broken her heart.

"I'll order refreshments in the drawing room," Lady Stokeford was saying to the group. "Unless you'd prefer to go up to your chambers."

"I wouldn't refuse a wee nip," Uncle Nathaniel said.

"Jabbar and I would like to see this marvelous house," Meg gushed. On cue, the chimpanzee clapped his hands.

But Kate felt compelled to safeguard her father's journals. "If you'll excuse me, I'd like to freshen up."

"I'll escort you," Gabriel said instantly.

That was a complication she didn't need. "I'm sure you'd rather visit with your family," she said, vainly attempting to extricate herself from his hold on her arm. "If you'll just give me directions . . ."

His laughter boomed through the foyer. "In this mausoleum, you'd be lost for days. We'd have to send out a search party."

"Quite so," Lady Stokeford concurred, making a shooing motion with her dainty hands. "Gabriel has been gone for four years. Another few minutes won't matter."

Exerting a firm pressure at the base of her back, Gabriel propelled her toward the grand staircase. Kate caught one last glimpse of the small party proceeding down a long corridor, the echo of their voices fading. Then she and Gabriel were alone, mounting the polished marble steps. Half of her wanted to stop short, but the other half refused to let him goad her into losing her dignity.

"Your grandmother's out of sight now, so your chivalry isn't necessary."

He flashed her a cocky grin. "Prickly Kate. Perhaps I like being with you."

He looked her up and down in a slow survey, and she found herself wishing she wore a prettier gown than the drab old black that was three years out of date. "Perhaps you hope to charm me into giving up my father's journals."

His gaze flitted to her lips. "I'd certainly enjoy trying."

Tension fluttered low in her belly. In a flash of memory, she recalled Gabriel in his chamber at the inn: a savage in his natural glory, his muscled chest gleaming like bronze in the morning sunshine. The mere thought made her breathless, and she blinked to dispel the scandalous image.

Logic told her that he was trying to bewitch her, to fool her into lowering her guard. Like the proverbial wolf in sheep's clothing, he would shed his civility when he realized how she meant to thwart his plans.

As they reached the top of the stairs and started down an ornate corridor, she said, "I shall need a carriage the day after tomorrow. I wish to pay a visit to Sir Charles in Cornwall."

Gabriel's air of good humor evaporated. "You're staying here with my grandmother. I forbid you to go anywhere without my permission."

The reminder of his power over her rankled Kate. "You may have maneuvered Uncle Nathaniel, but you can't maneuver me. I won't be left behind when you confront Papa's murderer."

Gabriel brought her around to face him. "So you truly believe Damson is guilty. What makes you so certain?"

"On the journey today, I read Papa's notebooks. In the final entry, he wrote . . ." Her throat tightened as she remembered his precise penmanship, infused with the vigor of life, the last words he'd ever written.

"Wrote what?" Gabriel demanded.

She drew a shaky breath, then said in a rush, "The day before he died, Papa encountered Sir Charles outside the inn. It was a chance meeting, or so Papa thought. They had a friendly debate about the origins of civilization, Sir Charles arguing for Egypt and Papa for Abyssinia. To prove his point, Papa showed him the statue of the goddess."

Gabriel swore under his breath. "Henry never told me."

Kate didn't know whether to believe that or not. "But you knew Sir Charles was in Cairo," she said. "How?"

"While I was at the harbor, making arrangements for our passage to Alexandria, I saw Damson's man, Figgins." The long rays of the setting sun poured through a window at the end of the corridor and illuminated his fierce expression. "At least it explains why Damson wants your father's journals. That entry incriminates him."

The fire of vengeance infused Kate. She pulled away, her fingers curling into claws. "I intend to see Sir Charles punished for Papa's murder. Promise you won't leave without me."

Gabriel's eyes took on the appearance of cold flat stones. Silence stretched out, a silence punctuated by the bonging of a clock somewhere. "I never make promises to women," he said. "Promises only get a man into trouble."

"You'll have trouble if you leave for Sir Charles's estate without me."

A brusque laugh rumbled from him. "How do you intend to stop me?"

"I'll follow you," Kate said with reckless bravado. "And don't think to sneak off. I intend to keep a watch on you."

That feral half-smile returned to his mouth. The corners of his eyes crinkling, he leaned closer so that his breath kissed her cheek. "Then prepare to stay close to me, my darling ward. Very close, indeed."

CHAPTER 8

CONFESSIONS OF A SLAVE

GABE intended to put his plan into motion as swiftly as possible. The trick was, he needed his grandmother's co-operation.

After dinner that evening, as the other ladies headed down the corridor toward the drawing room, accompanied by Michael and Uncle Nathaniel, Gabe took the dowager's arm. How small she seemed. Her elegantly styled white hair barely reached his shoulder. He'd always thought her a formidable woman, though of course, his memories were those of a youth.

His voice low, he said, "May I have a word with you, Grandmama?"

Her keen blue eyes studied him with a mixture of fondness and wisdom. "Certainly. It isn't every day that my wayward grandson deigns to come home."

He flinched inwardly. His grandmother had to be the only person on earth who still had the power to make him feel like a naughty child. But little did she realize, he had learned how to handle women.

As they proceeded down the passageway, the trill of laughter drew his attention to the lively group ahead of them. It was Meg who had laughed, of course. By her own admission, Kate no longer displayed such unseemly exuberance. She walked sedately at the rear of the party in the company of Lady Faversham and Lady Enid Quinton. With her wild tresses tamed into a knot and her curvaceous body swathed by a shapeless black gown, Kate seemed determined to align herself with the elderly tabbies.

That disguise didn't fool Gabe. His fingers itched to pull out all those pins and loosen her springy, red-gold curls. His mouth burned to coax a response from those prim, maidenly lips—

"Lest you forget," Grandmama chided, "she isn't one of your fancy pieces."

Annoyed at being caught staring, he deftly steered the dowager into an antechamber, where a single lamp cast a flickering glow over the rich crimson décor and the medieval stone walls. "I'm perfectly aware that Kate is a lady."

"Did I say Kate? Perhaps I meant Meg."

"Meg?" Gabriel exploded. "She's only sixteen. Why would you think I'd have any interest—" Then he noticed his grandmother's amused smile. "I've no interest in either of them. Other than providing for their welfare, of course."

"I see."

He doubted that; his grandmother saw what she chose to see. "I'm very pleased that you approve of the Talisford girls," he said, launching smoothly into his rhetoric. "You see, I'd like to leave them here with you for a short time while I'm gone."

"You're going away again?" Grandmama exclaimed. "But you've only just come home."

"I've business to attend to. It won't take long."

"Pish-posh. What could possibly be more important than your family?"

Gabe strolled to the mantelpiece and glanced up at the portrait of a pompous, bewigged ancestor. "I must ride to Cornwall and see to my estate there," he said glibly. "I'll be away for only a few days. A week at the most."

"A week!" The dowager sank gracefully onto a gold velvet chaise and arranged her pale blue skirts. "Sit," she commanded, patting the cushion beside her. "You will tell me what this is really about."

Gabe clenched his teeth around a curse. Grandmama had always been able to see through his lies. In particular, he recalled the time he had pilfered a bottle of gin from his father's stash in the study and sneaked out to the stables. He never knew how she'd found him out, but before he'd choked down more than one swig of the fiery liquor, Grandmama had marched into the stall and seized the bottle, carrying it outside and pouring the contents into a thicket of holly bushes.

Now he wondered what she'd say if he told her he intended to break into a nobleman's house and steal a statue. Not to mention, take revenge for murder.

Assuming a casual air, he sat down beside his grandmother and stretched out his arm across the back of the chaise. He flashed her a bedazzling smile. "You're right, I haven't told you everything," he said. "The fact is, I'm panicked by my responsibility. I haven't the slightest notion what to do with two respectable girls."

"So you'll shirk your duty? That's hardly the way I raised you."

"Come now, Grandmama. I *am* doing my duty by bringing them to you. What do I know of training young ladies?" Leaning forward, he grasped her wrinkled hand; it felt as small and fragile as a wren. "Kate and Meg need *you*. You're the perfect person to take them under your wing. They've led a sheltered life in a small cottage, and they would greatly benefit from your experience with society."

The dowager thinned her lips. "Something tells me there's more to your flattery than meets the eye."

He laughed easily. "I'm merely asking you for help. You can arrange for dancing lessons, teach them the ways of society, refurbish their wardrobes. And charge all the bills to me, of course."

Lady Stokeford harrumphed. "So you'll come home only when you need a problem solved, will you?"

"Of course not," he said, assuaging his guilt by kissing her papery cheek. She smelled faintly of lilac, a scent that evoked memories of his youth. Whenever his mother had been lost in prayer and his father drunk by noon, Grandmama had always been there to soothe his hurts and to encourage him. "I missed you very much," he said sincerely. "I'll be back as soon as my business is concluded at Fairfield Park. Then we can have a nice long visit." And with luck, once Grandmama grew fond of Meg and Kate, she would want to keep them here. He could pay their bills and be confident of their care, while he was free to go off as he pleased.

Lady Stokeford sighed. "Who knows if I'll still be here in a week? I'm old and feeble. Or are you so caught up in your own schemes that you haven't noticed?"

Her words jolted him. She looked as hale as any pampered elderly lady . . . didn't she? He regarded her snowy hair and patrician features, the slim form garbed in her favorite blue. Were the lines on her porcelain skin etched a little deeper now? Was her slenderness a sign of frailty? Was the rosy color in her cheeks a mark of health or the flush of fever? Gabe had always prided himself on his powers of observation. Either he'd been blind to her infirmity— or she was playacting to get what she wanted.

He'd cast his vote for the latter.

He sprang up from the chaise, gently grasped her ankles, and lifted her legs up onto the cushions.

"What are you doing?" his grandmother said testily, swatting him away.

"I'm making you more comfortable. I didn't realize that you've been ill." He pilfered a stuffed pillow from a chair and tucked it behind her back. "I'll send for the doctor. A session of leeches should improve your bad blood."

"I don't need a physician. I need my family around me."

"But I'm imposing on you. That's all the more reason for me to leave the Abbey."

"Leave! I suffer the complaints of the aged, that's all. Aching bones, flagging strength . . . and loneliness." She pressed a delicate hand to her brow. "But never mind me, you do as you like. You always have."

"Don't talk, Grandmama. You'll only tire yourself. I'll ring for your maid, and then inform Kate and Meg of our departure in the morning."

With uncanny agility, Lady Stokeford swung her feet off the chaise and sat up straight, her age-spotted hands gripping the folds of her skirt. "You will do nothing of the sort! A gentleman cannot travel alone with two unmarried ladies. Why, their reputations will suffer."

They'd traveled here with no ill effects. But he needn't add fuel to his grandmother's fire. "You're absolutely right. I'll borrow a female servant as chaperone. Michael must have someone he can spare."

"Balderdash! Where will you go?"

"To London, I suppose," he said, rubbing his temples. "I'll advertise for a companion. Yes, that's it. There must be some respectable woman who would be willing to sponsor them."

"You know nothing of choosing a lady's companion. I forbid you to take those sweet girls away from here."

"But if you won't watch them for me . . ."

"I will, you sly devil." He had only a moment of triumph before she narrowed her eyes at him and added, "But only if you tell me the real reason you're heading off to Cornwall in such a hurry."

"I own an estate," he reiterated. "After four years, it requires my attention." If it weren't for Damson, he truly might be curious to see the manor he'd inherited from his maternal grandfather. He'd enjoyed visiting the rambling old house as a child, sliding down the long, curved oak balustrade, examining the curios in the attic, exploring the priest hole cleverly hidden behind a wardrobe in one of the ancient bedchambers.

"You never cared about Fairfield Park before now. You were too busy wandering the countryside to be bothered with the responsibility."

"Then rejoice in my transformation," he said lightly. "I'll be departing on the morrow."

"No." She eyed him craftily. "We'll make a bargain, you and I. If you wish me to watch Kate and Meg, you'll stay here for a week first."

He reined in his impatience. He couldn't afford to stir her curiosity any further. "One day. The sooner I conclude my business, the sooner I can return."

"Five days."

"Two."

"Four."

"Three, and not a moment longer," he said firmly. "That's my final concession."

She smiled serenely. "Three days, then."

Chuckling wryly, Gabe bent down to kiss her cheek again. He'd been outfoxed this time. But at least Grandmama hadn't found out his true purpose.

God help him if she and the Rosebuds meddled with his plans.

AFTER sending her maid to deliver a message, Kate paced the cavernous bedchamber. She wondered if the recipient would come, or if he would ignore her summons. There was nothing to do but wait and see.

Compared to her spartan room at Larkspur Cottage, the guest chamber was a lavish paradise. The mahogany furniture had been carved with a delicate touch and polished to a rich sheen. Hangings of pale blue velvet draped the canopied bed, creating a pretty picture with the embroidered white counterpane and lace-edged pillows. The bed-side table and the adjacent shelves held a collection of the latest novels and books of poetry. She had secreted her father's precious mementos and Gabriel's sketchbooks in the spacious drawers of the wardrobe in the dressing room, beneath her extra chemise. Certainly she had little else to fill the space.

She paced to the windows, which were framed by great swags of blue damask. The darkened glass reflected the crackling fire on the hearth and the soft glow of several candles. Kate threw open the casement to let in the chilly night air. Huddling into her shawl, she looked down toward the front of the house, where yellow light from the drawing room spilled onto the neatly trimmed shrubbery.

A part of her had wanted to stay down there with Gabriel's family. Michael and Vivien, Lord and Lady Stokeford, had entertained everyone with amusing tales about their infant son and small daughter. Meg had been happy, too, playing cards with Uncle Nathaniel, Lady Enid, and Lady Faversham. How her sister had sparkled at the novelty of being a guest in a great house. Kate couldn't blame her. Looking back, she realized how dull their years alone must have been for her fun-loving sister, sitting in the evening in the old parlor, reading aloud or tending to the endless sewing.

But Kate had something more important to do than so-cialize.

She walked the length of the bedchamber, counting thirty-four paces from the windows to the arched doorway. Without the guidance of a servant, she would have been lost in the maze of corridors on her way to and from dinner. She'd passed dozens of doors, dozens of chambers. One hundred twenty in all, her maid had proudly informed her.

A pleasant, freckle-faced country girl of about Meg's age, Betty had been assigned to act as Kate's abigail. She had unpacked Kate's meager belongings and had been sitting by the fire, mending the lace on Kate's oldest gown, when Kate had returned from dinner. Kate had promptly sent Betty on this important errand.

What was taking her so long?

Clenching the edges of her shawl, Kate roamed the chamber and planned what she would say. At last a knock sounded. She whirled around as the door opened, and Betty's mobcapped head peeked into the chamber. The maid stepped inside, glancing back with nervous interest in her brown eyes. In a loud whisper, she said, "I brung him here, miss, like ye asked."

"Show him in, please."

"Do ye wish me to stay?"

"No, thank you." Seeing Betty's eyes widen with questions, Kate added, "However, I would appreciate your fetching a pot of tea." The long trip to the kitchen and back would give Kate time enough to accomplish her purpose.

The maid bobbed a curtsy and darted out. A moment later, a man entered the bedchamber.

Kate gripped the rounded back of a chair as the visitor advanced toward her. That tall, somber form raised the hairs on the back of her neck. Or perhaps her discomfort was a reaction to his foreignness, the impenetrable black eyes and the outlandish white robes.

Pressing his palms together, Ashraf bowed so low his headpiece almost brushed the carpet. "I am your servant, Miss Talisford."

Deliberately, she remained standing. It would be inappropriate to invite him to sit and intimidating for her to look up to him from her chair. "I hope you'll oblige me by answering a few questions in regard to my father's death."

He waited, his dusky features inscrutable.

"How long have you been employed by Lord Gabriel?" she asked.

"Since Ramadan two years ago."

"Ramadan?"

"A time of fasting and prayer ordained by the Prophet Muhammed."

She wondered if his foreign religion condoned theft and murder. "Tell me, where were you at the time my father was attacked?"

"On the dhow in the harbor that would take us to Alexandria, there to board the English ship. His lordship bade me watch their belongings."

Disappointment speared her. She'd been hoping he'd seen something that night, some overlooked clue. "There was a crate on the vessel that belonged to my father. What else?"

His lip curled slightly. "Jabbar, mistress."

"But why were you told to protect a few souvenirs and journals?" she asked in puzzlement. "Shouldn't you have stayed at the inn to . . . ?"

"To guard the goddess?" he said, finishing her question. "Your father believed that Lord Gabriel would return soon."

"Where was he?"

He lowered his eyes. "It is not for me to know."

Would Ashraf lie to protect his master? Kate wondered. Or was he himself the culprit? Perhaps he'd coveted the statue. Perhaps in the dark of night he'd crept back to the inn and murdered her father . . .

She steeled herself against a shudder. As the fire crackled into the silence, she was aware of how alone they were. He might think she had found him out. If he were to draw out a knife from inside those robes . . .

She banished her qualms. The man would scarcely slay her when her servant could attest to his presence here. "When did you find out . . . what had happened?"

"At dawn, when your father and my master did not

board the dhow, I went to the inn. There was blood on the floor of their chamber. The innkeeper, may Allah curse him, wailed about the cost of hiring litter-bearers to carry my master to the physician." Ashraf paused, bowing his head respectfully. "Your father had been taken to the palace of the pasha to be prepared for burial."

"The pasha?"

"The ruler of Cairo."

Her mind swirling with questions, she pressed her fingers into the back of the chair. What if this pasha had stolen the statue? Or was she merely grasping at straws, reluctant to believe her father had been killed by a fellow Englishman?

A man whom she had invited into her cottage as an honored guest.

Swallowing her queasiness, she regarded Ashraf. "Did you go after the murderers?"

"Nay, my lady. I was tending to the master's injuries. The pasha sent his guards to search the city, but alas, they found nothing."

"Tell me about this pasha. What manner of man is he?"

Ashraf spread his palms wide. "As a native of Khartoum, I know little of him. But his people seemed content."

The vague answer frustrated Kate. "And your master— what manner of man is he?"

"An infidel." Ashraf's thin lips twitched disapprovingly. "He is not fit to wash the feet of Professor Talisford's daughter."

She stifled an hysterical laugh. "If you think so little of Lord Gabriel, then why do you serve him?"

"I must obey his every command." The Arab swept another bow. "You see, he owns me. I am his slave."

CHAPTER 9

THE SKULL-FACED MAN

"WHAT will you have?" Michael asked, opening a glass-fronted cabinet in his study to display an array of crystal decanters.

Gabe settled into a wing chair by the fire. The study looked much the same as when he'd been a boy. Heavy green draperies framed the night-darkened windows, ledgers lined the shelves, and a branch of candles on the desk cast a flickering light. He half expected to see a worn place in the crimson carpet where he'd stood to endure a rambling lecture from his besotted father. "Anything but gin."

Michael grimaced. "It's a wonder none of us became drunkards."

"Or religious zealots like Mama."

As a child, Gabe had been forced by his pious mother to spend long hours on his knees in chapel. He could still remember the numbing hardness of the granite floor, the difficulty in keeping his head bowed and his hands folded. Instead of meditating on his sins, however, he'd been imagining dragons and other fantastical creatures in the striations of the stone.

At the age of eighteen, he'd escaped home, seeking the amusements of London, and in particular, the women. He'd wallowed in dissipation, evading the clutches of match-making mamas and taking the pleasures offered to him by lusty ladies. Until one morning he'd awakened in bed with an unfamiliar woman whose irate husband pounded on the door. Then and there, Gabe had decided that he had little taste for quick escapes through windows.

He'd tried his hand at portrait painting, but the discipline of laboring day after day on the same subject had bored him. Restless, he'd roamed the countryside, sketching, always sketching. His travels had taken him through the bustling town of Oxford, where on a whim he'd attended a lecture on ancient civilizations presented by Professor Henry Talisford. Gabe had offered to illustrate a book the professor was planning to write. Eventually, struck by wanderlust, Gabe had funded that ill-fated trip to Africa.

Propping his boot heels on the brass fender of the fireplace, he shut the door on the past and focused on the present. He idly picked up a notebook from the table beside him and flipped through the pages. Written in his brother's bold hand, it was a dictionary of English terms alongside words in a strange language.

As Michael handed him a glass of port, Gabe asked, "Is this the Gypsy tongue?"

"It's Romany," his brother confirmed, sitting in the opposite chair. Like Gabe, he had cast off his coat and waistcoat. Unlike Gabe, he wore a cravat. "I'm learning to speak the language of Vivien's people. With moderate success, I might add."

Picturing his vivacious, dark-haired sister-in-law, Gabe shook his head in amazement. "So you're married to a woman raised by the Gypsies. And Grandmama thought I was the one to flout convention."

Michael lifted his glass in a salute. "Let's drink to the power of love."

As they clinked glasses, Gabe didn't mention his own skepticism of love. The thought of marriage left a sour taste in his mouth, conjuring memories of his parents' unhappiness and the unwelcome secrets told to him by his father. Distastefully, he pushed that incident out of his mind and considered the change in his older brother. Four years ago, Michael had been a widower pursuing the pleasures of London to bury his grief. Now, his brother's contentment made Gabe wonder if something was missing from his own life.

For no reason at all, he thought of Kate Talisford with her cool green eyes and priggish manners. That shrew would make life hell for the man who was fool enough to wed her. Thank God it wouldn't be him.

Leaning back, he savored his freedom along with his drink. "A fine port. Makes me almost glad to be back in the civilized world."

"Tell me about your trip," Michael said. "In particular, what happened to Henry Talisford."

Gabe steadied himself with another sip of port, this time without tasting it. Even at the age of thirty, it galled him to admit his failures to his older brother. "It's a long story," he hedged.

Michael's keen stare demanded the truth. "I have all evening."

Turning his gaze to the darkened window, Gabe forced his thoughts back to that night, reliving it with gut-twisting aversion. "I went out that last evening in Cairo," he began, his voice thick with reluctance. "I met a woman outside the inn where we were staying. A beautiful woman . . ."

She had flashed him a sultry smile. Clad in robes, Yasmin was dark, sloe-eyed, nubile, a feast to a man who'd trekked through desolate lands for four years. She'd enticed him to a little house near the bazaar, poured him a chalice of thick, sweet wine, and disrobed in a sinuous dance that heated his blood and made time melt into a euphoria of pleasure.

Hours later, he was jolted to realize that it was well past midnight. Ashraf must have left for the dhow in the harbor.

Over Yasmin's protests, he stumbled out in a drunken haze and by some miracle found his way back to the inn.

And from the moment he stepped into the gloomy ante-chamber, he sensed danger.

His head reeling, he braced his fingertips on the wall. The rough clay bricks still held a trace of the day's warmth. The wine, he thought fuzzily. What had been in that wine?

He blinked, struggling to focus, slowly making out the black shapes of tables and stools, the earthen water jar near the doorway. Nothing unusual. Yet his neck prickled.

Stealthily, he reached for his knife. His fingers met the smooth waistband of his breeches. He'd forgotten the weapon at Yasmin's house.

Swaying a little, he walked toward the bedchamber. The place was silent. Too silent. The balcony doors were open, and the cool night breezes came through the moucharabie, a trellis of carved wood designed to protect the privacy of the room's occupants. Snakes of moonlight writhed over the darkened floor. The professor's sleeping mat was empty.

"Henry?" he whispered.

No answer.

Gabe focused his bleary gaze on the corner. Through the gloom, he could just see the dark outline of the opened trunk. That niggling of alarm crept over him again. The statue. Was the goddess there?

As he weaved a path toward the trunk, he spied someone lying crumpled on the floor. He dropped into a crouch beside the man. Horror struck him in the gut.

Henry Talisford lay unmoving. Numbly, Gabe probed Henry's neck, but couldn't find a pulse. A dark puddle stained the floor beneath his head. Like a noxious vapor, the coppery scent of blood tainted the air.

Gabe cursed. Murderers!

A small movement in the shadows alerted him. Fists clenched, he sprang to his feet, his senses distorted by drink. The robed figure of a man stood in the gloom of the corner. In the crook of his arm, he held the small gold statue. Moonlight penetrated his hood to touch pale, aristocratic features. There was something vaguely familiar about him . . .

"Who the hell are you?" Gabe demanded.

The man merely laughed, a genteel disturbance of the air.

Seized by a lethal rage, Gabe leapt toward him. Then something struck him in the back. The searing pain made him stumble. Pivoting, he caught a glimpse of another man in the moonlight. A ruffian with the skull-like features of an Englishman.

The knife flashed, slicing into Gabe again. His legs buckled. Through the agony, he felt the trickling warmth of blood. His vision wavered like a mirage. The last thing he remembered was that elegant laugh . . .

Gabe sprang from the chair. He stalked across the study to the window, threw open the casement, and gulped in lungfuls of cold night air. His fingers pressed against the white-painted sill. Staring into the darkness, he said flatly, "Yasmin was in league with the thieves. The wine she gave me was laced with opium. I was gulled."

He heard the clink of glass as his brother refilled his drink. "Did you look for her later?" Michael asked.

"She was gone. The house was abandoned. None of the neighbors knew her. Apparently, she'd leased the place for the day."

"And the murderers?"

"Vanished without a trace." Gabe slammed his palm onto the sill. "Damn my idiocy! If I'd been there, Henry would still be alive."

"You could have been killed," Michael said. "I'm thankful you're safe."

"Safe." Gabe drenched the word in the self-contempt that ate at him. Turning, he leaned against the window frame and regarded his brother. "I should have guarded the statue. And Henry."

"Why? Did you mention the goddess to anyone?"

"Hell, no. But Henry did. He was far too trusting." The professor had had a childlike enthusiasm for their discovery. If anyone showed an interest in their journey, he'd launch into a zealous account of finding the ancient temple. According to his last journal entry, he'd done so with Damson.

"The past can't be changed. What matters is now. What you'll do next." Michael sent him a piercing stare. "I suspect you know these men."

Gabe set his jaw. It was bad enough that Kate had learned the truth. "Yes," he bit out. "I intend to make them pay."

"Who are they?"

"Never mind. It's my battle, not yours."

"Don't be pig-headed. I've a right to know. You'd feel the same if the tables were turned."

Michael had a point, Gabe grudgingly conceded. Perhaps he could use an ally in case Kate or Grandmama proved troublesome. "The man who stabbed me is named Figgins. The other man, the one holding the statue, is his employer, Sir Charles Damson."

"Damson." Michael's blue eyes narrowed as if he were looking into the past. "Foppish fellow, fair hair, glib tongue. A few years ago, he was embroiled in a scandal involving a young lady. He tried to dishonor her, then managed to convince people that she suffered from hysteria."

"Like an alley cat, Damson always lands on his feet." Gabe clenched and unclenched his fingers. "But not this time. He won't get away with murder."

His brother nodded curtly. "Describe this statue."

"I'll do better. If I may have paper and pen . . ."

Michael waved him toward the desk. "Help yourself."

Gabe rummaged in a drawer and found a sheet of stationery imprinted with the gold Stokeford crest. Dipping a sharpened quill into a silver inkpot, he sketched an outline of the goddess, the oval face and lush mouth, the ponderous breasts and rounded hips.

Michael leaned over the desk to study the curvaceous form. "How big is the statue?"

"About twice the size of my hand. Here's the most impressive item." Gabe outlined the gemstone nestled at the top of the statue's thighs. "The largest yellow diamond I've ever seen."

Picking up the drawing, his brother whistled softly. "Your goddess is worth a tidy fortune, then. How do you know Damson hasn't already sold it?"

"Money isn't his purpose. He wants to add the statue to his collection."

"Collection?"

Gabe tossed down the quill. "Damson owns a vast array of ancient artifacts. His particular interest is erotica."

Michael grimaced. "I see. He gets his jollies from inanimate objects—as well as from misusing women."

"Precisely." Gabe's blood ran cold at the thought of Kate in the clutches of that villain. If Gabe had to lock her up, he'd never let her within ten miles of Damson.

"Once you find the statue," Michael said, "you'll need a warrant to recover it. Have you contacted the local magistrate?"

"Damson *is* the magistrate."

"Good God. Well, then, I'll accompany you to Cornwall."

Gabe shook his head. "Ashraf will be sufficient. He once served as guard to a desert prince." Taking the drawing, he rolled it into a tube. "However, there's one thing I'd ask of you."

"Anything."

"Order Grandmama to keep a close watch on Kate Talisford."

"Let me guess. She wants to go with you. To avenge her father."

His gut twisted into a knot. "She's too blasted stubborn for her own good. She refuses to accept that such a dangerous mission is best handled by a man."

Amusement shone in his brother's eyes. "A feisty woman can be a handful. Yet a blessing, too. You could do worse."

Gabe scowled. "Kate is my responsibility, that's all. I want only to keep her and her sister safe from harm—" A small sound came from the corridor. The scrape of a shoe on stone. His senses snapped to alertness. "Did you hear that?"

"What?"

Gabe didn't answer. The door stood open a crack, and he sprang toward it. Yanking back the heavy oak panel, he peered out into the passageway. On a nearby table, the tiny flame of a candle wavered inside a glass chimney. The empty, shadowed corridor stretched out to either side.

To the right, the corridor turned a corner. He strode there and peered into the darkness of a long, seldom-used picture gallery where the furniture huddled like gloomy shadows. Nothing moved.

Michael appeared beside him. "What was it?"

"I heard a footstep."

"A servant most likely."

"Perhaps." Gabe didn't agree, but he held his tongue as they returned to the study. There was no point in arguing. Yet he was certain that someone had been out here.

Listening.

LATER that evening, the three Rosebuds sat drinking sherry in the bedchamber of the dowager Lady Stokeford. Lucy had invited her friends to spend the night at the Abbey, and she'd just finished telling them the astonishing news.

"Really, Lucy, you should be ashamed of yourself," said Olivia, Lady Faversham. "Spying on your grandsons."

"Do loosen your corset, Olivia," Enid said. "If not for eavesdropping, one would never know half of what goes on in the world."

Despite Enid's defense, Lucy felt rather mortified by her actions. She hadn't intended to spy. She'd gone to bid her grandsons good-night—and to feast her eyes once again on her darling Gabriel. She couldn't believe her youngest rapscallion had grown into such a tall, handsome, masterful man.

When she'd heard him speaking about the death of Professor Talisford, why, she hadn't been able to help herself. To her shock, she'd learned that Kate's father had been brutally murdered during the robbery of an ancient statue. After a while, her limbs had gone stiff from standing so long, and she'd shifted position, inadvertently scraping her slipper on the stone floor.

"I nearly suffered an apoplexy, hiding in the gallery like one of Bonaparte's spies," she told her friends. "Though perhaps I should have stood my ground. Gabriel ought to have confided in me."

Olivia snorted. "Men never confide in women. They're too certain of their own superiority."

"Or afraid that we might talk sense into them," Enid added, bobbing her head. In the privacy of the boudoir, she had removed the ubiquitous turban, revealing an unkempt mop of graying ginger hair.

"Which is why we must resort to strategems," Lucy concurred.

"This is by far the most harebrained scheme that Gabriel has ever concocted," Olivia stated. "It's worse than the time he took Joshua's dare, climbed to the roof, and almost fell to his death."

"Gabriel always did love adventure," Enid said with a sigh. "But going after a murderer is far too dangerous. We must find a way to stop him."

Gazing at her longtime friends, Lucy didn't hide her sense of helplessness. "Alas, I can no longer force my grandsons to behave. Nor can I fault Gabriel's intent. He believes a wrong has been done, and he wishes to right it."

"But he can't possibly succeed," Olivia pointed out. "Sir Charles Damson is a member of the best circles. His family can be traced back to the Conquerer. No one would believe him capable of such a foul deed."

"There was that incident three years ago," Enid ventured.

Lucy sat forward. "What incident?"

Enid wriggled into a more comfortable position on the overstuffed rose chair. "At the Abernathys' ball, a young lady claimed that Sir Charles lured her into a deserted bedchamber. Fortunately, they were discovered before he could dishonor her. He insisted she was mistaken as to his intent, and she later recanted her story. The dash of impropriety only made him more popular with the ladies."

"Hmph," Olivia said. "If Gabriel is caught thieving from Sir Charles, he'll go straight to Newgate. And thence to the gibbet."

Enid gasped. "Surely the Kenyon name would save him."

Olivia dourly shook her head. "Not in these times. People still remember the bloody revolt of the French peasants. A noble-born thief would be judged even more harshly than a commoner. Any leniency due to rank might well start a riot."

Lucy's hand quivered as she took a bracing gulp of sherry. When she could speak, she said, "I fear my grandson will take more than the statue. He's consumed by a passion for justice. He'll seek retaliation for the murder of Henry Talisford."

A grim silence spread over the boudoir. For a moment, there was only the ticking of the clock on the bedside table and the snapping of the fire.

"Oh, dear," Enid said faintly, "surely he won't *kill* Sir Charles."

Too distraught to speak, Lucy shrugged her shoulders.

"We must act swiftly, then," Olivia said, using the cane to lever herself to her feet. "We must hire the Bow Street Runners. They can retrieve the statue and see that justice is done."

"Gabriel will never agree to such a course of action," Lucy fretted. "He doesn't trust authority."

"And what of Kate Talisford?" Enid asked. "You said she intends to go with him."

"She, at least, must be stopped," Olivia said, pacing the bedchamber, her gray gown swishing and her cane thumping. "We'll keep her here, as Gabriel asked."

Distressed, Lucy reflected on the quiet strength she'd sensed in Kate Talisford. The strength to tame her youngest grandson. "She's a very determined girl. And . . . I don't know that we *should* stop her."

A clamor of protests broke out. "We must," Enid said. "No lady should endanger herself so."

"It would be the ruination of her reputation," Olivia declared. "What can you be thinking?"

Lucy held up her hand. "Hear me out, Rosebuds. Did either of you mark the attraction between Kate and my grandson?"

"During dinner, he watched her like a sultan with a new concubine," Enid said. She poured herself another draught of sherry from the decanter on the table beside her chair.

"Just as we couldn't keep our eyes off her great-uncle. Did you see the way his eyes twinkled?"

"Nathaniel Babcock is a roué," Olivia said sourly. "His eyes always twinkle whenever he meets a rich widow. Especially an exceedingly silly one."

Enid put her nose in the air. "You're still jealous about the Christmas ball fifty years ago," she said, wagging a plump, beringed finger at Olivia. "You've never forgotten that Nathaniel danced twice with me and only once with you."

"Poppycock. He danced three times with Lucy, and I was happy for her—"

"Ladies, please," Lucy broke in. "We were discussing Kate and my grandson."

Olivia curled her thin fingers around the knob of her cane. "If this is another of your schemes, Lucy, I would beg you to recall the near disaster when we interfered with Vivien's life."

"And look at how well things turned out for her and Michael," Lucy said.

The Rosebuds shared a smile. The friendship between them had never been stronger than in old age, Lucy reflected. Always before there had been children to tend to, husbands to appease, households to run. But now they had the leisure to spend most days together, and they'd grown closer than sisters. She knew Olivia and Enid as well as she knew herself. And she also knew they would support her scheme no matter what.

With renewed resolve, Lucy leaned forward in her chair. "Gabriel has promised not to depart until three days from now. So let us put our minds to fostering a romance between him and Kate Talisford."

"But he'll never settle down with one woman," Olivia stated. "Some men are like that."

"I must concur," Enid fretted. "I fear he'll break poor Kate's heart."

"He won't," Lucy said with more hope than confidence. "*I* fear she's our only chance to reform his adventuresome nature."

CHAPTER 10

PISTOLS AT DAWN

THE next morning, Kate awakened early after a surprisingly restful sleep. At first, she blinked in puzzlement at the blue arch of the canopy and the magnificent four-poster bed. Then she remembered. She was a guest at Stokeford Abbey. It was the first time she'd slept anywhere but her tidy little chamber at Larkspur Cottage. There were no chores to be done, no sewing or cleaning or baking. Like a lady of leisure, she could lie abed for as long as she liked.

Indolence lasted all of half a minute. Gabriel. What if he'd left for Cornwall without her?

She splashed cold water on her face and hastily donned her second-best black gown. Running out of the chamber, she nearly knocked down Betty, who was toting a pile of linens. Kate muttered a swift apology, then said, "Have you seen Lord Gabriel this morning?"

The maid peered around the towering stack. "Aye, miss. He was talkin' to Mr. Ashraf downstairs."

"When?"

"Why, 'twas nigh on half an hour ago. I heard 'em mention the stables."

The stables. Dear heaven, Gabriel must be intending to order the carriage. If he set off without her . . .

Kate scurried downstairs, past the tall Ionic columns and the classical statues in niches along the walls. The scuffle of her slippers on the sand-colored marble echoed in the vast corridor. As she headed toward the rear of the house, room upon opulent room unfolded on either side of her.

She glimpsed a piano and a harp in one, a soaring library in another. There were antechambers and sitting rooms, and a dining room with a table so long it surely seated fifty guests.

Then the corridor split into two and, guessing which turn to take, she found herself in the ancient part of the house, where stone archways led to smaller, monastic rooms, including a lovely old chapel which she might have explored had haste not been crucial.

While she wandered around, lost, Gabriel might be leaving her behind.

As her frustration reached a zenith, she came upon an obliging footman who led her through a maze of passageways, then directed her down a small corridor, at the end of which stood an outside door. These were service rooms, she realized, storage for dishes and silver and crystal. As she reached for the outside door handle, she glanced into the last room.

Along the paneled walls stood massive, glass-fronted cabinets that held an array of weapons from old-fashioned muskets to modern rifles, hunting knives to wicked-looking swords. A man stood by the window with his back to her. The early morning sunlight glinted off his dark hair and powerful physique, his broad shoulders clad in a forest-green coat and his long legs in tan breeches with gleaming Hessians.

Gabriel.

Aware of a treacherous weakening in her knees, she braced her hand on the doorframe. It was relief, Kate told herself, relief that he hadn't absconded to Cornwall, after all. She certainly wasn't a ninny who swooned at the sight of a handsome rogue.

Stepping briskly into the gun room, she said, "Gabriel, I'd like to speak to you—"

The words died on her tongue as he pivoted, a long-barreled pistol pointed straight at her heart.

She stood paralyzed. His tanned features wore a murderous expression, and his finger caressed the trigger. The acrid scents of metal and gun oil hung in the air. A few dust motes danced in a beam of sunshine.

"My dear ward," he drawled. "You're late."

"To my own execution?" she said tartly. "Put that thing down."

"Afraid?"

"No," she said, though her heart was beating far too fast. "You . . . startled me, that's all."

He lowered his arm, the pistol gripped at his side. His glower eased into a watchful expression. "You promised to follow me everywhere. But I haven't seen you since last evening."

"Of course not. I can scarcely watch you all night."

"You could try." His gaze did a leisurely inspection of her serviceable black gown. Sensing a sharp edge to his mood this morning, she wondered how he viewed her. As an annoying duty? A dried-up spinster? The foolish girl he had once scorned? Probably all of those things.

"There was a time," he said, "when propriety didn't stop you. When you were more than willing to share my bed."

A flush stung her cheeks. "There was a time when I was young and naïve and couldn't read a man's true character."

"Naïve? Yes." He sauntered closer, the pistol held loosely in his grip. "But you did admire me, Kate. You still do."

His audacity robbed her of speech. Never had a man spoken to her so boldly. Never had she felt such a tumult of anger. There could be no other reason for her pulse to race and her breath to catch.

He stopped in front of her, so close she could feel the heat of his body and smell the spiciness of his cologne.

Though she was a tall woman, he topped her by half a head. His white teeth gleaming against his sun-burnished skin, he gazed at her with that wicked smile and those bewitching blue eyes.

In a wild surge of giddiness, she thought he meant to kiss her. She feared she might allow him.

Instead, he let the cold, smooth barrel of the gun glide down her cheek. "Admit it," he said with unabashed confidence. "You dream about me in your lonely bed."

Appalled by the truth of that, Kate fought back a shiver. She, who had sworn to never again rely on any man, did indeed feel an attraction to this adventurer. Stepping away, she took up a stance behind the table in the center of the room, where an opened leather case displayed another long-barreled pistol, the match to the one in Gabriel's hand.

"For a guardian, you're far too bold," she said. "You lack integrity and honor. This situation with Ashraf only confirms it."

"Ashraf?"

"He's your slave. You *own* him as if he were a . . . a horse or a gun."

His smile faded. Without denying the allegation, he said, "When did you speak to him?"

"Yesterday evening." She crossed her arms. "I shouldn't be surprised. You've little regard for the rights of others."

"In some cultures, slavery is a way of life."

"Not here in England."

"In the colonies, then. Jamaica. Barbados. The Americas."

"That's no excuse," she said. "How can you call yourself a civilized man?"

"I don't. You of all people should know that."

She wanted to slap the smirk off his too handsome face. "So you'll force that poor man to labor for you. Without wages, without hope of gaining his freedom."

"Have a care, Miss Katie. Things aren't always as they seem."

Her throat choked. For a moment she couldn't speak. "Miss Katie" had been Papa's pet name for her. "You're despicable. I wonder if your family knows your true nature."

His smile took on a feral quality. Through narrowed eyes, he stared at her until she felt uneasy, wondering what he was thinking. All the while, he caressed the tooled silver grip of the pistol. "Think what you will," he said, a terse edge to his voice. "But I won't have you upsetting my grandmother."

Kate swallowed a petty riposte. Better to act calm and aloof than to lower herself to his level of incivility. In a crisp, no-nonsense tone, she said again, "Will you kindly lay down that gun?"

He glanced down at the weapon. "So I do frighten you."

"A deadly weapon in the hands of an irresponsible man?" she said with pithy sarcasm. "Heavens, why would that alarm me?"

Gabriel beckoned lazily with the long barrel. "Come closer, then."

She stepped cautiously toward him, not because he'd ordered her to do so, but because she wouldn't let him intimidate her. "What are you doing with that thing, anyway?"

"It's a dueling pistol," he said. "A very expensive one, I might add. I was cleaning it." He picked up a cloth and polished the long barrel.

Her stomach curled in revulsion. "You're taking it . . . when we visit Sir Charles?"

"When *I* visit him."

She ignored that. "Do you intend to shoot him?"

"Let's say I'm doing this my way. Which is why you're

staying right here. Besides, you can't keep up with my mount."

"You're *riding*?" she gasped out. "But I thought . . ."

"You thought I'd take the carriage? This isn't a social call."

Truth be told, she hadn't stopped to consider his mode of transit. She'd simply assumed they could travel together. And unlike Gabriel's wealthy family, her father hadn't had the means to keep a horse. Consequently, there had been no opportunity for her to learn equestrian skills.

His grin broadened in a display of insufferable male gloating. "What's wrong? Don't you ride?"

She lifted her chin. "Like the wind, my lord."

IN frustrated silence, Kate accompanied Gabriel to the dining room for breakfast. He was remarkably jolly, the lout. As he chatted with his brother, Kate picked at her poached eggs and toast, wondering how quickly she could learn to ride a horse as well as a nobleman who had been riding all his privileged life. She would try, of course. Giving up wasn't in her nature. Especially conceding defeat to an arrogant lord.

But her riding practice had to be postponed when a maidservant summoned Kate to the dowager's chambers. As Kate stepped inside the sumptuous green and pink bedchamber, the chaos within drove all thought of Gabriel from her mind.

Bolts of fabric lay on the four-poster bed, over the pink-sprigged chaise longue, on the chairs and tables. The Rosebuds sat drinking tea by the hearth and smiling at Meg who stood in her chemise as a stout woman took her measurements. Nearby, Jabbar poked a stubby finger at a bobbin, sending it rolling across the carpet and leaving a trail of scarlet thread. The chimpanzee clapped as the seamstress's skinny assistant chased after the little wooden spool.

Meg danced forward and beckoned to her sister. "Kate, the most wonderful event has happened! Lady Stokeford says we're both to have an entire new wardrobe."

An eager yearning unfurled in Kate, catching her by surprise. Just as quickly, she stifled her errant greed. "We can't afford new gowns," she protested. "My lady, I'm afraid you've gone to much trouble for nothing."

The elder Lady Stokeford smiled indulgently. "Of course, *you* aren't expected to pay the bills. You and your sister are wards of my grandson, who happens to be a very wealthy young man."

"He *claims* to be our guardian," Kate clarified. "My father never mentioned the appointment to me."

"Surely you're not suggesting that my grandson would lie."

Yes, he would lie, prevaricate, finagle, and deceive. Kate swallowed the retort as the wounded look on the dowager's face struck her with remorse. Hastening forward, she curtsied before the venerable old woman. "Forgive me. It's a misunderstanding, I'm sure."

Lady Stokeford fluttered her fingers in a breezy gesture. "Pish-posh. The fact is, Gabriel wishes to provide for both of you. And that's that."

"But we mustn't accept personal gifts from a man we scarcely know."

"He lived with your family for a few months, did he not? Besides, it's the role of men to provide for a woman's wants and needs."

"Hear, hear," said Lady Enid, nodding vigorously from her chair by the hearth. "Men squander their fortunes on gambling and mistresses, so we must seize our share, too. Why, I could tell you of many men who shower jewels on their doxies—"

"Enid, really!" Seated across from her, the regal Lady

Faversham thumped the tip of her cane on the floral carpet. "Be mindful of innocent young ears."

Giggling, Lady Enid clapped a plump hand over her mouth. "Dear me! I quite forgot myself."

Lady Faversham picked up her companion's teacup and sniffed the contents, then wrinkled her sharp nose. "It's rather early in the day for French cream in your tea."

"You're entirely too stuffy, Olivia. I vow, sometimes you've no sense of fun."

Leaving them squabbling, Lady Stokeford took Kate's arm and led her toward a selection of fabrics draped over a chair. "My grandson is an admirable man," she said. "He's to be commended for honoring his pledge to your father. He could easily have shirked his duty to you."

"*I* think he's a wonderful guardian," Meg said, whirling around the bedchamber, trailed by the frustrated seamstress with her cloth measuring tape. "Imagine . . . we'll attend fashionable parties and meet handsome men. We'll drink champagne and dance until dawn. Oh, I can't wait to be a member of the *ton*."

In the face of Meg's excitement, Kate felt trapped between good sense and ill judgment. Her sister had been denied so much during her young life. What harm could it do to indulge this one wish? And for once in her life to garb herself in pretty gowns, too.

Yet it would be tantamount to admitting that Gabriel had the right to dictate their lives.

Kate feathered her fingertips over a plum-colored silk so soft and delicate that she instantly coveted it. "These fabrics are too rich for mourning. We must wear black to show respect for Papa."

"My dear girl," Lady Stokeford said in a kindly tone, patting Kate's hand. "Please know that we—the Rosebuds and I—have the utmost sympathy for your loss. However, out here in the country, the rules are not so stringent. It's perfectly acceptable for a young woman to wear half-mourning."

Groping for a handkerchief, Lady Enid dabbed at her moist eyes. "He would have wanted you to be happy," she said. "Why, on his deathbed, my own father told me I mustn't grieve, that he loved me too much to see me dress like a nun."

Even the dour Lady Faversham nodded. "There's nothing wrong with a bit of sober color, so long as you avoid the brighter hues. I would venture to guess your father would have agreed."

Aware of the emptiness of loss inside her, Kate bit her lip. The Rosebuds were right; Papa had cared little for convention. Truth be told, he'd been too involved in his studies to notice if she wore silk or sackcloth. Yet how she missed him, eccentricities and all.

"Please, Kate," Meg said. "Papa wanted us to be happy. He said so in his letters." She stood quietly, sniffling a little, her lower lip wobbly. The seamstress seized the opportunity to stretch the measuring tape from Meg's waist down to the floor, then made a notation on a scrap of paper.

Jabbar knuckle-walked to Meg and looked up at her, uttering a series of soft grunts that seemed to express commiseration.

"Come, see what we have for you girls," Lady Stokeford said gently, drawing Kate over to the array of fabrics on the bed. "This forest-green satin would make a pretty evening gown and set off your red-gold hair. The bronze muslin over here would be suitable for daytime. And look at these. Don't you agree that the marine-blue silk and the lilac crepe would suit Meg's dark coloring exceptionally well?"

Unable to resist, Kate lifted the silk, and the airy, cool fabric flowed like a cloud through her fingers. She fancied herself garbed in a gown of the latest fashion, her unruly hair tamed into smooth, stylish curls . . . and Gabriel on his knees gazing worshipfully up at her.

She crushed the fine cloth in her fist. Blast the man. She didn't want his regard. Rather, she would relish the opportunity to flirt with other gentlemen, to show him that he meant nothing to her. Dream about him, indeed!

Now that she considered it, why shouldn't the cad pay for taking Papa away from his family? It was the least Gabe could do.

She pivoted toward Lady Stokeford. "All right," she said recklessly. "We'll accept the garments."

Meg seized her in an exuberant hug. "Thank you, Katie. You're the best sister in the world."

Jabbar bounded up onto the fireplace mantel, where he hooted and clapped. Everyone turned to gaze at him, the Rosebuds laughing, Meg smiling like an indulgent mother, the seamstress's assistant fumbling with a basket of tangled skeins of thread.

With a serene smile, Lady Stokeford looked at Kate. "By the by, have I mentioned that Gabriel is going off on a trip?"

Struck by alarm, Kate tensed. "Is he leaving today, my lady?"

"No, he promised to stay here for three days," the dowager said, her blue eyes bright and observant. "May I say, you seem inordinately concerned with his whereabouts."

"I'm not," Kate said quickly. "It's just that . . . he hadn't mentioned anything about his departure to me."

She was relieved when Meg asked for an opinion on several bolts of cloth, and Lady Stokeford turned away to help her. It wouldn't do for the dowager to find out that Kate intended to follow Gabriel. *If* she could manage it.

Three days, Kate thought feverishly. She had three days in which to become an accomplished equestrian.

CHAPTER 11

JABBAR'S ESCAPE

"OVER here, miss. Ye mun't mount from the right side."

Kate cautiously walked around the dappled gray mare with the velvety brown eyes. The scent of horseflesh tickled her nose. "Why not?"

Raymond, a middle-aged groom with stooped shoulders, respectfully doffed his cap as he'd done a score of times already. " 'Tis how she's trained. Ye mun do what the horse expects o' ye."

"Yes, of course. Thank you."

At her smile, Raymond blushed, his weathered face turning red to the tips of his big ears. He stepped back, bumping into the white-painted fence of the paddock. Kate had tried to put him at ease, but he still seemed amazed that she'd asked a mere groom to give riding lessons to a lady.

Glancing from the mounting block to the sidesaddle, she pondered the best way to get herself onto the rather large and intimidating horse. Raymond seemed too shy to offer advice until she'd done something wrong. "Are you certain the mare is gentle?" she asked.

He bobbed his head. "Stormy belongs to Lady Amy. Lord Stokeford bought the mare himself."

If a five-year-old could handle this horse, then so could Kate Talisford, age twenty. Resolutely, she clambered onto the mounting block, grasped the pommel, and inserted the toe of her half-boot into the stirrup as she'd seen other ladies do.

Raymond hovered anxiously. "Other foot, miss."

"What? Oh." She gingerly switched feet, then levered herself upward, only to coast right off the slippery leather seat. "Lend me a hand, please."

The groom hastened to crouch down and cup her boot in his broad palms. This time, she managed to hoist herself into the sidesaddle and hooked her knee around the pommel. The mare danced sideways, and Raymond seized the bridle just in time.

Kate rearranged her black skirt to no avail. The gown wasn't designed for riding, and the awkward position revealed the bleached edge of her petticoat. But there was nothing to be done about that impropriety.

Beset by a twinge of vertigo, she closed her gloved fingers around the reins. Slowly she straightened her spine, and a spirit of exhilaration infused her. From the high perch, she could see over the yew hedge to the lush rose garden and the magnificent stone terrace that stretched across the rear façade of Stokeford Abbey. She could also observe the stables, which solved one sticky problem.

She didn't trust Gabriel to keep his promise to his grandmother. But he couldn't depart without his big black gelding, Kate reasoned. That meant she could pursue her riding lessons here in the paddock and, at the same time, intercept him if he tried to steal away without her.

"Hold them reins up tight," Raymond instructed. "Don't let 'em drag, or ye'll lose control."

Kate gathered up the leather ribbons. "Like this?"

"Aye. When ye want t' turn right, pull the reins t' the right. Or left t' go t'other way."

"Yes. I'll remember."

"Ready, miss?"

Inhaling a deep breath for courage, she nodded.

The groom slapped the mare on the rump, and the horse set out on a sedate walk around the perimeter of the paddock. Swaying, Kate clung rigidly to the reins. Her position felt precarious, as if she were about to slide off the mare. But after a few moments, she began to relax and enjoy the slow ride. It was a marvelous novelty after so many years of walking. Yet she wouldn't keep up with Gabe at this plodding pace.

"How do I go faster?" she called out to Raymond.

"Slap the reins."

She did so, and the mare launched into a trot. Immediately, Kate regretted the action, for she bounced up and down in a bone-rattling rhythm. Feeling herself slip a little with each jolt, she grabbed for the pommel. A gust of cool wind whipped back her bonnet so that it dangled down her back by its strings.

"Help! What do I do now?"

"Pull back," Raymond shouted.

Reluctant to let the metal bit hurt the animal's mouth, she gave a tiny tug on the reins. The mare kept up a jarring trot, circling the paddock while Kate fought to maintain the awkward seat.

Raymond waved his cap. "Harder, miss. Pull harder!"

This time, when she hauled on the reins, the mare came to an abrupt stop. Momentum sent Kate sliding from the sidesaddle, her feet striking the hard-packed earth. Staggering, she only just managed to hold herself upright.

Like a faithful hound, Raymond came loping toward her. "Criminy! Are ye hurt, miss?"

"No, I'm fine. Just a bit shaken." And her muscles ached already.

Hanging his head, the groom shifted from one hobnailed shoe to the other. "Mayhap ye'd like Lord Gabriel t'give ye lessons, instead. What with him bein' in charge of ye, and all."

Kate stiffened. "Who told you that?"

Raymond held his cap to his scrawny chest. " 'Tis the

talk o' the servants' hall, miss. Beggin' yer pardon for speakin' of me betters, that is."

"You've every right to speak. And while you're doing so, you may inform the staff that Miss Talisford has no master."

A peal of laughter rang out. "Well spoken," said a feminine voice with the hint of a musical lilt.

Kate turned to see Vivien, Lady Stokeford, leaning on the white fence, her small, bare feet perched on the lowest slat. Other than her lack of shoes—an odd habit of hers—she was dressed as a fine lady in a leaf-green gown with matching ribbons in her black hair. Jumping down from the fence, she opened the gate. As she approached, the bangles at her wrist chimed faintly in the breeze.

Mortified that Gabriel's sister-in-law had witnessed her tirade, Kate sketched a curtsy. "My lady. I—I didn't know you were watching."

"Please, you must call me Vivien," the marchioness said with a warm smile. "I don't mean to intrude, but perhaps you'll let me help with your riding lessons?"

"You? But surely you have more important things to do."

Vivien shook her head. "Little Will is napping, and Amy is at her lessons with the governess. So for the moment, I'm at loose ends." Turning to the groom, she said, "You may return to your duties, Raymond."

"Aye, m'lady." Bowing, he doffed his cap one last time and then trotted away to the stables.

Vivien stroked the mare's nose. "*Develesa!* These side-saddles are a nuisance, aren't they? I don't doubt they were invented by a man to torture us."

Kate laughed, wishing she dared rub her sore bottom. "Then it wasn't my inexperience?"

"Absolutely not." Her brown eyes sparkling, Vivien leaned closer. "If you wish to feel more comfortable on a horse, there's an easier way to learn to ride."

"What do you mean?"

"First, you must befriend the creature."

She whistled softly, and the mare came trotting up to nuzzle her hands as if looking for a treat. Vivien bent her dark head and crooned to the horse, and Kate marveled at the uncanny sense that they were communicating on some mysterious level. Vivien motioned Kate closer, encouraging her to rub the velvety muzzle and stroke the silken mane. Kate found herself curious about the marchioness. Not for the first time, she wondered how a Gypsy woman had come to wed one of the richest, most powerful lords in England.

It would be rude to inquire, so she phrased another question. "Did you learn to ride from the Gypsies?"

"Yes, though I confess, the women are forbidden to touch the horses. I had to sneak out during the night while the men were sleeping." Vivien smiled impishly. "Alas, my adventures ended when *miro dado* caught me returning one morning at dawn."

"*Miro . . . dado?*"

"My father. My Romany father." A wistful warmth shone on her dusky features. "I can see that you are burning to know my story. My natural father was a nobleman who had a love affair with the governess to Michael and his brothers."

Kate hardly knew what to say. "But how did you . . . ?"

"How did I come to live with the *Rom*? My *gorgio* father gave me away as an infant." With a wry smile, Vivien held up her hand. "Don't look so horrified. I never knew him, so it doesn't matter. And I love *miro dado* and *miro dye*— my mother. They doted on me like the best of parents, and I couldn't have had a happier childhood. In truth, I was so devoted to them that I even fought against falling in love with a *gorgio* lord."

The softness on her face made it clear that she adored

her husband, Michael. Kate grew aware of a loneliness inside herself, a yearning to know such happiness. Perhaps some men made good husbands. But how was a woman to know if she could trust her chosen mate? It was a question Kate couldn't answer. Even her quiet, honorable Papa had been lured into leaving his family. Lured by Gabriel's offer of funding for the expedition.

"Now," Vivien said briskly, "we've one more task before you can ride. We'll discard this horrid contraption."

To Kate's astonishment, the marchioness reached beneath the mare and unbuckled the cinch. In a matter of moments, she tugged off the heavy saddle, and Kate rushed to help her carry it outside the gate of the paddock.

Vivien clapped the dust from her hands. "There. Now it's time for your lesson."

"But . . . I'll need a saddle."

"It's far easier to learn to ride without one. You'll control the mare with your knees. Come, I'll show you."

In short order, Kate found herself mounted astride the horse with only the blanket to cushion her. The fact that her stocking-clad calves were exposed bothered her for only a moment. There was no one else around to witness the impropriety. And how much more gloriously free she felt.

Taking the bridle, Vivien led the mare around the paddock while Kate accustomed herself to the novel position. She could feel the mare's muscles bunch and release with each step, which gave her a greater sense of control. She still had the reins to give the animal guidance. After a few rounds, Vivien instructed Kate to crouch low over the long neck and hug the mare's body with her knees. Then Vivien lightly tapped the horse on the rump even as she stepped back.

The mare launched into a trot. This time, to Kate's delight, she no longer bounced. Instead, she felt at one with the mare. She could sense the animal's eagerness to run, and without quite intending to, she slapped the reins and the mare increased the gait to a canter. Watching from the center of the ring, Vivien smiled her approval.

In the cool breeze, several curls sprang loose, fluttering in Kate's face. The ride became even smoother, and she sat up straight, enjoying the glorious sensation of the wind and sun on her face, and the feel of the sleek gray animal beneath her. The equine scents mingled with the freshness of the air. All her life, she hadn't even known what she'd been missing. It was an indescribable joy to experience such speed, to watch the world flashing by. She could see outside the paddock to the magnificent grounds, the rustling green trees, the tall white cupola of the stables beyond the hedgerow—

Then she spied him. In the stable yard, a man swung onto a black horse. He sat tall and imposing, the sunlight glinting off his burnished brown hair.

Alarm jolted her. "He's leaving," she cried out. "Hurry, open the gate so I can stop him."

"Who?" Vivien asked as she hastened to unlatch the gate. "What's wrong?"

"It's Gabriel. He's going to Cornwall without me."

Kate caught one last look at the marchioness's baffled expression; then she urged the mare out of the paddock. As if sensing Kate's impatience, the horse cantered down the path to the stable yard. To her surprise, she saw her sister standing near a great oak tree, talking to Gabriel. Seated on the gelding, he glanced up into the spreading branches.

At the sound of hoofbeats, he turned his head. His smile vanished and his eyes widened. He looked utterly flummoxed to see Kate riding a horse. The most exquisite feeling of triumph eddied through her, a balm to past indignities.

The next few moments happened in a blur. As Kate drew on the reins and the mare slowed its pace, movement flashed in the branches of the oak directly above her. A familiar simian face peered down from the leaves. Half a second later, hairy arms latched onto a limb and a sturdy little body swung back and forth.

Jabbar dropped out of the tree and landed on her back.

The impact knocked the wind out of her. It was all she could do to keep her seat. Squealing at the unfamiliar scent of the chimpanzee, the mare reared.

Instinctively, Kate squeezed her knees and clutched the reins. She heard Gabriel's shout and saw Meg scramble to safety. Her heart thudding madly, she struggled to suck air into her empty lungs. It didn't help that Jabbar had a death grip on her neck. The chimp hooted as if in great enjoyment. Several grooms dashed around, adding to the confusion.

Gabriel angled his mount closer and made a grab for her bridle. But the mare danced away, bucking and snorting.

"Give him to me," he called out, controlling the gelding with one hand and holding out the other to Kate.

She would, if only Jabbar would cooperate.

The mare reared again, startling Gabriel's mount. The gelding's front legs pawed the air. At that precise moment, the chimp took a flying leap at Gabriel.

To Kate's horror, both man and monkey went tumbling to the hard-packed earth.

DEMONS danced in his skull. A devil's pitchfork prodded his tailbone. Burning in hell, he felt something cool and soothing touch his brow, but he shoved it away, seeking the darkness of oblivion.

A foul scent seared his nostrils.

Gabe turned his head, but the odor followed and the fumes made him cough. Forcing his eyes open, he saw the double image of a woman. He squinted, and the images

converged into an angel with green eyes and a profusion
of corkscrew curls framing her prim face.

No, not an angel. A virago named Kate Talisford.

"What the deuce is that?" he snapped, swatting away her
hand from beneath his nose. "Get it away from me."

She set the small brown bottle on a table. "It's hartshorn.
And since you're awake, it has accomplished its purpose."

"Bloody damned stuff nearly killed me."

Grandmama's face swam into view. Her finely etched
features were drawn with worry. "My dear boy, don't curse.
It's nothing compared to that nasty fall you suffered. You
gave us all quite a start."

Memory flooded him. Kate. Jabbar. The horses.

Only then did he notice his surroundings. He lay on a
gilded chaise by the fireplace in the huge drawing room,
his head propped on a tasseled pillow. The crackling blaze
on the hearth sent off waves of heat that made him sweat.

His brother came forward, his arm around Vivien. Behind them stood Uncle Nathaniel and the Rosebuds, the old
biddies clucking sympathetically.

Vivien frowned in obvious concern. "You've quite a
bump on your head," she said. "I saw you fall, but I was
too late to help you."

Michael quirked a chiding eyebrow. "The last time you
lost control of a horse, brother, you were ten."

Gabe gingerly probed the tenderness at the side of his
head. No wonder he had the Lucifer of all headaches. "I
didn't lose control," he said tersely. "Jabbar threw me off
balance. Where is the scamp, by the way?"

"Right here with Meg," Kate said.

Her sister ventured forward, hugging the chimp in her
arms. They wore comically identical looks of abashment.
"I'm sorry, my lord," she said in a small voice. "It's my
fault for not watching him properly. You won't take him
away from me, will you?"

"Huh," Gabe muttered. "You're welcome to him."

"Thank heavens Jabbar wasn't harmed," Kate said, pressing an ice-cold cloth to the throbbing lump. "You must have cushioned him as you fell."

Gabe pushed her hand away. Shavings of ice embedded with sawdust from the icehouse rained onto him, a welcome relief from the heat of the fire. "How long was I out?"

"Nearly an hour," she said, retrieving the ice and the cloth. "However, that's no excuse for behaving like a child."

This time, she held the makeshift bag in place with her palm. He almost thrust her arm away again, then reconsidered. Despite her thin-lipped glare, the gentleness of her touch and the chill of the ice felt soothing. He rather enjoyed the notion of her fussing over him. Perhaps he could finagle a transfer to his chambers and request her as his nurse.

"A groom went to fetch the physician," Grandmama said. "Ah, there's Dr. Lygon now."

A tall, lanky man bustled into the drawing room. In his plain black suit and carrying a leather satchel, he looked more like a mortician than a healer. "Is this our patient?" he said brightly. "I see he's awake now."

Disgruntled, Gabe pushed himself up into a sitting position. His tailbone hurt like the devil. He saw double again and blinked to focus his vision. "I'm fine," he insisted. "I don't need a doctor."

Her face drawn with anxiety, his grandmother hovered over him. "You've had a dreadful crack on the head, my dear. I shan't rest until I know you're all right."

"I am. So don't fuss."

"Nevertheless, you'll be examined," Michael stated. He aimed a steely glare at his brother. "Everyone, please leave us."

Muttering a curse, Gabe sank back down as the doctor

opened his case of instruments and tonics. He shuddered at the sight. It galled him to admit it, but he'd worried Grandmama enough.

Kate dropped the bag of ice into his hand. "Here, you can do this yourself. At least now you won't be going anywhere." With one last, saucy glare, she marched toward the arched doorway, following the others as they left the drawing room.

His gaze went to the feminine sway of her hips, and Gabe remembered how she'd looked riding toward him, her wild hair flying in the wind and her slim, stockinged legs hugging her mount. To his chagrin, he felt an undeniable stirring in his loins.

That fall must have damaged his sanity, he thought sourly. Only a corkbrain would want Kate Talisford in his bed. She had to be the most vexatious female he'd ever met.

CHAPTER 12

A DANGEROUS WOMAN

THAT evening, Kate carried a cup of tea into the drawing room with its Gothic arches and gold-striped furniture. Gabriel reclined on a chaise, his expression brooding as he watched Michael and Vivien play with their children. Lord Stokeford held the infant William in the crook of his arm. Five-year-old Amy was sprawled on the floor, doodling in a notebook.

At a nearby table, the Rosebuds and Uncle Nathaniel were engaged in a rollicking game of cards. Bathed by the glow of candles, they chatted and laughed as merrily as youngsters.

Kate's gaze fixed on Gabriel. The lump on his head was barely visible in the dark thickness of his hair. Yet she couldn't help noticing how drawn and pale he looked. Nor could she forget the awful, aching knot in her breast when she'd seen him sprawled unconscious in the stable yard. She'd slid off the mare and dashed to his side, her panic easing only a trifle when she'd felt the reassuring throb of his pulse. The grip of fear hadn't dissolved until he'd opened his eyes nearly an hour later and scowled at her.

Of course, any person of sensibility would have been concerned, she told herself. Under the circumstances, her intense reaction had been natural. Just as now, she felt an intrinsic compassion for him.

Even a lout deserved mercy when he'd been vanquished.

Gliding forward, she offered the cup to him. Those blue eyes pinned her with his customary, caustic charm.

"What's this?" he asked. "Poison?"

"Tea with sugar."

"How do you know I like sweetened tea?"

Drawing a footstool to the chaise, she sat down, aware that her muscles felt stiff from the riding lesson. "You forget. You lived with us for a time."

His eyelids lowered a little, giving him the hooded look of a hawk. "I haven't forgotten."

Their fingers brushed as he took the cup and saucer. A tingling awareness sped over her skin, sparking a peculiar tension in her bosom. Was he too remembering the time she'd come to his chamber and offered herself to him? Was he recalling how stupid and naïve she'd been?

Then she wondered if he'd ever regretted turning her down.

Kate pressed her fingers together in her lap. Foolish thought. Of course he had no regrets. As always, he'd done as he'd pleased. The following morning, he'd taken Papa on a grand African adventure, and now her father was dead.

"How is your head?" she asked briskly.

"Fine." His brusqueness suggested otherwise. His narrowed eyes studied her as he took a drink of tea. "But I thought you were fibbing when you said you could ride."

"Vivien gave me a lesson. The Gypsy way."

"So that's why you were sitting astride." His gaze slid downward in an intensely masculine perusal. "Nice legs. A pity they're covered now."

In defiance of her willpower, a blush heated her throat and cheeks. "You oughtn't have gawked."

"You oughtn't have behaved like a hoyden."

"I had to stop you from leaving without me."

"Leaving?"

"For Cornwall."

He burst out laughing, then winced, rubbing his temples. "I was riding to a neighbor's house to invite him to dinner."

"You'd say that, of course."

He shrugged. "If you don't believe me, ask Michael."

From a grouping of chaises a short distance away, his brother looked up from the infant cradled against him. "I trust you two aren't gossiping about me."

At his side, Vivien made a move to rise. "If you are, I should like to join in."

Catching her wrist, Michael drew her back down. "You'll stay right here, *vestacha*. Where you belong."

A profoundly personal look passed between them. Even from across the room, their tangible aura of love startled Kate, awakening the secret longing in herself to feel that closeness. She had never belonged to anyone, at least not like *that*.

Amy scrambled to her feet and brought over her sketch-pad. "Look, Uncle Gabriel. I can draw just like you."

With a surprising tenderness in his smile, he regarded the stick people scrawled on the paper. "Excellent," he said, reaching out to ruffle her hair. "Perhaps you'll be an artist someday."

Amy beamed. "I wanted to show my picture to Uncle Brandon. Why didn't he come for dinner, Mama?"

Vivien glided closer, reaching down to take the little girl's hand. "I'm afraid Uncle Gabriel never had the chance to ride over to his house and ask him. Now, it's time for you and your brother to go to bed."

Gabriel flashed a gloating smile at Kate.

So he hadn't lied about his destination. Kate hoped he didn't notice her mortification. She had ridden like a lunatic to stop him, when he'd merely been heading out on a visit to a neighbor.

Vivien drew Amy toward the doorway, and Michael and his family said their good-nights.

By the time they'd gone, Kate had recovered herself.

Summoning her best manners, she said, "I beg your pardon, my lord, for mistaking your purpose."

One eyebrow raised, he regarded her. "I'll forgive you on one condition. That you promise to make it worth my while."

She narrowed her eyes. "What do you mean?"

"First, you'll have to fetch my sketchbooks."

"You wish to draw?"

"No, I want the books you've stolen from me. The ones from Africa."

Kate bristled. "I haven't *stolen* them. I merely wanted the chance to look through the drawings. Perhaps there's a picture of another treasure you haven't told me about."

He sent her a scurrilous grin. "Get my artwork. Then I'll tell you what I have in mind."

LUCY knew when to seize an opportunity. Upon seeing Kate leave the drawing room, returning a short while later with an armload of sketchbooks, Lucy lost no time in maneuvering the situation—and the furniture.

"Move the table over here in front of the chaise," she said, directing two footmen. "And set a branch of candles at either end, behind the books. Thank you, that will be all."

As the servants departed, she spied Kate walking toward a nearby chair. Clearly, the girl needed a prod in the right direction.

Lucy took Kate by the arm and guided her to the spot beside Gabriel on the chaise. "Sit over here, my dear. That way, the two of you can look at the drawings together. I'm sure you'll find that my grandson is an extremely talented artist." She bustled around, selecting a sketchbook at random and handing it to Gabriel.

"How helpful of you, Grandmama," he said, his smile

holding a hint of irony. "And here I thought you'd order me up to bed early."

"Pish-posh. Dr. Lygon said you'll be fine so long as you confine yourself to quiet pastimes for a few days."

"If you like, my lady, I'll be happy to monitor his progress," Kate said.

Gabriel smirked at her. "You'll be my personal attendant?"

"I'll be your warden," Kate retorted. "Else you'll be riding off again without telling me."

Lucy hid a delighted smile. Kate Talisford was the perfect woman to tame her high-handed, daredevil grandson. What a shame she still wore her drab blacks, though. The somber hue turned her skin sallow and did little to enhance the red-gold hair that was scraped into an unattractive knob at the back of her head.

Patience, Lucy reminded herself. In a few days' time, she would fix those superficial details. She would teach Kate how to entice a man. Then she dared her grandson to resist the girl.

Resuming her seat with the Rosebuds and Nathaniel, Lucy picked up her cards. "There now," she murmured, keeping her voice low. "Don't they make a handsome couple?"

"But they look as though they're quarreling," Enid whispered, her brown eyes avid beneath the orange turban. "I wonder what they're saying."

"For pity's sake, don't stare," Olivia chided. Defying her own command, she stole a glance at the couple. "I do hope he doesn't break her heart."

Nathaniel shook his head. "You three will never learn," he declared. "You're still up to your old tricks."

Lucy sent him a cool stare. He grinned right back at her. Time had dealt too kindly with Nathaniel Babcock. He'd been handsome in his youth, but now, blessed with a full thatch of white hair and a smile that could make an unsuspecting woman's heart melt, he possessed an élan that was irresistible.

Almost irresistible. "Learn what, pray tell?" she asked.

"Not to mind other people's business," he said. "Leave 'em alone, I say. Live and let live."

His cavalier attitude annoyed Lucy. The cad would never understand her need for great-grandchildren to brighten her old age. "If Gabriel doesn't marry, he'll go off adventuring again."

"So let him. A man needs his freedom."

Olivia pursed her lips. "Speak for yourself," she said, slapping down a card. "A young man needs a family to settle him."

"And a woman to love," Enid added with a wistful sigh. "Don't you wish *you'd* married, Nathaniel? Don't you ever feel lonely?"

"Impossible," Lucy said with a cultured laugh, before he could spout another glib remark. "There's always another rich widow for him to gull."

As soon as she'd spoken, Lucy was appalled at herself. It wasn't like her to be cruel. She had learned long ago the value of social euphemisms, for the truth was too often unpalatable.

To her surprise, she fancied there was a flash of pain in Nathaniel's eyes. Yet his rakish smile remained fixed on his craggy features, and he threw back his head and chuckled. "You're a dangerous woman, Lucy. You always could see right through me."

Sincerely repentant, she brushed her fingertips over the smooth sleeve of his coat. "Forgive me. That was thoughtless and inconsiderate. I don't know what came over me."

"No offense taken. I believe in calling a spade a spade." He gathered up the cards, his long fingers expertly shuffling the pasteboard rectangles. His blue eyes twinkled with practiced charm. "Now, while I have you at my mercy, I'll remind you of our wager. If I win this round, you'll let me visit you in your boudoir."

A surprising warmth swept through Lucy, a sensation she immediately discounted. The only thing worse than an old roué was the woman who made a fool of herself over him. "You must be dreaming," she said airily. "I made no such wager."

"I suppose you're right." Leaning closer, he winked. "But 'tis you I'll be dreaming of."

KATE concentrated on sitting perfectly motionless on the chaise. If she dared to shift position, even a fraction of an inch, she would brush against Gabriel's arm or leg. It wasn't the notion of impropriety that held her immobile. Rather, any physical contact fed the disgraceful heat inside herself.

Lady Stokeford's blatant matchmaking didn't help matters. The dowager clearly didn't realize how ill-suited Kate and Gabriel were. Kate wanted a settled life, the chance to work on Papa's book undisturbed. Lord Gabriel Kenyon was an uncivilized wayfarer.

As he leafed through the sketchbook, she stole a long look at him. His profile showed the clean, chiseled lines of a classical sculpture: the strong slash of cheekbones, the high brow, the firm mouth with that hint of a world-weary smile, as if he were privy to secrets she could never fathom. The years spent outdoors had burnished his skin to a teak hue. His dark hair, sorely in need of a trim, grazed the collar of his white shirt. How she would like to have the right to reach out and tuck that wayward strand behind his ear—

He turned his head and his ocean-blue eyes pinned her. "Is something wrong?"

"Wrong?"

"You're staring at me."

"You're mistaken," she said quickly, fighting a blush. "I was looking at the drawing."

He cocked an eyebrow. "Then perhaps you'll have a comment on what I just told you about it."

Nonplussed, Kate whipped her gaze to the page that lay open on his lap. The inked lines showed a scene of tribal men gathered in a circle. They wore fantastical headdresses, bracelets circling their upper arms, and animal skins. The detail was exquisite right down to the tattoos decorating their half-naked bodies, and so real that she could imagine them dancing.

"It's . . . fascinating."

"I was just saying that this scene has a particular importance to our book."

She frowned. "Kindly remember that I haven't agreed to collaborate."

"Then you don't care to hear more about the drawing."

He started to close the sketchpad, but she stopped him, her fingers tensed around the leather cover. Swallowing her pride, she asked, "Will you please explain again? I must have been wool-gathering."

He smiled knowingly. "These Abyssinian natives led us to the lost city. Without their help, Henry and I would never have found the ruins. It's considered a holy, haunted place, the home of spirits."

With renewed interest, Kate pulled the sketchbook onto her lap and studied the illustration, wondering at the lives of these noble savages. "Why did they consent to take you there?"

"I convinced them that I could exorcise the ghosts, that I have powers over the spirit world."

She huffed out a breath. "Of course. You're a smooth-talking devil."

"With no gift for prose. At Eton, I was the despair of

my headmaster." Leaning an elbow on his knee, he graced her with a coaxing smile. "Think about it, Kate. With my artistic skills and your aptitude for the written word, we can publish a book that will have all of England talking."

"How do you know I have any talent for writing?"

"Henry liked to read your letters aloud around the campfire. Your descriptions of the neighbors were especially colorful. The gossipy Weasly Beasley, the pompous vicar, silly Mrs. Wooster."

Kate stiffened. She'd never meant for her whimsical meanderings to be read by anyone but Papa. She'd wanted to brighten his travels with all the neighborhood news, and in her heart, she'd also hoped to tempt him to come home.

Loath to let Gabriel see her vulnerability, she turned the questioning on him. "Why are *you* so eager to publish a book?"

When Gabriel lifted his dark lashes, Kate sensed that she'd struck a nerve. But he merely lounged against the chaise, stretching his arms out along the back. "Fame, of course," he said in a jaunty tone. "To see my name immortalized. Imagine how the women will flock to me."

He didn't need a book to make women flock to him. He had only to curve his mouth into that smoldering smile. Coolly, she said, "I doubt you can stay in one place long enough to see the project through to the finish."

"You're right, I don't like my freedom curtailed. But I'll remain here long enough to complete our book."

There it was again. *Our* book. Gritting her teeth, Kate fought the pressure of resentment. *She* wanted to compose the book Papa had always intended to write, but had never had the chance. It would be a labor of love, her last chance to atone for refusing to bid him good-bye.

No one must be allowed to interfere, least of all, Gabriel Kenyon.

Warm and solid, his hand came down on hers. "I admired your father, Kate. His work should be remembered."

She pulled her hand free. "I've no wish to discuss him with *you*."

"Then let me do the talking. Henry adored you and Meg. He spoke of you often. You were very important to him."

Not as important as you. "You're only trying to maneuver me."

"I'm trying to help you. This book *is* your memorial to Henry, is it not?"

His keen blue eyes stripped bare her emotions. Kate felt exposed, stricken, mortified that he could see into her heart. She laced her fingers in her lap. "*My* motives are not in question here."

"Nor should mine be." He gestured at the sketchbooks piled on the table. "Each one of these drawings has a story. Each scene was witnessed by your father. Whether you like it or not, you need me."

She feared he was right. How could she do a thorough job without Gabriel's sketches and anecdotes to fill in the gaps? Yet every fiber of her being resisted the prospect. She couldn't collaborate with the man who had used his wealth to lure Papa from his home and family.

"I can manage on my own by using Papa's papers."

A faintly calculating look replaced his charm. "There's something I haven't mentioned," Gabriel said in a soft growl. "In addition to naming me as your guardian, Henry also appointed me executor of his estate."

"Papa didn't own an estate. He was a university professor. We lived in a rented cottage."

"Nevertheless, he entrusted his possessions to my care. That includes you . . . and all of his papers."

"No," she said on a searing wave of shock. "*No.*"

"Yes. Those journals are mine." With a coolly confident expression, Gabriel regarded her. "So you can either accept me as your collaborator, or not write the book at all. The choice is yours."

Fury beseiged Kate. Wasn't it enough that he had destroyed her family? Now Gabriel would rob her of the one chance to vindicate herself, to make up for that painful parting with Papa.

She felt the wild urge to lash out at Gabriel with her fists, to give him another lump on his thick skull. But she couldn't do that, not with the Rosebuds sitting a short distance away.

She clapped the sketchbook shut. "If you expect me to meekly hand over Papa's notebooks, think again. You'll have to take them from me by force."

His gaze sharpened, showing a trace of his true savagery. "I'll do whatever is necessary, Kate. That's a promise."

Rising to her feet, she shoved the sketchbook at him. "Then be forewarned, my lord. I'll fight you every step of the way."

CHAPTER 13

MEETING AT MIDNIGHT

Two nights later, the Gypsies came to Stokeford Abbey. The merry sound of fiddle music drifted from their encampment. Through a misty veil of clouds, the cool face of the full moon smiled down from the midnight sky.

Toting a small knapsack, Kate kept to the deep shadows of the hedge as she made her way toward the stables. Pinpricks of light glowed in the distance. She could see people sitting around the campfires, clapping to the music and watching the dancing. Although it was too dark to distinguish any individuals, she knew that among the Rom sat the Rosebuds, Michael and Vivien, Meg and Jabbar.

And Gabriel.

You can either accept me as your collaborator, or not write the book at all. The choice is yours.

Kate burned to recall that ultimatum. It summed up his arrogant view of her as a mere possession, no more significant than a pet who must obey its master's every command. Then and there, she had decided to watch for her chance. That opportunity had come tonight with everyone distracted by the Gypsy banquet.

Though he'd been deep in conversation with a group of Gypsy men, she had sensed Gabriel watching her as she'd slipped away after the feast. She'd hastened to her chambers to exchange her old black gown for a pair of rough breeches and a man's homespun linen shirt, which she'd pilfered from the laundry room that afternoon.

All the while, she'd brooded on Gabriel. The three days

he'd promised to his grandmother were up, and Kate knew
the knot on his head wouldn't stop him for long. In the
morning, Michael, Vivien, and their children would be departing on a month-long trek with the Gypsies. It was very
likely that Gabriel would go to Cornwall then.

Now, in the gloom beneath the old oak tree at the edge
of the stable yard, Kate set down her knapsack and adjusted
the workman's cap that hid her curly hair. Her shirt felt
ridiculously huge, the sleeves swamping her hands. In contrast, the breeches were too snug, molding to her bottom
and thighs. She prayed the disguise would fool all but the
most discerning of strangers. A woman traveling alone at
night would attract undue attention.

Dangerous attention.

From inside the stables came the faint whinny of a horse.
Then all lay silent except for the lilt of distant music.
Thankfully, the yard was deserted. The outside servants
were enjoying their own revelry in the meadow beyond the
circle of caravans. She would never have a better opportunity to borrow a horse without being found out.

Picking up the knapsack, she tiptoed toward the double
doors. The Cornish coast lay less than a day's ride distant.
Earlier, she'd slipped into the library and consulted a detailed map of England. She'd traced the route to the ap-
proximate location of Sir Charles Damson's estate. Once
she reached the vicinity, it should be a simple matter to ask
for directions.

In her knapsack, she carried her feminine garb. She
would change in the woods, pay a call on Sir Charles, and
locate the statue. With luck, her absence here wouldn't be
discovered until mid-morning.

Gabriel wouldn't realize she was gone until it was too
late.

Reaching the building, she lifted the latch and stepped
inside. She paused a moment to let her eyes adjust to the

gloom. Then her heart tripped over a beat. A dim glow emanated from the rear of the stables.

Kate froze in place, listening. She could hear only the faint snuffling of the horses in their stalls, the scrape of a hoof. The heavy scent of hay and manure permeated the air.

After a moment, she chided herself. The grooms slept in quarters at the rear of the building. Likely, a lantern had been left burning so they wouldn't stumble on their way to bed.

Quietly, she made her way down the line of stalls. Now and then, a horse poked its head over the half-door to watch her progress. At the end of the row, she turned a corner and found what she was looking for.

The gray mare looked almost black standing in the shadows. With an eager snort, Stormy nuzzled Kate's hand.

Laughing softly, Kate produced a withered apple from last autumn's harvest. The mare crunched the fruit, and then whickered for more.

"Greedy beggar," Kate murmured, stroking the mare's long neck. "You've had your oats already, so you can't be hungry."

Aware of the need for haste, she found her way to the tack room and felt around in the darkness for the necessary equipment. She had to make two trips, first for the bridle and blanket, then the saddle, which was heavier than she'd expected. With effort, she managed to lug it to the stall. She would have preferred to ride bareback, but didn't want to do anything that would attract undue attention.

The previous day, she'd made a point of watching as a stableboy saddled a horse. Now, as she held the bit and urged it into Stormy's mouth, the mare accepted it with surprising ease. Remembering what Vivien had taught her, Kate crooned to the animal as she fitted the bridle over the nose and ears. Then she settled the blanket in place over the horse's back. Relieved at the ease of her tasks, she dusted off her hands.

The saddle, however, proved to be another matter. Kate lifted its awkward weight and staggered into the gloom of the stall. With a mighty push, she heaved the saddle upward, but at the last moment, the mare danced sideways and the saddle tumbled to the floor, sending up a shower of prickly hay dust.

"Blast," Kate muttered, invoking the most indelicate curse she knew. "Blast it all!"

"Need a hand?"

The sarcastic male voice startled her. Gasping, she spun around to see a tall, shadowed figure looming in the corridor. In the half-light, he looked as big and powerful as a demon from out of the night. His hands planted on his hips, he radiated an aggressive fury.

CHAPTER 14

LUCY'S PLAN

"WELL?" Gabriel said. "Are you now a horse thief?"

His baleful tone sent chills down Kate's spine. Taking several shallow breaths, she cast around for a logical explanation. "I needed fresh air. I was going for a ride in the moonlight."

"Dressed like that?" His gaze raked her boy's clothing. "You were leaving for Damson's estate."

Her stomach squeezed into a knot. His statement held a flinty, uncompromising note that frightened her. For a scant moment, she wished she were safe in her bed, under the covers.

Coward. Why are you letting him intimidate you? Outfox him.

She lowered her head as if in defeat. "Yes, I admit it. You've caught me, my lord, so I suppose that's the end of it. I'll return to the house, if you'll kindly allow me."

She stepped toward him.

He moved, but not in retreat. His fingers closed around her arm as he hauled her out into the corridor. The feeble light cast shadows on his unsmiling face. He looked fierce and angry, the brute behind the mask of the charming rogue. "So," he said. "Just like that, you'd give up. Somehow, I doubt you."

"I've no other choice," she said, injecting a note of bitter pride in her voice. "You'll stop me if I—" Abruptly, she noticed his appearance. He wore a greatcoat over his shirt and breeches, and his hands were encased in leather gloves.

The dueling pistol was stuck into his waistband. "You're wearing traveling clothes."

"So I am," he said unapologetically.

Stung by rage, she said, "You were intending to depart tonight, too. Without me."

He neither confirmed nor denied her accusation. He merely stood there, watching her in that contemptuous manner, as if she were a child defying authority.

Subterfuge flew out of her mind. "And you dare to chastise *me* for leaving!"

Whirling, she sprang toward the stall, determined to wrestle the saddle onto the mare's back. Gabriel's hands bit into her arms and swung her around to face him.

"Kate," he ground out between his teeth, "for the last time, I'm ordering you to stay here."

"For the last time, my lord, I don't take orders from you."

She tried to step away, but Gabriel was swifter. He kicked the stall door shut. Thrusting his hands under her knees and back, he lifted her into his arms. Then he strode down the corridor, carrying her as effortlessly as he would a sack of grain. He turned the corner and headed toward the big double doors of the stable.

In a panic, she pushed at his chest. The action dislodged her cap, which tumbled away into the darkness. "Put me down."

"If you behave like a disobedient child, I'll treat you like one."

Fear and fury tangled her tongue. "Where . . . what . . ."

He laughed, an unpleasant sound. "Speechless at last. I'm taking you to your chamber. You'll stay there until I return."

"No, I'll follow you."

"I'll lock you in." In one smooth move, he unlatched the door and carried her outside. The moonlight showed his grimly determined expression. "If I must, I'll bind you, hand and foot."

A frisson of alarm eddied through Kate. His jolting steps caused her bosom to rub against his chest in a disturbing rhythm that increased the tension inside her. She stared up at his forbidding profile against the starry sky. Gabriel meant what he said. He would force her to obey him. Once again, she had no choice, no free will. The bitter thought gnawed at her.

Unwilling to aggravate his temper any further, she seethed in silence, holding herself rigid in his arms, her fists balled against his chest. Let him play the wild savage for now. But he would not dictate to her as if she possessed no mind or will of her own. *He would not.*

"Unbridle the mare, Raymond," Gabriel said, nodding toward the stables. Under his breath, he added, "While I bridle this one."

Kate twisted her head to see the groom gawking from the pathway. A flush of mortification swept over her. Bug-eyed, Raymond doffed his cap as they walked past.

"Fetch Lady Stoke—" she began.

Gabriel tilted her closer, muffling her words against his coat. "A slight sprain to her ankle," he called over his shoulder to the man. "She'll be fine by morning."

Gasping for air, Kate reared back. "How dare you mistreat me."

"Give me cause, and I'll dare much more."

His ominous words raised a shiver in her. "Let me go. Now, before someone else sees us."

Gabriel bared his teeth in a feral grin as he headed down the path that led toward the house. "Everyone is still at the party."

Faint music floated from the Gypsy camp, mingling with the frantic beating of her heart. No one would hear her if she screamed. She had only herself to depend upon.

Dear God, he would lock her in her chamber. Then he would leave for Sir Charles Damson's estate. He would claim the statue for himself. Hadn't he said that all of Papa's belongings had been entrusted to him?

He shouldered open a side door and hauled her inside. Except for the hard click of his footsteps, the house was silent as a tomb. He made his way unerringly through the maze of dim-lit corridors, then mounted a staircase, taking the steps two at a time.

As if he were eager to be rid of her.

She wanted to flail her fists against his chest. But she conserved her strength. Recognizing the gold-striped paper on the walls of the passageway, she bided her time until they reached her chamber.

The instant he set her down, she shoved open the door and lunged for the inside lock. He made a dive for her, but she twisted away. Snatching the key, she ran across the darkened bedroom and tossed it out the window. It was a petty gesture, but the only one she could think of.

"There," she snapped. "You shan't lock me up."

The faint moonlight illuminated his furious features. "There are other rooms and other keys."

"I'll find a way out, then. I'll be right on your heels."

Gabriel swore under his breath. "Damson murdered your father. He's ruthless. I won't let you anywhere near him."

Her resolve quailed at that. But the statue represented financial independence for her and Meg. And it was also a direct link to Papa, the chance to hold his great discovery in her hands. "I've the right to make my own choices. You don't own me."

He took a menacing step forward. Catching her by the arms, he pinned her to the wall. "Then perhaps you'll heed this."

Lowering his head, he trapped her mouth beneath his. Kate stiffened, then struggled wildly to break free. His gloved hands cupped her face so that she couldn't turn away. His lips were hard, angry, vengeful, a blatant bid for mastery. Her futile writhings only made her more aware of him as a man, of the superior strength of his body.

And the ungovernable response in herself.

She fought as much against her own shameful weakening as him. But instead of pushing him away, her hands gripped the smooth fabric of his greatcoat. A scandalous thrill quickened her heartbeat, flooding her with an eagerness she shouldn't feel. As if sensing her inner turmoil, he altered the kiss with a subtle easing of pressure. The dampness of his tongue nudged at her mouth until she gasped for breath.

The moment her lips parted, he pressed deeper into her mouth, tasting her with a finesse that sent heat straight down to her loins. Never had she imagined such an intimacy. She could only cling to him, forgetting all the reasons to despise him, overwhelmed by a feast of the senses.

For so long, she had dreamed of his touch. In her secret fantasies, she had pictured Gabriel kneeling at her feet, professing his love and begging her forgiveness. Only then would she permit him a chaste peck on the cheek, or perhaps a tender embrace.

But there was nothing chaste or tender about this kiss.

Even as his mouth seduced her, his gloved fingers stroked over her face and down her arms. Instinctively, she pressed herself to him, reveling in the heat of his body. She wreathed her arms around his neck and slid her fingers into his hair, relishing its thickness. Still, she wasn't satisfied, and the need inside her grew by leaps and bounds.

What he did next nearly made her swoon. He curled his hand around her breast and stroked his thumb across the sensitive peak. His boldness should have outraged her; in some sensible remnant of her mind she knew that no lady allowed a man such license. But the maddening pleasure of his touch banished rationality.

When his mouth moved to her throat, she let her head fall back to allow him easier access. It was as if a creature of sensuality had taken hold of her. Never had she suspected that a man could make her feel so alive. And not just any man. "Gabriel," she murmured. "Oh, Gabriel."

He exhaled a harsh breath. Bringing his mouth up to hers, he subjected her to another deep, drowning kiss. He plucked at the hem of her shirt, and then abruptly broke off the kiss.

Giddy, she watched as he tugged at his leather glove with his teeth. His eyes glittered through the gloom. He removed first one glove, and then the other, dropping them to the floor, never once looking away from her. The directness of his stare was unnerving, promising dark secrets beyond her wildest imaginings.

He drew her away from the window and across the room. Realizing that he was steering her toward the bed, cold reality invaded her sensual fog. She was in her chamber in Stokeford Abbey. Ready to give herself to a notorious adventurer. To Gabriel.

"No," she whispered hoarsely. "This is *wrong*."

He caressed the curve of her bottom. "It's the only right thing you and I have ever done."

His questing hands slipped beneath her shirt, and Kate shivered at the contact of his fingers gliding over her bare back. Stunned by his boldness, she could scarcely form a rational thought. Except that she sensed a grim purpose in him. He cared nothing for her.

Lord Gabriel Kenyon would use passion as a means to subdue her.

With a cry of protest, she wrenched herself out of his arms, backing up until she met the bedpost. "You won't seduce me into doing your will."

He stalked after her, reaching out to stroke her cheek as he would gentle a skittish mare. "It's better than quarreling. If you'd obeyed me, none of this would have happened."

Obeyed. The word struck her like a dash of ice water, and she recoiled. "You profess to be my guardian. Yet you're the man I need to guard against."

His hand fell to his side. The harshness of his breathing filled the quiet air. "I can't deny that," he said in a low voice. "But it isn't without provocation."

"Without my permission, then."

He hissed with impatience. "Damn it, Kate. Don't make me out to be a villain. You desire me as much as I do you."

Unable to deny it, she said nothing. The knowledge of her passion coiled like a snake, and incredibly, an awareness of him stirred inside her again. That kiss. How hot and hungry it had been, as if Gabriel had wanted to consume her. And she'd wanted him to do just that. She still wanted it. What was wrong with her, that her body responded to the one man who would enslave her to his will?

The patter of footsteps came from the corridor. In consternation, Kate spun around to see several people crowd into the doorway.

The Rosebuds. And Uncle Nathaniel.

Lady Stokeford held up a lighted lamp. Her bright-eyed gaze flitted from Kate's rumpled, boyish garb to her grandson in his greatcoat. "Why, what's this?" she exclaimed. "Why are you dressed so oddly, Kate? Are you two eloping to Scotland?"

In the space of a minute, Gabe knew he'd stepped from trouble into disaster. "Don't be ridiculous, Grandmama. There is no elopement."

"I am never ridiculous." Sailing into the chamber, Lady Stokeford set down the lamp on a table near the hearth.

"Come, everyone, sit down. We may as well be comfortable while Gabriel explains himself."

Overriding his objections, she waved the others into seats. The Rosebuds shared a chaise near the hearth, with plump Lady Enid and grim Lady Faversham like gorgons flanking his grandmother. On a bench near a dainty writing desk, Kate sat with her hands primly folded in her lap.

Nathaniel Babcock threw himself into a nearby chair, crossed his arms, and aimed a suspicious glare at Gabe. "I'm waiting to hear your reason for being in my grand-niece's bedchamber," he said with the air of an outraged father instead of an old rascal who had invaded his share of ladies' bedchambers. "By jings, I should call you out for this."

Resting his elbow on the mantelpiece, Gabe assumed a casual pose, though his gut clenched with guilt. The force of his lust had taken him by storm. Kissing Kate had not been in his plans for the night. "There's no cause for alarm," he said smoothly. "I discovered Miss Talisford in the stables. She intended to go out for a ride, and I forbade her to do so. Then I brought her back here."

"A ride?" Grandmama asked doubtfully. "In the middle of the night?"

"But where would she be going?" Lady Faversham asked, leaning forward on her ivory-topped cane.

"And in such dreadful apparel," Lady Enid said. "Wearing the shirt and trousers of a workman, no less!"

All eyes turned to Kate, but she offered no explanation. She sat there as cool and remote as a queen. Not that her hoydenish appearance had any resemblance to royalty. Shorn of that ridiculous cap, a froth of red-gold curls encircled her stubborn features. The cuffs of her baggy white shirt hung down past her wrists.

Gabe had never known that a pair of ordinary brown breeches could look so fine on a female. Nor had he known that Kate Talisford could kiss like an erotic fantasy. The impact of it still shook him to the core.

Who was she, virago or vixen?

Both. Fool that he was, he wanted to hold her again, to coax forth her wildness, to take her to bed, his conscience be damned.

"Well, Gabriel?" Grandmama prompted. "Don't just stand there gawking at the girl."

"Yes," Lady Faversham said severely, "tell us what really happened here."

Lady Enid shook her finger. "And don't leave out any details," she added, her hazel eyes bright with interest.

With icy control, Gabe regarded them. "As I said, I escorted Miss Talisford here. There's nothing more to it."

Uncle Nathaniel harrumphed. "My grandniece is no corkbrain to go riding alone at night when there's footpads about."

"Pardon me, Lord Gabriel, but you two were quarreling," Lady Faversham said. "We can't help but wonder why."

"Your voices carried all the way down the passageway," Lady Enid added. "Though, alas, we couldn't make out your words."

"Miss Talisford resented my edict. I had to remind her not to endanger herself." Seeing Kate narrow her eyes and compress her lips, Gabe said pointedly, "She dislikes obeying the good advice of her guardian."

As if pricked by a pin, Kate broke her silence. "If you gave good advice, and if you really were my guardian, then I might heed you."

"My guidance is given for your own protection," Gabe said with a flare of anger. "You heard what your uncle said. Footpads prowl the roads at night."

"So do scoundrels."

Her gaze held his, and her tone clearly marked him as a knave. It was galling to admit she was right. Never before had he lost control of himself. Driven to the edge, he had been desperate to stop her from going to Damson.

Desperate to make her submit to his will.

"I'm still not satisfied as to why Kate would be riding out at such a late hour," Lady Stokeford said. She paused delicately, looking from Kate to Gabe. "Unless perhaps she was intending to call on Sir Charles Damson."

Jolted, Gabe swung around to meet his grandmother's calculating stare. "What the deuce—you were the one listening at the door that night."

The dowager lifted her hand in an imperious wave. "Not by design. But I'm gratified that I did. Else I wouldn't have known what really happened to Kate's poor father."

Kate made a small sound of distress, but said nothing.

"Henry died in Egypt," Uncle Nathaniel said with a frown. " 'Tis a tragedy, but one I surely mentioned to you."

"You did, but there's more," Grandmama said, her elegant mouth forming a determined expression. "You deserve to know the whole truth."

Clamping his teeth, Gabe thought back to his unwitting role in the murder. He'd let himself be lured away by a woman, leaving Henry alone to protect the goddess. It had been difficult enough to admit his culpability to his brother. Now Grandmama also knew, and without a doubt, so did all the Rosebuds.

And Kate?

His gaze veered to her. Surely if she'd known his whereabouts on the night of the murder, she'd have thrown it in his face.

Her attention on Nathaniel Babcock, Kate said quietly, "Papa was killed by thieves. They stole a valuable statue, his greatest discovery. Lord Gabriel has reason to believe that Sir Charles Damson is responsible. I'm sorry I didn't tell you earlier, but Meg has been with us, and I don't want her involved . . ."

Her green eyes held a watery sheen that tightened Gabe's chest. The prospect of her weeping made him restless and edgy, so he paced the bedchamber. "I won't have *you* involved, either," he said. "You're to remain here in the custody of your uncle."

Nathaniel leapt to his feet. "Dash it all, she can stay with the Rosebuds. If you're going after Damson, then I am, too."

"That won't be necessary. My man, Ashraf, will be assisting me. The fewer involved, the better."

"Quite the contrary," Grandmama said in a thoughtful tone. "There's safety in numbers."

"Have you come up with a plan, then?" Lady Faversham asked.

As if they were arranging a picnic, Lady Enid clapped her hands in delight. "Do tell us, Lucy. You always concoct the best schemes."

"So long as I'm included," Kate interjected. "I shan't sit home and twiddle my thumbs."

Rising from the chaise, Lady Stokeford went to hug Kate. "Of course not. Poor girl, I can't blame you for wanting to avenge your dear father."

Gabe battled a furious panic. He'd known all hell would break loose if his grandmother found out. "For pity's sake, don't encourage Kate," he snapped. "As her guardian, I command her to stay here. You and the Rosebuds and Nathaniel will remain with her. That is final."

Raising a silver eyebrow, Lady Stokeford appeared singularly unimpressed. She made an authoritative gesture at a chair. "If you're quite finished with your manly tirade, Gabriel, do sit down. I'd like to tell all of you my plan."

CHAPTER 15 •

SURPRISE IN THE ATTIC

THE day before their departure, Kate faced the unwelcome task of informing her sister that she was to be left behind.

Kate delayed the news for as long as she could, waiting until after the footmen had delivered all the boxes from the seamstress, and Meg had delighted in examining each new garment in her dressing chamber. While Jabbar hooted and clapped, she'd held each gown up to herself, twirling around the room and admiring herself in the pier glass.

But Meg's happiness vanished upon hearing that Kate, Lady Stokeford, Uncle Nathaniel, and Gabriel would be attending the house party given by Sir Charles Damson. Without her.

Beautiful in a deep lilac silk that set off her black curls, Meg crossed her arms mutinously. "It isn't fair," she wailed, thrusting out her lower lip in a pout. "Sir Charles invited me, too."

Kate felt a clutch of emotion in her breast. She longed to grant all of her sister's wishes, if only to make up for the loss of their parents, their money, their home. But Meg didn't know about the statue or the role of Sir Charles Damson in their father's death. For her own protection, she mustn't know this was anything more than a social visit.

Kate put her arm around her sister in a brief hug. "You're only sixteen, dear. You know it isn't suitable for you to mingle with strangers."

"I'll be seventeen next Tuesday. My birthday falls during the party. And Sir Charles is inviting his friends from

London. Surely any member of the *ton* would make acceptable company."

Kate shook her head firmly. "Nevertheless, this isn't the right time for you to make your début. When we return, Lady Stokeford has promised to hold a ball here at the Abbey. Then you can meet all the neighbors."

"But *I* want to meet people of fashion. I'll never have a better chance than this." With an air of dramatic tragedy, Meg wilted onto a hassock and placed the back of her hand to her brow. She didn't even seem to notice that Jabbar crouched on the dressing table and rummaged through her new hats. With a toothy grin, the chimpanzee jammed on a frilly yellow bonnet.

Kate took the hat from Jabbar and placed it inside a wardrobe. "I'm sorry, Meg. There will be other parties. Many of them. Besides, Gabriel has refused his permission."

"You've stood up to him before. Why can't you do so now?"

Because after that wild kiss, she had avoided his company. Lest she be tempted to fall into his arms again. "I'm afraid he won't budge on the matter. There's nothing more to say."

Promising to bring back all the latest gossip, Kate left her sister to brood alone. She had to supervise her packing. And she wanted to be alone with her thoughts, to prepare herself to play the role of admirer to the man who had murdered her father.

Papa, she thought in a torrent of guilt and grief. He had been on his way home. She'd been so close to seeing his crooked smile again, the ink stains on fingers cramped from hours of writing, the spectacles that too often slid down to perch at the tip of his nose. Finally, she would have had the chance to make amends with him, to tell him how much she loved him.

But no amount of wishing could ever bring him back.

Drawing a cleansing breath, Kate centered her mind on a clear, cold purpose. If nothing else, she would see his death avenged.

Her bedchamber was a short walk down the corridor, and the door was ajar. Absorbed in her plans, she walked inside and came to an abrupt halt.

She stood face-to-face with Gabriel's manservant. His *slave*.

For an instant, Ashraf's dark, thin features wore a look of startlement. Then his face smoothed into its typically bland expression, and he bowed, his hands pressed together within the sleeves of his long white robe. "Miss Talisford."

"Why have you come here?" she asked sharply.

"To deliver a message from the master. I placed it on the desk."

He made a move to depart, and on impulse, she stepped in front of him. "Wait. There's something I'd like to know."

He stood very still, his brown eyes watchful.

"How did Lord Gabriel come to purchase you?" she asked.

"He did not purchase me, mistress."

"But I thought . . . you said you were his slave."

Ashraf inclined his dark head. "The master shot a lion that was about to attack my previous master, Prince Faruq. I was given to Lord Gabriel in gratitude."

Startled, Kate imagined the wild beast about to pounce, Gabriel raising his pistol and firing with deadly accuracy. "Why won't he give you your freedom?"

"He has offered. Many times. But I must refuse him."

"Refuse? Why?"

"It is my duty to serve his lordship. The blood debt must be paid."

With that, the servant glided out the door and vanished

into the corridor. The faint odor of spice lingered in his wake.

Have a care, Miss Katie. Things aren't always what they seem.

Gabriel's admonition came back to plague her. She had judged him too hastily. Ashraf himself insisted on serving out a life sentence on behalf of his former master. Why hadn't Gabriel told her?

He seemed to prefer that she think the worst of him. Not that that was difficult, given his devil-may-care temperament.

Lost in thought, Kate shut the door. Only then did she notice the sound of humming that emanated from the adjacent dressing room. Recognizing Betty's off-key pitch, Kate went to the desk, where a sheet of vellum lay folded into a square. The jagged edge showed where it had been torn from one of Gabriel's sketchpads.

Snatching up the paper, she read the brief, scrawled message: *Lend your father's journals to Ashraf. I have need of them.*

The note was signed with a bold black letter *G*.

Kate stiffened as much from the nature of the request as its brusque tone. Ever since his grandmother had laid out a perfectly logical, perfectly brilliant plan to retrieve the statue and punish Sir Charles in the process, Gabriel had kept to himself. Sulking, Kate thought. His male pride had taken a blow, and now he would strike back by demanding Papa's papers. At least she'd taken the precaution of hiding them.

But why hadn't Ashraf asked her for the journals? The message implied that Gabriel had told him to do so.

The icy fingers of foreboding tiptoed over her skin. Hearing Betty's tuneless song drift across the large bedchamber, Kate half ran to the dressing room. It was nearly as large as the parlor at Larkspur Cottage, with more storage space in dressers and cabinets than Kate could ever hope to use. The open doors of a white-painted wardrobe displayed a neat row of new gowns that had been delivered that morning, with more to come. In the confusion, she hadn't yet had the chance to don the rich garb.

Then she spied another surprising sight, one that would have induced a smile had she not been so agitated. Like a dancer on May Day, her maid twirled in front of the mirror, a green cashmere shawl draped over her aproned work-dress.

"Betty."

The servant girl screeched in surprise. Consternation on her freckled face, she fumbled to remove the shawl while executing a wobbly curtsy. "I didn't mean no harm, miss. I was only borrowin' it." She hastily folded the shawl into a crooked square.

"Never mind that," Kate said, walking closer. "I must know. Did Ashraf come in here?"

A faint redness suffused Betty's plump cheeks. "Aye, miss. He knocked on the door, all proper like. He said Lord Gabriel sent him."

"Did he ask for anything?"

"Them books o' yers, the ones with all the scribblin' in 'em that was tucked behind the wardrobe."

A shock wave rolled through Kate. So Betty knew about the hiding place. "Did you give them to him?"

"Aye. 'Twas his lordship what wanted 'em, Mr. Ashraf said. He behaved nice and polite for a foreigner." Betty's blush deepened. "Smiled at me, too."

That dour man had smiled? Perhaps, like his master, Ashraf could be charming when he wished. He'd likely learned that trick by observing Gabriel.

Mentally flaying herself, Kate remembered the way Ashraf had kept his hands tucked inside his voluminous robes. She should have guessed he was up to no good.

Betty wrung her stubby fingers. "I hope I didn't do wrong, miss. Mr. Ashraf said his lordship would return yer books soon."

Kate doubted that. Though anger lacerated her, she shaped her lips into a reassuring smile. "You only did as you were told," she said. "You may leave any disputes with his lordship to me."

AN hour later, after a frustrating hunt through endless corridors and questions asked of numerous servants, Kate finally located Gabriel in the attic over the east wing of the house.

Late afternoon sunlight flooded the cavernous room, illuminating a curious scene. Leather trunks, crates of old schoolbooks, and discarded furniture had been pushed to the far end, making space for a long worktable. A snowstorm of paper littered the surface, and a number of drawings were tacked to the bare walls beside the huge dormer windows. They were Gabriel's sketches of Africa.

The object of her search stood a short distance away, leaning over the table, his back to her. His discarded coat had been thrown over a chair, and he'd rolled the sleeves of his rumpled linen shirt to his elbows. Her heart did an involuntary flip-flop. In defiance of good sense, she felt herself teeter on the brink of yearning. How perfectly she remembered the pressure of his body against hers, the expertise of his hand on her bosom. And that kiss. Deep and hungry, it had awakened her to sensations no proper lady should feel.

Gabriel didn't notice her standing at the top of the narrow staircase. With a jolt, she saw what held his attention. It was the leather-bound book in his hands. Papa's journal.

Her journal.

Spurred by anger, Kate started toward him. Oblivious, he reached down to switch the positions of two drawings.

Transferring the volume to the crook of his arm, he collected another sheaf of drawings and moved them to the end of the table.

Only then did he look up and see her approach.

His dark eyebrows lowered, and he threw down his quill pen. Without greeting, he said bluntly, "I didn't invite you here."

"But surely you were expecting me. After all, you sent your *slave* to steal Papa's journals."

"As I said in the note, I'm merely borrowing them."

"Ashraf entered my chambers without my permission. He took my possessions. I'd call that stealing."

"You forget," Gabriel said, "the journals belong to me."

Seething, Kate stopped by the table and held out her hand. "I'll have Papa's notebook, if you please. That one and the others."

"I'll return them when I'm done."

"When will that be? Next year? Five years from now?"

His wide shoulders lifted in a shrug. "However long it takes me to complete my book."

The piles of sketches in the attic took on a new meaning. In spite of her ire, she felt a spurt of surprise. And resentment. "You're organizing the illustrations."

Gabriel said nothing. His eyes were a fathomless blue, his handsome face set in stone.

"Why are you doing this now?" she asked, waving a hand at the loose sketches. "We're departing in the morning."

"It keeps me busy. So I'm not tempted to throttle you or Grandmama."

Her anger somewhat mollified, she said, "You shouldn't carry a grudge. We merely came up with a better strategy than yours."

"And threatened to go straight to Damson if I didn't cooperate."

Kate supposed his curtness was understandable. Men did so like to be in charge. "You should applaud the excellence of her ladyship's plan—and mine. It has a far greater chance of success than you sneaking like a thief into his house."

"Success? You'll get yourself killed."

"More likely, I'll avenge Papa's death."

Gabriel took a hostile step toward her. "You're to find the statue and leave the rest to me. Is that clear?"

Kate afforded him a cool shrug. It served no purpose to quarrel. She would do as she saw fit.

She eyed the notebook he held, weighing her chances of snatching back the precious volume. Prudence warned her against a tussle with Gabriel Kenyon. Not only would he emerge the victor, he would have cause to put his hands on her again. He might conquer her with a kiss.

She might submit without a struggle.

"You may go now," he said as if she were a servant. "I'm busy."

He turned his back on her, snatching up several sketches and striding to the wall to tack them up. Kate felt a guarded interest that he would forge on with the book despite her refusal to help him. She had scorned his dedication, accused him of lacking commitment to the project. Now she was abashed to realize that he'd accomplished more on the book than she had.

Curiosity warred with a gnawing rancor, a sentiment she recognized as jealousy. Papa had gone adventuring with Gabriel, leaving her behind. She burned to know more about their journey, to learn everything they had seen and done.

Looking over the table, she recognized many sketches of jungle and desert and mountain. A grouping of round huts with coned roofs. A string of laden camels trudging over a sandy dune. A lush forest teeming with plumed birds and wizened monkeys. There were people, too. Robed Arabs kneeling before a tall minaret at sunset. A lithe, dark woman balancing a huge basket on her head. A loinclothed man herding cows to a water hole.

Several illustrations included Henry Talisford. One in particular showed Papa crouched beside a shallow hole, cradling a pottery jar in his dirty hands, his bespectacled face alive with the joy of discovery. A lump in her throat, Kate recognized that small, nondescript jar. It had been packed in the crate.

Picking up the drawing, she carried it to Gabriel. "Where was this done?"

He cast it a scowling glance. "The lost city. In the short time we were there, Henry managed to dig up a few artifacts."

"While you found the statue of the goddess."

"By stroke of luck."

"Or mischance," Kate said bitterly. "If you and Papa hadn't been bringing the goddess to England for safekeeping, he would still be alive."

Pivoting on his heel, Gabriel walked to one of the dormer windows, where the brilliance of sunlight turned him into a shadowed outline. There, he propped his shoulder on the wall. "You should know something. We'd planned to return to the ruins at a later date. A thorough excavation of the site could take years."

Kate rolled the drawing into a tube. "I wish Papa *had* stayed there," she burst out. "Why couldn't you have brought back the statue alone?"

And died in his place. The unspoken words hung in the dusty air of the attic, leaving her with an uneasy sense of shame. She would not wish her father's fate on anyone, not even Gabriel.

"Henry was determined to leave Africa. No argument to the contrary could have stopped him." Gabriel paused, then added in a gruff tone, "He'd hoped to bring you and your sister back with him."

The sketch fell out of Kate's numb fingers, landing on the dusty floor. She took a step toward Gabriel. "He said that?"

"He missed his daughters. He thought you in particular might enjoy being his assistant." A corner of Gabriel's mouth twisted. "Of course, I did my best to dissuade him. I told you you were a frivolous girl lacking in common sense."

Kate bristled. Yet how could she blame him for having such an opinion after the spectacle she'd made of herself on that long-ago night? She had waited in his bed, thrown herself at him like a lovesick wanton. In the four years since his mortifying rejection, she had regretted her willfulness and learned the value of prudence.

Until that kiss. If she closed her eyes, she could still taste him on her tongue and feel the hard heat of his body against hers.

She kept her eyes wide open. "Do you still think me an irksome little girl?"

He strolled out of the blinding sunlight. "Little girl? No. Irksome? You don't really want me to answer that."

His wry mockery caused an odd melting inside her. To her surprise, Kate had the urge to laugh with him.

Instead, she walked briskly to a map of Africa that was tacked to the wall. The placement of pins traced a meandering route that went southward from Egypt into the eastern edge of the continent, and then looped back up again. Remembering what Gabriel had said, that Papa had wanted her and Meg with him, she felt an easing of the ache that had been her long-time companion. How she would have leapt at the chance to explore the ruins in her father's company.

"Where is the lost city?" she asked.

Stepping to her side, Gabriel planted his index finger on the route southeast of Khartoum. "Here. In the mountains of Abyssinia."

"What is it like there?"

"Wild and windswept. Uninhabited except for a primitive tribe or two. We had to bring in our supplies on mules. During the dry season, even our water was transported that way."

"Papa didn't mention that in his writings."

Gabriel idly riffled the pages of the notebook. "No, he didn't. Henry seldom thought about the practicalities of life." He flashed her an oblique glance. "That's an observation, not a criticism."

Instead of resenting Gabriel, she felt a great curiosity about his travels. A curiosity about *him*. She leaned back against the wall. "Why do you want to tell my father's story?" she asked. "Why not spend your days at idle pursuits like other noblemen?"

"It's something to pass the time, that's all." Moving away, he went to a drawing fastened to the wall, dipped a quill into an inkwell, and added some shading to a spotted beast with an unnaturally long neck.

"It has to be more than that," she said, following him. "Else you'd be off traveling again."

"I told you before, I admired Henry's dedication to his work. I don't want it to be forgotten. Isn't that what you want, too?"

"Of course." And yet, when he went over to the table, Kate again suspected that she'd probed a raw place in him. Going to his side, she picked up the drawing of a large, spotted, catlike creature that lurked in the bushes near a herd of grazing antelope. "What is this beast?"

He glanced at it. "A leopard."

The leopard's alert eyes and crouching stance held an unnerving reality that made her shiver. It looked as if it

were about to pounce. "Have you always had such an amazing talent for art?"

Gabriel grunted. "Amazing? More often than not, I got
in trouble for sketching instead of studying."

"But your parents must have been proud of you."

"My mother wanted me to join the clergy."

Kate laughed at the astonishing notion. "You, a vicar?
Preaching sermons from a pulpit?"

"Ridiculous, isn't it? My mother had me on my knees
in the chapel every day, praying for my own redemption."
The quirk of his mouth was more a grimace than a smile
as Gabriel tossed the quill onto the table. "It's no wonder
I was the rebellious one. I left home on my eighteenth birthday."

"What did you do then?"

"Wandered. Sketched. Seduced women."

By his smirk, it was plain that he meant to shock her.
But Kate was too curious for that. Tilting her head to the
side, she asked, "What about your brothers? What did your
parents want for them?"

"The military for Joshua, which suited him. He's now a
captain in the cavalry. As for Michael, he was groomed for
the title and the land. He never wanted anything else."

Something in Gabriel's tone caught Kate's attention. He
turned away again, sorting with studious interest through a
batch of drawings.

She moved some papers aside and then perched on the
edge of the table. "It must have been difficult, growing up
in the shadow of two older brothers," she mused. "Especially since they followed the path chosen for them, while
you veered away from yours."

He looked up sharply, his expression hostile. "What's
that supposed to mean?"

"I think . . . you must have envied your brothers, at least
a little. They had the support of your parents."

"It doesn't matter. It was a long time ago."

"Yes, but . . ." Kate struggled to form her intuition into words. "Perhaps you hope this book about your travels with Papa will prove you're more than a rebel or an itinerant artist. That you're as competent and worthy as your brothers."

A muscle worked in his jaw. He gripped the journal in his hands. "You presume too much. I haven't the time for your chatter. Run along now."

Kate didn't move. She imagined Gabriel as a defiant boy being pushed in the wrong direction. Like her, he'd yearned for approval; unlike her, he'd fled home to escape his decreed fate. A ray of understanding settled in her bosom, the feeling tender and tenacious.

On impulse, she asked, "What if I said I'd write the text for the book?"

His blue eyes narrowed, intense and suspicious. "Why would you change your mind?"

Because you need me. "Because there's no sense in us working at cross-purposes. And because I want this book to be the best that it can be." After a pause, she found the humility to add, "I can't do it without you, Gabriel."

Silence fell over the cavernous attic room as he stared at her, his stony expression giving no clue to his thoughts. Dust motes danced in the last beams of sunlight that pierced the dormer windows. She heard the faint buzz of a fly somewhere.

Tossing down the notebook, Gabriel extended his hand. "Truce, then."

Her pulse quickened. After they'd concluded the dangerous business with Sir Charles and returned here to the Abbey, she would work side by side with Gabriel. The project would likely take months to complete. Months in which they would be alone together. She already knew they were like spark and tinder.

Was she a fool for hoping they could ever find true accord?

Disregarding the clamor of common sense, Kate stood up and walked toward him. When she reached out, his big hand swallowed hers in a firm grip. "Truce," she murmured.

He held on to her hand a few moments longer. Deviltry glimmered in his ocean-blue eyes. With that obnoxious confidence, he said, "Just so long as you remember who's in charge."

"Of course," she retorted. "I am."

CHAPTER 16

THE FRAUDULENT FOOTMAN

As he rode the gelding over the hill and saw Fairfield Park nestled in its familiar wooded setting, Gabe felt a keen sense of homecoming. Set amid banks of rhododendrons, the sprawling Tudor mansion was built of gray granite with mullioned windows and a gabled roof. Ivy climbed the walls, and the setting sun painted the eaves in streaks of gold. From the garden drifted the cooing of doves in the dovecote.

The place hadn't changed a bit, though he'd been gone for more than four years. Longer than that, Gabe mused. Since he'd inherited the manor at eighteen, he'd either been carousing in London or wandering the world. Now he wondered why he hadn't returned here more often. He had good memories of the holidays he'd spent each summer with his maternal grandparents who had doted on him. Fairfield Park had been his refuge from a drunken father and a pious mother.

As he dismounted in front of the house, a stooped old man trudged around from the stables. When he spied Gabe, his grizzled features broke into a toothless grin, and he increased his amble to a jog.

"Welcome home, m'lord," he called out in a thin, raspy voice. " 'Tis been a month o' Sundays since we seen ye."

"Tom Wickett," Gabe exclaimed, clapping an arm around the ancient retainer. "I thought you'd retired already."

"Got a few years o' life left in these auld bones."

"So it would seem. Pinched any maids on the bum lately?"

Tom cackled. "I ain't in me grave yet."

While Tom led the gelding off to the stables, the stately black coach with the Stokeford crest trundled up the drive, followed by the baggage cart piled high with trunks containing enough garments to clothe half the population of London. Gabe's good humor soured.

He'd wanted to press on to Damson's estate on the coast, but Grandmama had vetoed him, decreeing they would stop here for the night. "We'll proceed the last ten miles in the morning," she'd said airily. "You can't expect us to present ourselves at the castle, all travel-stained and weary. We ladies are far more delicate than men."

Rolling his eyes, Gabe had deemed it wise to bite his tongue. He knew from long experience the futility of arguing with the dowager Lady Stokeford.

Waving away the footman, he opened the door of the coach and helped his grandmother descend the single step to the paving stones. She looked bright-eyed and cheerful, not the least bit weary from traveling since dawn. "It's been a long time since I visited here," she said. "What a pretty place it is, as warm and friendly as a cottage. Don't you agree, Kate?"

"A very *large* cottage," Kate jested as she stepped out of the coach. "You were right to sing its praises."

As he'd done that morning upon their departure, Gabe stared at her, amazed that shedding her crow's plumage could make such a difference. The deep bronze hue of her gown flattered her red-gold hair, which was drawn up in a new style that looked softer and more feminine than her usual spinster's knot. Her gown dipped low over her bosom and skimmed downward over womanly hips. He imagined himself stripping it off her, inch by slow inch.

Uncle Nathaniel gallantly took his grandniece's arm.

Admiring the stately old house, they started toward the steps. At the last minute, Kate cast a glance over her shoulder at Gabe as if she'd just remembered his presence. A come-hither smile played over her lips before she turned away.

That seductive expression caused an instantaneous reaction in him. Heat seared his body, centering in his groin. He hadn't felt such a hard, raging need since that night when he'd had her up against a wall with his hands on her breasts.

"She's a quick study," Grandmama said fondly. "I hope you don't mind that I suggested she practice on you."

Befuddled, he realized that the dowager stood at his side, watching him. "Practice?"

"Walk me inside, and I'll tell you all about it." Grandmama took his arm as they proceeded slowly up the steps to the broad front porch. "It's quite simple. To pass the time on the journey, I gave Kate a few lessons on how to entice a man."

Gabe stopped short. "What?" he exploded. "Why the devil would you do that?"

"It's all part of the ruse, of course. She'll be attending her first real party with the *ton*, and she must learn how to captivate the gentlemen."

"She needn't captivate anyone. We're searching for a statue."

Lady Stokeford fluttered her kid-gloved fingers. "Oh, that."

"Yes, that," he said through gritted teeth. Channeling his ill humor into anger, he walked her toward the door. "It's our sole reason for calling on Damson. That, and seeing him pay for his crime."

"I haven't forgotten that Sir Charles is guilty of murder and theft." Her gently lined face firmed into a steely expression. Just as quickly, she looked up at Gabe and smiled artlessly. "However, as we'll be spending the better part of a week in noble company, it behooves Kate to learn how to play the coquette."

"It's a waste of effort."

"Don't be silly," she said on a cultured laugh. "As her guardian, you should encourage her to flirt. After all, you're responsible for finding her a husband." With that, she glided through the front doorway.

Flabbergasted, Gabe stood on the porch and stared after his grandmother. He couldn't think of a single response. Find Kate a husband? He'd sooner shovel coal into the furnaces of Hell.

THE next morning, ready ahead of time and anxious to depart, Kate descended to the timbered hall only to stop in surprise with her hand on the newel post. Lady Stokeford and Uncle Nathaniel stood near a portly stranger and a white-wigged footman. Instead of politely taking the visitor's hat and cloak, the manservant reached out and shook his hand. Odder still, the newcomer bowed to the footman as if he were the Prince Regent.

She frowned at that tall, muscular form in the crimson livery of the Stokefords. Her heart beat unnaturally fast, and to her confusion, she experienced a deep, unmistakable throb of attraction. She curled her fingers around the carved post. Had that one kiss turned her into such a wanton that she could hunger for every able-bodied man she encountered?

Then the footman turned and she saw his face. Despite the formal white wig, he had the chiseled features and dictatorial air of an aristocrat.

Gabriel.

Kate bit back a laugh. He was disguised for his role in the ruse. Because Sir Charles knew him by sight, Gabriel couldn't attend the party as a guest. But with him clad as a servant, the nobility would simply overlook him. He would be another faceless menial, whose sole purpose in life was to serve his betters.

Bedeviled by humor, Kate headed toward the small party, her gown of forest-green silk swishing around her ankles. The tap of her slippers echoed in the entrance hall with its fine old tapestries decorating the oak-paneled walls. "Good morning," she said. "Footman, you've neglected your duties. Won't you take our guest's hat and cloak?"

Gabriel scowled, his gaze roaming over her in a most un-footmanlike manner.

Lady Stokeford's tinkling laugh filled the hall. "Kate is right, Gabriel. You would do well to practice a more humble demeanor. And for heaven's sake, don't glower."

"Now, Lucy, you mustn't tease the poor man," Uncle Nathaniel said, though his mouth twitched in a grin. "He cuts a fine figure. The serving maids will be all a-twitter."

Gabriel took the visitors' outer garments and tossed them on a chair. Making a mocking bow to Kate, he said, "Shall we proceed?"

As the small party headed down a corridor, she hung back to walk with him at the rear. Despite the crimson livery with its shiny gold buttons and the old-fashioned powdered wig, he had an imperious presence and a handsomeness that was almost godlike. "Servitude becomes you, my lord."

"That gown becomes you, my lady."

The unexpected compliment, coupled by his wolfish stare, caused a turmoil inside her. But she wouldn't let him get the upper hand. "You realize that henceforth, you must obey my every command."

"You've only to summon me, and I'll fulfill your every pleasure."

Soft and beguiling, yearning lurked within her. Those beautiful blue eyes held a promise that no lady should heed. How was it that he could so easily unnerve her?

They entered a large, comfortable drawing room decorated with old-fashioned wing chairs and fine walnut furniture. The ladies and Uncle Nathaniel sat down while Gabriel and the visitor remained standing. "Allow me to introduce Mr. Bickell, the Bow Street Runner who will be assisting us on this case," Gabriel said.

With interest, Kate studied their guest. The presence of a law officer brought a sobering reminder of the task that lay ahead of them. Though he didn't look at all as she had expected.

Bickell had gray eyes half hidden beneath shaggy eyebrows, and a florid complexion to match his red waistcoat. In contrast to his spindly legs, his stout chest strained the brass buttons of his vest. Except for the keenness of his gaze, he looked like someone's jolly uncle.

He swept a courtly bow, revealing a bald pate encircled by a tonsure of brown hair. "Barnabus Bickell, at your service."

At Gabriel's imperious wave, Bickell settled onto a bench by the unlit fireplace. His face solemn, he regarded Gabriel, who leaned an elbow on the mantelpiece, his pose entirely too casual for a servant. "With due respect, m'lord, perhaps you'll tell me why you've summoned help all the way from London."

Gabriel reached into his pocket and pulled forth a folded paper, which he handed to Bickell. "A valuable statue has been stolen. This one."

The Runner whistled softly as he stared at the illustration. " 'Tis a beaut," he said. "It must be worth a pretty penny."

"It's priceless. The statue is solid gold, about twice the size of my hand." Gabriel spread his fingers, his palm open. "The largest stone is a rare yellow diamond."

"That isn't all," Kate said on a surge of angry grief. "The thief also murdered my father." Unwilling to leave his journals behind, she had spent the previous evening leafing through them again, rereading the entry in which Papa had reported meeting Sir Charles on the day before his death.

Lady Stokeford placed a comforting arm around her as Gabriel told an abbreviated version of the events in Cairo. "Our plan is simple," he said. "Lady Stokeford, Nathaniel Babcock, and Miss Talisford will attend a party at the home of the thief. Once we find the statue, I'll send word to you here. You'll obtain the warrant as swiftly as possible and make the arrest." He eyed Bickell. "I trust you can handle that."

"All in a day's work," the man said, placidly resting his hands on his protruding belly. "But who is your thief?"

"A nobleman called Damson."

Bickell lowered his thick brows. "Damson, you say? Sir Charles Damson?"

"You know the name?" Lady Stokeford asked sharply.

"Aye, m'lady." Bickell cast a respectful glance at Kate and the dowager, then looked up at Gabriel. "This is a fine pickle, indeed. I can't say I like involving the ladies with such a man."

Gabriel aimed a look of insufferable smugness at the women.

Annoyed, Kate said, "Will you tell us what you mean, sir?"

Bickell shifted on the bench. "I feel it my duty to warn you, there've been strange goings-on reported in the vicinity of Damson Castle. Curious things, indeed."

His face alert, Gabriel propped his foot on a stool and his elbow on his knee. "Explain yourself."

"For one, some of the locals have seen odd lights on the beach at night near his castle."

"Smugglers?" Gabriel said.

"Perhaps there'll be a fine French brandy served at his house," Uncle Nathaniel said with relish.

Lady Stokeford slapped him with her closed fan. "No more than one glass for you," she chided. "We've a mission, and no room for drunkards."

Bickell cleared his throat. "Ahem. 'Tisn't smuggling, I fear. Rather, 'tis something far more sordid." Earnestness on his ruddy face, he leaned forward, his ample belly resting on his scrawny knees. " 'Tis devil worship."

Silence reigned in the drawing room.

Then Gabriel burst out laughing. "Satanic rites? What nonsense."

But Bickell's face remained anxious. "Last May Day, two farmlads spied some gentlemen prancing around a bonfire on the beach. They cast off their black robes and danced—" Glancing at Kate and Lady Stokeford, the Runner bobbed his balding head. "Begging your pardon, ladies, but the rest is too indelicate for your ears."

Gabriel gestured toward the door. "We'll speak in my office."

"No," Kate said. The idea of fussy, aristocratic Sir Charles dancing naked on a beach was simply too absurd to be believed. "Lady Stokeford and I would like to hear these allegations."

"Forewarned is forearmed," the dowager added, sitting up straight in her high-backed chair. "Kindly proceed, Mr. Bickell."

He rubbed his bristled chin. "At the last winter solstice, a young woman vanished from a nearby village. Upon returning the next day, she swore she'd been drugged and misused by a band of men dressed in black robes."

A chill coursed through Kate. Here was a far more serious claim. "Did she see their faces?"

"They wore hoods, miss, and devil's horns. When she screamed, they forced her to drink a potion that made her pass out. She remembered naught else until she awakened in a field the next morning, some five miles from home."

"Surely there was a hue and cry," Lady Stokeford said. "Why were these villains not captured?"

"Begging your pardon again, m'lady, this female wasn't any decent sort, but a poor serving girl in a tavern."

"That shouldn't matter," Kate declared heatedly. "The poor have rights, too."

"Of course," Bickell said. "I didn't mean to imply otherwise."

His hands clasped behind his back, Gabriel paced slowly, looking incongruous in the crimson livery and white wig.

"Devils and robed men," Uncle Nathaniel said with a snort. "The chit imbibed too much, went off with a man, and feared being found out."

"But if her story *is* true," Kate said, "then something must be done."

Bickell mournfully shook his head. "Without a warrant, I've no jurisdiction in these parts, miss. 'Tis a matter for the local magistrate."

"Who happens to be Sir Charles Damson," Gabriel said on a note of irony.

"This all seems rather far-fetched," Lady Stokeford said, her eyebrows quirked in doubt. "Men cavorting on beaches. And a strange, garbled tale told by a tavern girl."

"There's one more thing," Bickell said ominously. "There's been whispers afloat in London about Damson's club."

Gabriel frowned. "One of the St. James Street clubs?"

"Nay, m'lord." Bickell's ruddy face settled into a grim expression. " 'Tis said that Damson heads a secret society for certain gentlemen of quality. They call themselves . . . the Lucifer League."

CHAPTER 17

THE EGYPTIAN

DAMSON Castle brooded like a demon on a cliff over-looking the sea.

Peering out the window of the coach, Kate half expected to see a spiked tail twisting down the hillside. Pennants flapped atop the gatehouse, and a crenellated wall barri-caded the massive stone keep. The fortress looked like a perfectly preserved example of medieval architecture, al-though Gabriel had said it had been recently constructed by Sir Charles.

The four towers pierced the gray flesh of the swollen clouds. The day had turned dark and gusty beneath a sky that threatened rain. Mercifully, the storm had held off, sparing the servants who rode outside.

Including one counterfeit footman.

Despite her warm cloak, Kate shivered. For all that Ga-briel's disguise had amused her, she also dreaded the ordeal that lay ahead. In a few moments, she must greet her fa-ther's murderer with a smile.

"What a sinister place," Lady Stokeford said with a grimace. "I've always said that a man's home reveals much about his character."

Solemn for once, Uncle Nathaniel regarded her and Kate from his seat across the coach. "Mind you two don't wan-der away on your own. 'Twould seem this fellow and his companions are ruffians of the worst ilk."

The Lucifer League.

Kate remembered that Meg had heard gossip about the

sordid club and had even broached an innocent query to
Sir Charles himself. The baron had confirmed the group's
existence while denying any association with it. But was it
real? Kate wondered. Or merely an exaggeration?

The coach rattled over the drawbridge and into the castle
yard, where several other carriages discharged their occupants. As they waited for a position near the front door,
Kate gazed up at the tall, square keep, wishing she were
back at Gabriel's house. That fine example of Tudor restraint had exuded a warmth and coziness that reminded
her of Larkspur Cottage. She had fallen in love with the
place, from the wild gardens and the sweep of green lawn,
to the quaint rooms and the practical furnishings.

In a flash of avarice, she'd coveted Fairfield Park. She
couldn't fathom how Gabriel could spend his life wandering when he owned such a beautiful house.

The coach inched forward and then stopped before the
entrance to the keep. As the door swung open, Gabriel in
his white wig and crimson livery stood smartly at attention.
Lady Stokeford stepped out, followed by Kate. Gabriel
stared straight ahead, without so much as a flicker of a
glance at the ladies.

A gust of wind tossed a flurry of raindrops that struck
Kate like icy pinpricks. Shivering, she let Uncle Nathaniel
lead her and Lady Stokeford up the broad stone steps.
Looking back, she saw Gabriel leap up to the driver's seat
and sit beside the coachman, a dour servant with swarthy
features.

At a glance, Ashraf looked like any other coachman in
livery. Kate didn't quite trust the man, but they would need
him to fetch Barnabas Bickell when the time came.

Then the great doors opened, and the small party walked
into the keep. In startling contrast to the medieval exterior,
the modern foyer would have suited the finest mansion. The
plastered walls had been painted a marbled russet color, an

elegant backdrop for the many gilt mirrors and lighted torchères. Great sprays of orchids decorated the side tables. As a dramatic focal point, a curving staircase with an iron balustrade soared upward without any apparent support.

Kate's gaze riveted to the man who stood greeting several guests on their way upstairs. Sir Charles Damson cut a dapper figure in a peacock-blue coat and yellow waistcoat, his starched white cravat perfectly tied. He looked like the consummate gentleman of fashion.

A hard knot of rage pressed on her lungs, making it difficult to breathe. This man had ordered Papa's death.

Spying them, Sir Charles excused himself and made his way across the green marble floor. The flaxen curls of a choirboy framed his fine, pale features. His affable smile sickened her.

She couldn't do it. She couldn't go through with the scheme.

He bowed over her hand. "My dear Miss Talisford," he said effusively. "How very delighted I was to receive your note. I had quite given up hope that you would attend my humble gathering."

Kate's throat felt paralyzed. Her ears buzzed, and for a horrid moment, she feared she might fly at him in a frenzy, clawing that smooth, cunning, aristocratic face.

Sir Charles didn't seem to notice her agitation. "Where is your dear sister?"

He looked straight at her, awaiting her answer. To avenge Papa, she must play her role to the hilt. Drawing strength from the thought, Kate withdrew her hand and coerced a smile. "Meg remained at home, of course."

"Alone at Larkspur Cottage?"

He didn't know they'd moved to Stokeford Abbey. "She's staying with . . . friends. Do let me introduce my uncle, Nathaniel Babcock."

Ever the gracious host, Sir Charles turned his attention

to the couple standing beside her. "It's a pleasure," he said. "I didn't expect this lovely lady."

Placing a proprietary hand on the dowager's arm, Uncle Nathaniel gave her a look of soulful devotion. "This is my betrothed bride. Lucy, the incomparable Lady Stokeford."

The slight narrowing of Sir Charles's eyes betrayed his recognition of Gabriel's family name. Kate pressed her gloved fingertips into her palms. Would the baron suspect their purpose here? Or would he shrug off the presence of Gabriel's grandmother as mere coincidence?

Playing her part in the ruse, Lady Stokeford gazed rapturously at Uncle Nathaniel. "We've known each other since Nathaniel was a brash young cavalier, determined to charm all the débutantes. Who would have guessed all those years ago that we would end up marrying?" Turning to the baron, she smiled brilliantly. "You must forgive us, Sir Charles, for behaving like lovebirds. Nathaniel only just made his offer to me two days ago."

"Two days, three hours, and thirty-seven minutes," Uncle Nathaniel declared. "I couldn't bear to leave my beloved, so I persuaded Kate to include her. A young lady needs a female chaperone."

"You're wise to watch over her, my lady," Sir Charles said. "You're one of the famous Rosebuds, are you not?"

"Oh, la. That was long before your time." Looking around with bright-eyed attention, Lady Stokeford stepped across the foyer to examine a small figurine of a seated, cross-legged man with a strange, cone-shaped hat. "What an unusual object. What is its origin, pray tell?"

"It's an ancient Hindu god from Java," Sir Charles said. "The statue is fashioned of volcanic stone."

"Oh, my. And there's another one," she said, pointing to a bronze sculpture of Oriental origin. "Are you perchance a collector?"

"Yes, there are many more artifacts scattered all over

my castle." The penetrating glance Sir Charles cast at Kate made her skin crawl: "Miss Talisford, in particular, will enjoy seeing them."

"Then you don't mind if we have a look around?" Uncle Nathaniel asked.

The baron shaped his thin lips into a pleasant grin. "Explore to your heart's content. I want all of you to feel right at home here."

GABE did his best to be unobtrusive, a task that proved more difficult than he'd anticipated.

Led by the housekeeper, he and the cartman wrestled the trunks upstairs and deposited them in the appropriate bedchambers, first his grandmother's and then nearby, Nathaniel Babcock's, both situated in the east wing. Kate, however, had been assigned a large, airy bedchamber in one of the towers at the opposite end of the castle.

Gabe heartily disliked the arrangement. Had Damson separated Kate from her chaperones on purpose? What the bloody hell did that bastard have in mind for her?

Gabe let down the trunk with a loud thump in the dressing room, startling the apple-cheeked maid. Betty started to curtsy, then checked herself, casting him a frightened glance. He hadn't wanted to include her in the scheme, but Kate and his grandmother needed a maid. Back at Fairfield Park, he had lectured the girl so sternly she still looked petrified.

So much the better. The last thing he needed was a servant with a babbling tongue.

Rain drummed on the windows as he went out into the bedchamber, taking in the room at a glance. The circular walls and pale rose draperies made the place look like a scene out of a damned storybook. A gauzy white fabric veiled the four-poster bed, and he imagined Kate lying there asleep, her wild curls spilling over the pillows, her body soft and warm.

And naked.

The fantasy was so real that he heard her voice. A second later, he spied her speaking to Mrs. Swindon near the door.

He walked toward them, keeping his head lowered, though his gaze remained concentrated on Kate. She stripped off her pelisse, revealing the deep green dress that showed off her fine figure. His pulse leapt in utter disregard for his guise as footman.

As he approached, she flicked a cool glance at him, but continued talking to the housekeeper. "I prefer to be closer to my uncle and Lady Stokeford."

"I fear 'tis impossible," Mrs. Swindon said in an obsequious tone. "Begging your pardon, but I had a time locating a chamber for her ladyship."

"Perhaps she could share mine, then."

The housekeeper shook her head, the strings of her mobcap fluttering around her common, earthy features. "I fear such an arrangement would offend the baron. He gave orders that no one was to be so inconvenienced."

Gabe wanted to snap out his opinion of Damson's mandate. Compressing his lips, he stepped past the pair and went out onto the small landing.

"Whitcombe," Kate called after him, using his predetermined alias. "Fetch me a tea tray, please."

Gabe bowed. The request would give them a chance to speak in private. He relished the prospect.

The housekeeper followed him out, closing the door. He stepped back to allow her to precede him down the winding stone stairs. "How polite you are," Mrs. Swindon said, giving him an unmistakably coy glance over her shoulder. "Unlike some of these what think themselves so high and mighty."

Gabe shrugged. It was best to say as little as possible.

"Loyal to your mistress, are you? I like devotion in a man."

He could think only that he was angry about the room arrangements, and alarmed that Kate would be so isolated. Already, he had gleaned the names of the guests, noblemen he had known from his London days. Apart from a few ladies, they were men of unsavory reputation, knaves and scapegraces, aristocrats with nothing more productive to do than gamble and drink and whore.

And join secret clubs like the Lucifer League.

The thought enhanced his disquiet. At first, he'd doubted the club's existence—until he'd heard about the abducted girl. That was exactly the sort of titillating antic sought after by jaded noblemen. If Damson or one of his cohorts dared to lay a hand on Kate . . .

They reached the bottom of the stairs. "The kitchen is this way," Mrs. Swindon said in a chipper tone. "I'll show you."

"I'm sure I can find it," Gabe said. "You must have other guests to attend to."

"Nonsense. Your mistress was the last arrival."

The housekeeper smiled lustily at him as they started down the passageway. A full-figured woman in a gray dress that was cut a tad too low for her station, Mrs. Swindon eyed him with frank interest, her gaze roving up and down as if he were a choice cut of beef.

"A pity Miss Talisford has given you orders," she went on. "I'd hoped to invite you into my private sitting room for a spot of tea." She winked at him in blatant invitation. "You look like a man I'd like to become better acquainted with."

He forced a smile. "Perhaps another time," he said as they descended a small staircase.

"Tomorrow, then." Tilting her head, she gazed keenly

at him. "How fine your manners are. You must have had some education."

His muscles tensed. Had he betrayed himself? Surely she was only making conversation. "My father was a schoolmaster," he improvised.

Thankfully, they entered the kitchen and she could ask no more. The huge room was a madhouse of dinner preparations, with scullery maids and house boys scurrying here and there, and a French chef snapping out orders to the undercooks. Several footmen polished silver in the butler's pantry.

Flashing him an avid parting smile, the housekeeper swept into an adjoining room. Remembering the instructions he'd gleaned from Ashraf, Gabe found a teapot and cup in a cupboard, along with the tea leaves. He poured hot water from a steaming kettle on the hob. But when he reached for a tray of steaming rolls that had just come out of the oven, the chef threatened him with a dripping ladle. "*Merde!* Zat is for ze master's table."

Seeing a dark-eyed maidservant peeling a mound of potatoes, Gabe cajoled her into fetching him bread and butter and cake. She trotted eagerly to the pantry, bringing him the items and introducing herself in a broad country accent as Sally.

He politely thanked her and turned away. Instead of taking the hint and returning to her duties, Sally continued to gaze adoringly at him as he buttered the bread and arranged it on a plate. Her blushing attention irked Gabe, but he didn't have the heart to be cold.

Abruptly her face paled as she looked past him. Sally snatched up a potato, but it slipped through her fingers and bounced onto the flagstones, rolling away under a worktable.

Gabe turned to see who had frightened her so. Every muscle in his body went rigid.

A scowling man strode through the kitchen, eyeing Sally as she scrambled after the potato. The buzz quieted as everyone from the cooks to the kitchen boys watched the newcomer. A palpable fear hung in the air.

Although clad in a tailored suit and starched cravat, he looked nothing like a gentleman. He had a wiry build and narrow, skull-like features. His leathery face had a misshapen nose, obviously broken at one time, and deep-set black eyes. In his hand, he brandished a long willow switch.

Figgins.

Averting his head, Gabe fought back rage as he watched Damson's minion out of the corner of his eye. But Figgins didn't notice him. Towering over the girl, he raised the whip.

"Clumsy lout! The baron don't pay ye to stand idle, nor to waste his food."

As the switch came whistling down, Gabe reacted without thinking. He snatched up the plate, swung around, and lurched into Figgins. Thrown off balance, Figgins staggered against a worktable. The bread stuck to his black suit for a moment and then fell, leaving behind several greasy smears of butter.

Gabe wished he'd used a knife. Keeping his face lowered, he bent to collect the ruined bread. "Begging your pardon, sir."

"Bumblin' oaf!" Figgins snatched up a rag and scrubbed at the slimy mess. "Stand up and tell me yer name."

The command paralyzed Gabe. Their only other close encounter had been in a darkened room in Cairo. But if Figgins had a clear look at Gabe's face, there was a chance he'd see through the disguise.

"His name is Whitcombe, and I'm sure it was only an unfortunate accident," Mrs. Swindon said from behind him.

This time, the housekeeper's voice was music to Gabe's ears. Crouched down, he saw her gray skirt swish past him.

"Nitwit is more the like," Figgins snarled. "My best coat is ruined."

"Now, now, there's no real harm done, Mr. Figgins. Come, I'll have you set right in no time."

The two servants walked away, and with a sidelong glance, Gabe saw them vanish into the adjacent room and shut the door. The noise in the kitchen increased as everyone gossiped about the incident, some smothering laughter at the spectacle Figgins had made. Rising to his feet, Gabe collected the tea tray. Sally industriously peeled potatoes in the company of several other giggling serving maids. As one, they cast adoring glances his way.

Gabe suppressed a groan. So much for blending into the background.

Picking up the tea tray, he quickly strode into the narrow shaft of the servants' staircase. Alone on the wooden steps, he paused a moment to damn himself. He'd taken a foolish risk. Twice already, he'd almost betrayed himself. If he didn't take care, he would be found out.

He would lose his chance to make Damson pay.

THE guests gathered before dinner in a spacious chamber that reminded Kate more of an Egyptian temple than a drawing room.

Carved palm fronds decorated the tops of the tall white pillars. In a corner of the room stood a colorful mummy case similar to the pictures she had seen in one of Papa's books. The walls were painted with panels of ancient people at work and pleasure, some having the body of a human and the head of a falcon or a jackal.

More than thirty guests chatted in clusters, the gentlemen outnumbering the ladies. A glance told Kate that Lady Stokeford and Uncle Nathaniel hadn't come down for dinner yet. Several footmen were serving the guests, but Gabriel wasn't among them. They still hadn't had the chance to talk, for when he'd brought the tea tray, one of Damson's maids had been present, delivering some extra pillows.

Kate hesitated in the doorway, feeling a little shy at approaching these sophisticated strangers in their London finery. In the privacy of her chamber, she had fancied herself at the height of fashion in the new gown of dark blue silk with a pale blue gauze overskirt. But now, she was tongue-tied at the prospect of conversation. What did one say to such worldly folk?

Hello, I've come here to prove your host is a thief and a murderer.

"Miss Talisford. How positively angelic you look."

Kate gave a start as Sir Charles appeared out of nowhere. His haughty features regarded her from beneath his mop of pale curls. For the span of a heartbeat, she thought him an incubus from a nightmare.

Collecting her composure, she summoned a pleasant expression. "Good evening," she said. "I was admiring your drawing room."

"I'm pleased that it meets with your approval. Your good opinion holds great significance to me."

"You flatter me," she said in a light-hearted tone. "I'm certain anyone here would have more knowledge of the latest styles than I do."

"But yours is a fresh and unbiased judgment," Sir Charles said warmly. "After all, you are the daughter of the late, esteemed Henry Talisford. Come, I'll show you some of my treasures."

As he took her elbow, Kate hid a twist of revulsion. How could he act so nonchalant when her father's blood stained his hands? She was hard-pressed not to shrink from his touch.

Instead of taking her to meet the other guests, Sir Charles guided her over to a grouping of artifacts. Inside a glass case lay a long papyrus scroll, the edges tattered, the colored inks faded on the small figures and strange pictorial writing. "This is only a portion of a longer document," he said. "It appears to be a book about death, though of course, no one can read the ancient Egyptian script."

"The scroll must be very valuable. Where did you acquire it?"

"On my travels," he said offhandedly, "I've secured many a fine artifact."

Like the goddess.

Had he murdered other poor souls to procure these things? Kate subdued the vile speculation. Better to keep herself focused on her own goal, her own revenge.

She turned to the display of a miniature boat, long and slender, with a painted sarcophagus resting beneath an awning. "This piece is beautiful."

"It's a funeral barge. Once the corpse was mummified, it was transported down the Nile to a gravesite."

"What is that jackal-headed creature standing at the prow?"

"Anubis. God of the dead." Sir Charles smiled, his pale eyes alight with the passion of a collector. "The men and women you see sitting in the barge are slaves. They were destined to be killed so they could serve their master in the afterlife."

Kate shuddered, pretending it was a reaction to the display. "A cruel custom. How do you know of it?"

"You might be surprised at how well-read I am. Like your father, I've devoted my life to the study of ancient cultures."

How dare this murdering thief compare himself to an eminent scholar like Papa? She took a deep breath before trusting herself to speak. "You've so many fascinating relics," she said, stroking her fingertips over a stone plaque containing more of the mysterious hieroglyphics. "Perhaps you'd be kind enough to show all of them to me."

"That would take days, my dear. However, I might agree on one condition." He watched her, his eyes narrowed to slits of ice-blue.

"What condition?"

Taking her by the arm, he guided her to a chaise decorated with a gilt-and-ebony-winged sphinx at either end. He sat her down beside him. "The condition is that you help me out on my latest project. You see, I'm writing a book about ancient religions."

"You?" The question slipped out before Kate could stop it. She and Gabriel were writing a book, not him.

For a fleeting moment, his face tightened. "Few people know of my extensive studies, but that will soon change when I publish my first scholarly work. It shall be a far more comprehensive volume than any other. And it would aid in my research if I could consult your father's notes."

His gall strangled her. Who was Sir Charles Damson to think he had any right to use the life's work of the man he had killed? Or did he just wish to destroy that last incriminating entry?

"I can see you're hesitant," Sir Charles went on. "Let me assure you on my honor as a gentleman that I would merely borrow the journals for a short time. And I would pay you exceedingly well for the privilege."

She mustn't voice the acid retort that soured her tongue. Rather, she must play to his vanity. The success of her plan depended upon it. "I'm flattered that you'd include Papa's work in your book. You seem to know so much about history." Kate feigned a worried look. If only he knew, the journals were in the tower room, hidden at the bottom of her trunk. "But I don't have the journals with me. Does that mean you won't show me around?"

He snapped at the bait. Picking up her hand, he clasped it in his cool, soft fingers. "My dear, it's your vow that I seek. Then, of course, I would be happy to give you a tour of my castle."

This was her chance. Without compunction, she told another lie. "As you wish, then. When I return home, I'll send you the notebooks."

"You *are* an angel." He raised her hand to his lips and kissed the back. "Please bring the journals yourself when you and your sister return."

As she politely disengaged herself, Kate was tempted to scrub her hand against her skirt. "Return?"

"You and Margaret must both come here for a nice long stay. After all, I *am* your guardian."

Shocked, she blurted, "But . . . you never showed me the document . . ."

"I had to fetch it from my solicitor." Reaching inside his coat, Sir Charles drew forth a folded paper and pressed it into her hand.

Numbly she opened the parchment. Her disbelieving eyes scanned the legal paper, fixing on the neatly penned name at the bottom of the page. *Henry Leyton Talisford*.

Papa's signature. She knew his precise script as well as she knew her own. Either it was an exceedingly clever forgery, or Papa really had signed over guardianship to this monster.

Her mind scrambled to grasp the ramifications. Sir Charles mustn't find out that Uncle Nathaniel had ceded the right of protector to Gabriel. As much as that fact had appalled her, this new development held a far greater danger.

She lifted her eyes to find Sir Charles staring at her, his face all the more sinister for its refined appearance. "I'm afraid your document is worthless," Kate said in as calm a voice as she could muster. "My great-uncle is our guardian. Since he's our blood relation, his claim takes precedence."

"We'll let the Chancery Court decide that," Sir Charles

said, briskly plucking the paper from her nerveless fingers. "I hesitate to say this, my dear, but Nathaniel Babcock has a rather sordid reputation. And I will do everything in my power to protect you and Margaret from all wickedness."

His voice held an eloquent zest that sent a chill crawling down her spine. Sir Charles was an articulate man, his words smooth and fluent, his manner gentlemanly. What if he convinced a judge to rule in his favor? What if she and her sister were forced to endure his guardianship? Meg already viewed him with the starry eyes of an innocent, and it horrified Kate to imagine how easily he might misuse her rash, impetuous sister . . .

A man sauntered to them. "It isn't fair for the host to claim the prettiest lady all for himself," he said. "Introduce me, Damson."

Concealing her inner turmoil, Kate forced a polite smile at the stranger. Long-limbed and leanly handsome, he carried a drink in his hand. A small, half-moon scar drew up the corner of his mouth in sly amusement. He looked like a man who kept secrets. Dark secrets.

Standing up, Sir Charles gave him an intense stare. "This is my dear friend Miss Talisford," he said, helping her to her feet. "Miss Talisford, may I present—"

"Brandon Villiers," Lady Stokeford said, sailing toward them, Uncle Nathaniel at her side. "What on earth are you doing here?"

The man bowed over her dainty hand. "I could ask the same of you, my lady." Frowning, he slid a glance beyond her. "Pray don't tell me that Grandmama is present. It would quite ruin my expectations of this party."

"This is the infamous Earl of Faversham," the dowager told Kate. "His grandmother is Lady Faversham." She sent him a severe look. "Who, I might add, is not here. But if she had been, *she* would have been delighted to see *you*."

He shrugged without repentance. "She wouldn't like my crowd. Nor should you."

A smile transformed Lady Stokeford's delicate, aging face as she slipped her arm through Uncle Nathaniel's. "I'm here with my fiancé, Nathaniel Babcock, lately of Italy. I'm helping him chaperone his niece, Miss Talisford."

"Fiancé?" A stunned look altered Lord Faversham's jaded expression. Then with a surprisingly genial grin, he leaned down to kiss Lady Stokeford's cheek. "Well, well. It seems congratulations are in order." He shook Uncle Nathaniel's hand. "To you, too."

"I'm the luckiest man in the world," Uncle Nathaniel declared, clasping the dowager's hand.

"And I'm the luckiest woman." She gave him a look so adoring that Kate stared in surprise. Did Lady Stokeford feel a true devotion that went beyond the ruse?

She musn't. Uncle Nathaniel was an incurable rascal who lived off the generosity of his mistresses. When he grew bored, he simply found another rich woman to gull. If he dared to set his sights on Lady Stokeford . . .

Kate resolved to lecture him on the matter. More than that, she ached to tell him about the document, to pour out all her fears and beg him for help.

"Now, Brandon," the dowager said. "You must tell me how Charlotte fares."

The brief flicker of lightness vanished from Lord Faversham's face. More than ever, he looked cold and cruel and cynical. "How the devil should I know? I haven't seen the chit in two years. And good riddance."

Lady Stokeford smacked him on his sleeve with her closed fan. "Do not speak of Lady Enid's granddaughter with such disrespect."

"She earned that and more," Lord Faversham growled, radiating a chilly intensity. "You know that as well as I."

"Are you speaking of Lady Charlotte Quinton?" Sir Charles inquired, an eyebrow raised.

"Lady Stokeford is," the earl said tersely. "I'm not." Downing the rest of his drink, he set the glass on a table.

His scornful manner intrigued Kate. What had Lady Enid's granddaughter done to earn his contempt? Unfortunately, it wouldn't be polite to ask.

Just then, a foreign lady glided to Sir Charles's side. Strikingly beautiful in a low-cut emerald gown of the latest fashion, she had dusky skin, coal-black hair, and dark almond eyes. Diamonds sparkled from her earlobes, and a musky perfume eddied around her like a veil.

"You look as fierce as a lion, my lord," she said to the earl in a low, musical accent. "But perhaps I am intruding." Arching a languid eyebrow, she glanced around the small party as if daring someone to send her away.

Lord Faversham gave her a predatory smile. "I like it when beautiful women intrude."

"May I present Yasmin," Sir Charles said with a flourish. "She's a visitor to our fair shores from Egypt."

"My stars," Lady Stokeford said lightly. "All this way for a party."

Everyone laughed, even Kate, who felt the niggling of an ugly suspicion. The Egyptian woman must have accompanied Sir Charles to England. Did that also mean she knew of his treachery?

Yasmin made a graceful curtsy. "I have come to observe your customs, my lady. They are so different from my own."

"I've heard the Arabic ladies are closely guarded and hidden in harems," Uncle Nathaniel said with a devilish wag of his white eyebrows. "Were you in a harem, Miss Yasmin?"

"If so, I'd like to hear all about your experiences," Lord Faversham said, offering Yasmin his arm. "In private."

This time, Lady Stokeford used her fan to jab both Uncle Nathaniel and the earl in the ribs. "Behave yourselves. Yasmin will think Englishmen are a lot of fools."

Yasmin looked as if she thought nothing of the sort. She eyed the men, her lashes half lowered, a mysterious smile on her lips.

The baron gave a cultured laugh. "Hear, hear, Lady Stokeford. We gentlemen are soundly chastised."

Yasmin's catlike gaze veered to the dowager. The Egyptian seemed very aware of her effect on men, Kate decided, though the woman had said nothing to substantiate that opinion. Rather, it was her sultry manner, the confident way she moved and the way she smiled as if she knew men wanted her. As much as she wanted them.

But as the dinner gong sounded, Yasmin eluded both Lord Faversham and Sir Charles. To Kate's surprise, the woman drew her aside. "I beg a moment of your time, Miss Talisford."

"I . . . of course," Kate murmured. She caught one last glimpse of Sir Charles smiling benignly as he offered his arm to another lady.

"Come where no one will overhear us." The Egyptian glided toward a stand of potted palms, and Kate followed, intensely curious and more than a little wary. The moment they were alone, Yasmin whispered, "You are with Lady Stokeford, are you not?"

"Her fiancé is my great-uncle, Nathaniel Babcock."

Yasmin shrugged as if the distinction didn't matter. "I know this name, Stokeford. Perhaps it belongs to the Kenyon family?"

The bottom dropped out of Kate's stomach as she stared at the extraordinarily beautiful woman. "Yes. Why do you wish to know?"

Yasmin's face showed a feline satisfaction. "It is as I believe, then."

"What?"

"In Cairo, I met the kinsman of Lady Stokeford." As if relishing a private, cherished memory, Yasmin ran the tip of her tongue over her ruby lips. "Perhaps you know him. He is a handsome Englishman named Lord Gabriel Kenyon."

CHAPTER 18

THE LOCKED ROOM

WHILE the guests were at dinner and much of the staff enjoying supper in the servants' hall, Gabe used the opportunity to search the castle. Truth be told, he didn't expect to find the goddess sitting out in plain sight. But he would have a look, anyway, and get a feel for the layout of the castle.

Driven by ruthless purpose, he started in the east wing, making a methodical inspection of each room, including every bedchamber. Not surprisingly, there were few ancient artifacts in the guest chambers, only an occasional urn or a decorative bust. Otherwise, Damson had spared no expense on the lavish furnishings, and Gabe grimly confirmed that Kate had indeed been given the finest chamber.

He brooded on the anomaly. Did Damson hope to soften her into selling him Henry Talisford's artifacts? Was he trying to impress her with his wealth for the purpose of courting her?

Or did he have an even more nefarious purpose in mind?

Gabe breathed deeply to ease the pressure in his chest. The sooner he found the goddess, the sooner they could depart. If anything happened to Kate or his grandmother, he would never forgive himself.

Though the disguise was a nuisance, the wig hot and itchy, and the livery stiff with its formal, starched collar, now he could admit to the cleverness of his grandmother's plan. On his own, he would have been forced to enter the castle like a thief, with an extremely limited time to locate the statue. Instead, he could walk freely through the corridors, for few people would question the presence of another servant.

Proceeding to the main rooms in the keep, Gabe cupped his hand around the candle to keep the drafts from extinguishing the flame. He passed only a carbuncle-faced maid who smiled bashfully as she toted a coal scuttle up the back stairs. Nodding to her, he continued on his way as if he were tending to an errand for his mistress.

His mistress. How he'd like to have Kate welcome him with a smile, to show an eager, bright-eyed interest in him as she had so long ago. He wondered if that impetuous girl still lurked inside the woman she'd become: prudish, disapproving, cautious. He wanted to hold her in his arms, to kiss her again, this time without anger. He wanted to coax her into bed and find the wildness in her.

As swiftly as the fantasy had arisen, he banished it, though the tension in his loins remained. He was bound by vow to protect Kate. He must never forget that. Besides, he didn't need any distractions from his mission here.

Entering the library, he peered into every nook and cranny, spying a range of ancient curios from a porcelain Buddha to a bronze plaque of a man with the body of a horse. He searched a music room, a sitting room, and a ballroom. His frustration mounting, he went down passageways and subcorridors, checking in every chamber along the way. Although he saw other artifacts, there was little to support Damson's reputation as a collector of ancient erotica. The most risqué object was a life-sized Roman statue of a near-naked gladiator in one of the staircase halls.

Reaching the top floor, Gabe tried several doorknobs, but to his aggravation, all were locked. These weren't guest chambers, for those had been open. The expensive paintings and gold-striped wallpaper would suggest that Damson used this floor himself. Did he keep his most valuable relics in one of these rooms? The probability of that invigorated Gabe.

He needed a key. Quite likely, the housekeeper and Figgins had a set—and Damson himself.

Pondering various ways to achieve his goal, Gabe strode down the corridor to the nearest staircase. The plush crimson carpet muffled his footsteps. As he turned the corner, he almost collided with someone.

He caught her arm to steady her. "Mrs. Swindon. Forgive me."

In the pale candlelight, the housekeeper's eyes looked almost black and more than a little suspicious. She clutched a sheaf of papers to her voluptuous bosom. "Whitcombe. What are you doing up here?"

"Lost my way," he said glibly. "Perhaps you could direct me to the back staircase. I was going to Lady Stokeford's chamber."

She looked him up and down, her earthy features taking on a bawdy appreciation. "If I may first leave these menus in the master's study." Moving past him, she walked to one of the locked doors and reached for the ring of keys that jingled from her waist.

Keys.

With studied casualness, Gabe went to her side. He held his candle close as if to aid her task. "There, that should help you see better."

She gave him a predatory smile, making him notice the sparse moustache that garnished her upper lip. "How thoughtful of you. Are you always so attentive?"

"Women often say so." He glanced down as if to ogle her bosom. Unfortunately, the key was half-hidden in her hand. "Allow me."

He took the slender bit of metal from her fingers, then slowly tugged her and the attached key closer to the door.

"Mr. Whitcombe!" she said in a breathy squeal. "Why, I never!"

"I'm happy to be of service to you, madam."

He inserted the iron key in the lock and turned it. The tumblers clicked, and as he released the key, he noted that it had a scrolled top with a small numeral 2 engraved in the metal.

He opened the door with a flourish, taking a swift look around the gloomy chamber. "I can see you'll need my help in here, too."

Pretending not to hear her sputtered objection, he walked inside, the candle held high to illuminate a spacious study dominated by an impressive marble desk on which sat an array of quills and a silver inkwell. Gabe's attention veered to the walls, where tall glass cases displayed a profusion of shadowy objects.

His pulse surged. Damson's private treasure trove.

Striding to the nearest case, he let the candle illuminate a Greek vase decorated by a series of copulating couples. Moving quickly down, he shone the flame over shelves that contained figurines of men and women in various sexual positions.

"Whitcombe! You're not allowed in here." Mrs. Swindon bustled to the desk and deposited the menus. "None of the servants can enter this chamber, except for myself and Mr. Figgins."

"I won't tell if you won't," he said, eyeing the stone figurine of a Hindu male in full arousal, and then one of a bare-breasted tribal native with a huge pregnant belly. Pretending surprise, Gabe whistled. "This is a corker of a display. Who'd think the quality would collect such naughty things?"

"Come along," the housekeeper said, sounding almost frightened. "The master will be furious if he catches you in here."

"He's with his guests," Gabe said, stepping to the next case to see an alabaster sculpture of a woman fondling her privates, her head thrown back in rapture. "Look at that. What do you suppose Damson does with all these statues?"

"That's none of our concern." Mrs. Swindon grabbed his arm and pulled him out into the passageway.

Gabe almost rapped out a command to desist, then remembered his place. He was a footman, dammit. He had no right to give orders to the housekeeper.

The key rattled as she relocked the door, and then tried the handle. As she picked up her gray skirt and started down the corridor, she glanced around as if fearing they'd been observed.

"There's no one here but us." Goaded by razor-sharp purpose, Gabe leaned down to whisper in Mrs. Swindon's ear, "Let's have another look, my little dove. It might inspire us."

He could see the indecision in her, the lust in her greedy features. But she resisted. "Dinner will be over by now. The master might take a mind to bring his guests up here."

"Does he do that often?"

"Yes." She cocked her mobcapped head toward the staircase. "Egad! I hear voices."

Indeed, a burst of hearty male laughter echoed from somewhere below them. The faint tramping of feet sounded hollow in the cavernous stairway hall.

"Make haste," Mrs. Swindon said, prodding Gabe along the corridor. "You mustn't be seen here."

Gabe moved stiffly, his muscles tight with anger. He'd throttle Damson if he dared to expose Kate to that lewd display. Not even to find the goddess did he want her in that study.

"Surely he won't bring all the guests up here," Gabe said. "My mistress is an innocent lady."

"He's a gentleman, the master is," Mrs. Swindon hissed.

"And don't you be questioning your betters." With that, she touched the paneling and a cleverly concealed door swung open. "In here, now. Spit-spot."

With one last glance back at the closed door of the study, he reluctantly followed her into the narrow shaft of a staircase. The candle flame cast wavering shadows over the unadorned stone walls. As he allowed the housekeeper to descend the steep steps ahead of him, he knew she'd expect a few comments on the unusual display. "That's quite a collection your master owns," he said over the tapping of their footsteps. "I would never have guessed his vices by looking at him."

"It isn't my place to question the master. I do my duties, that's all."

"Always dutiful? Confess now, you must have sneaked a closer look at all those statues."

She glanced over her shoulder, a hint of that avaricious smile playing on her full lips. "And if I have, what would you think of me?"

"I'd think that like most folk, you enjoy taking a bit of a peek now and then."

She gave him a coquettish scrutiny from his powdered wig down to his knee breeches and buckled shoes. "I'd like to take a peek at *you*, Whitcombe."

Gad, she was undressing him with her eyes. "How about we return there very soon and inspect the room together?"

She shook her head. "Not while the master is in residence. And that's that."

Her decisive tone warned him not to press the issue. Biting off a curse, he tried another tactic. "Sir Charles must go away often to collect more statues. Does he always bring some back?" She may have seen the goddess. Too bad he couldn't ask her outright.

"Can't say yea or nay. He surely doesn't show me."

"But perhaps there's one or two in particular that stand out in your mind."

She winked. "Now that you mention it, I'm partial to the naked men."

"And jewels?" he persisted. "Most women like pretty baubles."

"Why would you ask?" she said, peering suspiciously at him. "If you're a thief . . ."

He laughed. "I meant a man's jewels, of course."

Mrs. Swindon's face brightened as she surveyed his breeches. "Aye, those are my favorite sort."

They reached the bottom of the stairs and stepped into the kitchen. Though the dim-lit room was vacant, he could hear several maids chattering in the adjacent scullery, accompanied by the clanging of pots and pans.

As he was casting about for another line of questioning, Mrs. Swindon stepped closer so that her pillowy bosom brushed his arm. "You're a handsome devil, Whitcombe. May I ask your Christian name?"

He picked the first one that came to mind. "George."

"George," she murmured in a caressing tone. "How very lovely. You may call me Agnes."

He'd call her a none-too-subtle hussy. "I doubt that would sit well with the rest of the staff."

"But you can do so in the privacy of my chamber." Crooking her finger, she beckoned to him. "Follow me, my virile footman. I've some sweets for you to sample."

Gabe concealed his distaste behind a smile. Now what? A tryst might be the only way to get her to let loose of that damned ring of keys. But he wasn't that desperate yet.

A jangling noise came from the board over the door. Distractedly, he frowned up at the array of bells, each one connected to a different room in the castle. With a jolt, he realized whose bell it was.

"It's Miss Talisford's chamber," Mrs. Swindon said, her

mouth settling into a sour line. "Why would she summon you at this late hour?"

To hear what he'd found out thus far. Eager to see Kate, he had the very devil of a time keeping his expression bland. "She probably wants me to carry a message to Lady Stokeford or her uncle." He winked at the housekeeper. "She has an abominable sense of timing, though."

"So ignore her," Mrs. Swindon said, running her hands over his double-breasted coat. "Let her think you've already gone . . . to bed."

"I can't afford to lose my post." With a supreme show of regret, he bowed. "But don't be too disappointed, madam. We'll meet again soon."

WENDING a path around the many hassocks and brass braziers, Kate paced the confines of the tower room. The round walls were draped with tapestries depicting veiled women in harems and fierce desert warriors on fine horses. With the tentlike gauze swathing the bed and the mosaic tile of the fireplace, she felt trapped in an Arabian fairy tale. But her stay here was no work of fiction where men were heroes.

Going to one of the windows, she leaned on the cold stone sill and peered out into the night. The darkened glass showed only the reflection of the fire on the hearth. From far below came the crashing of the surf. The storm had passed, but waves still churned against the rocky shore, a counterpoint to her agitated emotions.

By pretending to be a friend, Sir Charles had coerced Papa into signing that guardianship deed. Then he had murdered Papa and stolen the goddess. Now Sir Charles wanted her and Meg to live here, for what foul purpose, Kate didn't want to imagine. The legal document made her all the more desperately determined to bring about the baron's downfall.

Her feverish thoughts turned to the meeting with Yasmin. She had to warn Gabriel that the Egyptian woman was here. Yasmin might recognize him and give away their plot.

But that wasn't the entire cause of the turmoil inside Kate. Yasmin had enjoyed a tryst with Gabriel. That meant she must have been in Cairo at the time of Papa's murder.

And Gabriel hadn't bothered to mention that fact to Kate.

The omission had gnawed at her during the lengthy dinner. Sitting to the right of Sir Charles, she had smiled and conversed without remembering anything she'd said. She'd sampled the many rich dishes without tasting any of them. When the meal was finally concluded, Sir Charles had taken the men somewhere to drink brandy and smoke cigars. The ladies had retired to the drawing room, and Kate had made her escape.

She had come straight here and rung for Gabriel. Where was he?

By way of answer, there came a light rapping on the door, and then Gabriel stepped into the chamber. She was flustered anew by the change in his outward appearance. The crimson uniform emphasized the expanse of his shoulders, the narrowness of his waist, the powerful legs encased in knee breeches and white stockings.

No other man could look so splendid in livery. Or so arrogant.

As he walked with a bold stride across the Persian rug, his pirate's gaze demanded her attention. She should resent his domineering male attitude, yet her insides dissolved into a swamp of yearning. How well she remembered the strength of his body pressed against hers. How dearly she wanted him to kiss her again, to drown her in passion.

How foolish of her to desire any man. Let alone one who had betrayed her trust.

Kate crossed her arms. "I hope you act more servile

around other people," she said coolly. "Your haughty manner quite ruins the disguise."

"Devil take it. Being a servant is more difficult than I'd imagined. When this is all over, remind me to speak to Grandmama about raising the salaries at the Abbey." Reaching up, he yanked off the powdered wig and tossed it onto a hassock. Then he combed his fingers through his hair, leaving the thick brown strands attractively rumpled. "However, you'll be pleased to hear, I may have found the goddess."

That news distracted Kate. "*May* have?"

"There's a locked room upstairs," he said, loosening his collar with an impatient tug. "It's Damson's private study. I was able to walk inside with Mrs. Swindon."

"What did you see?"

"More decadence than you could imagine. Glass cases everywhere, crammed with artifacts. They must be worth a fortune."

Eager in spite of herself, she took a step toward him. "What about the statue?"

He shook his head. "There wasn't time to view more than a few things. I'll have to procure a key and take a closer look later." Walking to her, he caught her shoulders. "But I'm sure it's there, Kate. It has to be."

His jubilation was infectious, and she couldn't help smiling. "Oh, Gabriel, I hope so. I hope you're right. Now more than ever."

His gaze went to her mouth, a look of male appreciation that made her tingle all over. "What do you mean, more than ever?"

The sobering reminder banished her good cheer. She took a breath to calm herself. "Sir Charles showed me a guardianship deed signed by Papa."

"It's a forgery," Gabriel said flatly.

"It's *not*. And even if it is, the signature looks exactly

like Papa's." Agitated, she walked back and forth, her skirt brushing the hassocks. "He intends to challenge my uncle's claim in court. If we don't find the goddess, we'll have no proof to incriminate Sir Charles. Meg and I may be forced to live here."

Gabriel approached, settling his hands on her shoulders and bringing her to a halt. "We'll find the statue," he stated. "I promise you, Damson will never, ever have any power over you or Meg."

His closeness as much as his words blanketed Kate in the comfort of security. Yet cold logic denied her any warmth. "I summoned you with other news. I had an interesting encounter with one of the houseguests."

Gabriel's face hardened. "If any man has made an indecent proposal to you—"

"No," she broke in. "I'm referring to an Egyptian woman. A woman who claims to have known you very well."

He went still. Those ocean-blue eyes narrowed slightly, his dark lashes guarding his thoughts. "Who?"

So there were more than one? Reining in her ill humor, Kate said, "She calls herself Yasmin."

Looking confounded, he cocked an eyebrow. "Yasmin is *here*?"

Struck deeply by his implied admission, Kate walked away and then spun around to face him. The muffled roar of the sea underscored her seething anger. "Yes, and as you can guess, I was very surprised to meet her. Especially since she was in Cairo at the same time as you and Papa."

His face settled into an expression of closed vigilance. "Why would Yasmin speak of me to you?"

"Lady Stokeford is one of my chaperones. Yasmin recognized the name and correctly assumed that you and I had met."

"What exactly did she say?"

"She asked after you. In particular, if you had any lingering effects from your wounds."

Crooking his arms, he flexed his back. "What did you tell her?"

"That she would have to ask her questions of you. Because obviously you don't confide in me."

His face tightening, he took a step toward her. "You didn't say I was here, did you?"

"Of course not. Do you think me a dolt?"

Again, he laid his hand on her shoulder, his touch warm and heavy. "No, I think you're a very bright young lady. I've long admired your"—he looked her up and down—"intelligence."

Kate shook off his hand. She'd had enough of his calculated charm. "Don't placate me. Yasmin is an associate of Papa's murderer. Yet never once did you see fit to mention her to me."

"There was no need."

"Then you can vow that she had nothing whatsoever to do with Papa's death?"

He hesitated, averting his eyes as if he were casting about for an appropriate lie.

Seizing on that moment of silence, Kate snapped, "So she *was* involved. Tell me, did she wield the knife that took Papa's life?"

"Don't be ridiculous." A muscle worked in his jaw. He gave her a glower like a sulky boy facing up to a transgression. "If you must know, Yasmin was with me that night. She was a decoy to divert me from the inn."

Kate drew in a breath and slowly exhaled it. She had suspected as much. Yet her insides still twisted into a painful knot. Gabriel had lain with that ravishing temptress. How could such a man ever look twice at a naïve spinster who had spent her life in the country?

Then her shallowness appalled her. That wasn't why she

ached. It couldn't be. It was his concealment of the truth.

"So you were gulled," she said. "You will tell me how it happened."

Gabriel grumbled under his breath. He started to turn away, but she caught his arm, her fingers wrapping around his smooth sleeve. "Sit," she said, pointing at a gold hassock with crimson tassels.

His lips thinned as if he contemplated refusal. Then with a sardonic wave of his hand, he said, "Ladies first."

She drew up another hassock and sat down, coolly arranging her green skirt. He flung himself down opposite her, his jaw clenched as he grimaced at the fireplace. "There isn't much to tell," he said.

"I'll hear it anyway. And look at me while you're speaking."

Aiming his sullen gaze at her, he leaned forward, resting his elbows on his knees. "Earlier that evening, I'd met Yasmin outside the inn. We went to her house. I meant to stay only for a short time, but the wine she gave me was laced with opium."

"Why did you drink it, then?"

Gabriel scowled. "Because she didn't tell me what was in it. One doesn't when one is drugging another."

Kate didn't want to imagine what they'd done together. The mere thought filled her with burning resentment. "How long were you gone?"

"It was past midnight when I returned. By then, it was too late."

She kept her spine stiff. "So. If not for this liaison, you would have been at the inn, guarding the statue. Papa might still be alive."

Her statement hung like a foul vapor in the quiet bedchamber. The only sound was the rhythmic thunder of the surf outside.

"Yes." Gabriel sprang to his feet and stalked to the fireplace. Snatching up the poker, he stirred the coals so that the flames leapt higher.

Kate watched him in bemusement. His terse voice had held an edge of self-loathing. Did he regret his actions? Was he tormented by what he might have prevented?

That probability made her feel slightly more charitable toward him. Yet she couldn't forgive him so easily. "You should have seen the deviousness in Yasmin," she said. "Any woman who would take a strange man to her house has no scruples."

With a metallic clang, he set the poker back on its stand. He looked at her again, a faintly wolfish charm in his gaze. "Scruples, my dear ward, have no place in the bedchamber."

"So speaks a man with a wicked reputation."

He strolled toward her, his dark hair mussed as if he'd just arisen from bed. "There's something to be said for wickedness."

"There's nothing to be said for a man who can't see beyond a woman's outward beauty. I can only hope you'll have the sense not to go to Yasmin tonight."

Gabriel subjected her to an unsettling scrutiny. Instead of showing annoyance, he gave her that grin, the one she detested. The one that said he had experience in things she could only imagine.

Leaning down, he caressed her cheek with the backs of his fingers. "You're jealous."

Kate clamped her lips shut, mortified that he'd guessed her private, shameful wish to be as lovely and desirable as Yasmin. And as free to give of herself to Gabriel.

Retreating behind the façade of old maid, she said, "I'm merely concerned that you'll give away our purpose here. Otherwise, it's of no consequence to me if you bedded the entire female population of Egypt."

Her tirade only served to sharpen the gleam in his eyes.

"Prickly Kate. The dilemma is, I'd rather bed you."

With predatory swiftness, his big hands caught her by the waist. He lifted her from the hassock and carried her to the bed, where he thrust aside the gauzy drapes and laid her down on the white silk counterpane.

She tried to sit up. "Gabriel!" she said indignantly. "What are you doing?"

"An inane question from a keen-witted woman." He came down over her, half on and half off, his heavy leg draped over her thighs. Even as she gathered her breath for another protest, her senses greedily absorbed the heat and strength of him. His spicy scent had a narcotic effect that made it difficult to think. The filmy bed hangings enclosed them in a private bower, lending the scene the softness of a dream.

"Get off, you lout." Appalled at her feeble tone, she added more firmly, "At once."

"Not until you cease acting like a puritan." He stroked his hand up and down her bare arm. "You're quick to judge me, Kate. Yet there's passion in you, too. I felt it when I kissed you."

"A momentary lapse."

His smile deepened, creating the hint of a dimple beside his mouth. His chiseled, masculine mouth. "A lapse," he mused. "Then explain why I've done nothing but think about you ever since. You've tied me in knots, kept me awake at night. You've made me want no other woman but you."

She struggled against a shiver of pleasure. Four years ago, she'd longed to hear such a declaration from him. Now, she feared to trust in it. She shook her head. "You claim to be my guardian. But now you'd take advantage of me."

"Am I taking advantage? I doubt it." He settled more comfortably against her, making her aware of his hard-hewn muscles, his virile body. "You've been thinking about me, too. I can tell by the way you look at me."

"That's your conceit."

"It's proof of your desire. Nothing else could make your eyes soften so." His fingertips stroked along her brows. "Or your mouth." With a lazy thumb, he traced the moist contour of her lips. "Or your body." His hand moved to her midsection, as if he knew the heat that burned there. The heat that burned for him alone.

"Gabriel, please . . ." She meant to rebuke him, but the words died on her tongue as he brought his face closer to hers. His warm breath feathered her lips, making her lightheaded. Dear God, she wanted his kiss. She could almost taste it.

Yet still he watched her as a tomcat stalks a mouse. His fingers did a slow, tantalizing massage over her gown, finding the indentation of her waist, the flare of her hips. "Please what?" he said, the vibration of his rough voice making her breasts tingle. "Finish what you were going to say, Kate."

Her resistance teetered like a house of cards. To shore it up, she had nothing left but her pride. "You know what."

"Say it. I want to hear the words."

Beset by roiling emotions, Kate curled her fingers into the stiff fabric of his footman's coat. She felt frustrated by his insistence, confused by her inappropriate longing, and uncertain of his affection for her. She knew only that she craved his mouth on hers.

"Please kiss me." Closing her eyes in giddy anticipation, she lifted her face to him. "Kiss me, and be done with it."

CHAPTER 19

A Chance Encounter

LOOKING down at that puckered mouth, Gabe felt something deep and unexpected tug at his chest. Humor. Tenderness. Fascination. Meanwhile, his muscles were clenched, his skin burned, and his loins demanded release. In the throes of all that lust, he ought to avail himself of her offer.

Instead, he rolled onto his back, bringing her with him, so that she sprawled over him in a lavish heap of obstinate woman. To keep himself from caressing her, he tucked his hands behind his head.

Her lashes lifted. Eyes the shade of spring ivy stared straight into his. Tumbled, red-gold curls framed her wary expression. "Don't you want to kiss me?" she asked.

"This time, I want *you* to kiss *me*."

A mist of pink tinted her cheeks, and her rosebud lips wilted into a familiar prim line. But she made no move to lift herself from him. Soft and womanly, her breasts reposed against his chest. He doubted she realized that he could see down her bodice, or that her slim hip brushed his arousal.

Nothing could come of this encounter. She was right; he couldn't seduce his ward. It was madness to lie with her like this, tempting himself with what could never be. Yet he had a powerful need to strip away her thorny exterior, to know . . .

To know that he didn't have to force their second kiss.

"Why?" she asked.

The blunt question took him aback. "Why? Because I want to know you're willing."

"Or perhaps you want to conquer me. To crush my will entirely."

Not a disagreeable notion, he thought with dark mirth. And yet, without her strength of will, she wouldn't be Kate. She wouldn't amuse him, intrigue him, excite him to the verge of pain.

"See, I'm right," she crowed before he could reply. "You can't deny it. This is just another way for you to exert your authority over me."

"No, Kate."

"Then what other glib explanation can you give me?"

"That I'm worn out from my duties as servant. I need you to minister to me."

She eyed him skeptically. "For once, I'll have the truth from you."

Intensely frustrated, he blew out a breath. He didn't want to say that by telling her about Yasmin, he feared he'd destroyed their fledgling truce. But there didn't seem to be any way around it. "All right, then. I want to know . . . that you don't despise me."

His craving for Kate's favor was a hard admission to make, even to himself. Setting his jaw, he braced himself for her flippant response.

But he must have shocked her, for she didn't speak. She merely regarded him with both wide-eyed innocence and typical suspicion. Then her gaze flitted to his mouth. Her lips parted, the tip of her tongue tracing the curve of an inviting path.

Sweat dampened his skin in a fresh wave of lust. He swallowed the dryness in his throat. With each breath, he inhaled the subtle womanly scent that belonged to her alone. He was keenly aware of her supple body, the slender legs, the warm skin, the enticing breasts. Torture had never felt so agonizing . . . or so welcome.

Lifting her hand, she feathered her fingers over his face in a tender caress. In a needy, un-Kate-like voice, she murmured, "I don't hate you, Gabriel. Not anymore."

To his rampant satisfaction, she lowered her mouth to his, and that first tentative touch sparked a fuse of fire down to his loins. He steeled himself not to move lest she change her mind. With an inexpert charm, she kissed him, and all the while, her hands drifted over his face, tracing the curve of his ear and the length of his jaw, threading into his hair. Tense with control, he returned her kiss with small, teasing sips that seemed to please her. Uttering a husky sigh, she stirred on him, snuggling closer, parting her lips to taste him deeply.

With that untutored action, his enjoyment flared to dangerous, white-hot passion. Gabe could no longer keep from touching her, and he brought his arms around her, his hands finding silken shoulders, slender back, delectable breasts. Ah, her breasts. Lush and full and tempting. He slipped his fingers inside her bodice, seeking her warm secrets. Brushing his thumb over her nipples, he took command of the kiss, showing her what he liked, titillating her in return. With a questing fervor, her mouth drank from his, her body melting over him in trembling surrender.

Her responsiveness plunged him into a rushing river of madness. Groaning, he cupped her rounded bottom, rolled her over, and pressed himself deeply into the cradle of her hips. He couldn't get enough of her, his soft, submissive Kate. Freeing the sensual woman inside the thorns didn't satisfy him. He wanted to brand her with himself, to make her recognize that she belonged to him and him alone.

Reaching down, he slid his hand beneath her tangled skirts, up the slim muscles of her calf, past the tender crook of her knee, and over the frilled garter that secured her stocking. Like any decent young lady, she wore no drawers, and his fingers brushed the triangle of tight curls that guarded the gate to heaven.

She gasped, breaking the kiss by turning her head, exposing the slender column of her throat. "Gabriel!"

His loins ruled him, but his mind fought a valiant battle. Letting his hand rest lightly on her thigh, he kissed the fragrant skin of her throat. "Let me touch you," he coaxed in a low, raspy voice. "Just a touch and no more . . . I promise you."

"I . . ." Her bosom rose and fell as she watched him, her lashes half lowered over dreamy eyes. Then she placed her hand over his, so that only a thin layer of skirts separated them. Fiercely she whispered, "Yes."

Her consent broke the bounds of his restraint. Parting her nether folds, he traced a path through velvety dampness. A soft cry escaped her, and she arched to him in sweet entreaty. His breath came harder and faster, his lust more torture than pleasure. But he concentrated on pleasing her, stroking her with a slow, deliberate hand. She was hot and eager, her legs fully open to his caresses, and he longed to put his mouth there, but knew he'd frighten her. Lost in delight, she lay with her eyes closed, her fiery hair spread over the white coverlet, her head moving back and forth as if to deny the unfamiliar, coiling tension in her body.

Sensing her resistance, he muttered words of encouragement, hardly knowing what he was saying. "Let go, love. Let yourself fly. I'll be there to catch you." Bending down, he kissed the creamy skin mounded above her bodice, while his hand remained beneath her skirt, continuing the relentlessly sensual assault until, with a keening sob, she convulsed in his arms.

The look of rapturous wonder on her face filled Gabe with savage exultation. He had only to tear open his breeches, to sink into her and take the release his hot blood demanded. In her soft, defenseless state, she wouldn't deny him. But a fragment of sanity barred that course. Already, he'd far overstepped his bounds. He'd sworn to protect Kate. He could not claim her maidenhead, for that would tie him to her forever.

With a groan, he flung himself to his feet. His legs unsteady, he stalked to the window and pressed his fevered brow to the cold glass, his fingers to the stone sill. His chest heaved as he sucked air into his starving lungs. His body shook from the effort it took to conquer his instinct to return to the bed.

To Kate.

Slowly, the madness eased its grip on him. The desire still burned, but he could control it. He couldn't so easily control his guilt. Never before had he touched a virgin. There had always been many experienced women who were delighted to satisfy him. Worldly, sophisticated women. So why had he taken complete leave of his senses over Kate?

He turned to see her sit up slowly, still half in a stupor. Through the filmy draperies, she looked adorably rumpled with loosened curls cascading past her shoulders. Intercepting his gaze, she flushed, hurriedly restoring her skirt so that not a hint of flesh showed. Then she lifted her hands to her rosy cheeks, and he saw the awareness in her eyes, an awareness of their wrongful intimacy.

Gabe swore under his breath. He would give his entire fortune to erase that look of mortification from her face.

He walked to her, stopping a few feet from the bed. He wanted to kiss away her regrets. But he knew where that would lead. "Kate," he said, his voice low and grating, "I took advantage of you. I should not have done so."

"I let you." Her whisper was throaty, fraught with shame.

He wrapped his fingers around the bedpost, squeezing

until his knucles showed white. "You're not to blame. The fault is entirely mine."

She shook her head. "No. I encouraged you. I wanted it."

A cynical humor invaded Gabe. Even in this, Kate would quarrel with him. "As the man, I've the benefit of experience," he said tersely. "I nearly lost my head over you—and I'm not even sorry. So rail at me if you like. Denounce me. I want to hear you do so."

She remained stubbornly silent, her fingers laced in her lap and her gaze on him. He didn't know how to interpret that frown. Had she accepted his liability? He had always been able to read women, to charm them and get his way. But with Kate, he felt on treacherous ground, now more than ever. Now, the awareness in her eyes held the mysteries of a woman.

A thought struck him like a thunderbolt. In every sense but the physical, he *had* stolen her innocence. And he should offer her marriage.

BY the fourth and final day of the party, Kate still hadn't found the goddess.

The late April weather had remained cloudy and cold, precluding any outdoor activities. The company spent the days in card playing and billiards and endless drinking, which Kate had avoided. The other guests had a hard-edged sophistication that made her uneasy, even the ladies, who liked to gamble and tipple sherry along with the gentlemen while laughing and gossiping, many of their comments barbed with cruelty. If this was high society, Kate didn't care for it.

As he had promised, Sir Charles had escorted Kate on a tour of the castle. Uncle Nathaniel and Lady Stokeford had strolled behind them as the baron pointed out the various relics he owned. To flatter Sir Charles, Kate had made a point to admire the exquisite quality of each piece. A medieval bishop's staff cast in gold. A chess set carved from walrus ivory. A glass case containing a finger bone reputedly belonging to the Apostle Peter.

Yet all the while, she had concealed her dark thoughts. Had Sir Charles stolen these things, too? Had he committed murder to get them?

In late afternoon on the last day, Kate felt the frantic prod of desperation. Finding the goddess was the only way to punish Sir Charles for his crimes. And to stop him from claiming guardianship of her and Meg.

But time was running out. Tomorrow morning, the party would be over and all the guests would depart.

She found Sir Charles in the first-floor hall as he was coming downstairs. His suave face lit up with an admiration that she might have appreciated in another gentleman. It sickened her to greet him with a smile and pretend to be flattered by his attention.

She loathed how he'd touched her in seemingly innocuous ways over the past few days, taking her elbow to escort her or brushing against her arm, too often to be a mere accident. Any contact with Sir Charles made her recoil, quite the opposite of her reaction to Gabriel.

How she longed to feel Gabriel's hands on her body again; how she tossed and turned at night from hot, restless dreams of him. It was as if he'd opened the cage of a wild creature in her, a sensualist who craved him. Because of that, ever since their tryst, she had avoided his company. It wasn't him she couldn't trust.

It was herself.

"You're just the person I've been wanting to see," Sir Charles said, taking her hand between his smooth palms.

"I'm delighted to see you, too," she said with determined charm, though she made haste to tug her hand free. Feigning a flirtatious smile, she went on. "I've discovered you're hiding something from me."

His fair lashes flickered over pale blue eyes. "What do you mean?" ·

She was right; his manner betrayed a faint tension. "I hear from my uncle that you've more treasures that you didn't show me the other day."

Chuckling, Sir Charles hung his head. "I confess, you've caught me in a fib. I do keep some other artifacts in several private chambers upstairs."

Several chambers? Uncle Nathaniel had visited only the study along with the other gentlemen guests, and he had reported seeing many vulgar objets d'art. Much to Kate's frustration, however, he'd found no golden goddess on display.

But if Sir Charles kept artifacts in other locked rooms, too . . . "I wish to see them. You did make a bargain with me."

The baron shook his head. "I'm afraid I must refuse. Those things aren't suitable for viewing by innocent young ladies."

"Why, I'm all of twenty," she said lightly. "I promise you, I'm not so easily shocked."

Except when Gabriel had put his hand on her privates. Shock had swiftly exploded into pleasure at the first stroke of his finger. Overcome by passion, she had behaved like a wanton, opening her legs to him, permitting him unspeakable liberties. The culminating waves of rapture that had surged through her seemed now like a glorious dream.

Sir Charles smiled benignly. "You're pure in body and spirit," he said. "I shan't allow you to be sullied by improper sights."

The experience with Gabriel hadn't sullied her. That was her guilty secret, the reason she felt so alive now, awakened to the joys of physical love. No wonder young ladies were sheltered until marriage; they would hunger for the act as she did. Whenever she thought of Gabriel—and that was far too often of late—she felt her need for him as a warm, liquid throbbing in the place that he had touched.

Noticing that Sir Charles was staring rather oddly at her, she thrust her mind back to the statue. "My father was a professor of antiquities. I can certainly view any type of ancient artifact with a professional eye."

The baron patted her hand. "No, my dear, it's out of the question. Remember, it's my sworn duty to protect you. I am your guardian, after all."

She clenched her teeth against a denial. It wouldn't do to anger him. "But you're not a dull, conventional guardian. You're so much more advanced in your intellect. Surely you can overlook the common proprieties."

A slight frown marred his smooth brow. "Modesty in a young girl is a virtue beyond compare. I'll hear no more talk of this inappropriate request."

His patronizing refusal irked her. How was she to locate the goddess now? She could only hope that Gabriel had been able to procure a set of keys.

I nearly lost my head over you—and I'm not even sorry.

Dear God, how deeply his avowal had pierced her. What had Gabriel meant by those words? That he too had been swept up in the firestorm of passion? Yet he had stopped. He'd left her on the bed, and she'd seen him go to the window, his powerful body bowed as if in pain. Despite her naïveté, she had grown up in the country and seen her share of mating animals, enough to know there had been no consummation between her and Gabriel. He must have been wracked by the same cataclysmic urges as she had been, but had denied himself any relief.

She should be grateful for that. She could so easily have become a fallen woman, a subject of gossip, as Mrs. Beasley, their next-door neighbor at Larkspur Cottage, had whispered in scandalous outrage about poor, homely Mary Dutton who had trysted with a peddler.

That could have been her, Kate thought with a sickening lurch, left pregnant while the man went on his merry way. Yet she wasn't sorry, either, to have known the stunning joy that Gabriel had aroused in her. To her shame, she wanted to experience it again.

Sir Charles sighed heavily, the sound echoing in the vast hall. "Dear me, I can't bear to see you looking so glum," he said, taking her arm and leading her to the grand staircase. "If you'll come with me, I'll show you something very special."

Her senses sprang to the alert. "Special? What do you mean?"

"It's a treasure I only recently acquired." Teasingly, he shook his finger at her. "Now don't ask any more questions. I want this to be a surprise."

Anticipation bubbled inside Kate as she joined him in mounting the curving flight of stairs. A treasure, recently acquired. That could only mean one thing. Finally, Sir Charles would take her to the goddess.

"GEORGE. Hsst, George!"

The whispering voice barely registered with Gabe as he stood in the library, trimming the last lamp and watching Kate. She and Damson stood talking out in the hall. The murmur of their voices carried to him, though he couldn't make out their words. The baron sidled closer to Kate, and Gabe was sorely tempted to stride out there and throttle the lecher. Restrained by his role, he could only glower at them.

Or rather, at Kate.

Tall and proud, she wore a dress of flowing blue stuff that skimmed her fine figure. She stood to the side, and he feasted his eyes on her lovely profile. Her head was tilted, her attention focused on Damson. A primal possessiveness gripped Gabe. She belonged to him—no, she didn't. Touching her didn't mean he had to marry her. A nagging female would complicate his life and put an end to his freedom. Especially Kate with her sharp tongue and critical manner.

Kate with her tender kisses and passionate nature. The prospect of having her in his bed every night could almost make him welcome the noose of wedlock.

Then Damson took her arm. To Gabe's fury, the two of them went up the stairs.

Leaning forward to watch them go, he tipped the oil can too far forward. Muttering a string of profanity, he mopped up the greasy puddle with a rag, only just catching the oozing mess before it dribbled onto the rug.

Where the hell had Damson taken Kate? The next floor held only bedchambers, and above that, the baron's study. Another of the locked doors led to Damson's suite of chambers, as Gabe had ascertained by asking around in the servants' hall.

He threw down the oil-soaked rag. He couldn't stand here, twiddling his thumbs, while Kate went upstairs with a murderer.

As he started toward the door, the voice came again, this time snapping him to his senses. "George Whitcombe!"

Pivoting on his heel, Gabe saw Mrs. Swindon making her way from the servants' staircase. He compressed his lips. Much to his chagrin, the housekeeper had been as difficult to shed as a nasty rash. After three futile days spent attempting to get the keys, he had finally resigned himself to the chore of seduction, only to be saved by a last-minute reprieve.

Late yesterday evening, when he'd gone into the steward's cramped room to do the lamps, he'd had the good luck to happen upon the man's ring of keys lying on the desk. Quickly, Gabe had whipped out the softened lump of beeswax from his pocket and had made impressions of several keys. Although Nathaniel Babcock had reported not seeing the goddess in the study, Gabe wanted to search the other locked chambers.

Carefully wrapping the wax, he'd delivered it to Ashraf in the stables. Ashraf had departed at dawn, ostensibly to fetch ribbons for Lady Stokeford from a nearby village. Gabe expected the manservant to have returned from the locksmith by now.

Then tonight, while everyone else was at the final ball, Gabe would conduct his search.

"There you are, my naughty man," Agnes Swindon trilled. "I've been searching all over the house for you."

He forced a smile. "I was tending to my duties, of course."

Replacing the glass globe, he positioned the lamp in front of him. God help him if the housekeeper noticed the swelling in his breeches, his reaction to seeing Kate.

With the familiarity of a fishwife, she grabbed his arm and examined his hand. Black soot and oil smeared his palms. She made a grimace that drew attention to her mustachioed upper lip. "Trimming the lamps is Potter's duty," she fretted, naming one of Damson's footmen. "Such beautiful hands as yours oughtn't be dirtied. They're better kept for . . . other things." She winked lasciviously at him.

"Potter and I exchanged duties. He prefers polishing the silver." While this task gave Gabe the freedom to move around the castle.

"Come downstairs with me," Mrs. Swindon cooed, sidling closer and rubbing up against him, no doubt to give him a look at her bovine bosom. "Let me trim *your* wick."

"I need to finish here."

"Nonsense, there's only this one lamp left to light." She fetched a burning fagot from the hearth, lifted the glass chimney, and touched the tiny flame to the wick. "There, I've done it for you," she said, blowing out the lighted twig with an exaggerated pucker of her lips. "Now, to return the favor, you may light *my* lamp."

He'd like to give the slattern a swift boot in the arse, for she was keeping him from following Kate and Damson. "I'll have to put my mind to the matter."

"It isn't your mind that interests me." Mrs. Swindon waggled her eyebrows. "Come along, my handsome blade. There's naught to keep you here."

If only she knew. As Gabe reluctantly picked up his tray of supplies, he pondered yet another pretext to avoid her bed. Between her and the swarm of adoring housemaids, he couldn't get a moment's peace. But at least her crude seductiveness had had one welcome result.

He no longer had to worry about her stealing a glance at his breeches.

BESET by trepidation, Kate accompanied Sir Charles up the stairs. With his froth of fair curls and his pale, patrician features, he looked like a gentleman any mother would be thrilled to have court her daughter.

Yet he and his cronies were members of the secret sect known as the Lucifer League. Sir Charles would steal and kill to get what he wanted. And she was alone with him.

A window on the landing gave a view of the gray skies and the white-capped surf pounding at the base of the cliff, where the jagged teeth of boulders bit at the oncoming waves. Gulls screeched, diving for fish in the churning waters. Kate remembered that the Bow Street runner had mentioned a pagan rite taking place there on the rocky shore.

"How do you get down to the beach?" she asked. "Are there steps?"

"Gracious, no. It's far too steep." Pausing on the landing, Sir Charles looked at her curiously. "Surely you don't wish to stroll along the seashore in this gloomy weather, Miss Talisford. There's nothing but caves and rocks down there, anyway."

"Caves?"

"These cliffs are honeycombed with subterranean caverns. I believe they're connected somehow to the dungeons."

Kate suppressed a shiver. "I didn't realize you'd built dungeons."

He chuckled, seeming to enjoy frightening her. "I didn't. You see, my castle was constructed on the ruins of an old medieval keep. The workmen reported seeing tunnels and such, though I don't know where they all lead."

She pondered that as they progressed up the stairs. Did Sir Charles know a route through the tunnels down to the beach? Was that how he and his cronies had made their way there?

As they reached the top floor, another sight drove that speculation from her mind. A lamp flickered in a sconce on the wall, shedding an eerie illumination over the plush crimson carpet and the gilded woodwork. Down the corridor, a man stood locking one of the doors.

He was a foxlike chap in a fine suit of clothing. When he turned around, Kate bit back a gasp. She recognized him from Gabriel's sketch: the skull-like features, the misshapen nose and hollow black eyes.

Figgins. He had been there on the night of Papa's murder. He had stabbed Gabriel in the back.

An impotent fury choked her throat. But he gave her no more than a glance, his groveling attention on Sir Charles. "Beggin' yer pardon, sir. I brought up the wine from the cellars, like ye ordered."

"And the brandy?"

Figgins bobbed his head up and down. "Filled all the decanters."

"Excellent. You may go."

As Figgins scurried away down the corridor, Sir Charles drew a key from his pocket and unlocked the door. "If you don't mind, my dear," he said to Kate, "please wait out here for a moment."

Going inside, he pushed the door almost shut. Through the crack, she caught a glimpse of a spacious chamber with glass-fronted cases set against the walls. She could make out only a few shadowy shapes of curios.

This must be the study where Sir Charles met with the Lucifer League, Kate thought, taking a deep breath to clear her mind of anger. She tapped the toe of her slipper on the carpet. Would Sir Charles bring out the goddess? Perhaps he'd hidden the statue in a safe or strongbox, where Uncle Nathaniel hadn't seen it.

The door swung open, and she stepped back. But Sir Charles held only a ring of keys. "I'm ever so sorry to make you wait. I misplaced my other key and had to fetch these from my desk. Come with me."

He led her farther down the corridor to an ornately gilded door. Selecting a key, he stuck it in the lock and turned it with an audible click. "Now," he said, his eyes dancing with dark mysteries, "if you'll be patient just a moment longer."

His secretive manner alarmed Kate. "What is this chamber?" she asked. "Why is it kept secured?"

"It's my private sitting room. As for the locks, it's all the fault of thieves."

"Thieves?"

Tut-tutting, Sir Charles nodded. "You see, a few years ago, a servant made off with a number of valuable objects. They were recovered, of course. And I watched the black-guard hanged by the neck."

Was he giving her a warning? Or was she just imagining that hint of relish in him, as if he were anticipating her aversion? "You're wise to be cautious, then."

"Do have a seat, if you will." He waved at a rush-bottomed chair across from the door. "I'll be back straight-away."

The door began to close behind him, and unable to restrain her curiosity, she moved forward to steal a glance inside. Abruptly, the painted panel flew open again, causing her to stop dead.

Sir Charles poked out his head, his urbane features showing a boyish glee. "No peeking now," he admonished. "Lest you spoil my surprise."

"You're a dastard for keeping me in suspense."

He grinned. "I am indeed a devil."

As he went back inside, the door clicking shut, Kate seated herself on the edge of the chair. A tomblike silence spread over the deserted corridor. Then a muffled screech made her jump.

She pressed her hand to her thumping heart. Had that inhuman noise come from behind the closed door of the sitting room? Had Sir Charles hurt himself? With any luck, it was a fatal injury. Not that fate had been so kind thus far.

Thinking caustic thoughts, she waited, her fingers knotted in her lap. If he brought out the goddess, she mustn't let her wild agitation betray her. She must be prepared to school her face into an expression of polite admiration, even though he would be handing her the means to his downfall.

When the door opened again, Kate stood up gracefully, a civil smile pasted on her mouth. Sir Charles walked out, fairly beaming with merriment. For a moment she stared at him in confusion.

His manicured hands were empty. He carried no golden goddess.

Then someone stepped out from behind him.

Kate froze in absolute, dumfounded shock. There in the doorway, her dainty chin jutted defiantly and her hand clutching Jabbar's, stood her foolish, disobedient sister, Meg.

CHAPTER 20

THE PURLOINED KEY

PETRIFIED with horror, Kate gripped the folds of her skirt. This was her worst nightmare, seeing her sister here at Damson Castle. Questions tumbled pell-mell through her mind. How had Meg eluded the Rosebuds? What had she told Sir Charles? And dear God in heaven, what was Kate to do with her?

"Won't you even say hullo?" Meg asked, a little wobble to her voice. "Jabbar and I have traveled a very long way."

Jabbar. That explained the screech Kate had heard. Aware of Sir Charles's watchful eyes, she walked forward and jerked her sister into an embrace, her dismay intensified by Meg's trusting warmth. "What are you doing here?" Kate said in a raspy whisper. "I'm astonished . . ."

"So you are," Sir Charles said, rubbing his palms together. "She is my recently acquired treasure. I must say, Miss Talisford, the expression on your face was priceless."

As the baron stepped closer, Jabbar emerged from behind Meg's skirts and hooted a warning at Sir Charles. With leathery fists, the chimpanzee beat on his small, hairy chest.

"Pray excuse his behavior," Meg said to Sir Charles. Scooping up the animal, she hugged him close. "Quiet, dearest. Sir Charles won't hurt you. He's a very kind gentleman to take us in at short notice."

The baron chuckled. "I daresay, the little nipper is jealous of me."

Clinging to Meg's neck, Jabbar lowered his complaint

to a mutter as his dark eyes continued to glower at Sir Charles.

The little interlude had given Kate a chance to hide her trembling dread. She had to ascertain if any damage had been done. "How long have you been here?" she asked her sister.

"Not half an hour before you came upstairs."

Sir Charles nodded. "I was positively overjoyed when the gatekeeper sent word of her arrival. I went down there myself to escort her inside."

Meg gazed cautiously at Kate. "Sir Charles asked me to wait here. He said he wished to surprise you."

Kate was more than surprised. She was shocked, aghast, and afraid. The first order of business was to spirit Meg away before she said anything damning, such as asking after Gabriel.

If she hadn't done so already.

Kate took hold of her sister's arm. In a severe tone, she said, "Come along to my chamber, please. You and I have matters to discuss."

Meg balked. "You mustn't send me home. Sir Charles has already given me permission to stay for the ball to-night."

Crossing his arms over his apple-green coat, the baron smiled indulgently. "Indeed I did. Such a lovely girl as you will be an unparalleled success with the *ton*."

Meg lifted eager blue eyes to him. "Do you truly think so?"

"I know so. You'll dance with every man present. You'll have a veritable entourage of admirers."

His high-handedness infuriated Kate, and she fought to keep her voice even. "I'm afraid I must disagree. My sister is far too young to attend this party."

"But it's my seventeenth birthday today," Meg said plaintively. "Have you forgotten?"

Amid all the intrigue, Kate *had* forgotten. She felt a treacherous softening at her sister's woebegone expression, the tearful eyes and the jutting lower lip. Poor Meg. How left out she must have felt, having no family there to celebrate with her.

Yet how dangerous a dilemma her rebelliousness had created.

"If you'll excuse us, Sir Charles," Kate said, "I really must speak to my sister alone."

"As you wish," he said, bowing to them. "But let me add, there's a storm brewing to the west. I shouldn't like to see a lady set out in a coach in such uncertain weather."

Shivering, Meg sent Kate an appealing look. "You know how afraid I am of lightning and thunder. Won't you *please* let me stay?"

The added impetus of a rainstorm pushed Kate into a corner. What other choice did she have? None, she thought bleakly. None at all. "All right, then," she forced out. "But you must promise to behave yourself."

"I will. You're the best sister in the *world*." Her eyes shining, Meg threw her free arm around Kate, drawing her against Jabbar, who babbled happily and patted Kate on the shoulder.

A tangle of emotion caught at her breast. Tenderness, for she had missed her sister's companionship and cheerful chatter. Anxiety, for when Kate returned here tonight to search for the statue, she would have to leave Meg with Lady Stokeford. And fear, for Meg didn't know the terrible risk she had taken by coming here.

She had to be told, Kate knew. It was the only way Kate could protect her sister. Then Meg would realize that the man standing with them, smiling so affably, had murdered their father.

* * *

"MY very first ball," Meg sang, pirouetting in front of the mirror while admiring her gown of royal-blue sarcenet. "I can scarcely believe it's about to begin."

"You look like a princess," Lady Stokeford said. "Both of you do."

The dowager's fond gaze encompassed Kate, who sat on a stool in her ladyship's dressing room while Betty tamed her unruly curls into a presentable style. Usually, Kate envied Meg her smooth black hair, which was caught up in an elegant chignon that showed off her swanlike neck. At the same time, she was proud of Meg's beauty. But tonight, she wished fervently that her sister looked like a hag.

"Is this bodice too high?" Meg asked, tugging at it. "I don't want anyone to think I'm just out of the schoolroom."

"They *should* know," Kate said tartly. "After all, it's the truth."

High color tinted Meg's fair face. But she also had a determined gaiety of manner. "Tra-la, tra-la. I'll look as fine as these London ladies."

"You'll look finer, for none of them are as young and beautiful as you are," Lady Stokeford said sagely. "And beware, their claws will be out tonight."

"As for the gentlemen," Kate said, thinking of the Lucifer League, "you must take care not to let any one of them lure you from the ballroom."

"Gentlemen of the *ton*," Meg said, pressing her hand to her bosom. "At the mere thought, my heart is beating so fast I vow I may swoon."

Kate exchanged a worried glance with Lady Stokeford. The dowager had received a frantic message from the other Rosebuds, alerting her to Meg's disappearance. She'd sent a prompt reply informing Lady Faversham and Lady Enid of Meg's safe arrival and asking them to wait at Fairfield Park, for they would all be journeying there on the morrow.

"These men are gamblers and rakes," the dowager said. "They are not to be trifled with."

"They're only men," Meg said with a careless wave of her fan. "I'm not afraid of any of them. Not even Sir Charles."

Kate had told her sister an abbreviated version of the truth, that Gabriel was posing as a footman in an attempt to gather proof to apprehend Sir Charles. Meg had been shocked and disbelieving, unwilling to accept that such an elegant aristocrat could be a thief and a murderer. She'd been fretful and sullen for a while, and now her breezy manner troubled Kate.

Conscious of Betty's listening ears, she rose from the stool and dismissed the maid, sending her out to the bedchamber. Then she took Meg by the hands, fiercely wishing that her headstrong sister had not been so foolish as to enter this viper's nest. "Remember what I told you, Meg. Sir Charles might appear to be a fine gentleman, but he is responsible for Papa's death."

Her lips pursed, Meg drew her hands free. "You've already said so, but . . . surely I can be pleasant to him. He's shown me nothing but courtesy."

"Men are often not what they seem to be," Lady Stokeford said, coming to stand beside them. With her snowy hair and the pale blue silk that matched her eyes, she looked like a wise old angel. "You must be especially cautious of their flattery and compliments."

"And if you don't behave as you're told, you'll be banished here with Jabbar," Kate said sternly. "Is that understood?"

A faintly rebellious spark shone in Meg's blue eyes. But to Kate's relief, her sister looked away and nodded.

"Excellent," Lady Stokeford said, linking arms with both of them, her finely wrinkled face blooming with vivacity. "Now, shall we all go down and join the party?"

* * *

COLLECTING empty champagne glasses in the ballroom, Gabe kept his back turned to the throng of guests.

He had been assigned to clean-up duties, much to his annoyance. It was all due to his bogus confession to Agnes Swindon. To put an end to her lustfulness once and for all, he'd told her bluntly that he preferred boys.

He'd rather enjoyed her shriek of disgust. As for the chores she'd heaped on him in retaliation, he had no intention of completing them all. Only this one, because he needed to assure himself that Kate was safely ensconced at the party while he did his skulking.

Where the devil was she?

Crouching to wipe a puddle of spilled champagne from the parquet floor, he imagined he caught a whiff of her flowery scent. His blood heated, but he clamped his teeth and finished his task. Then he sensed movement beside him. Jerking his head around, he saw dainty slippers, a sea-green gown, and a shapely feminine form that caused an instantaneous, combustible reaction in his body.

Kate frowned down at him. "Gabriel. I must speak to you."

He muttered, "It isn't safe and well you know it."

"This is important. Meg is here."

If she'd drawn a pistol, he couldn't have been more shocked. He sprang to his feet, motioning her to step into an alcove behind a grouping of leafy ferns. "The devil you say—"

"It's true. She ran away from Stokeford Abbey. She's over there in the doorway with your grandmother."

Biting off a curse, he slid a glance over the fancy, gilded ballroom with its tall pillars and glittering chandeliers. The orchestra was tuning its instruments, and the guests were gathering in the center in preparation for the dancing, but thankfully, the bushy foliage half hid him and Kate. To his anger and alarm, he spied an animated, dark-haired Meg by the doorway, already surrounded by men.

He snapped his attention back to Kate. "Does she know about Damson?"

Her small white teeth sinking into her lower lip, she nodded. "I had to warn her. Though I said little about our plan. I let her think we were here only to spy on Sir Charles."

"Blast it all." Gabe started to run his fingers through his hair, remembered the cursed wig, and made a fist instead. "Tonight is my last chance to find the statue. If she gets in the way, it could be a disaster."

"She won't." Kate's beautiful green eyes studied him. "Did Ashraf get the keys made?"

"They're in my pocket."

"When are you going upstairs?"

Wheeling around, he pretended to busy himself with the tray of glassware. "Later," he lied. "After the dancing is well under way. In fact, I don't think I can get away until suppertime."

"But that's midnight," she exclaimed.

"Yes. I've a lot of duties tonight." He would head upstairs right after he left this tray in a convenient closet. But Kate didn't need to know that. She'd only interfere and endanger herself. And distract him.

As she was distracting him now.

She moved closer. So close that her body brushed against his with spectacular results. "I want to go with you."

"No," he muttered. "Now get away from me. Before someone sees us together."

"No one can see us behind all this foliage." She touched his sleeve, stroking him in a beguiling dance. "Please, Gabriel, take me along."

"It isn't safe. Just watch over your sister."

"Lady Stokeford will do so." Her fingers slipped in between his arm and his coat, rubbing up and down his side. "You can't go without me. I want to be with you."

Her words were spark to his tinder. He burned to toss her over his shoulder, carry her off to the nearest bed, and show her in no uncertain terms who was in charge. Damn the minx for using her seductive powers on him.

"Miss Talisford. How lovely you look this evening."

Bent over the tray, Gabe froze. That deep, sardonic male voice sounded naggingly familiar . . .

"Lord Faversham," Kate said warmly. "What a pleasure to see you."

Gabe went rigid. Brand Villiers. He'd seen the scoundrel's name on the guest list, but until now, hadn't encountered him.

Kate moved away, and with any luck, Brand would think she'd just set down an empty glass. That is, unless Gabe swung around as he hungered to do, and warned Brand that Kate was off limits.

Only the memory of the statue stopped him. Tonight was his last chance to have revenge on Damson. Playing the decorous servant, Gabe stiffly picked up his tray of glasses and walked away.

"THAT footman looks familiar," Lord Faversham said musingly. His gray eyes narrowed, he stared after Gabriel, who moved through the crowd of guests as if he belonged among them.

Kate's heart gave a jolt. It wasn't inconceivable that the earl might see through Gabriel's disguise. According to Lady Stokeford, Brandon Villiers had grown up knowing the Kenyons, though he had been of an age with Gabriel's brother Michael. "Do you mean Whitcombe?" she said carelessly. "He serves at the Abbey, so perhaps you've seen him there."

He raised a dark brow. "Perhaps."

Kate tried to gauge his reaction. Did he believe her? She couldn't be certain. The best thing to do was to change the subject. "Are you enjoying the party, my lord?"

A faint smile touched his scarred mouth. "What's more the question, are you?"

His knowing gaze dropped to her hand. In instinctive alarm, she made a move to hide her closed fingers behind her back.

The earl's hand flashed out, snaring her wrist. She stiffened, trying to draw back. But with a calm, relentless touch, he opened her gloved fingers and plucked out an object. He held it up to the candlelight, turning the slender bit of metal in his long fingers.

"A key," he said with sham surprise. "Fancy that."

"I . . ." Though her heart was pounding, she affected a laugh. "I forgot I was carrying the key to my chamber. How silly of me."

She reached out, but he closed his fingers, locking the key inside his big palm. Short of wrestling him, she couldn't get at it.

"I saw you take this out of Whitcombe's pocket." His charcoal-gray eyes, rife with cynical amusement, glinted at her. "Is the proper Miss Talisford making assignations with the help?"

So that was it. He thought her a strumpet. She ought to go along with the handy explanation, for she desperately needed that key. Yet her pride rebelled at being classified as having the morals of the *ton*.

Meeting his stare, she coolly extended her hand. "I'll thank you to give that back to me."

He didn't move. His saturnine face hinted at secrets that should make any decent woman run away screaming. But Kate held her ground. She couldn't depend on Gabriel to find the statue, especially as he intended to delay until midnight. If he waited too long, the male guests might go up to the study.

Men like Lord Faversham.

After a moment, much to her surprise, he gently placed the key in her palm. Closing her fingers around it, he brought her fist up to his mouth and kissed her knuckles. Then he made a mocking bow. "May I offer you one piece of advice, Miss Talisford?"

She stood in a dignified pose, cloaking her jubilation at having the key, though quickly slipping it inside her glove. "Go ahead. But don't expect me to follow it."

Rather than laugh, he gave her an intense, sober look. "My advice is that you and your sister depart from here at once. And never return."

CHAPTER 21

A Narrow Escape

MEG felt the music shimmer through her veins, sparkling inside her like the champagne she'd sipped for the first time in her seventeen years.

Hundreds of twinkling candles veiled the ballroom in a golden sheen of light. It didn't matter that old Uncle Nathaniel had insisted on partnering her for the first dance. It didn't matter because the other noblemen were watching her with admiring glances. Graceful as a swan, she performed the complicated steps of the country dance, dipping and swaying to the airy tune played by the musicians, her slippers floating over the shiny parquet floor. Her heart soared with the certainty that she'd found her rightful place in the world, here in the fellowship of the *ton*.

When she'd walked into the ballroom, Sir Charles had taken her by the hand and announced the celebration of her birthday to the entire company. The adjacent supper room held a three-tiered cake iced with pink roses in her honor. The gentlemen had thronged around her, handsome, worldly aristocrats vying for a scrap of her attention. She, Margaret Anne Talisford, a rustic nobody who had grown up in a simple cottage!

At the head of the line, Kate danced with Sir Charles. For a moment, Meg's good humor soured, and she wanted to stick out her tongue at her sister. It wasn't fair that Kate, who harbored such a mean opinion of Sir Charles, had been granted the honor of the first dance with him. Kate was always suspicious of people, always overly protective, always certain she knew best.

But Meg knew that if she displayed one smidgen of rebellion, her stern sister would send her straight back to Lady Stokeford's chamber, there to sit alone while everyone else had fun. Meg would let nothing mar the perfection of this marvelous evening.

With determined vivacity, she turned her gaze to Kate's partner. Fair-haired and lordly, Sir Charles Damson was the epitome of a London gentleman in his pale blue coat and matching pantaloons. His elegant cravat cascaded like a waterfall from his throat. Meg thought he looked as dashing and intense as a poet, as polished and proficient as a courtier.

He simply *couldn't* be a thief and a murderer. His manner was too well-bred, his behavior too refined. Blue-blooded aristocrats didn't commit crimes, especially not against her dear papa.

Papa. Sometimes Meg feared she'd forgotten his face, and she'd strain to recall him by bits and pieces. The kindly blue eyes magnified by his spectacles. His scent of pipe smoke and dusty artifacts. The threadbare cuffs of his favorite brown coat.

Tears threatened, but Meg blinked them away. She couldn't imagine anyone but a vicious, horrid criminal killing her papa. Kate had made a dreadful mistake, that was all. After her sister had watched Sir Charles for a while, she would realize her error of judgment.

As the dance drew to a close, Uncle Nathaniel bowed to Meg. "I'll take you back to Lucy now," he said, his eyes twinkling. "No doubt you'll be wanting to dance with the young bucks, instead of a creaky old gent like me."

"Yes . . . no!" Meg exclaimed, afraid she'd hurt his feelings. "I enjoyed our dance very much!"

Impulsively, she hugged him, liking his scent of shaving

soap. Uncle Nathaniel hadn't been around much in her childhood, only popping in for a visit every few years. But he was a merry gentleman and rather handsome with his thick white hair and courtly, old-fashioned manners.

Chuckling, he released her. "You make me wish for my youth again. The days when the prettiest girl was always mine."

As they strolled through the throng, Meg realized he was smiling rather pensively at Lady Stokeford, who stood in conversation with a group of ladies. An amazing thought took root in Meg. Was her great-uncle in love with the dowager marchioness of Stokeford? Would their pretend betrothal become truth?

The notion filled her with delight, for she liked Lady Stokeford, who had welcomed her with the warmth of a grandmother. It was due to her ladyship's intervention that Meg had so many pretty dresses to wear, including this midnight-blue sarcenet that made her feel like a true lady of fashion.

A tall man with a headful of russet curls stepped into her path, flashing his large white teeth in a smile. "Hark! I see an angel standing before me."

A short, stocky young man with intense brown eyes approached from her left side. "I beg your guardian to introduce us, fair lady."

Even as Uncle Nathaniel opened his mouth to speak, yet another handsome gentleman swept an extravagant bow. "May I offer you many happy returns of the day."

Surrounded by admirers, Meg laughed from sheer happiness. It was her birthday! She was a woman now. She could have suitors and flirtations, kisses and courtships. How pleasing it would be to accept love letters and poems written by ardent gentlemen. She might even receive a marriage proposal or two.

"There you are, Miss Margaret," Sir Charles said, step-

ping past the other men to take her gloved hand in his.
"May I have the honor of this dance?"

A fluttery excitement took wing in her stomach. The
baron's warm gaze made her feel special, and Meg only
just restrained herself from blurting out an assent. She
mustn't appear too eager.

She coyly looked up at Uncle Nathaniel. "May I?"

Uncle Nathaniel didn't respond with his usual alacrity,
and Meg was afraid that he too believed the worst of Sir
Charles. What if he denied the request? Dizzy with anticipation, she held her breath.

Then he nodded, although Meg noticed a troubled expression on his weathered face.

With steadfast gaiety, she put him out of her mind. Sir
Charles had singled her out for his attention! The mere
touch of his gloved fingers on hers as he led her to the
dance floor was enough to make her heart beat faster.

They joined the line of dancers forming in the center of
the ballroom. The music began, the sprightly melody stirring her blood. Sir Charles was much older than her, at
least in his middle thirties, but that fact only enhanced his
glamour. No doubt, he had courted many women. He had
kissed them . . . perhaps even on the mouth. What would it
be like to have those male lips pressed to hers? The daring
thought made her giddy.

As the dance steps brought him closer, his admiring blue
eyes held hers. "You are the most exquisite woman here,
Margaret. May I be so bold as to address you so famil-
iarly?"

"Yes, please! But my family calls me Meg."

"I prefer Margaret. It suits the virtuous maiden that you
are."

Though she'd always thought her full name to be staid
and dull, Sir Charles made it sound as if it belonged to a
medieval princess. Indeed, she felt like royalty, gliding

around him as he bowed to her in accordance with the dance. "Perhaps from now on," she said, "I shall tell everyone to call me Margaret."

"Or you might allow me alone that honor." He deftly caught her hand, drawing her closer. As they stepped in a circle, his amorous gaze bewitched her. "If you'll permit me, Margaret, I'd like to show you my castle later. We could become better acquainted."

For a moment, she forgot to breathe. Did Sir Charles mean to pay her court? Should she let him? Her most cherished dream was happening so fast . . .

Then Meg remembered her vow to Kate. And Lady Stokeford's warning: *Men are often not what they seem to be.* "I—I don't know if that would be wise."

"My dear girl, rest assured that my intentions are honorable. You'll be quite safe in my company."

"But I promised my sister . . ."

"Then don't tell her," Sir Charles whispered in her ear, his warm breath making her shiver. "It'll be our little secret."

UPSTAIRS in the shadowed study, Gabe swore under his breath as he turned his pockets inside out. The rumble of distant thunder made a counterpoint to the anger that resounded in him. By the meager light of the candle, he scanned the plush gold-and-blue carpet.

The blasted key had vanished.

Time was running short; already he'd been delayed in the kitchens by Mrs. Swindon. Finally, he had come up here only to discover he had two keys instead of three— the one to the study and another to an ornate sitting room that he'd explored a few moments ago, without finding the goddess.

He was missing the key to Damson's private bedchamber.

It could be anywhere. Down in the kitchen . . . in a dim-lit corridor . . . in the ballroom . . .

The ballroom.

With a jolt, he remembered Kate standing close to him, asking to go with him, smoothing her hand over his coat as if to coax him to her purpose. Ever since their encounter in her bedchamber, she'd acted cool toward him, and her unexpectedly seductive manner had sucked him into the quicksand of lust. Once again, he'd been gulled.

Intending to find her, he stalked out into the gilded corridor. A sound stopped him. A quiet click from the direction of Damson's bedchamber.

Gabe pinched out the candle flame and melted into the shadows. A flash of lightning lit the empty passageway in either direction.

He'd heard a door opening; he was sure of it. Was it Figgins on an errand? Damson, answering a call of nature?

Or Kate, disobeying him again?

Gabe stood perfectly still, listening. As the minutes ticked by and he heard only the occasional grumble of thunder, he drew the dueling pistol from inside his coat and crept down the corridor. Outside Damson's bedchamber, he paused, his muscles taut.

The ornate door that had been locked only moments ago now stood slightly ajar.

THE candle cast a small circle of light as Kate tiptoed through the vast, shadowy bedchamber. She could scarcely contain her excitement at having had the good luck to possess the right key. Shrouded in dark hangings, a massive four-poster bed loomed to her left. To her right, she could discern several low, Roman-style couches arranged in a circle with large pillows scattering the center, as if Sir Charles liked to loll on the floor. Kate puzzled over that oddity for only an instant; then she turned her thoughts to finding the goddess.

The feeble candlelight frustrated her. Spying a lamp on a low table by the ring of sofas, she lifted the glass chimney, using the taper to light the oil-soaked wick. A blessed brightness banished the gloom at this end of the chamber, at least.

Only then did she notice the artifacts lying on the table. She frowned, baffled by their purpose: smooth, sausagelike objects carved from either dark wood or pale ivory.

Turning her gaze away, she inspected the rest of the room. On the shelves that abutted the black onyx fireplace stood a collection of figurines. Walking closer, she saw they were naked men and women locked in scandalous positions. A flush suffused her. In defiance of decency, her imagination conjured images of her and Gabriel engaged in these forbidden, carnal activities.

Appalled at herself, she moved briskly away, her slippers making no sound on the soft Persian carpet. She must hurry. Although Lady Stokeford would make excuses for her absence from the ball, Kate didn't want to stir suspicion in Sir Charles. Nor did she wish to chance him popping in here and surprising her.

Lord Faversham's words came back to haunt her. *My advice is that you and your sister depart from here at once. And never return.*

What had the earl meant? If he was a member of the Lucifer League, and if they planned to do something wicked . . .

A bone-deep shiver coursed through her. Thank goodness Lady Stokeford and Uncle Nathaniel were keeping a close watch on Meg. But Kate couldn't depart yet. She couldn't leave the castle until she'd accomplished her mission. Sir Charles's threat of guardianship made her all the more desperate.

Where was the goddess?

She made a quick sweep of every tabletop, peering into nooks and crannies where other erotic objects resided. She averted her eyes from the worst of them—humans mating with beasts, and even a marble statue of a woman being ravished by a hideous demon.

What sort of man collected these evil things? With a sickening lurch in her stomach, Kate knew the answer. A man who had stolen her father's greatest discovery. A man who would commit murder.

A man who deserved her rightful revenge.

Angry and frustrated, Kate scanned the gloomy bedchamber. Perhaps the statue had never even been here at Damson Castle. Sir Charles could have left it at his London home. Or elsewhere, for such a wealthy man surely owned other estates.

Then she spied a curtained area in the corner near the bed. A window? Or did it hide a door that led to another chamber?

Hastening forward, she grasped the folds of cloth, the deep blue velvet rich and cool to her fingertips. A shiver swept over her skin, raising the fine hairs at the back of her neck. Then slowly she drew back the draperies.

GABE blessed the well-oiled hinges that allowed him to slip quietly into the bedchamber. Gripping the ivory butt of the pistol, he paused in the shadows by the door. By a curtain in the far corner of the murky chamber, a woman held a lamp aloft.

Kate.

Anger constricted his chest; a violent heat assailed his loins. The lamplight made her skin glow like alabaster. She looked delicate and sweet, but he knew her to be strong and keen-witted. And far too disobedient for her own good.

As she parted the curtains, he stalked toward her, his

footfalls muffled by the thick carpet. Then he stopped again, frozen.

Instead of a window, the draperies hid an arched alcove. Within stood a marble pedestal holding an exquisite golden figurine.

The goddess.

Jeweled loops adorned the ears, and rose quartz gems marked the tips of her generous breasts. The essence of sensuality, she cupped her slender belly, her fingertips caressing an enormous yellow diamond nestled at the top of her thighs.

The air seared his lungs. He'd last seen the statue in Cairo more than two months ago. But not even a flood of elation could drown his ire. "My compliments," he snapped.

Kate whirled around. "Gabriel!"

He shoved the pistol inside his coat. "You stole the key. After I gave you strict orders not to come here."

"But I found the statue. Aren't you glad?"

"I'm glad you weren't caught." He stepped toward her, seizing her upper arms. "Blast you! Damson killed your father. If he found you here, he'd kill you, too."

Memory hurled him back to that darkened chamber at the inn, to Henry Talisford lying dead in a pool of blood. Gabe broke out in a cold sweat to imagine Kate doomed to the same end. He couldn't fail her as he'd failed her father.

"Papa died for the goddess," she said fiercely. "I intend to use the statue to have my revenge."

"You shouldn't have come here alone. That was foolish, Kate. Damned foolish."

"I don't care. Only the goddess matters to me." Pulling away, she whirled around to regard the statue.

The hell of it was, he could understand her angry ambition. It was the same ambition that had spurred him ever since he'd awakened in a hospital bed, his back throbbing with pain, his thoughts dark with hatred.

Yet now he cared more for Kate's safety. He felt an affinity for her that he'd never felt for any other woman. Not even the goddess was worth Kate's life.

Stepping past her, he picked up the statue. The heavy artifact felt almost warm and alive in his hands. He let his exaltation come to the fore. At last he had it. The proof of Damson's treachery.

Holding the lamp, Kate leaned over his arm to get a better look. "She's beautiful. Papa's treasure."

With studied care, Gabe set the statue back on the pedestal. "And the means to Damson's destruction."

Kate's eyes glittered in the lamplight. "Oh, Gabriel, we've done it. By morning, Sir Charles will be locked in prison, awaiting trial for murder."

His gaze clung to hers, and the joy there altered into something softer, a budding sensual awareness that he found more intoxicating than wine. Need overriding logic, he took a step toward her.

She cocked her head to the side. "Listen!"

Amid the growling of thunder, the sound of approaching voices came from the outer corridor.

Gabe blew out the lamp. Then he thrust her into the alcove, yanking the curtain closed.

There was barely enough room for the two of them. Kate sidled into the corner, and he pressed himself against her until they were wedged between the cold stone wall and the pedestal. His heartbeat surged, as much from an untimely arousal as the danger of discovery.

Velvety darkness enclosed them. His jaw rested against her soft curls, and he breathed in her light, feminine essence. Her lithe form imprinted him, small shoulders, slender waist, rounded bottom. When she made a slight shift of position, her hip brushed against his stiffened cock. It was madness to fantasize about making love to her. Yet his imagination played out ways he could take her standing, drawing up her skirts, parting her legs, lifting her onto him—

A faint rattling sound jerked him back to reality. The outer door opened and feet tramped inside. "It wasn't locked, I tell you," said a sharp female voice. Agnes Swindon. "You were up here last. You must have forgotten to secure the door."

"Shut yer blinkin' trap," a man growled. "And stand back. There could be thieves in here." Figgins.

His muscles tensed, Gabe spied a faint light beneath the curtains. He could hear the valet skulking around the bedchamber, peering into cupboards and creeping through the adjacent dressing room. Then the light beneath the draperies brightened as Figgins approached.

Quietly, Gabe drew his pistol.

AT the start of the next dance, Lucy paired Meg with another partner. None of these wastrels were suitable company for an innocent girl, Lucy knew, but after tonight, Meg needn't encounter them again. Noting the sparkling enjoyment on the girl's face, she allowed herself a wistful smile.

How wonderful to be so young and carefree. Let the girl flirt all she liked within the confines of the crowded ballroom. She was safe so long as she remained here, under Lucy's strict vigilance.

Sir Charles Damson was leading the Egyptian woman, Yasmin, out to the dance floor. Lucy's gaze hardened on them. How gentlemanly he appeared to be, the perfect host. But she knew from the wisdom of years that depravity came in all guises. She had long relied on feminine intuition in determining the character of a man. In only one instance had perception confused her . . .

Someone goosed her on the waist, and Lucy whirled around, an icy reprimand poised on her tongue. Her anger turned to pique when she spied the ruggedly handsome face of her nemesis. "Nathaniel Babcock. Kindly keep your hands to yourself."

"And spoil our pretense?" His manner jaunty, Nathaniel slid his arm through hers, weaving their fingers together. "Come walk with me, my darling. We'll steal a few moments alone. People expect an engaged couple to behave as lovebirds."

Though her heart beat faster, Lucy balked. "We mustn't leave the ballroom."

"Ah, Meg will be fine. We'll hear when the music stops."

This time, when he drew her toward the arched doorway, she let him lead her out into the echoing expanse of the grand corridor. Like the rest of the castle, it had an aura of lush drama, the high ceiling painted as a midnight sky strewn with stars, the candles in the wall sconces adding to the illusion of twinkling lights. Yet upon closer inspection, gargoyles and demons lurked in dark corners as if waiting to pounce. The sight made Lucy shudder.

She was glad for Nathaniel's companionship, for it distracted her from the ever-present worries. His playful nature was evident in the deep creases around his blue eyes and sensual mouth. She'd enjoyed the pretense of being his fiancée more than she could have imagined. It had brought to mind the days of yore, when they had carried on a light flirtation that had never quite deepened into love.

Nathaniel had always kept himself just beyond her reach. Half a century ago, he had teased her with flowery compliments instead of heartfelt truths, involved her in mischievous pranks rather than serious conversations.

Intrigued, she gazed up at him. What lay in his heart?

The shallowness of a rake? Or the fascinating depths she had glimpsed in him from time to time?

The muted sound of music drifted from the ballroom. As they strolled arm in arm into a small, dim-lit chamber, he looked at her and cocked a white eyebrow. "There's a mystery in that smile of yours, Lucy."

"I was remembering the time we went up to the roof and dripped water on the departing guests," she improvised. "The Duke of Devonshire swore it was raining."

"Though there was nary a cloud in the starry sky." They shared a laugh as Nathaniel guided her onto a chaise and sat down beside her. "We did have some good times. My biggest regret is that I wasn't there the night you became a Rosebud."

Lucy smiled to recall how as débutantes, she and Enid and Olivia had had the madcap notion to put rouge on their nipples. They hadn't stopped to consider the ballroom would be sweltering, or that the color would bleed through their white bodices. In the ensuing whirl of male attention, all three of them had become betrothed to dashing young aristocrats.

If Nathaniel had been there, might she have chosen him, instead?

It served no purpose to speculate. They were here only to help Kate and Gabriel achieve justice in the death of Professor Talisford. Even now, Kate was upstairs, searching for the statue. Lucy breathed a little fervent prayer for her success. And then another, that Gabriel would find Kate.

As if he'd seen into her thoughts, Nathaniel growled, "I've a good mind to go after Kate."

Lucy curled her fingers around his sleeve. "Don't you dare. She has Gabriel to protect her."

"Bah. I've seen the way he looks at her. He wants to seduce her."

"I pray he does." Ignoring his sputter of angry incre-

dulity, Lucy said calmly, "I've high hopes for a match between the two of them. That's why I told Betty to stay away
from the tower chamber tonight. If my grandson has any
wits at all, he'll take advantage of the opportunity."

Nathaniel bristled. "The devil you say. I won't allow the
cad to ruin my grandniece."

"Pish-posh. Gabriel will marry her, of course. He *must*."
Lucy made an airy wave of her gloved fingers. "So save
your blustering, Nathaniel. Not every man is like you."

As the barb struck, his eyes widened slightly, giving her
another tantalizing glimpse into his depths. He recovered
swiftly, a rakish grin tilting his mouth. "You always were
a tart-tongued beldam. 'Tis no wonder you've never taken
a lover."

"How do you know I haven't?" she retorted. "Perhaps
I've had dozens."

He chuckled, his shrewd gaze sweeping over her
powder-blue gown and styled white hair. "I recognize a
woman with principles. You've never been touched by any
man but your husband."

His direct gaze demanded the truth from her, and she
gave it in a roundabout manner. "I'm not averse to male
companionship."

"Nor I to the company of an intelligent woman." Lifting
her gloved hand, he kissed the back, never once taking his
compelling gaze from her.

Lucy's heart fluttered. Was he hinting at his desire for
a liaison? No, surely his tastes ran to younger women,
women who had not yet experienced the change of life,
women who didn't have wrinkled skin and sagging breasts
and great-grandchildren.

She extracted her hand. "So long as the woman is
wealthy, and willing to support you in the manner to which
you are accustomed."

He winced. "Such a cold woman you've become, Lucy.

There was a time when you looked on me with favor."

"That was before you frolicked off to Paris with the widowed Lady Ramsgate."

His deeply chiseled features showed amusement rather than shame. "So you even recall her name."

"Only because she was twice your age and opened her legs as easily as her purse strings."

He threw back his head and laughed. "By jings, what a memory you have. I wonder what else you recollect?" That impish light in his gaze, he sidled closer to her, his fingers stroking the nape of her neck. "I seem to recall a moonlit garden, an arbor of roses—"

"Honeysuckle."

"Ah, yes, I remember it well, that honeysuckle. And a sweet young girl who'd never been kissed."

His large hands settled over her shoulders. Lucy didn't protest; she couldn't protest. She was too enraptured by the memory of stealing outside with a dashing rake, nearly swooning at her first taste of a man's lips . . .

Nathaniel touched his mouth to her brow. "Lucy," he murmured. "My dear Lucy. If I hadn't gone off to Paris, perhaps we would have wed."

She shook her head. "You aren't the marrying sort."

"Then tell me why I've been pining for you all these years."

For once in her life, Lucy couldn't think of a single thing to say. He took her in his arms, and his tender embrace stirred a mélange of feelings in her, hope and yearning and excitement. Oh, she had missed a man's attentions. It had been so many years since her husband's death; she'd raised her son and then her grandsons, suppressing the ache of loneliness, making herself believe she needed only the companionship of the Rosebuds.

But now she wondered. Was she foolish to long for love at her advanced age?

Then she noticed something alarming. "The music has stopped."

"Let's make our own, then," Nathaniel murmured in her ear.

"Scoundrel," she said, slapping him away and rising to her feet. "We must see to Meg."

Grumbling, he escorted her back to the ballroom. There was a swagger to his manner that demonstrated his pleasure at their revitalized closeness. But did Nathaniel truly care for her? Or did he simply want another rich widow to gull?

Distractedly, Lucy looked around the ballroom for her charge. But she couldn't spy dark-haired Meg anywhere in the milling throng.

Her buoyant mood altered to a burgeoning dread, and she lifted her gaze to Nathaniel's grim features. "Dear heavens. She's gone."

"So is Sir Charles Damson."

CHAPTER 22

THE LIGHT IN THE WINDOW

"YOU forgot to lock the master's chambers again," Mrs. Swindon accused, her voice slightly muffled beyond the curtained alcove. "When Sir Charles hears about your carelessness—" Her words ended in a choking gasp.

"Ye won't live to tell the tale, bitch."

With a jolt, Gabe realized the valet was throttling the housekeeper.

Huddled against him, Kate shivered. Gabe swore silently, viciously, his grip tightening on the pistol. In a moment, he'd have to burst out of their hiding place and stop the bastard. And ruin their plan to snare Damson.

Thankfully, there came a muffled thump as Figgins released Mrs. Swindon. Her ragged breaths rasped through the chamber.

"Say one word to the master," Figgins snarled, "and I'll gut your innards and throw 'em over the cliff to the fish."

"I . . . won't," the housekeeper muttered hoarsely.

Kate let out a whispery sigh of relief. Gabe held her close, rubbing his cheek against her hair. She responded to the comforting gesture by lifting her face to him, her hands seeking his collar and gripping hard. Her mouth was so close he could feel the warmth of her breath.

Outside the alcove, Agnes Swindon coughed. "Mr. Figgins," she said in a much subdued tone, "there's no need for threats. Haven't I always kept your little secrets?"

His guttural laugh slithered past the curtain. "Ye don't know my secrets."

"There was that serving maid you ravished here while the master was away."

"Bide yer tongue. Lest I blacken yer eye like I did hers." Drawers opened and closed. "Where's that tin of goose grease? The master wants it put downstairs."

"Bottom drawer." The housekeeper's footsteps scuffled over the carpet; then there were more rummaging sounds. "Here 'tis. Oooh, Mr. Figgins!" she squealed. "You pinched me!"

"That'll teach ye to wiggle yer bum in me face."

"You used to like my bum. Remember?" In an abrupt switch, a slavish seductiveness entered her voice. "Mayhap you'll come to my room. We could play dragon and maiden."

"What of that fancy footman of yers?"

"Whitcombe?" she scoffed. "Huh, I've no interest in *him,* pretty as he is."

"So he refused ye, did he?"

"He has a liking for the lads."

Kate made a sound suspiciously like a giggle.

At the same moment, Figgins guffawed. "Oh-ho! All that simperin' ye did, and he's a buggerin' arse peddler."

"Never mind him," Mrs. Swindon said huffily. "I'd sooner have a real man betwixt the sheets."

"Then lift yer skirts fer me right now."

There was a gasp, then the sound of smacking lips and rustling clothes. Gabe groaned inwardly. If those two went at it right here, he and Kate could be stuck in this alcove while time ticked relentlessly away.

A playful slap resounded. "Mind where you put your hands," Mrs. Swindon said on a giggle. "The master could walk in at any moment."

"He'll join us, then," Figgins said with a nasty laugh. "Though he likes his chickens young and fresh, not tough old birds like ye."

"But you like a seasoned hen," the housekeeper said cajolingly. "Come along, my handsome cock, I'll give you much to crow about in my chambers."

Their voices faded as they tramped out, taking the candle with them. Kate shuddered against Gabe. "I feared they'd never go," she whispered, tucking her face to his high collar.

Velvety blackness enveloped the alcove. Gabe brought his hand up to cup her cheek, rubbing lightly over her satiny skin. An intense rush of feeling flooded him. Relief that she was safe in his arms. The desire to claim her. And something more. Something soft and tender and unmanly. For one wild moment, he forgot that he was holding a pistol, that they stood in an alcove with a stolen statue, that they hid in the bedchamber of a murderer.

Until he tried to get closer to her, and the awkwardness of their position snapped him to his senses.

"Let's go," he said, nuzzling her brow. "It's time to signal Ashraf."

"The light in the window . . . of my bedchamber."

"Yes." By a prearranged signal, when Ashraf saw the lamp burning in the tower window, he would depart the castle and notify Bickell. The Bow Street Runner would obtain a search warrant from a magistrate in the neighboring county. If all went as planned, Damson would be behind bars by morning.

Gabe squeezed out from behind the pedestal and stuck the pistol inside his coat. As he held the curtain aside and Kate stepped into the shadowy bedchamber, he took one last look at the alcove.

He could barely see the statue. Without the benefit of candlelight, the goddess neither glittered nor gleamed. Not even the occasional flash of lightning could penetrate the deep obscurity therein.

Gabe hated like hell to leave the statue. To let it out of

his sight, even for a few hours. But he had no choice.

As they started toward the door, a burst of raindrops spattered the windows. "The storm is worsening," Kate said. "What if Ashraf isn't watching for the signal?"

"He will be."

"The rain could delay him."

"He'll go, anyway. You can count on that."

"You really do trust him."

"With my life." Grasping her hand, he drew her to the door and turned the handle. Locked. "Dammit, they took their key. I hope you have yours."

Through the gloom, he saw Kate reach inside her glove and extract a slender bit of metal. Bending down to unlock the door, she said, "It must be your lucky night, my lord."

His mouth went dry. Kate could have no notion of the hot images evoked by her words. She was too innocent to know.

And he was too jaded to forget that.

Stepping in front of her, he peered into the dim-lit corridor. Figgins and Mrs. Swindon had vanished, and Gabe hoped to hell they were swiving each other blind. It would keep both of them out of the way for a while.

Tense, he walked ahead of Kate. He couldn't shake a core uneasiness. As they went down the passageway, he felt the need to hurry, to get her safely away from here.

They took the broad staircase that curved downward in a gilded stairwell. The far-off strains of music indicated that all the guests were still in the ballroom. It struck Gabe that he'd never danced with Kate, though it seemed they'd known each other forever.

When this was all over, when he shed this damned wig and livery, he'd rectify that omission. That, and others. He'd court her, woo her . . .

His palms broke out in a cold sweat. No, he wouldn't marry Kate or any other woman. Long ago, he'd vowed to avoid that trap. He could pinpoint his aversion to a night when he'd found his drunken father sobbing on the staircase, ready to pour out his troubles with his cold wife to his eleven-year-old son. The burden of those marital secrets had weighed on Gabe, and in time, his shock and bewilderment had given way to a deep-rooted distaste for the institution of matrimony.

Of course, Kate wasn't like his mother, nor was he like his father. He relished Kate's combination of prim spinster and feisty female. He'd harbored fantasies of her writing the book with him, amusing him with her lively conversation . . . and making love with him.

In the wilds of Africa, when he'd lain beneath the starry sky, he'd thought of her, half-girl and half-woman, determined to become his mistress. He'd wanted Kate then, but now he desired her with a single-minded recklessness. More than that, he craved her respect and the impossible dream of her love.

The intensity of his feelings choked him. When this was all over, he'd leave Kate with his grandmother. He'd strike out for the open road, live his life as he pleased, without any encumbrances. He'd forget Kate Talisford, once and for all.

He ushered her down a deserted corridor, where closed doors marked the many guest bedchambers. At last they reached the winding stairs that led to the tower room. One foot on the bottom step, he paused to look back at Kate. The ballgown skimmed the perfection of her slim figure, the bodice cut low over her full breasts. Her lips were parted, her upswept hair tousled as if she were going to meet her lover.

Her lover.

"I'll take care of the signal," Gabe said abruptly. "You should return to the ball, lest Damson become suspicious."

Her fine brows winged together in a frown. "Lady Stokeford will make my excuses."

"As your guardian, I'm telling you to go. Now."

Her spine stiffened. "Sir Charles killed my father. *I* will light that lamp." With that, she brushed past him and marched up the stairs.

Short of throwing her over his shoulder, he couldn't stop her, so he followed in her wake, gazing balefully at the flick of her skirts, the sway of her hips. Didn't she realize the danger of being alone with him? If she had any inkling of the things he'd like to do with her . . .

The circular chamber was dim and shadowed, lit only by the fire smoldering on the tiled hearth. Studiously, he kept his gaze averted from the gauze-draped bed. But he remembered the softness of her skin. The satiny dampness at the juncture of her legs. Her wild cries of delight.

He wanted to make her come alive with passion again. This time, he'd be inside her, sharing the pleasure, binding her to him forever. The urge was so powerful, he ground to a halt in the middle of the room, his lust striking a blow at decency and good judgment.

Kate took a candle from the mantelpiece and bent down to light the taper at the hearth. The gracefulness of her action fed the beast inside him. The flames painted a fiery sheen over her upswept hair, and his fingers itched to pull out those pins, to let her curls ripple down to her waist in a glorious waterfall.

Rising, she went to the bedside table and used the candle to light a brass lamp, which she carried to the third window and set on the stone ledge. The placement of the beacon would tell Ashraf where they'd found the goddess: the first window meant the study, the second indicated Damson's sitting room, the third his bedchamber. The fourth and final window implied a location elsewhere in the castle and signaled Ashraf to wait in the stables for Gabe's instructions.

Gabe wished he had that excuse to leave here.

Lightning flared with an eerie glow, briefly limning Kate's womanly form. As if she'd forgotten his presence, she stood with her back to him, peering out the night-darkened glass.

They had accomplished their purpose to rousing success. Now all they had to do was wait. Somewhere else.

"Kate," he said.

She didn't answer.

A certain rigidity in her bearing lured him to her. His footfalls silent, he walked to her and laid his hand on her shoulder. Her warm, bare skin delivered a charge of heat to his body. He fought the compulsion to run his hands all over her, to find out if she felt so silky everywhere.

"Kate, let's go."

She bowed her head in uncharacteristic silence. As he brought her around to face him, he noticed the luster of tears in her eyes. *Tears.*

She made a move to walk away, but he held her in place. He usually avoided a woman's tears, for they were too often artifice designed to manipulate a man.

But this was Kate. His beautiful, strong, invincible Kate. "What is it?" he asked gruffly. "What's wrong?"

She averted her face. "Nothing."

Cradling her cheeks, he tilted her head up. "Tell me. Please."

Her green eyes formed pools of anguish. She hesitated, then her words tumbled out in a rush. "I never said good-bye to him. To Papa."

Gabe set his jaw. "What happened in Cairo is my fault. Hate me if you must, but don't weep."

"I meant four years ago. On the morning of Papa's departure, I . . . kept to my chamber."

He frowned, thinking back to that sunny dawn. He'd felt a guilty relief at not having to face Kate again, and he'd been filled with high spirits and an eager impatience to set out on an adventure into the unknown. "Of course. You didn't want to see me."

"I didn't want to see Papa." Kate swallowed as if it pained her to speak. "I was so angry at him. He knocked on my door, but I . . . refused to come out and embrace him, to wish him well. I let him go without a single, kind, loving word . . ." Her voice choked to a halt, and a tear rolled down her cheek.

Disabled by tenderness, Gabe put his arms around her, stroking her hair, wishing he knew how to comfort her. "You were distraught. I'm sure your father understood that."

"But if I hadn't been so stubborn . . . so childish . . ."

"You *were* a child," Gabe said roughly. "That's why you shouldn't blame yourself. I know you loved him—"

"Not enough," she cried out. "Never enough."

"More than enough." With his thumb, he caught another tear that trickled down her cheek. "You loved him enough to offer yourself to me. Enough to wish me dead for taking him away."

I loathe you, Gabriel Kenyon. I'll loathe you forever. I hope you die in that jungle!

Her lashes lowered slightly, as if she too were remembering the intensity of her hatred. He wished bleakly that he could do it all over. Back then, she'd been young and impressionable, and if he'd taken her to bed, he could have made her love him, too. Instead, he had inspired her revulsion.

He forced himself to step back. "I must go."

"Where?"

He couldn't let himself be swayed by that wounded, needy look. Or by the fact that they had little to do now but wait. Recalling the nebulous disquiet that had nagged at him, he said, "I'll watch Damson's chambers. Make certain the statue doesn't disappear."

Kate curled her fingers around his arms. "Be careful."

The little catch in her voice disarmed him. Was she truly concerned for his safety? "And if something happened to me?" he found himself asking. "Would it matter to you?"

Her lips parted as if to deliver a tart rejoinder. But she didn't speak, didn't move. She simply gazed at him, her large green eyes conveying an eloquent warmth and a sense of wonderment. He was rendered powerless by that look. Incapable of rational thought. Unable to stop himself from tasting her soft lips.

At that first sizzling touch, he knew he needed more. Much more. Kate did, too, for she trailed eager fingers over his face and chest, sliding her hands inside his coat. Her scent wafted to him, something feminine and infinitely mysterious. He drank deeply of her, his desire flaring with a violence that strained the bonds of his self-control.

He couldn't get enough of her . . . his Kate. She was a fire in his blood, a feast to his starving senses. He surrounded her with his body, his hands memorizing her supple curves. When he moved his lips to her cheek, she arched to him in wanton innocence, her desire toppling his strong defenses.

"God help me," he muttered, the words torn from him. "I want to make love to you, Kate. Here. Now. And damn the consequences."

CHAPTER 23

THE GUARDIAN'S DEMAND

KATE heard him as if through a dream. She loved his embrace, the pressure of his body against hers. This was Gabriel, the man who had fascinated her since girlhood, the man who made her body kindle with the fire of passion.

Yet her mind whispered against him. Nothing but shame could ever come of surrendering to him. Gabriel was a libertine, a reckless adventurer who walked a wild path. He would use her and then go on his merry way.

But would it be so wrong to steal a little pleasure for herself? To just once know the fullness of womanhood? She had been the rational, principled one for so long, and now she wanted to let go, to give in to her yearnings. Before her courage could falter, she murmured, "I want you, too, Gabriel."

He reared back, his eyes a fathomless blue in the dim light. "Enough to go to bed with me?"

"Yes," she said without hesitation.

He studied her with that hard, burning gaze. "I won't just caress you this time, Kate. I'll take your innocence."

"I'll give it to you of my own free will." Reaching up, Kate removed his powdered wig and dropped it onto a nearby hassock. His hair was mussed as if he'd just rolled out of bed. A few dark, sun-kissed strands dipped onto his brow, giving him the appearance of a scoundrel after a long night of sin. Oh, how she wanted to sin with him. She pressed her lips to his jaw, the tip of her tongue flicking out to taste his warm, salty skin.

Inhaling a breath through his teeth, Gabriel caught her face in his palms. "Once we start this, there's no turning back. So for God's sake, tell me to leave."

"I'll die if you leave." Bemused by her audacity, she loosened his cravat, then tugged off the starched linen strip and let it fall to the floor. She slid her fingers inside his collar, shaping her hands around the breadth of his muscled shoulders. Obeying instinct, she pressed her body to his. "Don't refuse me, Gabriel. I'm no longer sixteen."

A wolfish appreciation entered his eyes, the force of his stare raising prickles over her skin. "So you aren't."

With that, he peeled off her long white gloves and kissed the inner crook of her elbow, his mouth nipping at the tender skin he exposed. Infused with delight, Kate bit down on her lip to stifle a gasp.

Turning her, he wrested open the buttons of her gown, then thrust his hands inside, letting the garment slither to the floor in a sea-green puddle. His palms rubbed possessively over her midriff before ascending to her bosom, kneading her through the chemise and corset. As his fingers brushed her flesh, she was helpless to stop a shiver.

"Cold?" he asked, his breath tickling her ear.

A fever burned in her secret depths. A heat born of passion for him. She shook her head. "No," she whispered. "Never with you."

It was true. Gabriel had always possessed the power to awaken her feminine yearnings. She had longed for him since the moment of their first meeting four years earlier, when he'd been an itinerant artist whom Papa had brought home for dinner. Back then, she'd been awestruck by Gabriel's skill with a pen, and she'd dreamed of those clever fingers tracing over her body. As he did now.

He removed her corset and chemise, rendering her naked except for garters and stockings. She gasped when his hungry mouth closed over her breast, his tongue laving her, causing a tension so sharp and sweet she felt on the verge of swooning. He shifted to her other breast, suckling, then blowing lightly on the dampness. The sensation seared like liquid fire down to her most private place, where a gathering moisture left her soft and ready.

But he didn't assuage that primal ache. He unpinned her hair so that it tumbled in an untidy mass down to her waist. Burying his face in the curls, he breathed deeply. "The day I came back to Larkspur Cottage, you had your hair down. I wanted to carry you straight to bed."

He had? Kate remembered how self-conscious she'd felt after Jabbar had stolen her comb, and Gabriel had seen her in unflattering disarray. "My hair is too wild."

He flashed her a roguish smirk. "Wildness becomes you, darling."

With charming subservience, he knelt before her and untied her garter, rolling the wisp of silk stocking down her thigh, over her knee, and off her calf and foot. He did the same to her other leg, kissing her bare skin along the way, finding sensitive spots that she hadn't known existed.

Boneless with desire, she braced her hands on his broad shoulders to keep from dissolving into a pool at his feet. She could scarcely believe that she stood naked before Gabriel, that he could stir such an eager tumult inside her. Crouched on his knees, he looked up at her in an appreciative survey.

A belated flush of vulnerability swept over Kate. Without thinking, she covered herself with her hands.

"You're too lovely to hide." He caught her wrists so that he could view the curves and valleys that no other man had ever seen. "My beautiful, perfect Kate." Leaning forward, he planted a kiss . . . *there.*

A moan of helpless surrender rose from her depths. Her knees buckled, but Gabriel was there to catch her. He stood up, taking her weight against him, his lips nuzzling hers.

The fabric of his coat caused a delightful abrasion against her bare bosom. She felt as if she'd been born for this pleasure, as if she hadn't been truly alive until Gabriel had probed the deep reservoir of passion hidden within her.

He swung her up in his arms and strode to the bed, laying her down on the cool satin coverlet, bending over to kiss her before he drew away again. She opened slumberous eyes to see him stripping off his clothing, his movements feverish, the filmy bedcurtains lending him a dreamlike quality.

Kate rolled onto her side, her breasts heavy beneath the scant protection of her unbound hair. Like a wanton woman, she felt free to fulfill her desires. And all she desired was Gabriel.

She watched hungrily as he shed the footman's disguise, pitching his coat and shirt to the floor. The lamp in the window cast a glow over the sculpted musculature of his shoulders. The sprinkling of dark hair on his chest narrowed to an enticing line that disappeared into the waistband of his breeches. When he placed the dueling pistol on the bedside table, she felt a fierce satisfaction at the success of their mission. Tonight they celebrated their triumph in finding the goddess.

The mattress dipped beneath his weight as he sat down to kick off his shoes and stockings. Only then did she notice his lower back, where several livid scars marred his smooth skin. Newly healed wounds.

Her insides coiled into a painful knot. In that moment she realized how severely he'd been injured on the night of her father's death. And she hadn't trusted his word on that.

Crawling across the bed, she knelt beside him. With trembling fingers, she lightly traced one upraised mark.

He flinched away.

Stricken, Kate drew back her hand. "Did I hurt you?"

His gaze, dark with secrets, flashed over her. "Of course not. You startled me."

Had she reminded him of the attack? Remorseful, she bent down to soothe his scars with her lips. With a little tremor in her voice, she murmured, "You could have died that night, Gabriel."

"Perhaps I should have."

His eyes revealed a stark self-loathing, the proof that he'd endured more than physical wounds. In a rush of understanding, Kate saw beyond the insouciant charmer to the tormented soul inside him. He felt responsible for the tragic events of that night. So acutely that he despised himself.

"You mustn't speak so." Sliding her arms around his bare torso, she pressed her cheek to his warm back and let the words pour from her heart. "I couldn't bear to lose you, too."

She didn't dare try to untangle the powerful emotions that wrenched at her. She knew only that she craved his vitality, his strength. As much as she resisted it, a dangerous thought flitted through her mind. Was she falling in love with Gabriel?

Then she could think no more as he reacted with stunning swiftness. Twisting around, he came down on her, covering her with his hard, virile form. Only his breeches kept him from utter nakedness.

Kate reveled in the sensation of skin against skin, his expansive chest firm against her breasts. As his mouth trapped hers in another long and luscious kiss, she clung to him in trembling anticipation. Looping her arms around his neck, she threaded her fingers into the density of his hair. Though his large body nearly crushed her, she couldn't get close enough to him. She lifted her hips in mindless entreaty, wanting, aching, needing.

"Gabriel, please," she whispered. "Touch me."

"Patience," he murmured against her mouth. "You'll have all you desire . . . and more."

More? How could there be more than the marvelous sensations he'd aroused in her the last time they'd lain in this bed? She wanted him to stroke her again, craved it with an indelicate greed. But he seemed determined to savor the seduction, kissing her breasts and throat and belly, his head bent over her, the lamplight picking out the dark gold strands in his brown hair. Like an adventurer in uncharted territory, he explored every inch of her skin until she squirmed beneath him, her passion mounting to a fever pitch. She explored him, too, seeking out the solid contours of him, so beautifully different from her own softness.

His weight lifting, Gabriel peeled off his breeches and flung them aside. Then he reached for a pillow, yanked off the linen case, and tucked it beneath her.

Half-dazed, she blinked at him. "What—?"

He brushed a tender kiss to her brow. "A woman can bleed a little her first time, love."

Her heart melted at an astonishing revelation. Did he love her? Or did he speak such platitudes to all his women? Then he caressed her between the legs, and any doubts or fears she might have felt vanished in a torrent of intense pleasure. She closed her eyes, giving herself up to his masterful touch. His slow, torturous stroking made her desire coil tighter and tighter, so that she strained upward, her breath coming in panting whimpers. She became a creature of pure sensuality, striving for release from the exquisite tension.

Even as the glorious spasms exploded inside her, his hands grasped her hips to hold her still, and through the extremity of rapture, she felt a heated pressure filling her. With one smooth thrust, he broached the barrier of her virginity. She cried out, the sting of his entry somehow sharpening the fading ripples of pleasure.

Though his chest heaved and his breath came swift and harsh, he held her gently, anointing her face with soft kisses. "I was too rough. Are you in pain?"

"No," Kate sighed, barely able to articulate. "You feel . . . wonderful."

Instinctively, she tilted her hips to take him deeper inside herself. Her hands skimmed up the corded muscles of his back to touch his face, her fingertips absorbing his chiseled features, the stubble of whiskers. The fervor in his gaze reached past the bitterness and pain to a place hidden deep inside her, a place she hadn't known existed until tonight. She felt one with Gabriel in a bond that went beyond the physical act of joining. It was as if their souls had merged as well as their bodies.

He began to move in her, slow and easy. A sheen of sweat dampened his skin, and she sensed the effort it took to hold himself back. In the semi-darkness, his face bore a look of relentless masculinity.

"I've wanted you . . . dreamed of you . . . ever since I found you in my bed four years ago." His lips nuzzled her cheek; then he lifted his hand to brush back her hair and kiss her ear. "You're mine now, Kate. Mine alone."

A wild elation leapt in her. Right or wrong, she rejoiced in his possessiveness. "You're mine, too, Gabriel."

He groaned, his movements surging harder, faster, elevating her to unbearable heights. Clutching at him, she turned her head on the pillow, desperate for release from the surfeit of sensation. At last, when she could bear no more, he reached between them and with one stroke of his hand, she shattered with bliss. She was dimly aware of Gabriel stiffening in the throes of exultation, hoarsely growling her name.

GABE lay in a hedonistic sprawl over Kate. The vast contentment he felt left no room for regrets. He'd lost control, he'd done the unforgivable, he'd taken her virginity. He'd doomed them both with this act. Yet a foolish part of him wanted to crow in triumph.

Shifting slightly, he smoothed his hand over her hip and waist, her skin like warm silk. "Well, Miss Katie. We're quite a match, you and I."

Her long lashes shaded soft green eyes. "Isn't it always . . . like that?"

"It's life's greatest pleasure. But I never thought—" He'd never thought the act could be so earth-shattering with Kate. He'd never imagined he could feel this dangerous need that went beyond the physical. But he couldn't admit that aloud. "I never thought I'd find myself in bed with my ward."

"You're not my guardian," she said rather lazily.

Gabe curved his palm around her breast, a perfect mound of creamy flesh. "Yes I am," he said, his thumb flicking across the pink tip. He watched it tighten, enjoyed her sigh. "And it puts me in a peculiar dilemma."

Contented as a purring cat, she murmured, "Mmm?"

He forced himself to concentrate, to say what must be said. "I'm the adventurer who deflowered you. As well as the man whose sworn duty it is to protect your honor."

"I absolve you of all responsibil—" Kate gasped as he slid his hand downward over her belly to the place where they were still joined. "Gabriel, *stop*. You're making it impossible for me to think."

He obeyed, though he let his hand cover her mound in an unsubtle statement of ownership. "Forgive me," he said, not meaning it in the least. "The adventurer wants to make love to you again."

She smiled at that, the coquettish smile of a woman who knows how to entice a man. Her fingertips glided down the sweat-dampened muscles of his chest. "Why doesn't he?"

His chest expanded in a deep breath. Her willingness

didn't make it any easier to act honorably. To take the leap he'd sworn to avoid. With a wry grimace, he leaned down and kissed the tip of her pert nose. "Because the guardian insists upon a betrothal first."

CHAPTER 24

THE LOST BUTTON

TOURING the castle with Sir Charles, Meg fancied herself a grown-up lady escorted by her suitor. The baron hadn't paid such solicitous attention to her since they'd sat together and watched the tightrope dancers at the fair in Oxford. But here, she thought with a delicious thrill, they were alone.

As they strolled along a ground-floor passageway toward the rear of the castle, he related tales of ghosts and eerie sounds witnessed by the servants. "You're jesting," Meg said flirtatiously, clinging to his strong arm. "I do believe you enjoy alarming me."

His white teeth flashed in an enigmatic smile. "If you've any doubts, ask my housekeeper. She swears she saw an apparition floating in the darkness of the dungeons."

"Perhaps she has poor eyesight."

"There's one way to find out." Sir Charles stopped, his celestial blue gaze gleaming in the meager light of the candlestick he held in his gloved hand. He indicated a doorway that loomed to their right. "That staircase descends to the dungeons. Shall we go explore for ourselves?"

Meg turned her gaze to the narrow flight of steps that vanished into a pitch-dark obscurity, and a lovely shiver tiptoed down her spine. While they'd viewed the library and the other formal chambers, Sir Charles had behaved like the perfect gentleman. Now, from his smoldering regard, she sensed he had other plans for her, perhaps an embrace in the darkness . . . or even a stolen kiss. With every scrap of her romantic heart, she yearned to experience those secrets of womanhood.

But Kate's voice sounded in her mind. *Sir Charles might appear to be a fine gentleman, but he is responsible for Papa's death.*

Meg didn't believe her, of course. Kate was always overly cautious, a fussbudget who cast a suspicious eye at all men. Yet a twinge of apprehension caught at Meg. "But I promised my sister that I wouldn't trust you—" She swallowed the impulsive words.

"Not trust me?" Sir Charles asked, a certain alertness on his patrician features. "Why would she say that?"

"I—I'm sorry for how that sounded," Meg faltered. "She said I wasn't to go off with *any* man. Perhaps we should return to the ballroom."

Sir Charles sighed as if she'd disappointed him. "My dear Margaret. I thought you were different from the other ladies. I admired you for being the brave, adventuresome sort."

"I am! It's just that . . . we'll be all alone down there in the dungeons."

A tender warmth entered his gaze. Reaching out, he stroked his gloved fingers over her cheek. "Are you afraid, my dear?" he asked. "I'll protect you from harm. You have my word as a gentleman."

His kind manner made her misgivings melt away. She leaned into him, drawn by his aura of affection. "I'm never afraid when I'm with you—"

A missile exploded out of the gloom of the stairway. Something small and dark launched straight at Meg.

Staggering back, Sir Charles cried out in surprise.

Meg screamed. The creature leapt for her neck, throttling her with furry arms. In a panic, she reached up to free herself—and recognized the sturdy form of Jabbar.

The chimpanzee babbled nonsense in a high-pitched,

frantic tone. Aware that he was shivering, Meg stroked the back of his little shirt. "Why, darling! You nearly frightened me out of my wits. What's the matter?"

The chimp gave a drawn-out wail that raised prickles on her skin.

Sir Charles stooped down and picked up a scrap of paper, studying it with a fierce glower.

Idly curious, Meg asked, "What's that?"

"A note dropped by one of my servants," he said, shoving it into his pocket. "Now, I'd like to know how that creature escaped. I thought he was confined to Lady Stokeford's chamber."

"More to the point, what was he doing down there?" Meg said as she soothed Jabbar. "He must have seen something that scared him."

Sir Charles narrowed his eyes. "I wonder what it could be."

"Do you think he saw . . . a ghost?" she whispered.

Before the baron could reply, Jabbar did something even more peculiar. He jumped out of Meg's arms and took hold of her hand, tugging her toward the shadowed stone steps that led down to the dungeons. "Sir Charles! I do believe he wants to show us something."

With alacrity, Sir Charles stepped forward. "Then by all means, let's go."

But the sound of voices intruded from the end of the passageway. To Meg's surprise and chagrin, Lady Stokeford and Uncle Nathaniel hastened toward them.

"What's happened?" the dowager asked, her delicate features drawn with apprehension. "We heard you scream, Meg. You sounded terrified."

Uncle Nathaniel scowled at Sir Charles. "If this knave has harmed you—"

"Oh, no!" Meg said. "Jabbar jumped out of the darkness, that's all."

"Then you're quite certain you're all right?" Lady Stokeford asked anxiously, coming forward to touch Meg's cheek.

"Yes, I'm perfectly fine." Feeling guilty for having worried her chaperones, Meg picked up the chimpanzee again as a shield against their distress. "Sir Charles was giving me a tour of his castle."

"It's entirely my fault," the baron said gallantly. "I would have asked your permission, but I couldn't locate either of you. Nor Miss Talisford. She seems to have disappeared."

The dowager exchanged a veiled glance with Uncle Nathaniel. "Kate developed a headache, so she went to her chamber," Lady Stokeford said. "Nathaniel and I merely stepped out of the ballroom for a few minutes. When we left, Meg was dancing and needed no chaperone."

"Damme, you risked my niece's reputation," Uncle Nathaniel accused Sir Charles. "I won't allow you to dishonor her."

The baron bowed his head, his fair hair gleaming in the candlelight, his smooth features showing a polite regret. "I humbly beg your forgiveness. But as you can see, no harm was done."

"Sir Charles acted the perfect gentleman," Meg said. "Truly, he did!"

Ignoring her, Uncle Nathaniel shook his fist at the baron. "I'll call you out for this, Damson. Pistols or swords, take your pick."

Meg gasped, but Sir Charles's noble features wore a look of suave composure. "I've no wish to duel with a man of your age. It's an archaic way to settle a misunderstanding."

"A man of my age?" Uncle Nathaniel said, bristling with outrage. "Why, I'll show you what's what—"

"No you won't," Lady Stokeford said firmly. She placed

her hand on his sleeve and frowned at the older man, and Meg had the oddest sense that a secret message passed between them.

His movements jerky, Uncle Nathaniel motioned to Meg. "Come with us," he said through his teeth. "You'll go to her ladyship's room and remain there."

Meg dug in the heels of her blue dancing slippers. "But I want to see the dungeons. We were just now going down there."

Lady Stokeford pursed her lips. "Why on earth would you do that?"

"Jabbar saw something," Meg said. In her arms, the chimpanzee had quieted, observing the others with intelligent black eyes. "I don't know how he escaped your chamber, my lady, but he came up the staircase at a dreadful run, and he was screeching with fright. I do believe Sir Charles and I should investigate the matter."

The dowager flashed a keen stare at the baron. "Pishposh," she said crisply. "It must be filthy and damp down there, and you'll only ruin your ballgown. Not to mention your reputation." On that, she took Meg's arm and drew her away.

Hugging Jabbar, Meg opened her mouth to make one last desperate plea. She couldn't leave Sir Charles, not now, when he'd been about to fall in love with her!

But when she turned a beseeching look at him, the baron gave her a small, encouraging nod. A nod that sent her spirits soaring, for it promised this wasn't the end of their friendship.

It was merely the beginning.

"BETROTHAL?" Kate repeated, her mouth dry. Gabriel's leg lay heavily over her thighs. His chest touched her bare breasts, and his body heat penetrated her. Those physical signs gave solid proof that she wasn't dreaming.

But she had to be.

He nodded rather stiffly. "I'm asking you to be my wife, Kate."

His wife. He was offering her a proposal of marriage. Gabriel, who had been both her friend and her enemy. Gabriel, who had made love to her with compelling expertise. Gabriel, who had the soul of a wayfarer, the heart of a wanderer.

He raised her hand to his lips, his gaze resolute as he kissed her fingertips, one by one. "We'll wed by special license," he went on. "As soon as I can make the arrangements."

His confident manner caused a treacherous melting inside her, casting her adrift in a sea of love. Foolish, fickle *love.* Against all wisdom, ardor leapt in her bosom, urging her to take him on any terms. Dear God, she could wed him, love him, keep him close to her forever . . .

Sharp awareness burst the bubble. She could never hold Gabriel Kenyon because she could never change his basic nature. Men were unreliable, self-centered creatures who abandoned their families on a whim. And Gabriel—her charming, exciting lover—was an adventurer who could never be satisfied to settle in one place, to commit himself to one woman.

She wriggled out from under him, scooting up against the headboard and hugging a feather pillow to shield her bosom. "No," she whispered. "I won't marry you. So you needn't feel obligated."

Into the silence came the muffled crashing of the surf at the base of the cliff. The rain had slowed to a patter, the thunder fading in the distance.

Something flickered in Gabriel's eyes, but he lowered his lashes slightly to hide his thoughts. "I'm not the marrying kind, Kate. I'll admit that. My parents didn't set a very good example."

"What do you mean?"

"My mother was obsessed by prayer. After bearing three children, she rebuffed my father in the bedchamber. Her coldness drove him to drink."

Kate blinked. She herself had never even pondered the private intimacy of her parents. "How do you know that?"

"My father told me once, when he was dead drunk on gin. I was eleven years old and rather shocked to hear of his troubles."

He spoke offhandedly as if the incident didn't matter. Compassion and anger flared inside Kate. "No parent should burden his child with such secrets. Not only does it destroy the child's innocence, it's a betrayal of the trust between husband and wife."

Gabriel shrugged. "Perhaps."

"There's no perhaps about it." At least now she knew why he'd shunned commitment, why he'd left home to wander the world. "That was wrong of your father, Gabriel. Utterly *wrong*."

He sent her a level, concentrated stare. "I'm glad to hear you've such strong feelings about parenthood. You may have conceived my child."

A baby. The possibility both stunned and delighted her, driving out all other thought. Beneath the pillow, her hand stole over her belly. In the torrent of physical need, she had neglected to consider the consequences of their mating. Now she felt a wondrous craving to have a baby grow inside her. Gabriel's child. A tiny blue-eyed girl with a charming manner. Or a dark-haired boy with a winsome smile . . .

Mistrust reared its bleak head. "But you won't stay," she whispered. "You'll leave us." *And I couldn't bear that pain.*

"Nonsense," he said, his mouth tight. "We're going to write that book together."

"And when it's finished? Can you vow that you'd never

go off on another lark? That you'd be content to make your home in England and never travel abroad again?"

He hesitated for a moment. A telling moment. "I swear I would never forsake you."

"But you wouldn't be happy," she said, swallowing a bitter dose of reality. "You love to wander. It means more to you than I ever could."

He didn't deny it. Abruptly, he rolled to the edge of the bed. His scars shone faintly in the shadowy lamplight. Beset by the ache of yearning, she admired his tough male beauty. Sleek muscles delineated his shoulders and back as he stretched an arm down to the floor and snatched up his coat.

Was he leaving her already? she wondered with a piercing regret. Had she driven him away with her mistrust? It was for the best, Kate told herself. Best that he leave now, rather than shatter her heart later.

But Gabriel didn't don his clothing. He probed an inner pocket of the coat, then dropped the garment. Returning to the bed, he sat down beside her, the feather mattress sinking under his weight.

He pressed something into her hand. "Perhaps this will convince you."

She stared down at the small, round object in her palm. A plain ivory button. Confused, she lifted her gaze to him. "I don't understand."

"It fell off your nightdress a long time ago."

The memory came swooping back. The night she'd gone to his chamber at Larkspur Cottage. When she had torn open her gown and offered herself to him. Remembering that foolish, innocent girl, she felt a blaze of bewilderment. "You kept this?" she whispered. "For four years?"

A certain wariness in his manner, he inclined his head in a nod. "I took it to Africa with me."

"But . . . why?"

"It was a memento. Of the girl I never forgot."

Kate's fingers closed around the lost button as she fought against the rise of hope. She must have meant more to Gabriel than she'd ever imagined. But it didn't mean he loved her.

I'm not the marrying kind.

Kate couldn't quarrel with that. Yet she wanted desperately to believe Gabriel felt more for her than duty. If he would, just once, speak from his heart, perhaps it would ease her doubts . . .

He sat beside her on the bed, his arm resting on his crooked knee, his body taut and glistening in the pale lamplight. Her gaze catalogued his strong chest, flat belly, lean waist, coming to rest on his loins. Nature had shaped him superbly, her perfect mate.

To her astonishment, his male member thickened and grew before her eyes.

His mouth quirking in wry humor, Gabriel glanced down. "The cursed adventurer. He wants you again."

Kate felt a sweet, involuntary clenching inside her, a sensation she now recognized as the stirrings of desire. It was disconcerting, this effect he had on her. Clutching the button to her heart, she said, "I want you, too, Gabriel. But I don't know yet . . . if I can please the guardian."

A muscle tightened in his cheek. For a moment he looked impatient, intensely frustrated at not getting his way. "I won't give up, Kate. One way or another, I intend to marry you."

Perversely, his arrogant insistence pleased her. She felt an undeniable pride to know that this powerful man had chosen her, above all other women, to be his wife. That he'd kept her token all these years.

"Then convince me," she murmured.

Dropping the button, she brought her leg over so that she sat astride his lap. Her slim thighs embraced his, and she could feel his arousal, firm and hot beneath her. With a sigh, she melted against him.

Gabriel skimmed his hands up and down her spine, cupping her bottom in his big palms. "My God, Kate. Where did you learn that move?"

"There were statues upstairs . . . I thought about you and me . . ."

A smile in his voice, he pressed his brow to hers. "Let me fulfill your every fantasy. Tonight belongs to you."

With that, he took her mouth with a hungry passion that transcended her romantic dreams. There was no past and no future, only the glorious present. He caressed her most sensitive places until she cried out in a quest for satisfaction. With a smooth, upward thrust, he joined their bodies, filling her completely. His face reflected the potent vigor of his passion for her. Seduced by that look, she gave herself up to mindless indulgence, relishing the freedom of movement the position lent her. She looped her arms around his neck and clung tightly to him as they rode together to paradise.

Awash in contentment, Kate slid into an exhausted doze, her face tucked into the crook of his shoulder. Sometime later, she had a hazy awareness of Gabriel lifting her, laying her down on the linens. She stirred, protesting feebly at the loss of his warmth. Then he settled down beside her and drew the coverlet over them.

Gathering her to him, he pressed a kiss to her hair. His voice was a mere breath of sound. "Sleep, love."

Sighing, she snuggled closer, preferring his hard form to the soft pillows. The last thing she remembered was the steady beating of his heart against her breasts.

A sharp noise awakened Gabe.

He thought at first that he'd died and gone to heaven. Kate lay curled into him, her breath feathering his arm, her hair draping the pillows. Her fragrance mingled with the scent of their lovemaking, and longing caught his groin in a hot fist. Even in slumber, she aroused him to the verge of pain. His prickly, sweet Kate.

The sound came again. A rapping on the door.

His senses at instant alert, he shot into a sitting position. The watery sunlight of mid-morning streamed into the tower room. The lamp in the window had burnt out, and the sight galvanized him.

Damn, had Bickell arrived? Had he found the goddess?

Bending down, he shook Kate's shoulder. "Wake up, darling."

Moaning a protest, she stretched luxuriously against the sheets. A veil of red-gold hair enveloped her nakedness, her breasts peeking through the lush, curly strands. Her eyes opened, sleepy and heavy-lidded. Fighting the powerful need to ignore the world and make love to her again, he muttered, "Someone's at the door."

Although urgency nagged at him, he felt the greater need to protect her reputation. God forbid anyone should know he'd spent the night in her bed.

"Kate," called a familiar voice. "Are you in there?"

His grandmother. The situation was going from bad to worse.

Cursing, he snatched up his breeches and stepped into them, catching his toe on the cuff and hopping to keep his balance. As he pulled them up and fastened the buttons, Kate leapt out of bed and dragged on her chemise.

"Dear, sweet heaven," she whispered frantically. Then louder, she cried out, "I'll be there in a moment, my lady."

She looked so charmingly flustered that Gabriel forgot his irritation. Catching her close, he stole a swift, heartfelt kiss. She responded, her lips soft and warm, her fingers sliding into his hair. Unable to resist, he cupped her bottom and pressed himself into the cradle of her hips.

She pulled back. "Gabriel! Don't *do* that."

"Don't look so tempting, my sweet."

Her blush deepening, she gathered up his things, wig and shoes and shirt, and thrust them at his bare chest. "Go into the dressing room. Lady Stokeford mustn't know you're here."

Gabriel despised the need to hide, to skulk in the next room like an illicit lover. Dammit, if he had to marry her, he'd stand proudly at her side as her husband.

But he nodded, touching her cheek. "Whatever you do, don't let Grandmama into the bedchamber," he advised. "She'll guess at once that I've been with you."

Their gazes held for an eloquent moment. Calling himself every kind of fool, Gabe knew that he wanted Kate to wed him of her own free will. Not because she felt obliged, as he did, hypocrite that he was. After a moment she nodded, then went to don a bronze-hued dressing gown, tying the sash around her slender waist. The sunlight lent a fiery sheen to her long, tousled curls.

She looked like a woman who had been thoroughly loved.

Veering to the bed, Gabe snatched up the crumpled linen pillowcase that bore a trace of her virgin's blood. He wouldn't give his grandmother any more ammunition with which to trap Kate. Then he strode into the dressing room as Kate went to answer the door.

Though he strained to hear, the women stood outside on the small landing, and he was unable to discern their words. Tense and edgy, he finished dressing, stepping in front of the pier glass to straighten his collar and don the annoying powdered wig. When he returned home, he'd banish all wigs at Fairfield Park and convince Michael to do likewise at the Abbey. No servant ought to suffer the stupidity of outmoded tradition.

In the mirror, Kate appeared in the doorway behind him.

She put her hand to the wall as if to steady herself.

He wheeled around, struck by the pale delicacy of her features. "What is it?" he asked, closing the distance between them in two long strides. "Did Grandmama guess that we spent the night together?"

"It isn't that. Mr. Bickell is here. And something terrible has happened." Her gaze stricken, Kate went on, "The goddess has vanished."

CHAPTER 25

IN THE DUNGEON

PRECISELY three minutes later, Gabe strode through the open door of Damson's bedchamber.

Sunshine streamed through the recessed windows, highlighting the sordid décor, from the rumpled bed to the lewd artifacts. A knot of people were gathered in the center of the room. His stout back to the door and his arms akimbo, Barnabus Bickell stood in an authoritative stance before Sir Charles Damson. The baron looked coolly amused in a black silk dressing gown, as if he enjoyed being rousted out of bed and accused of theft by a Bow Street Runner.

The darkly sensual Yasmin clung to Damson's arm, her full lips forming a petulant pout. Figgins lurked in the background.

Gabe surged past them and stopped in front of the alcove. On the marble pedestal stood the statue of a naked woman.

A cheap clay figurine.

Fury throttled him. How the hell had Damson found out their plan?

His skull-like features drawn in a glower, Figgins stomped toward Gabe. "What d'ye think ye're doin'? Get belowstairs. This is the master's chamber—"

Gabe gave him a hard shove. The valet staggered backward, cracking his head on the marble pedestal. The clay statue teetered and crashed to the floor. Figgins stood swaying, bleary surprise in his sunken eyesockets before he crumpled to the floor like a broken marionette.

An exclamation of collective surprise came from the others. Damson's soft mouth formed a sneer of fury. "Who the devil are you?"

Skulking and trickery had brought Gabe nothing. Craving a confrontation, he yanked off his wig.

Even as Damson's eyes widened with recognition, Gabe swung his fist. The baron ducked too late, the blow glancing off his cheekbone. Gabe followed up with a punch from the left that struck Damson's nose with a satisfying crunch. Blood spurted and he howled, diving behind Yasmin.

Red droplets stained the white silk sleeve of her wrapper. Yasmin screeched at Damson in her foreign tongue.

Gabe intended to move her aside, but Bickell stepped into his path. His hands gripped like iron manacles around Gabe's arms. Despite his well-fed appearance, the Bow Street Runner had the strength of an ox.

His ruddy features conveyed a stern censure. "Nay, m'lord. 'Tisn't the way to settle matters."

"The hell it isn't," Gabe snapped. "I want the goddess."

"So do I," Bickell said with thinly veiled frustration. "But it isn't here. I've searched this chamber from stem to stern."

In the act of thrusting a handkerchief at Damson, Yasmin took a closer look at Gabe. Her avid gaze scoured his footman's garb. "Allah be praised!" she said, clasping her hand to her bosom. "It is you, Lord Gabriel."

Gabe hardened his gaze on her. She was eyeing him with a lascivious greed that turned his stomach. As if she expected him to fall into her arms after she'd tricked him into drinking opium-laced wine in Cairo.

He'd use her lust to his advantage.

Striding to the Egyptian, he took her slender hands in his. With cold, calculated charm, he said, "It's wonderful to see you again, Yasmin. If you tell me where Damson hid the statue of the goddess, I'll make it well worth your while."

Her dark velvet eyes lit up. "I—"

"Get away from her," Damson choked out, holding the handkerchief to his bloodied nose. "You've no right to badger my guests."

Gabe stroked Yasmin's palm with his thumb. "Answer me," he commanded softly. "You'll be glad you did."

Licking her lips, Yasmin glanced almost fearfully at the furious baron. Then her gaze slid to the shattered clay statue. "I know only of that one, my lord."

She was lying, dammit. "Come with me," Gabe said in his most alluring tone. "We'll speak alone, you and I."

A potent look flashed between Yasmin and Damson. As if he had some sinister hold on her, she drew her hands free and glided to his side.

"I demand that you arrest Kenyon at once," Damson told Bickell. "He's your villain. You saw him attack me. He entered my home under false pretenses."

"I'll show you a damned villain," Gabe snarled.

He lunged at Damson, who scuttled backward, taking refuge behind a chair. Again, the Bow Street Runner nimbly blocked Gabe, putting up ham fists to hold him at bay. "M'lord, you must hold your temper. Lest he press charges against you."

"He can't press charges if he's dead."

"There, you see? Kenyon's threatening my life." Damson's show of outrage was somewhat spoiled by his gingerly dabbing at his nose. "Seize him, I say. He's trespassing."

"The goddess was here last night," Gabe said, his voice tight. "That proves you killed Henry Talisford."

"These allegations are ridiculous. As the local magistrate, I'm ordering you to depart this house or be arrested for thievery and assault."

"I'm afraid you'll have to comply, m'lord," Bickell said glumly. "I'll continue searching, for the warrant allows me to remain here."

Gabe grasped at the opportunity. "Then appoint me your assistant."

Bickell rubbed his bristled jaw. "A highly irregular notion, m'lord. But not altogether impossible."

"This is an outrage," Damson sputtered. "You do this, Bickell, and I'll take it up with your superiors in London."

"Go ahead," Gabe taunted. "You'll do so from Newgate Prison."

"He belongs in prison." Kate's voice came from the doorway.

Gabe spun around to see her marching into the bedchamber with his grandmother. Anger and attraction fused in his chest. Kate looked composed and confident in a forest-green gown, her hair secured in a spinster's knot. No one would guess she'd just had the night of her life. Or that he had, too.

The new-found tenderness inside him intensified his desperate need to protect her. Surging forward, he herded the two women back toward the door, his arms outstretched. "I told you both to stay out of here."

"Don't bluster," Grandmama chided, sternness on her wrinkled features. "Clearly, the pretense is over. You've shed your disguise."

Kate ducked under his arm. "I wish to know the fate of the goddess."

Damson appeared beside her, the blood-spattered handkerchief clutched to his nose. "I suspected you were in on this plot," he said, his ice-blue gaze pinning Kate. "Leave this house at once."

She regarded him coolly. "Not until you pay for murdering my father."

Shaken by the cruel vindictiveness on the baron's face,

Gabe stepped between them, shielding her. "She's departing at once."

Damson ignored him, staring at Kate. "I won't forget this betrayal, my dear. You'll pay for deceiving me."

LATE that afternoon, Kate perched in the window seat of the drawing room at Fairfield Park. It was the last day of April, and a pleasant breeze drifted through the open window along with the scent of newly scythed grass. The sunny afternoon seemed to mock the dark turmoil inside her.

From across the room came the murmuring of voices as Lady Stokeford and Uncle Nathaniel related to Lady Enid and Lady Faversham everything that had happened at Damson Castle. A much subdued Meg had pleaded a headache and trudged upstairs with Jabbar. More than an hour ago, Ashraf had brought them here in the Stokeford coach, and then returned to the castle to wait for Gabriel and Mr. Bickell.

Although she knew it was far too soon for the men to return, Kate kept her eyes trained on the front drive. If not for her restless anxiety, she would feel right at home here on Gabriel's estate, with the bees buzzing in the rhododendrons beneath the windows and the great sweep of green lawn leading down to a thicket of elm trees at the base of the hill.

But she wouldn't feel secure until Gabriel returned. Until he put his arms around her and held her tightly. As much as she craved revenge for her father's death, she didn't want it at the expense of Gabriel's safety. The very thought of losing him filled her with a frantic dread.

Because she loved him.

Despite her misgivings, Kate could accept that now. Their lovemaking had satisfied her only temporarily; her desire for him was stronger than ever, enriched by their night together and the silken bonds of intimacy. A part of her yearned to accept his offer of marriage. If he left her someday, at least she would have many happy memories to sustain her. She would have his children, too, a family to love. She would survive as she'd always done.

Yet Kate was greedy enough to covet everything. She wanted from him what the marriage vows stated, *in sickness and health, and forsaking all others . . . so long as ye both shall live . . .*

A soul-deep longing ached in her heart. Could Gabriel keep such a promise to her? She could believe in his faithfulness in regard to other women. It was the alluring mistress of adventure that she feared.

Uncle Nathaniel sat down beside her. "Don't fret, my dear," he said, patting her on the shoulder. "Your young man will return, safe and sound."

"I should have stayed at the castle," Kate said, focusing on her anger lest she burst into foolish tears. "I shouldn't have let Gabriel send me away."

A grim look intensified the lines on Uncle Nathaniel's face. "You had no choice. None of us did. Damson ordered us all to leave."

I won't forget this betrayal, my dear. You'll pay for deceiving me.

She fisted her fingers in her lap. "I wish I knew how he found out."

"The man's shrewd as a snake, that's how. He seemed especially interested that you'd left the ball last night." His face stern, her great-uncle studied her. "I must say, I was surprised that you never returned to the festivities."

A flush warmed her cheeks. Shifting her gaze to the empty drive, she said, "I stayed in my bedchamber to make sure the beacon didn't go out."

"And where was Gabriel, hmm?" Uncle Nathaniel caught her chin and turned her face back toward him. His frown darkened, giving him the aspect of an irate father.

"Don't deny that he was with you, Kate. I recognize that soft look on a woman's face."

Unwilling to share her most cherished memory, she said, "He asked me to marry him."

That glower eased into astonished approval. "Well, well. Lucy said he would. To think I didn't believe her."

"But I refused him," Kate felt compelled to add.

"Refused him!" The glare returned in full force. "Damme, the man's nobility. He's rich enough to keep you in silks and diamonds."

She glared back. "Do you really think that matters to me?"

He gave a sheepish shake of his head. "The fellow loves you. That should count for something."

Did Gabriel love her? More than adventure? A soaring hope lifted her heart; then her practical nature grounded it.

Biting her lip, she glanced away. "I wish I could believe that. But even he admitted that he's not the marrying kind. He's a wanderer, and I can't rely on him."

Uncle Nathaniel sat silent for a moment. The conversation of the Rosebuds across the drawing room sounded rather like the cooing of doves outside the opened window. "Ah, well," he said on a sigh. "I suppose I'm to blame, at least in part. Always footloose and fancy free. Didn't set much of an example for you gels. But not all men are like me."

Seeing his remorse, Kate reached out to touch his age-spotted hand. "It's never too late to set a good example."

"What are you saying?"

"I'm saying you could wed Lady Stokeford."

He jumped as if she'd poked him with a pin. "See here now. I can manage my affairs without your interference."

"An affair? Is that all you intend for her?"

Glancing across the drawing room at Lady Stokeford,

Uncle Nathaniel shifted uncomfortably on the window seat. "Who says I intend anything at all?"

"I recognize that soft look on a man's face," she paraphrased.

To her amazement, he blushed. There could be no other explanation for the ruddy color that swept his weathered cheeks. Despite her tension, Kate fought against a smile. Never in her life had she seen her worldly great-uncle appear so flustered.

He sprang to his feet. "This is not a topic for your discussion, young lady."

"What are you two quarreling about?" Lady Stokeford called out.

Uncle Nathaniel stood frozen, glancing at the door as if he'd like to escape. Taking pity on him, Kate rose and faced the Rosebuds, who sat in a circle of comfortable, stuffed chairs near the unlit hearth. "You misconstrue, my lady. We weren't quarreling. My uncle is merely too modest to accept my compliments on how well he conducted himself . . . in your mock betrothal."

"Yes, he did play his role to the hilt," the dowager said with a mysterious smile. She waved them onto a nearby chaise, then picked up the blue-and-white china teapot. "Come sit with us. I'll pour you both a bracing cup of tea."

Uncle Nathaniel's feet dragged as if he were being led to the gallows. But he sat down beside Kate and accepted a cup, scowling down into its amber depths.

"Lucy was just telling us about the Lucifer League," Enid said, her shudder causing the feathers on her yellow turban to sway. "Those wicked men. Holding pagan ceremonies, indeed."

"I understand my grandson was at that party," Lady Faversham said, austere in gray broadcloth, her clawlike fingers curled around the ivory top of her cane. "I've a good mind to go after the boy. Imagine, a Villiers associating with such riffraff."

Kate would hardly call the lean, sinister Lord Faversham a *boy*. She accepted her teacup and distractedly stirred in a few crumbs of sugar. "If it comforts you, my lady, he did warn me to take Meg and depart the castle."

"Did he?" Lady Stokeford asked, her dainty white brows arching. "When did he say that?"

"At the ball. There wasn't an opportunity to tell you." Because Kate had been lost in the heaven of Gabriel's love-making.

"But what was Brandon warning you about?" Enid asked.

"That hellfire club, no doubt," Lady Faversham said darkly. "At least he had the decency to alert you."

Lady Stokeford's eyes hardened with an unladylike savagery. "It only confirms Sir Charles did indeed have a heinous plan that involved Meg."

Feeling a lurch of fear, Kate said, "There's something else I haven't yet told you. Sir Charles claims to be guardian to Meg and me. He has a document signed by Papa."

A barrage of protests exploded from the Rosebuds.

"That can't be true," Lady Enid gasped.

"Sir Charles is lying," Lady Faversham declared.

"It must be a forgery," Lady Stokeford said in a horrified tone.

"But I saw it myself, and it's authentic," Kate said with more than a little trepidation. "Or at least it appears to be."

Gripping his teacup, Uncle Nathaniel snorted. "Henry wouldn't give his daughters to the care of a stranger. He trusted Gabe to do the honors."

In that, Kate trusted Gabriel, too. If only she dared to trust her heart. "If Gabriel doesn't find the statue, there'll be no evidence to convict Sir Charles of theft and murder. His way will be clear to assume guardianship."

"Nathaniel will contest it," Lady Stokeford stated. "You'll take his claim to Chancery Court, won't you, Nathaniel?"

"At once," Uncle Nathaniel said, shaking his fist. "The blackguard won't stand a chance. My rights—and Gabriel's—will take precedence."

The Rosebuds nodded, their voices rising in a clamor of support.

But Kate couldn't share their certainty. They hadn't inspected the deed that her father had unwittingly signed. Given Nathaniel Babcock's reputation, the judge might rule in favor of Sir Charles. She feared not so much for herself, but for Meg. Sweet, naïve, susceptible Meg.

"Sir Charles can be very charming," Lady Stokeford said in a crisp tone. "He enticed Meg away yesterday evening. Thank heaven Nathaniel and I found them in time."

Although Kate had heard the story in the coach, a stranglehold of emotion gripped her anew. She felt an angry disbelief that her sister could behave so rashly. Horror at what might have happened. And guilt, for while Meg was being lured away by their father's murderer, Kate had been in bed with Gabriel.

"Damson," Uncle Nathaniel said, setting his teacup down with a clatter. "I should have finished off the wretch with my bare fists."

"You'd have been charged with his murder," Lady Stokeford countered.

"And the statue of the goddess would still be missing," Lady Faversham said.

"Perhaps it's down in the dungeon," Lady Enid ventured.

Kate gave a start of surprise and nearly burned herself as hot tea sloshed in her cup. "The dungeon?"

Uncle Nathaniel narrowed his eyes. "Didn't we tell you that part? Damson wanted to take your sister down there last night. But Jabbar jumped out and she screamed, and that's how we found her."

"She was gazing at Sir Charles as if he were Zeus on a mountaintop," Lady Stokeford said, shaking her head in disbelief. "The dear girl is too innocent to realize his depravity."

Perched on the edge of the chaise, Uncle Nathaniel glowered. "Damson was looking at her as if she were made of strawberries and cream. I must say, we took her out of that castle in the nick of time."

"She'll come to her senses now that his influence is gone," Lady Faversham said comfortingly. "We'll all do our best to distract her."

The Rosebuds murmured their agreement.

Yet Kate felt the niggling of disquiet. Something wasn't quite right. If Sir Charles had intended to violate Meg, it made more sense that he would have coaxed her upstairs to his bedchamber. So why would he take her sister down to the dungeon, of all places?

Unless he had other plans for her. Plans that involved the Lucifer League.

Tasting bile at the back of her throat, Kate stood abruptly. "I believe I'll sit with Meg for a while. To keep her company."

"An excellent notion," Lady Stokeford said, eyeing her keenly. "There's nothing like family and good friends to bolster one's spirits."

The Rosebuds looked fondly at one another.

Kate hastened out of the drawing room, her thoughts surging along a troublesome path. Sir Charles had mentioned that a network of subterranean tunnels and caves honeycombed the cliff beneath the castle. They were accessed through the dungeon. She also remembered the tale told by Mr. Bickell of the tavern girl, who had been ill-used by a throng of black-robed men wearing devil's horns.

Men who had made their way down to the rocky beach by way of those tunnels.

I won't forget this betrayal, my dear. You'll pay for deceiving me.

Kate hurried upstairs, her slippers tapping on the wooden risers. The mahogany balustrade slid smooth and cool beneath her fingers. Medieval tapestries graced the old paneled walls, and the air held the pleasant aroma of beeswax polish.

But she took only scant notice of her surroundings. She was too caught up in a pressing urgency to see Meg.

On learning of her sister's indiscretion during the coach ride here to Fairfield Park, Kate had hugged her close, terrified by what might have happened. Then she had soundly chastised Meg.

"You went off with Sir Charles when I warned you not to do so. How could you have been so foolish?"

"I wasn't foolish. We were merely touring the castle."

Kate leaned forward, grasping her sister's arm beneath her traveling cloak. *"Meg, he could have done you harm. Grave harm. He's a murderer."*

"You always think the worst of men," Meg flared, pulling away. *"Well, I don't want to be so sour. I want to marry, to find love and happiness."*

The rebuke had arrowed into Kate, piercing her heart. Was that how her sister viewed her? As a disagreeable shrew who didn't know how to love? If so, then her bitterness had influenced Meg to rebel.

Instantly contrite, Meg had apologized, the defiance draining from her. For the remainder of the ten-mile journey, she'd sat in uncharacteristic silence, either gazing out the window or looking down at the slim volume of poetry gripped in her gloved hands.

Kate brooded on her sister's denunciation. If only Meg knew how the wondrous night with Gabriel had changed

Kate, awakening her to the sharp, sweet pain of love. With him, she'd found the joy that had been missing from her life. Now she could even understand the restlessness that drove him, the distaste for family life that had been instilled in him by his father. But could she ever accept Gabriel's wandering ways?

Then an insight jolted her. She had to marry Gabriel; it was the only way to eradicate Sir Charles's claim to guardianship. No court in the land would deny the rights of a husband and brother-in-law. A foolish, imprudent exhilaration filled her, tempered only by a natural caution. She would ponder the situation later, wait to see if Gabriel found the goddess. In the meantime, she had enough on her mind with worrying about her sister.

She couldn't forget the peculiarity of Meg's restrained behavior. Did her sister regret the risk she'd taken? Or did she cling to the stubborn belief that Sir Charles had been wrongfully accused?

Kate feared the latter. She knew how persuasive Sir Charles could be. She too had trusted him when he'd first come to their door, bringing the news of Papa's death and offering his sham condolences. He'd presented himself as a colleague of Papa's, and for a short while, she'd accepted his lies. How much more credulous and naïve was her sister.

Meg had been a girl of twelve when Papa had departed on the expedition. The experiences of life that had made Kate wary of men had had the opposite effect on her sister. Too easily, Meg let her head be turned by a handsome face or a bold smile. She fell in love at the wink of an eye, often changing her affections from one day to the next.

But now, Meg had set her sights on a master manipulator.

I won't forget this betrayal, my dear. You'll pay for deceiving me.

Haunted by Sir Charles's threat, Kate hurried along the upstairs corridor. She tapped on the door to her sister's bedchamber. The echo faded away to silence. She waited impatiently, shifting from one foot to the other.

"Meg? Are you in there?"

There was no response, no sound of movement inside the room. Kate opened the door, and a shaft of late afternoon sunlight blinded her for a moment. Blinking, she shaded her eyes and walked inside, glancing around at the old Tudor furnishings, the four-poster bed with its brocaded hangings and the cozy blue wing chairs by the hearth. The tall windows were open, and a soft spring breeze stirred the draperies.

Meg's book of poetry lay abandoned on a footstool. It was the only sign that she'd been here at all.

Despite the tranquil scene, a knell of fear struck Kate's heart. She walked swiftly through the bedchamber and into the dressing room. There was a silver hairbrush that had belonged to their mother, a pink ribbon draped over a chair, and an opened, leather-bound trunk that had yet to be unpacked.

But her sister and Jabbar were gone.

GABE and Bickell searched Damson's study, rapping on the walls, listening for a hollow sound that might indicate a hidden aperture. They'd already rolled back the large Persian rug in a vain hunt for a trapdoor. They'd pushed aside the lewd artifacts and checked the cabinets for a secret compartment. They'd examined every stick of furniture in the entire castle, every bookshelf, every closet and cupboard and cubbyhole. The one repository they'd found in Damson's private sitting room had held an assortment of jewelry and stacks of banknotes.

But no golden goddess.

Reaching the end of the wall, Gabe bit out a string of

profanity that provided only a moment's respite from his angry frustration.

Bickell glanced up from his examination of the baseboards. The red waistcoat of the Bow Street Runners stretched across his stout belly. Like Gabe, he'd shed his coat and rolled up his shirtsleeves hours ago. "No luck, m'lord?"

Gabe shook his head. "When Damson returns, I may just throttle the truth out of him."

"I may just help you," Bickell said wearily.

Half an hour ago, Mrs. Swindon had entered the study. Curling her mustachioed upper lip, she'd stared at Gabe while she and the baron had held a whispered conversation. A covert gleam in his cold blue eyes, he'd quickly excused himself, the housekeeper marching after him.

Where the hell had Damson gone?

"Perhaps we should face facts," Bickell said, rising to his feet and flexing his knees as if they pained him. "The statue isn't here. The baron must have smuggled it out of the castle during the night."

"I'm not giving up."

"But we've run out of places to look. I fear we've been led on a merry chase."

Gabe bitterly wondered that, too. All afternoon and into the early evening, Damson had hovered over them, offering taunts and caustic hints to thwart their search. "Look under the mattress," he'd suggested. "That's where commoners hide their valuables." Or he'd point to a desk, saying, "There might be a hidden compartment if you two buffoons can find it."

By force of will, Gabe had held his temper. His sole compensation had been the sight of Damson's bruised, puffy nose and blackened eye. But that wasn't enough to satisfy Gabe. He had worked silently, efficiently, driven by his determination to locate the goddess. Not just for himself but for Kate, who deserved to have her father's death avenged.

Perhaps then she would love him.

He clenched his jaw. Their one night together had only intensified his damn-fool hopes. Denial was useless; he wanted Kate in his bed, by his side for the rest of his life. The thought warmed him, a strengthening flame that had been steadily burning away his distaste for commitment. Somehow, when this was all over, he would convince her to marry him. He had to make her trust him, to convince her that he would abandon his wandering life and settle down with her at Fairfield Park to raise a family. The fantasy of her suckling their baby at her breast vitalized him. He couldn't fail. He couldn't lose Kate.

I won't forget this betrayal, my dear. You'll pay for deceiving me.

The memory of Damson's threat provoked fury and fear in Gabe. With their plan exposed, she'd been in peril of retribution from that villain. Thank God she was safe at his estate. She hadn't been happy to leave, but in the end, she'd had no choice.

The sound of running footsteps approached from the corridor. Ashraf burst into the study. Instead of his traditional white robe, he wore the garb of a coachman. His thin, dark features showed an uncharacteristic agitation. "Master!"

The urgency in his tone caught at Gabe. He stalked forward, meeting the servant in the middle of the study. "What is it?" he demanded. "You took Kate home, didn't you?"

"Yes, master. As you commanded, I brought the coach back here to wait for you." Ashraf prostrated himself on the floor. "But I no longer deserve to live. I have displeased you."

"Get up, for God's sake. Explain yourself."

Ashraf compromised by rising into a crouched position

at Gabe's feet. He clasped his hands in supplication. "I did not know she had crept back into the coach. I swear I did not. She must have done so while I was at prayer."

"She?" Gabe seized the servant by the arms and hauled him to his feet. "Who?"

The image of misery, Ashraf hung his head. "The younger Miss Talisford."

"Meg? She's *here*?"

Even as Gabe absorbed that shock, Ashraf hit him with another one. "I did not realize I had been fooled until the elder Miss Talisford galloped into the courtyard. She was riding *your* horse," he added, his judgmental brown eyes conveying a scandalized astonishment.

A cold sweat broke out on Gabe's skin. He glanced toward the outer corridor in the vain hope of seeing them waiting out there. "Where are they?"

"The elder Miss Talisford went after her sister. She said Sir Charles Damson told the younger Miss Talisford to meet him in the dungeon."

The news struck Gabe like a punch in the gut. No wonder Damson had left in such gleeful delight. He'd learned of Meg's arrival.

BRUSHING aside a sticky cobweb, Kate held tightly to the candlestick. Its meager light failed to penetrate the deep gloom. The hollow drip-drip of water sounded somewhere, though she couldn't locate its source.

The castle had been built on the site of an old fortress, and the stone floor had been worn smooth in places, showing the patterns of traffic over the centuries. She'd half expected to see the ghosts of prisoners clad in filthy rags, their skeletal hands thrust through the iron bars. Instead, empty cells stretched out on either side of her, most of them unbarred, only the hinges showing where a door had once hung. A few cubicles contained casks of wine and brandy, while others held an accumulation of bric-a-brac.

"Meg?" she called out softly. "Are you here?"

Only a faint echo answered her.

Icy terror gripped her breast, her sense of foreboding stronger than ever. She'd found a letter from Sir Charles tucked inside the book of poetry. Every deceitful word of it was burned into Kate's mind:

My dearest Margaret,
Do you believe in love at first sight? Until I met you,
I thought it the invention of poets & fools. But now
my world has been turned upside down, for I cannot
bear the thought of never seeing you again. All other
ladies pale beside your chaste beauty. I must declare
myself hopelessly enamored, unable to think of any-
one but you, my dearest love.

If your heart beats as strongly for me as mine does
for you, I beg you to come to me tonight. Meet me in
the dungeon, lest Kenyon find out you are here. Take
care, my love, for he & your sister would only try to
separate us. As a token of your love, please bring
your father's journals, for his work has long fasci-
nated me. I shall have a token for you, too, my dar-
ling, a gift that will prove my great admiration for
your purity & virtue.

Until then, dearest Margaret, I shall count the
hours until I can hold you in my arms.
Always your servant, Charles

As she went deeper into the dungeon, dread churned in Kate's belly. Perhaps she ought to have enlisted the aid of Uncle Nathaniel and the Rosebuds. That had been her first impulse. But they'd have required a carriage and she could travel so much faster on horseback. Besides, she'd banked on having the help of Gabriel and the Bow Street Runner.

What was taking them so long? Maybe Ashraf hadn't been able to locate them. Maybe she was on her own.

The thought spurred her. Meg must have already met Sir Charles somewhere in this labyrinth of cells and storerooms. Had he lured her into a secret passageway that led down into the bowels of the cliff?

Scurrying down yet another corridor, Kate turned a corner and came to a dead end. The sound of dripping water grew louder.

As she wheeled around to examine the place, the candle flame wavered, and she swiftly cupped her hand around it. If the taper went out, she'd be plunged into total darkness.

Chilly air whispered against her face, the draft coming from the last cell. As she walked closer, the pale circle of candlelight showed a carving in the stone wall: a six-pointed star inside a circle, along with other strange symbols. Was it the work of a long-ago prisoner?

From the darkness at the rear of the cell came a snuffling noise. She faltered to a stop, the fine hairs lifting at the back of her neck. Visions of ghosts and demons crowded her mind. "Who's there?" she whispered.

Silence.

Her hand quivering, Kate lifted the candle. Its scant illumination caught something shining in the shadows.

A pair of watching eyes.

CHAPTER 26

THE INMOST CAVE

KATE'S heart slammed against her ribs. The moment seemed to stretch into forever. She heard the plop of a water droplet, smelled the damp mustiness, felt the hiss of air on her skin like the clammy breath of a fiend.

Then a small, furry animal bounded out of the shadows. In a rush of relief, she recognized him. "Jabbar!"

With a soft grunt of greeting, the chimpanzee came forward, balancing on his knuckles. He peeled back his lips in a grimace, and his rapid-fire chatter conveyed agitation and fear.

Kate dropped down to peer into his leathery face. "Where's my sister, darling? Where's Meg? Can you take me to her?"

As if he understood, the chimpanzee turned around and headed into the darkness at the rear of the cell, glancing back as if to beckon Kate. Straining her eyes, she saw the black outline of a small doorway.

The secret entrance.

Not daring to wait for Gabriel, she pulled out the ivory comb that had belonged to her mother. Pins popped out as the wild mass of her hair tumbled down her back. She placed the comb at the entrance of the cell. With luck, Gabriel would find it and realize where she'd gone.

Then she took a deep breath and followed Jabbar through the doorway.

Ducking her head to avoid the low ceiling, she entered a tunnel that was wide enough for a man. It twisted and turned on a slightly downward slope. According to Lady Stokeford, the chimpanzee had escaped yesterday evening and had gone exploring in the dungeon. He must have learned his way about, and that fact gave a boost to Kate's spirits.

Jabbar would lead her to Meg. He must know where Sir Charles had taken her sister.

As they traversed on a steep, descending path, Kate dropped a hairpin every now and then to mark a trail for Gabriel. Other tunnels led off into the pitch darkness, but Jabbar never deviated from the main path. The candle lent an eerie illumination, and she tried not to think about the flame blowing out. Then the tunnel widened and they emerged into a small cavern.

Her pulse leapt. A lighted torch illuminated the rocky area, proof that someone had been here a short time ago. There was no other sign of life. Water dripped from a fissure in the ceiling, plopping with unceasing regularity into a murky pond in the center of the chamber.

Jabbar looked back, hooting softly to her, seemingly anxious to go on. Then he loped through a natural doorway in the rocky wall. Kate blinked as she spied another faint gleam of light ahead. Was Meg there with Sir Charles? What had he done to her sister?

Fearful and angry, Kate braced herself for the inevitable confrontation. She had no weapons, only her wits. Somehow, she must make Meg realize her folly. She must convince Sir Charles to let her sister go . . .

The chimpanzee went through yet another large opening and stopped just inside, looking up at her with bright black eyes. Her heart in her throat, she stepped through the doorway and came to an enforced halt.

A wall of iron bars confronted her, transforming a natural grotto into a prison cell. Hanging from the low ceiling, an oil lamp shed a golden light over a scene of disconcerting domesticity.

A low bedstead stood against the back wall. A tattered Persian carpet cushioned the rocky floor. Near a worn leather wing chair, a plain wooden shelf held a sparse array of books.

Her gaze riveted to the man who sat hunched over a desk, absorbed in writing on a sheaf of paper. His wire-rimmed spectacles gleamed in the lamplight. He blew on his fingers to warm them in the damp, chilly air. Then he dipped his pen into the inkwell, scribbled madly, then dipped again, the action so familiar she had to be dreaming. Or seeing a ghost. The pipe clamped in his mouth emitted a thin curl of smoke that drifted to her, teasing her with an impossible awareness.

Kate blinked, then blinked again. Her throat tightened, making it difficult to breathe. Her lips moved, dry and disbelieving, as she uttered his name.

"Papa?"

THE moment the old groom stepped into the drawing room, Lucy felt a premonition of disaster. Exchanging a glance with the Rosebuds and Nathaniel, she saw worry in their eyes, too.

She'd had a vague sense of unease ever since Kate had gone upstairs to join her sister. There had been something unusual in Kate's manner, a tension that Lucy had noticed and attributed to concern for Gabriel's safety.

The two had, after all, made love the previous night. The glow on Kate's face this morning had warmed Lucy's heart. At last she would see Gabriel settled and contented, his restless urge to wander tempered by the love of a spirited woman.

But perhaps she had grown too complacent too soon.

The stooped old man doffed his cap. Clad in hobnailed

boots and homespun clothing, he looked like a duck out of water in the genteel surroundings of the drawing room.

"You're Tom Wickett, are you not?" Lucy said. "I thought you'd retired years ago."

"Ain't dead yet," he said, flashing a brief, toothless grin that vanished as swiftly as it had come. Clearly disquieted, he shifted from one booted foot to the other.

"You asked to see her ladyship," Nathaniel prodded. "Tell us what's on your mind."

Tom Wickett turned his cap in his gnarled fingers. "The young lady told me not to tell. But 'tis summit I can't keep secret."

"Which young lady?" Olivia demanded, leaning forward on her cane.

"The younger one or the older one?" Enid added.

"Both," Tom Wickett said. "First, the black-haired one sneaked into the coach while the foreigner was kneelin' on his rug and prayin' his mumbo-jumbo. Then a little while ago, the fire-haired miss come marchin' into the stables, tellin' me to saddle his lordship's bay gelding. I told her I wouldn't do it."

Lucy gripped the arms of her chair. "As well you shouldn't."

"So she saddled the horse herself," Tom Wickett went on, a glint of admiration in his rheumy old eyes. "She went ridin' off, hell-for-leather. Left me tastin' her dust."

Lucy drew a labored breath. "Thank you for telling me. You may go now."

As the groom trudged out of the room, Olivia thumped her cane on the rug. "Foolish Meg! She's gone to Sir Charles. And Kate is off to rescue her."

"We must save them," Enid said, her beringed hands clasped to her plump cheeks. "Lucy, you always have a plan. What shall we do?"

Before Lucy could collect her panicked thoughts, Nathaniel's hand came down firmly over hers. "The three of you will stay here, where it's safe. I'll go after them myself."

His misguided chivalry prodded Lucy into action. She shook off his hand and rose to her feet. "We are not shrinking violets, Nathaniel Babcock. We're the Rosebuds, and we're going, too."

NUMB with disbelief, Kate gripped the iron bars. Her father lifted his head and stared at her. As if he couldn't quite grasp her presence, his brow furrowed in befuddlement. The spectacles magnified his blue eyes into a familiar owlish look. Despite the burst of wild jubilation inside her, she could tell that his mind was still half on whatever it was he'd been writing.

Then the pen dropped from his fingers, spattering ink on the foolscap. He pushed back his chair, set down his pipe, and stood up, his hands braced on the desk. "Katie?"

That deep, raspy voice reached past her stupefaction. The dam around her emotions broke, and her eyes flooded with happiness. A sob broke from her. "Papa!"

A broad smile transformed his gaunt features. He looked painfully thin, ill-fed and garbed in old, worn clothing. He hastened around the desk, limping and slightly stooped over, but incredibly, her father.

Her dear, beloved Papa.

Their fingers met and clung through the bars. Tears coursed down her cheeks as she laughed and wept all at once. Reaching inside the enclosure, she stroked his whisker-roughened cheek, noting a few silvery strands among the brown of his hair. She ached to throw her arms around him, but the barricade stood between them.

"Papa . . . Oh, Papa, you're alive! How is it possible—? We were told you'd died in Cairo."

"I did almost die," he said grimly. "I suffered a nasty

gash at the back of my head and a fractured leg. When I regained consciousness, I was aboard a ship to England."

"But . . . there was a gravesite," Kate exclaimed, rubbing warmth into his icy, ink-stained fingers. "Gabriel gave me a sketch of it."

"Some other poor soul must be buried there. No doubt Damson made the arrangements." His frown deepened the creases that the past four years had chiseled into his beloved features. "But what are you doing here? Did you intercept my note?"

"Note?"

"When Jabbar wandered down here yesterday, I knew Gabe had to be here at the castle, searching for me. I scribbled a note and gave it to Jabbar."

Hearing his name, the chimpanzee jumped up and down, clapping his leathery palms.

Kate shook her head in bewilderment. "I never saw a note. And I don't understand . . . why did Sir Charles stage your death? Why has he imprisoned you?"

Henry Talisford grimaced. "He has a mad plan for me to write a book, a study of ancient religions. Damson intends to claim credit and have it published under his own name."

The explanation sickened her. Sir Charles had tried to enlist *her* in his evil plan, too. "So that's why he wanted your journals so badly."

"I told him I couldn't proceed without them. He craves recognition as a serious scholar, and he'll stop at nothing to get it."

"And then what?" she asked, her voice faint with horror. "Does he intend to kill you?"

"No doubt. I've been delaying as long as I can." His lean face drawn with anger, he tightened his fingers on hers. "That villain stole my greatest discovery. Gabe's discovery."

Kate wanted to confide in him about her love for Gabriel. Yet she could think only of the urgent need to find her sister. "I know about the goddess. Gabriel is looking for the statue right now. But Papa, there's something important I must tell you—"

"I knew I could count on Gabe. Pray God he finds the priceless artifact." A faraway fire in his bespectacled eyes, her father limped back and forth in the cell. "The goddess is a perfectly preserved artifact of ancient Abyssinian culture. It will prove my theory that the pharaohs of ancient Egypt rose to power from an even more ancient civilization. The statue is the link between the wild tribes at the source of the Nile and the beginnings of a civilized world—"

"Papa, listen! Something terrible has happened. Meg is missing."

He stopped pacing to stare at Kate. "My little Meggie?"

"She's seventeen now, and Sir Charles has abducted her. He brought her down here to these caves."

"Damn him!" Henry rattled the iron door, the sound echoing through the cavern. "I must get out of here. We must find them."

"Do you know where the key is kept?" Holding up the candle, Kate glanced around, her gaze frantically scouring the shadowy crevices of the rocks. Someone had to be bringing Papa food and drink. Did they take the key away each time? Or leave it nearby?

Then Jabbar loosed a drawn-out wail that sent a chill down her spine.

An instant later, a cultured male voice said, "Is this what you're looking for?"

Kate whirled around to see Sir Charles Damson looming in the stone doorway, carrying an armful of her father's notebooks. Limned by torchlight and smiling benignly, he dangled a ring of keys from his fingers.

CHAPTER 27

RITUAL SACRIFICE

TAKING a step toward him, Kate looked wildly into the adjacent cavern. "Where is my sister?"

"In a safe place," Sir Charles said affably. "Come, I'll take you to her."

Henry Talisford gave the bars another violent shake. "Don't go with him, Katie. Don't trust him. Damson, leave her be."

Still smiling, the baron strolled toward the prison cell. As he drew closer, Kate saw that his eye was blackened, his nose swollen.

Savaged by fear, she eyed the keys in his hand. If she could get the keys to her father, he could unlock the door while she held off Sir Charles. Then together they could overpower him, throw him into the cell, while they searched for Meg . . .

"I have your journals right here, Henry. Margaret was kind enough to deliver them to me. You've no more cause to delay your work on the book."

"I'll do nothing until you let both my daughters go free."

"Quite the contrary. If you value their lives, you'll do as I say."

As Sir Charles made a move to lay the notebooks on a shelf of rock near the enclosure, Jabbar loosed a feral cry. Hair bristling, he made a mock charge at Sir Charles. The baron kicked at the chimpanzee, and Kate lunged.

She knocked Sir Charles off balance so that his blow

went wild. With a whimpering cry, Jabbar ran away, vanishing into the next cave.

Her fingers closed around the iron ring of keys in the baron's hand. She jerked hard, and for one victorious moment, possession was hers. Then her father shouted, "Katie, watch out!"

Before she could do more than look up, Sir Charles swung one of the notebooks and struck her head with a sharp blow. The keys dropped as pain exploded behind her eyes. Black dots swam in her vision. Helpless to catch herself, she slid into oblivion.

KATE returned to awareness in slow stages. She lay on a hard, flat surface. Frost encased her body, restricting the movement of her limbs. Her uncontrollable shivering intensified the dull throbbing in her skull. From a distance came the muffled crashing of the sea.

Forcing her eyelids to lift, she saw the brilliance of two burning torches on a nearby wall. When she blinked, the images converged into one. Her gaze traveled up a rocky wall to the shadowed ceiling of a huge cavern, and a sense of disorientation made her dizzy. The last thing she recalled was Fairfield Park . . . the Rosebuds . . .

A faint sigh eddied in her ear. The ghostly sound prickled over her skin, and she turned her head.

Beside her, Meg lay sleeping, her face angled toward Kate. Her sister's loose hair formed a sleek black veil around her pale form. She wore only a thin white chemise, and her breasts rose and fell with her steady breathing.

Kate tried to move, but ice gripped her limbs. No, not ice. Lifting her arms, she realized that her wrists were bound with leather thongs. So were her ankles.

Like her sister, she'd been stripped down to her calf-length chemise. Her legs had been shorn of shoes and stockings. Her hair curled freely in a red-gold cloud down over the edge of the stone slab on which she lay.

Memory slapped Kate, bringing painful clarity to her mind. Meg. Sir Charles. Papa.

Papa . . . he was alive! Or had she only dreamed their encounter? No, she distinctly recalled his smile of joy upon seeing her, the touch of his ink-stained fingers, the deep lines on his beloved face.

Where was he?

Disciplining her shivers, she rolled onto her side to examine the cave. It looked nothing like the enclosed grotto where her father was imprisoned. Long fingers of rock reached down from the high ceiling. Across the cavern, the glassy black surface of an underground lake reflected the torch lights that were set at intervals in the stone walls. Close to her, several rows of empty stone benches gave the eerie impression of a house of worship.

Then she saw Lucifer.

Stepping out from behind a boulder, the black-robed figure glided toward her. Terror swamped Kate. To keep from screaming, she bit down hard on her lip. His head was hooded, and a pair of wickedly sharp horns sprouted from his forehead. As he drew nearer, she noticed the pewter band that encircled his head, securing the horns in place.

"I see you're awake," Sir Charles said.

Rage filled Kate that he could frighten her, even for a moment. That he could imprison her father and beguile her sister. She wanted to leap at him, to scratch out his eyes. But the bonds hobbled her.

He stopped at the foot of the stone slab. His satisfied gaze traveled over her and Meg. "I must beg forgiveness for striking you, Miss Talisford. However, you've only a slight bruise. It really won't matter."

"Matter?"

"You must be perfect, both of you. Tonight is the eve of May Day. You and Margaret will have the great honor of participating in a ritual sacrifice." He made a sweeping gesture at the stone wall behind her. "You'll offer your innocence to the goddess of fertility."

As she turned her aching head, she noticed a gleam of gold in a rocky niche. The goddess stood proudly, her fingertips touching the huge diamond nestled at the apex of her thighs.

Sacrifice. May Day.

She and Meg lay upon an altar. Sir Charles intended to defile them. He would subject them to a vile parody of the closeness she and Gabriel had shared.

Horror and fury threatened to choke her. Swallowing the sickness in her throat, Kate forced herself to think, to find a way out. In order to accomplish his foul purpose, Sir Charles would have to untie her ankles. Then she'd have her chance. She'd kick him in the face. She'd thrust her knee into his groin. She'd act swiftly, taking him by surprise. It was her only hope.

Out of the shadows, Figgins appeared. He wore a black robe but no horns, his hollow eyes and gaunt features looking as fleshless as a skull. In his hands he carried a silver goblet, which he offered to Sir Charles.

"The potion, master, prepared by the Egyptian wench. 'Tis mixed with yer finest wine."

"Give it to her."

The servant approached the altar. His gaze roamed over Kate, his leer making her feel unclean. He held out the cup.

Sir Charles stood watching. "Drink deeply," he urged. "Soon, you'll be asleep like your sister. You'll lie docile and submissive. By the time you awaken, the ceremony will be concluded."

Figgins pressed the cold metal rim to her lips, forcing a measure of sweet wine into her mouth. She spat it out, spewing the liquid at his bony face. Droplets of red wine fell like blood onto her chemise.

Figgins jumped back. "Hellfire bitch!"

He raised his hand as if to slap her. But Sir Charles caught his arm and shoved him away. "I forbid you to mark her features. Begone now."

"Ye let me watch the other time. Ye even let me have a go at her when ye was done."

"Miss Talisford is no tavern slut. Get back upstairs."

As Figgins reluctantly trudged out, Sir Charles smirked at Kate. "So, Miss Talisford, you choose to stay awake for the ritual. Perhaps you'll enjoy it."

She pretended to cower. "Let us go, I beg you. We won't tell anyone."

His cultured laughter echoed in the cavern. "Go ahead and tell. No one will believe you've been deflowered by Lucifer, then used by two score of his demons." He tilted his hooded head in a listening pose. "Ah. There they are now."

The hollow chanting of male voices drifted from a distance. Jolted by panic, Kate realized that other men were descending the webwork of tunnels, making their way down to the cavern.

The Lucifer League.

She had a chance at fighting off Sir Charles. But not an entire throng of attackers.

"Your ceremony will be a sham," she blurted out in desperation. "I'm no longer a virgin."

Frowning, Sir Charles stepped closer to the altar. "Liar. You're as pure as Margaret."

"No," she said fiercely. "I've given myself to Lord Gabriel. So you may as well untie me. I'm of no use to you."

The dirge of deep voices neared the chamber. She prayed he would heed her. It was her only chance.

The disbelief on the baron's face altered to a livid rage. "You let that scoundrel swive you?" he said, his voice vibrating with fury. "I honored you with my finest accommodations. I commanded my men to leave you be. I guarded your chastity so that I could have you first."

"Well, you've failed," Kate said. "Your plan is worthless now. But if you release me, I won't tell anyone what you've done."

His mouth twisted. "You must be punished. I'll call Figgins back. Let him have you—"

"The horns suit you, Damson," Gabriel's voice rang out. "At last you're showing your true nature."

Sir Charles wheeled around, his robe flapping.

Struck by a thunderbolt of hope, Kate saw Gabriel standing beside the inky expanse of the underground lake. The dueling pistol gleamed in his hand. The sight of him, his face hard and dangerous, filled her with exultation.

Motioning with the long barrel of the gun, Gabriel said, "Step back now. She belongs to me."

"No! My men are coming. You can't fight all of us."

"Bickell and Ashraf will intercept them. I'll take care of you myself. Now walk slowly. Should you make one false move, I'll shoot to kill."

"You wouldn't dare," Sir Charles blustered. "You won't risk striking her . . . your slut."

Gabriel's jaw tightened. "Move!"

Sir Charles started to sidle away. Abruptly, he dove behind the altar, using the great stone monolith as a shield. Kate could hear his feral, panting breaths. Across the cave, Gabriel started toward them, keeping to the shelter of the boulders alongside the lake.

Kate squirmed, wriggling herself to the verge of the altar. She could see the baron's hood and horns. If she could incapacitate him somehow . . .

Then Sir Charles drew a pistol from inside his robe. She saw the shiny barrel flash in the torchlight as he whipped out his arm. His finger curled around the trigger. In a frenzy, she kicked out with her bound feet to knock off his aim. She hit his arm, heard him curse.

Too late.

The shot deafened her, reverberating through the cave. The bullet struck Gabriel and his body stiffened from the impact, his gun falling into the shallows.

Staggering backward, he toppled into the lake. Water splashed as he disappeared beneath the black surface.

CHAPTER 28

THE RENEGADE DEMON

KATE struggled to sit up, her frantic gaze anchored to the widening ripples. But Gabriel didn't reappear. He had vanished into the cold, dark waters.

"He's dead," Sir Charles said with glee as he threw aside the gun and straightened his robe. "If my shot didn't kill him, he'll drown."

A disbelieving horror throbbed in Kate. She could scarcely breathe for the tightness in her breast, for the crushing sense of loss. *Gabriel.*

At the far end of the cavern, a throng of hooded men poured through the natural arch of a doorway. Like Sir Charles, they wore horns and black robes. Their chanting had ceased, and their agitation proved that they'd heard the gunshot.

Where were Ashraf and Bickell? Had they, too, been killed?

"You'll hang for this," Kate said, her voice tight with anguish. "For murder. For abduction. For all your unspeakable crimes."

Sir Charles bared his teeth in a grin. "And who will tell the tale? Certainly not you or your lovely sister."

He intended to kill her and Meg, she thought numbly. After he and his minions were finished with their monstrous rite.

The men surged toward the altar. A clamor of indistinguishable voices echoed in the vast chamber. Wanting to protect Meg, Kate edged closer to her unconscious sister and tried not to sink into a mire of grief and despair.

Regrets battered her. If only she hadn't rejected Gabriel's offer of marriage. If only she could have a second chance to tell him how much he meant to her. If only she'd cherished Gabriel as he was ... a charming adventurer whom she loved beyond reason. A strong, caring man who hid vulnerabilities just as she did.

But now it was too late.

Raising his arms, Sir Charles said in a booming voice, "Silence, brethren. All is well. There is no cause for alarm. Sit down, and we'll begin our ceremony without delay by passing the unholy chalice of wine—"

He faltered suddenly. There were shouts. Another gunshot.

Kate blinked, realizing that the hooded men weren't settling down on the stone benches. They scattered in all directions, disappearing into the many tunnels that led off from the cave. In the center of the chamber, Ashraf and Bickell grappled with several of the men.

Sir Charles stepped to the edge of the dais and shouted in a vain attempt to stop the mass exodus.

In the confusion, one of the demons surged up to the altar. Tall and menacing, he loomed over Kate. In his hand glinted a knife.

A scream gathered in her throat. Then the torchlight penetrated the shadows of the hood, and she saw his ice-gray eyes and the scar that drew up one corner of his mouth. With a few flicks of the blade, Lord Faversham sliced through her bonds, then did the same for her sister.

"Next time," he growled, "you'll heed my advice." Spinning around, he melted back into the mêlée.

Kate lost no time in sliding off the altar. When her bare feet met the stone floor, she grabbed at the stone slab to steady herself. The blood tingled through her icy, half-numb feet.

She shook her sister's shoulders. "Meg. Wake up."

Her sister moaned. Her eyelids fluttered, but remained shut. Kate lightly slapped Meg's cheek. To no avail.

She glanced wildly around for help. Ashraf and Bickell were still fighting a group of robed men. Then she saw a sight that chilled her blood.

His face grisly with anger, Sir Charles headed straight for her.

KEEPING to the shelter of a boulder, Gabe pulled himself out of the frigid water. Violent shivers gripped him. At least the cold dulled the pain in his side where the bullet had creased his flesh.

In the split second of being hit, he'd acted on instinct. He'd fallen into the lake on purpose, letting Damson believe him dead.

Now, the shouts and noises confirmed that Ashraf and Bickell had routed the bastards. Gabe had to find Damson. To make him pay for touching Kate. And for killing her father.

He stepped out from behind the boulder. Blood trickled down his side, liquid fire on his cold flesh. In a glance, he took in the scuffle in the center of the cavern. Ashraf had brought down two of the villains. Bickell had another in a headlock.

Then Gabe spied Kate by the altar, bending over her sister. Sir Charles was heading straight toward them.

A white-hot fury consumed Gabe. His gaze focused on Kate, he set out at a run. A blur streaked out from behind a rock, crashing into him. He went down hard onto his injured side, agony shooting through his chest and emptying his lungs. Fists pummeled him, and a sharp undercut to the jaw rattled his teeth.

"Ye shouldn'ta hit me this mornin'," Figgins snarled. "Ye'll die fer that."

Gabe surged upward, driving his shoulder into the man's gut, using momentum to throw him over onto the stone floor. Figgins fought back with a wiry strength, his fingers tearing viciously at Gabe's wound.

The searing pain temporarily disabled Gabe.

Figgins took advantage, his thumbs seeking to gouge out Gabe's eyes. But Gabe hadn't trekked through the wilds of Nubia and Abyssinia without learning some dirty tricks of his own. Trapping Figgins to the ground, he shoved his forearm against that scrawny throat in a chokehold that had Figgins gasping for air.

A robed man appeared beside them. His muscles bunched, Gabe eased up on Figgins, ready to face the new threat. But it was Brand Villiers who crouched down beside him.

A knife lay in his outstretched palm, the torchlight glinting off its razor edge. "Will you do the honors, or shall I?" he asked.

"I will." Snatching the weapon, Gabe slit Figgins's throat.

Blood spurted, and Gabe leapt back. Figgins made a gurgling sound, his hands clawing at his neck before he went still. Without another word, Brand strolled toward one of the tunnels that led out of the cavern.

Staggering to his feet, Gabe ignored the throbbing in his side as he searched the pandemonium. Meg lay on the stone altar. But Kate was gone.

Then he spied her retreating toward the underground lake. Stalked by Damson.

KATE clutched the heavy statue of the goddess to her bosom. As she inched her way backward, she kept her gaze trained on the baron. In a last-ditch attempt to protect her sister, she had seized the goddess from the niche and lured Sir Charles away from the altar.

"Give the goddess to me," he demanded. "It's mine."

She shook her head. "The statue belongs to Papa."

And to Gabriel. A salvo of sorrow threatened to cripple her. She took a steadying breath and forced herself to think, to find a path across the rocky terrain. If she could only distract Sir Charles for a few more minutes, surely Ashraf or Bickell would come to Meg's aid.

Then her bare feet sloshed into icy water.

"Take care," Sir Charles called out. "Don't venture any farther."

Kate slid a little on the smooth rock edging the lake. Hugging the goddess, she caught her balance, her heart thudding.

Sir Charles scooped up a rock and surged toward her.

She hefted the statue over her head. "Stop," she warned. "Lest I drop the goddess in the water."

He halted. All the color leached from his face. "By the devil! The goddess is sacred. What do you think you're doing?"

Kate took another step backward. Water lapped at her calves, numbing her feet and wetting the hem of her chemise. "I'm bartering for my sister's freedom. And mine."

"You have it," Sir Charles said instantly. "Just give the goddess to me."

Kate let him think she was considering it. Her arms shook under the weight of the statue and the bone-deep chill of the water. She knew that handing him the artifact wouldn't ensure her safety or Meg's. Given half a chance, he would smash in her skull with that rock.

"Do as he says, Kate."

That gritty male voice stunned her. Looking beyond Sir Charles, she saw Gabriel advancing on them.

A disbelieving joy lit her heart. His dark hair was plastered to his head, his clothing was soaked, his linen shirt stained with blood. He was hurt. But oh, praise God, he was alive.

Eyeing Gabriel, the baron tightened his fingers around the rock.

On instinct, Kate called out, "Sir Charles, help me. I'm slipping." Swaying, she held out the statue as an enticement.

His eyes avid, he veered toward her, gripping the rock, his robe floating in the water around his ankles. "Hand me the goddess. Quickly!"

"Fetch it yourself." With all her might, she flung the figurine out over the water.

At the same instant, Gabriel hurled something. Steel flashed. The knife blade caught the baron in the neck just as he leapt after the statue.

Loosing a strangled cry, Sir Charles plunged into the lake, his outstretched fingers grappling for the golden goddess. Thrashing madly, he went under, the statue in his grip.

CHAPTER 29

KATE'S DECISION

KATE stood there, shuddering, unable to believe it was over.

Gabriel splashed into the shallows and gathered her in a fierce embrace. He brushed back her hair and moved his lips over her face, murmuring, "Kate. My love. Are you all right?"

She nodded, uncaring that his soggy clothes were soaking her chemise, that her limbs trembled, that she stood in several inches of icy water. The shock of it all resonated in her. "Sir Charles . . . ?"

Gabriel gently touched her cheek. "He's dead."

"God forgive him," she whispered. Burying her face in his wet shirt, she let Gabriel hold her until the queasiness inside her settled and her legs regained a measure of strength. "We lost the goddess."

"We'll recover it. The lake can't be more than ten feet deep."

But she didn't care about the statue anymore. Only Gabriel mattered to her now. Her heart brimmed with a giddy thankfulness. Unthinkingly, she tightened her arms around his solid form, and he flinched.

Kate drew back, lifting his shirt to see an ugly, oozing gash along the side of his ribs. Her insides clenched. "Dear heavens, you're bleeding. And here I am clinging like a ninny."

With a hint of masculine appreciation, he eyed her dampened chemise. "That isn't all that's clinging."

"Hush. You need a doctor." Sliding her arm around his waist, she urged him toward Ashraf and Bickell who waited across the cavern with a few prisoners. "I'll find something to dress your wound."

Drawing her close, he nuzzled her neck. "I'd rather you undress me."

"Gabriel, please," she said, though her heart beat faster. "You mustn't strain yourself. Enough has happened already—"

"More than enough." His expression serious again, Gabriel tilted up her chin. In the flickering torchlight, his face revealed an unguarded regret. "I'm sorry, Kate. If only I'd been there that night in Cairo, none of this would have happened. I can recover the goddess for you. But I can't ever replace your father."

A miraculous perception bubbled up in her, bursting forth in a joyous laugh. "You don't know, Gabriel. Papa is alive. I saw him myself."

Gabriel regarded her as if she'd gone mad.

She laughed again. "It's *true*. Sir Charles was holding Papa prisoner. It's a long story, and I'll tell you while I'm tending your wound. We'll send Ashraf to find the ring of keys that I dropped."

To her delight, that wasn't necessary. The sound of voices echoed in one of the tunnels as a small party marched into the cavern.

Jabbar and Papa were in the lead. Then came Lady Stokeford, Uncle Nathaniel, and Lady Enid. Bringing up the rear was Lady Faversham, one hand gripping her cane, the other pulling her tall grandson along by his ear.

"Let go, Grandmama," the earl said testily. "I shan't run away."

"You were running a moment ago," she snapped. "Fleeing like a fool from his own shadow. Look at you, dressed in robes with those silly horns." Lady Faversham released him only to smack his legs with her cane.

Muttering a curse, he removed the horns and flung them into the gloom. "But I did leave. You should be glad of that."

"I'll be glad when you finally marry and have a wife to take over the task of scolding you."

The others hastened to the altar to see to Meg, who made a wobbly attempt to sit up. Papa removed his coat and draped it around her shoulders. Meg blinked in confusion, gave a cry of wonderment, and fell into his arms. The sight of their happy reunion brought a lump to Kate's throat.

As if seeing a ghost, Gabriel stared at Henry Talisford. "My God. It isn't possible . . ."

"It *is*." Mindful of his wound, Kate gently drew him forward. "Come, you'll want to greet Papa."

The two men embraced, and Kate swore she saw the sheen of tears in Gabriel's eyes. Their camaraderie touched a place deep inside her, making her aware that their years together had forged a bond as close as father and son.

Then Lady Stokeford scurried forward, her mouth dropping open in horror. "Good gracious! You're bleeding, Gabriel. You and Kate."

Kate looked down in surprise at a damp red smear where she'd leaned against him. And embarrassment, for as Gabriel had pointed out, the wet chemise adhered to her curves. Lady Enid kindly tucked her voluminous mantle around Kate.

She accepted its warmth gratefully. "I'm not hurt, it's Gabriel. He's been shot."

"Shot!" the Rosebuds said in unison, and they surrounded him, clucking questions and offering advice. "How badly?" "You must lie down." "Someone fetch a doctor."

"It's merely a scratch," Gabriel insisted.

But when Lady Stokeford folded her fine cashmere

shawl, and Kate used it as a compress to cover the wound, his face went pale and he sucked in a breath between his teeth. The dowager made him sit down, Uncle Nathaniel seconding the order.

Wrapped in the vast mantle, Kate joined Meg and her father. Meg leaned against him, her eyelids heavy from the aftereffects of the drugged wine. When she saw Kate, her face lost its smile and her lips quivered. "I was so foolish, Katie. I should have listened to you. Can you ever forgive me?"

"Always. I love you, dearest." Teary-eyed, Kate kissed her sister's smooth cheek. "Besides, I've been foolish, too, in my time."

Turning to her father, Kate put her arms around him for the first time in four years. She pressed her face to his whiskered cheek and breathed in his scent of pipe tobacco and ink. Her voice raw, she murmured, "I never said good-bye to you, Papa, all those years ago. I've regretted it ever since."

" 'Tis I who erred." Behind his spectacles, moisture glinted in the blue eyes that were so like her sister's. "I shouldn't have gone off and left my family. I mustn't ever do so again."

"You're back now, and that's all that matters. We'll let the future take care of itself."

Kate knew that clearly now. She wanted to enjoy the glorious present, to treasure the gifts that had been given to her. She wanted Gabriel.

Her gaze veered to him. Lady Stokeford had secured the shawl around his broad chest in a makeshift bandage. As everyone prepared to leave the cavern, Uncle Nathaniel and Lord Faversham stationed themselves on either side of Gabriel, helping him despite his protests. In his sodden clothes, his hair mussed, he looked surly and irritated and so utterly adorable that her heart swelled with yearning.

But she also saw pain in the lines around his mouth, in the way he favored his left side. He'd lost blood and he needed time to recover his strength. A few days at the very least.

Then, and only then, would she tell him her decision.

CHAPTER 30

THE GODDESS

THE following afternoon, Gabe leaned against the doorjamb of the conservatory and watched Kate.

His maternal grandparents had created a tropical paradise inside the domed, glass-walled chamber. The lush vegetation included acacias, orange trees, and date palms. Eucalyptus scented the air, along with the damp richness of earth and humus. Whenever he'd visited Fairfield Park as a child, he and his brothers had frolicked here among the lush foliage. Michael and Joshua had played knights on crusade, while as the youngest, he'd been coerced into acting the heathen infidel. Perhaps that had fed his spirit of adventure. The desire to visit exotic lands, to see all their wonders.

Now he desired only Kate.

On a stone bench in the center of the conservatory, she and Meg sat on either side of Henry Talisford, the three of them laughing at the antics of Jabbar, who had shinnied up the trunk of a palm. Perched among the leaves, the chimpanzee hooted, clearly enjoying his freedom.

Kate's face glowed as she spoke to her father. She touched Henry's hand and adjusted the blanket over his legs. Something ached inside Gabe. Something that had nothing to do with his bandaged side or his disgruntled mood.

Kate had her father back now. She didn't need a guardian anymore. And she certainly didn't want a husband. She had made that fact perfectly clear. The hell of it was, now

Gabe *wanted* to wed her. Wanted it with his whole heart and soul.

With a searing pain, Gabe didn't know if he belonged in their family group. He was the outsider, the footloose adventurer who now craved roots. But he had yet to convince Kate of his reformation. Or to find out if it would even matter to her.

It had been well after midnight when they'd returned from the castle. Grandmama had sent ahead for the doctor, and between the fussing of the physician and the Rosebuds, he hadn't had a moment alone with Kate. He'd have borne any agony to feel the soft touch of her hands. But she'd remained with her father and sister, and Gabe had faced the daunting realization that he no longer had any rights to her.

"What are you doing out of bed?" Grandmama demanded.

He turned to see her sailing toward him down the corridor, Nathaniel Babcock sauntering at her side. The dowager had that scolding look about her, her lips compressed and blue eyes flashing.

"I feel perfectly fine," he lied. He felt dispirited and out of sorts, but she needn't know that.

"This is no time for male bravado," she chided. "You've suffered a terrible injury. You need to conserve your strength."

"Give up," Uncle Nathaniel said, winking broadly. "What Lucy wants, Lucy gets."

Grandmama gave him an intent stare that hinted at hidden meanings. "I'm pleased you realize that. Now come, Gabriel. You'll lie down on the chaise in the drawing room."

Gabriel cast a frustrated glance back at the conservatory. The sound of their voices must have carried to Kate, for she looked up, straight at him.

For a brief, sizzling moment, their gazes held, her eyes widening slightly, conveying an unmistakable ardor for him. His knees weakened under the heat of that look. Then she lowered her eyes before glancing back at her father.

Shaken by a firmness of purpose, Gabe didn't object when Grandmama led him away. Kate felt a strong physical desire for him. It wasn't love, but it was a foundation nonetheless.

And by damn, he would use it to win her heart.

AFTER dinner that evening, Kate stood in the dim-lit corridor outside Gabriel's door.

It was a tall panel of solid oak with wrought-iron fittings. She had ventured inside his chambers the previous night. Drawn and weary, he'd lain in the master bed with its blue satin hangings while the Rosebuds fluttered about him, chattering like magpies, firing questions at the bleary-eyed doctor. Kate had yearned to stay, yet she'd been keenly aware that she lacked the rights of a wife. So she had left, resolving to visit Gabriel in the morning.

But he'd slept late, and halfway through the afternoon, when she'd looked up to see him standing in the doorway of the conservatory, her heart had filled with love and longing. He'd given her an enigmatic stare. She'd been on the verge of standing up and hastening to him when her father had spoken to her. When she looked back, Gabriel had gone off with his grandmother.

Deflated, she'd hoped to see him later, but he hadn't come down to dinner. Lady Stokeford had made his excuses, explaining that he was exhausted from the effects of his injury. She'd looked directly at Kate, smiling as if to reassure her.

The trouble was, Kate wanted reassurance from Gabriel. In spite of her resolve to wait for a few days, she needed desperately to tell him that she was ready to accept his marriage proposal. She wanted to put her arms around him, to kiss away his hurts and find happiness with him. Though she'd believed herself to be a sober, sensible woman, now Kate knew the fanciful dreamer still lurked in her, for she ached to hear him speak tender words of love.

But as she lifted her hand to knock, she hesitated. What if Gabriel was sleeping? It was selfish of her even to think of disturbing him. She mustn't impede his recovery.

Resolutely, Kate pivoted on her heel and walked away, heading toward her own chamber at the opposite end of the house. The floorboards squeaked now and then, and the faint aroma of beeswax hung in the air. A lamp flickered on a table, lending an aura of intimacy to the night-darkened old house. Sometime, she'd like to take a closer look at the antique portraits on the walls. She'd like to explore every chamber, every nook and cranny. How she yearned to be Gabriel's wife, to be mistress of this fine house, to see their children run and play in these corridors.

Her home was with Gabriel, wherever he might be.

The merry sounds of laughter rose from the drawing room downstairs, where Papa and Meg and the others caught up on all the family news. Uncle Nathaniel was openly courting Lady Stokeford, who sparkled at his attentions. If only she could be so happy, Kate reflected wistfully. She wouldn't feel at ease until she could speak to Gabriel, to know he still wanted her as his wife.

Reaching her bedchamber, she paused, looking back, though the turns in the corridor hid his door from view. Had he thought of her today? Did he feel the same torturous longing for her companionship as she did for his? She mustn't hope for too much. It was enough that she would commit herself to him, to accept the happiness he could give her, however long it lasted. She would live for the moment, savoring all the richness and joy of love.

On that resolve, she stepped into her bedchamber and

closed the door. A low fire burned on the hearth, though the rest of the cozy room lay deep in shadow. Ignoring a little twist of loneliness, Kate picked up a candle and went to the hearth to touch the wick to the flames. She would read for a while, divert her mind from distressing thoughts of Gabriel. As she straightened, the candlelight gleamed on something golden perched on the mantelpiece. Something she hadn't seen since the tumultuous events of the previous day.

The goddess.

Transfixed, Kate stared at the statue with its exotic features and curvaceous form, the huge diamond glinting like a star.

On a surge of impossible hope, she whirled around. Her gaze locked on the figure of a man reclining in the four-poster bed. The counterpane covered his lower extremities, and a bandage wrapped his bare chest, the bleached linen pale against his dark flesh. Through the gloom, his familiar cocky expression made her heart flutter.

"Gabriel!"

He beckoned to her. "I've been waiting for you, my lady."

Afraid to blink lest he vanish, Kate hastened to the bed and, with shaking hand, set the taper on the table. He looked so incredibly masculine against the lace-trimmed linens. His hair was rakishly mussed, the candlelight gilding his strong, sun-browned features. Her body reacted with a powerful pulse of yearning.

Denying herself, she touched his cheek, its rough warmth assuring her that he was real. "You're flushed. Do you have a fever?"

"Only for you." Taking her hand, he kissed her palm.

"You shouldn't be here," she scolded. "You're supposed to be resting."

"I'm in bed, aren't I? But I'd heal so much quicker if

you'd minister to me." Gabriel gave her arm a tug, bringing
her down onto the mattress.

Kate sat primly upright. "Are you in pain?"

His fingers traced a meandering path over her skirt.
"Sheer agony," he drawled. "I need a devoted nurse."

"You need a dash of cold water." To hide temptation,
Kate drew the covers up to his chin. Brightly, she said, "I
didn't expect to see the goddess again so soon."

He pushed the covers back down to his waist. His lean,
naked waist. "You can thank Bickell and Ashraf," he said.
"They retrieved the statue for you and your father."

"And you." She kept her gaze focused on his. "Gabriel,
I was wrong to claim the goddess for myself. You deserve
it as much as Papa."

"Never mind the damned statue. I've something to tell
you, Kate. Something very important."

In the midst of her longing, memory tugged at her.
"That's what I said to you . . . that night four years ago."

"Yes." An intense smile flashed and vanished. "But
there's one significant difference between then and now."

"Only one?" She ticked them off on her fingers. "*I* came
to *your* bed, not vice versa. I was a girl of sixteen, and you
were a man of twenty-six." Unbidden, her gaze dipped to
the broad expanse of his chest. "And I was clothed in a
nightdress."

"You're forgetting the most important difference of all,"
he murmured, his blue eyes serious. "You said that night
that you loved me."

She glanced away. For years she'd regretted that foolish
confession, and she'd suffered from his humiliating rejection of her. But now the memory had lost its sting, for she
had come so far since then. The love within her had sur-
vived and matured, enhanced by her experiences with Gabriel. "Yes," she whispered, "I did."

He caught her chin, bringing her face back toward him.

"But I never returned those words. So I'm saying them now. I love you, Kate."

Oh! Nothing else could have caused such a lifting of joy inside her. She leaned closer, mindful of his injury. "I love you, too. Oh, Gabriel, we didn't have a chance to talk today. I've done a lot of thinking—"

"To hell with thinking. Concentrate on this."

He brought his hands up to her breasts, caressing her through the bodice of her gown, making her thoughts scatter. She took firm hold of his wrists and pushed them away. "But there are things we need to discuss—"

"Yes, you're right," he said, nimbly sliding his hand beneath her skirts. "First and foremost, that I don't care for skulking around anymore. I had enough of that when I posed as a footman."

His fingers were doing delicious things to her legs, stroking her calves, rubbing lightly behind her knees. "I . . . yes," she breathed. "No more skulking."

"I mean it, Kate. There'll be no more of me visiting your chamber like this." As he spoke, Gabriel moved his hand a little higher on her leg. "I won't carry on an affair with you under your father's nose."

"But you're doing so right now," she said in bemusement.

"Only to make my point. To remind you of what you'll be missing."

Kate edged closer to him. "Missing?"

"I won't make love to you again until you become my wife." Heavy and warm, his hand came to a halt on her thigh. "However, if you marry me, we can send everyone away and enjoy a long honeymoon."

"As you wish," she murmured.

His face stern, Gabriel went on as if she hadn't spoken. "I realize that it'll take time for you to trust me. I told you myself I wasn't the marrying kind. But all that's changed now that I've fallen in love with you—" He stopped and stared at her. "What did you say?"

Laughing, she leaned toward him, cupping his cheeks in her palms. "That I accept your proposal. I went to your chamber tonight to tell you so."

He looked stupefied. "You did?"

"Yes. That's what I've been trying to tell you. But you're too arrogant to listen to a mere woman."

A slow smile spread over his handsome face, and his pirate eyes held a dissolute promise. Reaching out, he pulled her to him, nestling her against his uninjured side. He pressed his lips to her brow. "Woman," he said, his voice a soft growl, "you've yet to learn your place."

Tipping up her chin, he joined their mouths in a tender kiss that bound them, both body and soul. He held her as if she were a goddess, and Kate melted against him, wondering if he realized just how much she was already in his power. Better he not find that out too soon, she thought with a dash of giddy humor. It would only feed his charming lack of modesty.

When she felt his hands at her back, nimbly unfastening her gown, she curled her fingers around his muscled arms. Drawing back, she chided, "The doctor left strict orders for you to avoid any exertion."

His teeth flashed in a bawdy grin as he lifted the gown over her head and tossed it to the floor. "Then I'll lie here and let you have your wicked way with me."

Demurely, she said, "But you told me we can't make love until we're married."

"It's enough that I have your promise. I trust you'll not renege."

The uncertain note in his voice caught at her heart. Did this strong, indomitable man really love her so much that he could worry about losing her? "I'm all yours," she said softly. "Gabriel, I want you to know that I trust you, too. I want us to be together always."

"A woman after my own heart," he stated. "We'll help your father write his book. There's plenty of room for all of us here at Fairfield Park."

"Yes." A profound yearning brimmed in her breast. "But if someday you feel the need to travel again—"

"I won't leave you, Kate." He brought her hand to his mouth and kissed the back. "You have my solemn vow on that."

She arched an eyebrow. "There you go, not listening again. I wanted to say that I'd travel with you. I'll follow you to the ends of the earth."

A guarded light shone in his eyes. "But we'll have a family."

"We'll take our children with us, m'lord. We'll see the world together. I insist upon it."

Pulling her to him, he tilted his mouth in a smile that stirred her most idyllic dreams. "Prickly Kate. Right now, *I* insist we start on begetting an heir."

"Or heiress." Brushing aside the counterpane, she decided that in all the ways that mattered, she and Gabriel were in complete accord.

As the night deepened, neither of them had any further inclination to quarrel. And from her perch on the mantelpiece, the goddess smiled down at them.